IN WORLDS AFLAME
WITH SCHEMES OF CONQUEST—

RENNO—Born among white men, raised among Indians—he had the polished ways of a great gentleman and the raw nobility of a Seneca brave.

BETSY—Virginian beauty, she gave herself to Renno freely, leaving her people to become his woman in the untamed wilderness of his tribe.

NED—Betsy's brother and Renno's sworn friend, joined with Renno by a common cause on a mission of uncommon courage.

CONSUELO—The beautiful victim of a Spanish viceroy's lust, until she is rescued by Renno and Ned.

VAN DER KUYT—Freebooter and scoundrel, he wears the guise of loyalty, but betrayal is the only thing on his mind—and only Renno, Ned and Consuelo can put an end to his treachery.

The White Indian Series
Ask your bookseller for the books you have missed

The White Indian Series
Book III

WAR
CHIEF

Donald Clayton Porter

™ **BCI** Created by the producers of
**Wagons West, Children of the Lion,
Saga of the Southwest,** and
The Kent Family Chronicles Series.
Executive Producer: Lyle Kenyon Engel

BANTAM BOOKS
TORONTO • NEW YORK • LONDON • SYDNEY • AUCKLAND

WAR CHIEF

A Bantam Book / November 1980

2nd printing	*. November 1980*	*6th printing*	*.... March 1981*
3rd printing	*. November 1980*	*7th printing*	*... October 1981*
4th printing	*.. December 1980*	*8th printing*	*..... April 1983*
5th printing	*... January 1981*	*9th printing*	*.... August 1984*

Produced by Book Creations, Inc.
Chairman of the Board: Lyle Kenyon Engel
Drawings by Clay Ghiosay.

ISBN 0-553-24751-4

Published simultaneously in the United States and Canada

PRINTED IN THE UNITED STATES OF AMERICA

H   18 17 16 15 14 13 12 11 10 9

WAR CHIEF

Chapter I

The sound of the throbbing drums that began in the main town of the Seneca rolled across the fields of corn and squash and beans grown by the women and echoed through the endless forest of evergreen and elm, oak, and maple that surrounded the community. Seneca emerged from huts and longhouses to watch the solemn procession of the nation's leaders.

Leading the group was Ghonka, the Great Sachem of all the Iroquois, wearing the beaded buffalo robe and headgear of many hawk and eagle feathers, symbols of his exalted rank. Revered as the wisest of the wise and renowned for his exploits in battle, he was tall and muscular, and though in his middle years, he was still unmatched by any of the other fighting men.

Next, with clusters of feathers from his scalp lock trailing down his brawny back, came Sun-ai-yee, the main town's war chief, whose skills and acumen belied his portly appearance. Then marched the chiefs of the lesser Seneca towns, along with the principal medicine men and elders who were also members of the nation's highest governing body, the potent council of the Seneca.

Bringing up the rear was an impressive young man. The elderly nodded their approval, the younger warriors looked at him in admiration and awe, and the unmarried women brightened, casting provocative glances at this most eligible of bachelors. Renno, the son of Ghonka and his wife, Ena, was the only Seneca other than the Great Sachem himself ever to have achieved the distinction of being made a war chief prior to his twenty-third summer.

Renno was truly extraordinary. He stood more than six feet tall. He wore a magnificent headgear made from the feathers of the hawks who watched over him on behalf of the supernatural spirits of earth and sky and netherworld. Around his neck was a necklace of bear claws that not only identified him as a member of the Bear Clan, but served as a reminder of his extraordinary relationship with the huge brown bear Ja-gonh, now deceased.

But in addition to these marks of distinction, there was something else about Renno that made him truly unique. His bare torso and face, although browned by the sun, revealed that his skin was not as dark as that of other Indians. His eyes were an intense blue, and the hair of his scalp lock, although heavily greased, was the color of sand. He was the son of Ghonka and Ena, adopted when one of the first English settlements in Western Massachusetts Bay had been destroyed in an Indian raid in the late 1600s. He was born of white settler parents.

Renno learned of his parentage after he had achieved manhood and become a warrior. Since that time he had become a vital link between the Iroquois and the northern English colonies of the Atlantic Seaboard. He had earned his high rank by leading his Seneca at the side of the colonists in an attack on the French at Quebec and in the successful siege of the great French fortress Louisburg on Cape Breton Island. He had traveled to far-distant England to win the support of King William III to insure the success of the joint military campaigns. Thanks to him the Seneca and three other Iroquois nations—the Mohawk, the Oneida, and the Onondaga—now possessed and had become expert in the use of firearms, and trade between the northern English colonies and their Iroquois allies was flourishing.

He had learned English and had become familiar with English customs and manners. But he felt truly at home only in the land of the Seneca. So at this moment, knowing the reason the Seneca council had been called into session, his heart was heavy.

A war chief of the Seneca never revealed his feelings, however, so Renno's handsome features remained immobile, his expression wooden. As the procession moved past Ena, Renno paid homage to his mother by inclining his head to the dignified, graying woman in the dress of supple buckskin. Only she knew, when she saw his eyes, that he was unhappy. Beside her stood her younger son, El-i-chi, recently promoted to the rank of senior warrior. Although he and Renno were inseparable, even he could not guess that his brother was steeling himself for the ordeal that lay ahead.

Renno's composure was threatened just once, when he marched past a girl in her teens and a slightly older boy. Ba-lin-ta, his younger sister, was defying Seneca tradition as usual, her broad grin making plain her unbounded pride in Renno. He needed his lifetime of rigorous training to prevent himself from returning her smile or, even worse, laughing aloud.

He noted with satisfaction that her companion was appropriately somber, despite his shining eyes. Walter Alwin. son of a Fort Springfield woman, was a deaf-mute who somehow had a strong affinity to Ba-lin-ta from the time they had first met. Renno was convinced that the manitous, the spirits of the wilderness, were responsible, and at his instigation Walter had been living with the Seneca for many moons. The youth had become remarkably self-reliant in this land where his affliction was not regarded as a handicap. Walter had

3

even insisted on becoming a candidate for the Seneca manhood trials, tests of strength, courage, and endurance, and if he passed them he would become a full-fledged junior warrior. Renno would sponsor him and felt certain he'd succeed.

A fire burned in the log council house, the smoke escaping through a hole in the ceiling, and as the members entered, they sat in a circle around it. Ghonka filled a clay pipe, lighted it with a coal from the fire, and after puffing on it, passed it to Sun-ai-yee. Not until every member of the group had taken a puff did the Great Sachem speak.

"My brothers," he said in his deep, resounding voice, "I have called you to this place to solve a new problem that confronts the Seneca. May the manitous who watch over us guide us and help us to make the right decision."

The war chiefs, elders, and medicine men folded their arms across their chests, and during the long silence that followed, each in his own way implored the manitous for their help. Every Seneca of high rank had seen visions at one time or another, but because of the disparity of experiences, no two prayed alike.

Renno thought of the hawks that had led him out of trouble, and then an image of Ja-gonh appeared in his mind. The spirit of the bear who had been his companion since both had been very young had mingled with his own spirit and, he knew, would guide him now.

"My brothers," Ghonka said at last, "you who fought against the French at Louisburg and conquered them well remember Austin Ridley. To you who stayed at home, I will explain. Austin Ridley is the war chief of the colonists from Virginia. He fought beside us and became the comrade of the Seneca. He is a man of honor and courage."

Sun-ai-yee nodded in sober agreement, as did Renno and the others who had participated in the long, arduous campaign.

"Wilson," Ghonka said, "has sent a message to me,

4

a message of grave importance, which must be weighed carefully by the members of this council."

This time Renno was the first to nod. Brigadier Andrew Wilson, a wealthy western Massachusetts Bay landowner and commander of that colony's militia, had demonstrated repeatedly that he was the staunch ally of all Iroquois.

"The English of Virginia seek only peace with their neighbors," Ghonka said. "But the strongest of their neighbors, the Pimlico nation, are sending their warriors to raid the towns and farms of the colonists. It is the hope of Ridley that the Seneca will send a special messenger to the Pimlico, asking them to exchange the wampum of peace with the people of Virginia."

A grizzled elder was the first to reply, his voice querulous. "The Seneca live far from the land of the Pimlico," he said. "Even the swiftest of our warriors would need to march for almost a moon before he would reach that land. Why should the Seneca interfere in the wars of others?"

"It is because we are the strongest of all nations that the Pimlico might listen to us. Those who make war against our allies need to understand that they also make war against us."

"The land of the Pimlico is too far from the land of the Seneca," the old man said.

Several of the other elders and medicine men nodded to indicate that they agreed with him.

Renno looked at his father, who inclined his head a fraction of an inch, granting him the right to speak.

"The Virginia colonists," Renno said, "like the colonists of Massachusetts Bay and New York, swear fealty to William, the Great Sachem of the English. It is William who has given firesticks to the Seneca and the other nations of the Iroquois. He has given us knives and tomahawks and other weapons of metal. He has given us blankets that warm us when the weather is cold. He has given us cooking pots of metal and fine tools to cut the wood of the forest so we can make

5

better homes and stronger fences. William is our firm friend. We would lack honor if we refused to come to the aid of his subjects."

"Men with white skins," Sun-ai-yee declared, "have come to the lands of the Indians in such large numbers that we cannot drive them into the Great Sea. Of these, only the English are our friends. The French have become the allies of our ancient foes, the Huron and Ottawa. We cannot desert our friends in their time of need."

"The men of all nations tremble when they see the war paint of the Seneca," Ghonka said. "None seek combat with us. So it is my hope that the Pimlico will agree to make peace with the English of Virginia."

"Who among us will make the long journey and reason with them?" the querulous elder demanded.

The Great Sachem's reply was blunt. "Wilson of Massachusetts Bay has told us they have asked tnat Renno be sent to them."

Everyone seated around the circle turned to stare at the youngest war chief.

"Is it the wish of Renno that he go to reason with the Pimlico?" the principal medicine man asked quietly.

Renno shook his head, feeling the need for complete candor in this company. "I will go if it is the order of the council," he said. "If I did that which pleases me, I would stay home, hunt in our forests, and fish in our lakes and rivers. I have fought in two long wars against the soldiers of French. I spent many moons in London, the great city of the English. It is true that I have prospered, but now I would like to find the pleasures that I have earned. Even so, I will not shrink from my duty."

"When any ally cries for help, that cry must be answered," Ghonka said. "But Renno has made so many sacrifices for our people that I have told him I will not command him to make another. If this council wishes to send an emissary to the Pimlico, I would rather choose to take his place."

6

His son shook his head. "I alone speak the language of the English and know their ways. If it is the wish of the council to send a mission, I will accept."

The Great Sachem called for a vote.

A twig lay on the ground beside each member's place. Those who wanted to send an emissary voted by throwing a twig into the fire, while those opposed would refrain.

Renno folded his arms across his chest to indicate that he would not vote. He had stated his position bluntly, and now he awaited the verdict with Seneca stoicism.

Custom decreed that the Great Sachem vote last, so Sun-ai-yee cast the first ballot. Renno was his friend and protégé, the most dependable of his subordinate commanders, but Sun-ai-yee unhesitatingly placed duty above personal considerations. His face masklike, he threw his twig into the fire. The other war chiefs voted as he did. Only some of the elders and medicine men well advanced in age could afford to show sympathy.

By the time Ghonka's turn came it was decided. The vote was more than two to one in favor of sending Renno. A lesser man might have been tempted to make a gesture on behalf of the son he loved. But the Great Sachem always thought in terms of high principle and cast his twig into the flames.

Renno bowed his head in submission to the council's will, and the meeting came to an end. Within a short time those who lived in other Seneca towns would be homeward bound, accompanied by their escorts of warriors.

Everyone saw the bleak look in Renno's eyes, and no one halted him as he made his way across the fields and deep into the forest. He did not halt until he came to a tiny clearing that only he and El-i-chi knew. It was here that he had held his private meetings with Ja-gonh after the bear had grown too large to continue to dwell with humans.

Studying the sky with unblinking eyes, Renno

caught no glimpse of a hawk anywhere, even though he was renowned for vision greater than that of other warriors. So be it, he thought. The manitous were choosing not to reveal whether they approved of his mission and would offer him their protection.

Then he spoke aloud in a clear voice, "Spirit of Ja-gonh, my brother, return from the land of our ancestors and hear my plea. Lend me your strength and your wisdom in the moons that lie ahead. Keep watch over me, and help me to stand again if I should stumble."

He remained in the forest for a long time, and dusk was falling when he finally returned to town. Although he lived in his own small dwelling, a privilege of his rank, he continued to eat most of his meals at the house of his parents, and he arrived just as the others were seating themselves around the cooking fire in front of the hut. Renno inclined his head to his father, then to his mother, and took his place between them.

The family of the Great Sachem ate a special meal that night, which was Ena's quiet way of demonstrating the depth of her feelings for her elder son, who once again was sacrificing for the nation.

Ba-lin-ta had cooked the first course, a large fish with white flesh that Walter had caught in the lake that afternoon. Everyone in the family knew the baked fish was one of Renno's favorites, and Ba-lin-ta served him a portion as large as that which she gave to her father, a breach of Seneca custom. But although Ghonka ordinarily insisted on the observance of protocol, he conveniently pretended not to notice.

Ena had cooked the main dish in a large iron pot that Brigadier Andrew Wilson's wife, Mildred, had given her on her one visit to Fort Springfield. Chunks of smoked venison had been stewed with wild onions, dandelion greens, and beans for hours and were served with baked squash and still-steaming cornbread. Only Ena ate sparingly and enjoyed watching the others relish the meal.

Not until Ghonka was done and wiped his mouth

with the back of his hand did he break the silence. "When will you leave for the land of the Virginia colonists, Renno?"

"As soon as I can."

"I suggest you go in two mornings' time," Ghonka replied, settling the question.

Renno nodded. He had made up his mind to confer with Colonel Austin Ridley in the town the settlers called Norfolk before contacting the Pimlico.

"You will want to impress the Pimlico with the might and majesty of the Seneca," the Great Sachem said, "so I have decided to send an escort of two times ten men with you. Choose your own companions, of course. Let two or three be senior warriors."

El-i-chi promptly cleared his throat.

Renno grinned at him. "I choose my brother. The season of growing is farther advanced there than it is here, so perhaps the manitous will guide us to some plump ducks and fat deer."

Walter Alwin, sitting cross-legged like his Indian hosts, strained forward.

Ba-lin-ta instantly interpreted for him. "Wal-ter wants to go with you, too, Renno."

It was easy to understand the boy's eager desire, but Renno regretfully shook his head. "No one less than a junior warrior will march with me," he said. "One never knows what foes one will find in the forest, or what hardships one will encounter."

Renno smiled at the boy. "I promise I will take you with me on a mission, Walter, as soon as you have passed your manhood trials and become a junior warrior."

The girl took hold of her good friend's wrist, and by applying a series of pressures known only to the two of them, translated what her brother had said to the deaf boy. Walter reacted admirably, folding his arms across his chest and concealing his disappointment. Even Ghonka glanced at him approvingly for an instant.

Renno quickly gave El-i-chi the list of the warriors he wanted to take with him, and the younger brother, acting the familiar role of his brother's deputy, hurried off to tell them their good fortune. Ba-lin-ta and Walter were excused so they could swim in the nearby lake with the children before bedtime, and Renno was alone with his parents.

"Your father and I," Ena said, "wish to discuss with you a matter that long has been on our minds."

The ordinarily imperturbable Ghonka looked uncomfortable. Renno saw the subtle determined expression in his mother's doelike eyes and braced himself. Ena, as everyone in the family well knew, was an extraordinary woman. She worked in the fields with other wives, and in most matters she subordinated herself to her husband's will, but she had a backbone as hard as metal, and when there was something she deemed important she invariably got precisely what she wanted.

"My son," she said, "few warriors are chosen as war chiefs, and many are men of twice your summers before they reach such a high place."

"That is true," he murmured and tried not to look apprehensive.

Ghonka began to fidget, which wasn't like him.

"The time has come," Ena said with calm finality, "for you to be married."

"I know of no one I want to marry, my mother." Renno tried without success to match her serenity.

"The mothers of as many young women as I have fingers on my hands have come to me, offering their daughters to you. Some of the fathers are war chiefs. Others are medicine men. You may choose from the highest level of our people."

Renno wanted to protest that he knew virtually every eligible young woman in the entire Seneca nation and wasn't interested in any. But there were times when it was best to retreat into silence, his only defense.

"You have had two women, as far as I know," Ena said. "Perhaps you have taken others, too, but they meant nothing to you and I prefer not to hear about them. I wonder if the thought has ever come to you that both of the women you have loved have pale skins."

It was true. Deborah Jenkins was now happily married to Fort Springfield's leading clergyman, and Adrienne Wilson, a French Huguenot refugee, had found contentment as the wife of his closest friend in Massachusetts Bay, Jeffrey Wilson. He was delighted for both of them, but he could not ignore his mother's observation.

"It may be," Ena said, "that the destiny the manitous have in store for you is a marriage to a woman with pale skin. If that is so, you are responsible for finding her and making her your wife."

Ghonka cleared his throat. "Renno," he said, "I have tried to explain to your mother that no white woman would be at home in the land of the Seneca."

"That is so," Renno said. "I have never met any woman in the English colonies or in England who would be happy to live in this town. But I am a Seneca, and a Seneca I shall remain, even though I no longer find the ways of the pale-skinned people strange."

Ena had her own logic. "Then you should be married to a woman of the Seneca," she said.

"Renno goes on a mission that is important to all nations of this land," Ghonka said, trying not to show his irritation. "The Seneca cannot afford bad feelings between the English colonists and tribes that do not understand how difficult life will be for us if the French drive out the English. Yes, and Andrew Wilson has told me the men of Spain are even worse than the French! So do not fill Renno's mind with thoughts of women when he has a mission to establish peace."

"I will be silent," Ena said. "But while Renno is absent from home on his mission, I will study each of the young women whose mothers have come to me with offers. I will determine which of them would be the best wife for Renno. When he returns I will tell him what I have decided."

A flicker in Ghonka's eyes indicated that, although he sympathized with his son, in this case his own ordinarily unlimited authority was meaningless. Renno would have to deal with his mother alone.

Ena went off to wash the gourds and iron pot in a small stream, and her husband and son relaxed. Now they could turn their attention to matters they regarded as significant.

"When you speak with the sachem, war chiefs, and medicine men of the Pimlico," Ghonka said, "do not threaten them unless you find it necessary. But make it plain to them that the English colonists are the firm allies of the Seneca and all five of the other nations of the Iroquois League."

"They may not believe," Renno replied thoughtfully, "that we would go to war against a nation that lies so far from our own land. That is the weakness of our position. But I intend to make it clear to them that we traveled just as far when we fought the French at Louisburg."

"It is important for you to remember at all times that the reputation of the Seneca is at stake. No Indians, not even the Huron or the foolish Erie, would willingly go into battle alone against our warriors."

"I understand, my father. We have given our word to the English colonists, and we shall not fail them. How far may I go in making our position plain to the Pimlico?"

The Great Sachem removed two strips of wampum from his belt, one decorated with white shells, the other studded with black. "Take these," he said, "and use them as you see fit."

Renno was stunned. He was being granted a power Ghonka normally reserved for himself. The white shells meant that the Seneca and other Iroquois would remain at peace with the Pimlico. But if he presented the black, he would openly declare war. Renno realized his father had complete faith in his judgment, and he vowed to live up to it.

Three Virginia rivers, the James, the Nansemond, and the Elizabeth, came together about eighteen miles from the Atlantic Ocean, and the estuary formed one of the greatest natural harbors on the face of the earth. Colonel Austin Ridley stood at the base of the one small wharf that jutted out into the Elizabeth, with the town of Norfolk behind him.

One of the wealthiest citizens of the colony, the commander of the Virginia militia had already spent more than two decades in the New World. No man in the English colonies owned a larger fleet of merchant ships, none had grown so prosperous in so short a time. His hair graying at the temples, his body still trim in his worn blue uniform, he stared out across the water, his face stern. Then he caught sight of the small brig moving up the estuary and he relaxed.

"That's our ship," he told his son, who stood beside him.

Ned Ridley, who wore the uniform of a militia captain, was a younger version of his father, tall and spare, with rugged features and a shock of dark brown hair under his helmet. The only one of the three Ridley children to have been born in England, he had come to Virginia as a small boy and had only hazy memories of the Old World. He was completely American, as much at home in the wilderness as he was in the mansion his parents had built in the hills behind Norfolk.

"We're not sure Brigadier Wilson is on board, Papa," he said.

A broad grin creased Austin Ridley's craggy face. "Andy Wilson always keeps his word," he said. "He and Mildred are on that ship. I'll wager my last gold sovereign on it."

The brig loomed larger on the horizon, and Ned chuckled when he caught sight of a couple standing at the starboard rail. The lady wore a silk gown, an extravagance when most women he knew wore coarse linsey-woolsey, and the man was dressed in a blue and buff uniform. Impulsively drawing his pistol, Ned fired it into the air as a greeting. Andrew Wilson returned the fire, sending several gulls following the brig soaring high into the air.

The ship's master maneuvered his vessel expertly into her berth, a gangplank was lowered, and the white-haired Andrew led his still lovely wife ashore.

The Ridleys saluted, then bowed to Mildred Wilson. "Welcome to Virginia," Austin said. "Andy, I see you've been promoted."

"Yes, our colonels have elected me commander in chief of the Massachusetts Bay militia, and the governor promoted me to major general, but I'm not so sure I like the responsibility. It strikes me there's far too much trouble ahead."

Mildred intervened quickly. "You two will have ample time to discuss your problems," she said. "Right now I want to enjoy being ashore again."

"Quite right, ma'am." Austin Ridley led the visitors to his waiting carriage, attended by a servant in livery. Ned mounted his own gelding and rode beside the coach as they started inland on a rutted dirt road.

"I'm afraid I can't point out many sights of interest," Austin said. "Yonder is our Anglican church, with the highest steeple in town. Off to your left is the factory where tar is made, and to the right are my own warehouses. Norfolk has a population of fewer than two thousand right now, but soon we expect to have at least twice that many people here. But it will be a long time before we give Boston any real competition."

"Fort Springfield is a small town, too," Andrew replied. "We prefer rural living to cities. Both of us had our fill of London before we moved to the New World."

"So did I," Austin replied.

Leaving Norfolk behind them, they soon came to a clearing in the pine and cedar woods, and directly ahead, surrounded by a smooth lawn of short-cut grass, stood a three-story clapboard mansion, painted white. It reminded the Wilsons of their own farmhouse outside Fort Springfield, with one major difference. Here the portico over the front entrance was supported by four impressive Doric columns, each fashioned from the trunk of a large tree.

Mary Ridley, in a taffeta gown, her dark blond hair piled high on her head, stood at the entrance to welcome her guests. Mildred Wilson knew immediately that her hostess was like herself, a born lady who had also had to deal with the abrupt change from civilized living in England to the rigors of the frontier.

The two women smiled warmly at each other in mutual understanding.

"Your luggage will be along in an hour or two, when the brig's hold is unpacked," Mary Ridley said. "Please make yourself at home."

The visitors saw that the furnishings, like their own, had come from England. As yet there were few cabinetmakers in America, and carpenters were only capable of fashioning crude tables and chairs fit for kitchen use. Passing through several anterooms, the party came to the main drawing room, where portraits of King William III and Queen Mary stood above the mantel. Comfortable chairs faced each other in front of the brick hearth. Everything was in quiet good taste.

Andrew and Mildred Wilson both were pleased. Their host and hostess were people much like themselves.

A servant was summoned to bring cups of sherbet, and Mary sent Ned to fetch his sisters. He hurried out of the room.

The young woman who came into the chamber a few moments later was a startling beauty. Betsy Ridley was tall and stately, remarkably poised for a girl of twenty. Her enormous green eyes were luminous, her wheat-colored hair cascaded down her back in waves, and her figure, revealed in a simple gown of green velvet, was perfect. Mildred was reminded of her own daughter-in-law, Adrienne, when she saw the girl's high, firm breasts, tiny waist, and sleek lines.

Betsy curtsied to the guests, then frowned slightly and said, "Annie knew General and Mrs. Wilson were coming, Mama, but she isn't in her room."

"I reckon I know where to find her," Ned said, and again left the room.

At ease in the presence of her elders, Betsy joined in the lively conversation of the two couples who acted as though they had been friends all of their lives. The men, to be sure, had served together in the Louisburg campaign, but the ladies, meeting for the first time, struck an instant rapport.

Ned returned, trying not to smile. "I found Annie," he said. "She's in the tree house I built for her in the old oak in the backyard, and she won't come down."

Austin Ridley laughed aloud. His wife was not amused. "I'll get her," she said.

Betsy rose swiftly. "Stay where you are, Mama," she said. "I'll attend to this." Lifting her long skirt to reveal shapely ankles, she left the room, made her way through the dining chamber and pantry, and went out through the areaway that connected the main house and kitchen outbuilding.

There was a slight movement in a tree house of boards high above the ground in a towering oak. Betsy stood near the foot of the tree. "Anne Ridley," she called, "I know you're up there, so it's no use pretending. Come down this instant so you can meet the company."

There was neither sound nor movement above.

"If you don't come down immediately, I'll climb up there after you, and I'll tan your behind!"

A small, grubby face peered out through thick leaves. "Do I have to, Betsy?"

"Now!" The older girl impatiently tapped a high-heeled slipper on the grass.

A lugubrious sigh sounded from above, and then a girl of nine appeared and deftly made her way to the ground. She was wearing trousers, an old shirt of her brother's that was far too large for her, her chestnut hair was tangled, and her bare feet were as smeared

16

with dirt as her pert face. "I hope you're satisfied!"
Anne said.

"You're coming with me."

The little girl became alarmed. "Not looking like
this! Then Papa will tan me!"

"It's what you deserve." Betsy caught hold of her
ear. "March!"

"You're hurting me," Anne complained.

Her older sister laughed. "I'm doing no such thing,
and you won't win any sympathy that way. Now mind
your manners in front of General and Mrs. Wilson."

"You know what I wish?" Anne demanded. "That
you'd marry one of those suitors who hang around
here all the time. Then I'd be the only girl in this
family!"

"None of my beaux happen to appeal to me, and I
do wish you'd stop shouting." Betsy led her into the
drawing room.

The adults surveyed the grubby child in startled
silence for an instant.

"This," Austin Ridley announced dryly, "is my
younger daughter, Anne."

"We're comforted by the knowledge that she'll
change. It wasn't so long ago that her sister was a
tomboy," Mary said.

Betsy had the grace to redden. Anne curtsied deeply
to the guests before fleeing up the central staircase to
change. By the time she returned, immaculate in a
starched linen dress, dinner was served.

After the meal the men retired to Austin's library
for port. "Now we can get down to business," he said.
"I hope you won't mind if my son comes with us,
Andy. He's just returned from a scouting trip into
Pimlico country, so he can give you a first-hand ac-
count of our present situation."

"I'll be delighted to hear what Ned has to say. From
what Jeffrey tells me after working with him at Louisburg, Ned is in a class with Renno."

"Hardly," Ned replied with a modest grin. "But
thank Jeff for the compliment. He knows even better

than I do that Renno is unique. I swear, he could make his way blindfolded through a forest without making a sound or losing his sense of direction."

They settled themselves in armchairs in the book-lined room, and after toasting King William, Austin said, "The Pimlico are still confining their attacks to isolated farmhouses, but I've put two full battalions on alert, ready for immediate mobilization. I'm convinced they intend to make a full-scale attack, in strength, on Norfolk."

Andrew Wilson shook his head. "Can you handle them?"

"That depends on how many warriors they send against us," Austin replied "Ned can give you a better account than I can on that score."

"I just came home yesterday after spending almost two weeks in the wilderness with a dozen of my scouts, General," Ned Ridley said. "We made our reconnaissance in pairs, as usual, and every team had the same report. Pimlico warriors from their smaller communities are making their way to their main town in twos and threes. I saw several such groups myself, and although they weren't wearing war paint, they were armed to the teeth with bows and arrows, knives, spears, and tomahawks."

"Ned believes they're definitely planning to attack us with as many warriors as they can muster," Austin said.

"There's no doubt of it, sir," Ned declared. "They'd have no other reason for mobilizing so many fighting men, and the mere fact that they're bringing warriors into the main town in small groups proves they don't want to alarm us with mass movements."

"If you need help," Andrew said, "I can muster as many as three battalions of experienced wilderness fighters and get them down here in three to four weeks, provided you'll supply sea transportation for them, Austin."

"I'm grateful for your offer. But I'd hate to see other

tribes of the area joining in on the side of the Pimlico, so I'd rather contain them exclusively with my own Virginians. If I can."

"What's their grievance against you?"

"I'm damned if I know, and I'm damned if I can find out. I've made three requests to them for a parley. But their sachem—acting through their principal medicine man, for reasons I can't figure out—has turned down every offer."

"Our settlers," Ned added, "have been scrupulously careful not to invade the Pimlico hunting grounds. We prefer not to have an outright confrontation with them until we can double our strength. Which means a delay of years while more settlers come here from the British Isles and we have a chance to train them in the techniques of forest fighting."

"From what you tell me," Andrew said, "the Pimlico aren't likely to oblige you by waiting that long."

"Hardly," Austin replied.

"If my estimate is correct, they'll attack in another six weeks or so, when our farmers begin to take in their first tobacco crop of the season," Ned said. "The Pimlico are shrewd enough to know that the economy of Virginia rests on a base of tobacco. We do export other crops, of course, but the tobacco we send to England is the main source of our cash."

"Six weeks doesn't give much room for maneuver," Andrew Wilson said. "But with Renno's help and a bit of luck there might be time enough to bring some of my Massachusetts Bay battalions down here in the event that his intervention effort fails. I estimate that Renno has been on the trail for Virginia for approximately two weeks now."

"Knowing the way he travels, he ought to be here at any time," Ned said.

Andrew Wilson nodded. "Quite so. But I hope you aren't counting too heavily on his ability to call off the Pimlico."

"That's anybody's guess," Austin said. "There's a

branch of the Tuscarora, one of the six Iroquois nations, living not far from here in North Carolina. The other tribes of the area avoid them like the plague and give them no excuse to go to war. No sachem in his right mind wants a horde of Iroquois to descend on his tribe."

"The determining factor, as I see it," Ned said, "is whether Renno can persuade the leaders of the Pimlico that the Seneca actually would come to the military assistance of this colony. The best that Virginians have ever achieved in the eighty-five years since we began to settle here has been an armed truce with such tribes as the Chickahominy and the Potomac. We've never been able to form an alliance with any Indian nation, so the Pimlico may refuse to believe that the Iroquois, particularly the ferocious Seneca, have agreed to a treaty of friendship with the colonies."

"It's a waste of time to speculate," his father said crisply.

"So it is," Andrew Wilson agreed. "If Renno arrives during the few days I intend to spend here, I'll willingly delay my departure until I see how he fares. If I've gone, and he fails, send word to me by the fastest sloop in your fleet, Austin, and I'll send out the mobilization order that same day. In the meantime, Ned, perhaps you'll take me out to the wilderness tomorrow while the ladies become better acquainted here. I'd like to see this Pimlico mobilization for myself."

"I'll be delighted to escort you," Ned declared.

Renno stalked alone at the head of the single-file column, with El-i-chi directly behind him and two other senior warriors bringing up the rear. Seventeen junior warriors, most of them in their late teens and early twenties, occupied the middle, and day after day they marveled at the blistering pace the young war chief set.

They, like him, were in their physical prime, but as they struggled to keep up, they were awed by his seemingly inexhaustible energy. Except when he detected the presence of others, he always trotted, never walking, and on occasion he did not halt from sunrise until sundown.

Occasionally he or El-i-chi paused to bring down a deer or a wild pig, or wild geese. But, when necessary, Renno seemed content to eat only a few handfuls of parched corn and a few strips of smoked venison. Apparently the tales the junior warriors had heard about him were true. He had the eyes of a hawk, the sensitive hearing of a buck, and the cleverness of a fox.

He had a sixth sense for knowing when he had pushed his subordinates to the limits of their endurance and always called a halt before anyone collapsed. He had a sure instinct for game, and although they were traveling through unfamiliar country, he always avoided the sentry outposts of hostile tribes.

One incident demonstrated vividly that he well deserved his recent promotion to the high rank of war chief. When only a few days' march from their destination, traveling about fifty miles inland from the Great Salt Sea, Renno was leading the line at his usual untiring pace at an hour when the sun stood directly overhead. He made no sound, and he always managed to avoid hidden tree roots that might trip the unwary.

Suddenly he raised a hand in warning, halting the column, and dropped to the ground, holding one ear close to the mossy earth. El-i-chi stood silently, and the others followed his example.

Then Renno leaped to his feet and silently indicated that he wanted the warriors to climb quickly high into the branches of the tallest trees around. They lost no time obeying the order, and soon after they were hidden in the leafy branches they heard the approach of many men.

A large band of warriors appeared below, heading northward. They were wearing war paint. Even the most inexperienced of the juniors knew, after counting the warriors, that they formed a force that badly outnumbered the Seneca.

These strangers wore alternating streaks of white and

black war paint. Only the seniors among the Seneca realized they were Conoy, members of a small, belligerent tribe that rejected all alliances with other nations and adamantly refused to permit other Indians to cross their territory for any reason.

Only Renno's alert, instant reaction to danger prevented a small war. The main body of Conoy marched past the trees, unaware of the presence of aliens above them, and the juniors were ready to descend. Fortunately, however, Seneca discipline was strict, and none dared to move until their war chief gave the signal.

Renno remained hidden and made no move. Some of the juniors thought he was being too cautious. But a short period of time elapsed, and then a Conoy rear guard of ten senior warriors made its appearance. These veterans were well-trained, and as they moved, they conducted a thorough search of the terrain.

The last warrior in the short line dropped to one knee and examined the bent grass that the Seneca had trampled. In a moment the warrior would call out to his companions, and a battle appeared inevitable.

But Renno acted swiftly. Before the Conoy could make a sound, the young Seneca drew the bone-handled knife of double-edged Sheffield steel that Colonel John Churchill had given him in London and threw it with unerring accuracy. It plunged hilt-deep into the unsuspecting warrior's back, and he pitched forward, dying silently.

His companions, unaware of his fate, moved on and soon passed out of sight. At any moment, however, they would realize he was missing and would turn back for him.

Renno lost no time. Quickly dropping to the ground, he beckoned, and as his subordinates obeyed, he removed his knife from the dead Conoy's back and scalped him. He was on his way southward at a run before he could place the dripping scalp in his belt.

Now he was in earnest, well knowing that a band of eighty Conoy would be certain to seek vengeance when they found the senior warrior's body, and the mission of the Seneca was to prevent war, not start one.

Renno ran at a sprinter's pace, his eyes constantly searching the ground ahead, his ears straining for the possible sounds of other Conoy in the area. His subordinates kept up only because of their grueling training since early boyhood. Most were relieved, however, when night fell. Now, they believed, Renno would halt and give them at least a brief rest.

Instead he continued to run until his heart hammered in his ears and he found himself gasping for breath. Only then, in the middle of the night, did he finally call a halt. The exhausted Seneca dropped to the ground without delay and fought for breath. Before Renno permitted them time to rest, however, he circled the area to make certain there were no foes lurking nearby.

Renno let them rest only a short time. Then he silently roused them, and the rapid march was resumed. Not until long after the sun rose, when they reached the bank of a broad river, did he call a longer halt.

The warriors immediately spread out, each seeking his own cover, and promptly dropped off to sleep.

Renno continued to study the ground. The tired El-i-chi was curious and watched him as he leaned against a tree.

"Our Seneca will be hungry when they awaken," Renno said quietly, and pointed to the tracks of a deer.

His brother grinned at him. Together they went off down the river bank in search of the deer.

When the warriors awakened, they smelled roasting meat. They ate their fill beside the fire that Renno and El-i-chi had made and were pleased when they learned that the march would not start again until the following morning. Most of them had grown to manhood believing that the legendary Ghonka possessed powers greater than those of mere humans, and now they were convinced that his sons were similarly endowed.

Chapter II

General and Mrs. Andrew Wilson spent a week at the Ridley home outside Norfolk, but as Renno had not yet appeared, they decided to return home without further delay. Not only was Andrew needed at his own large farm, but he wanted to organize a contingency mobilization of his frontier battalions in case the Virginians needed them. The time he spent in the wilderness with Ned convinced him also that the Pimlico were planning a major campaign against the colonists.

Austin and Mary Ridley escorted their guests to the Ridley brig at the Norfolk wharf. Ned and Betsy went along, but Anne was in school.

Andrew Wilson's last words to Austin were strong and uncompromising. "If you decide you need help against the Pimlico," he said, "don't hesitate to let me know. I can mobilize in a week's time."

24

The Ridleys waited until the brig set sail before they started home, and dusk was falling by the time they arrived.

Mary was surprised and concerned to find that little Anne, who should have come home from school two hours earlier, had not yet appeared. Ned, who had not yet had his gelding unsaddled, immediately went in search of the child. The one-room schoolhouse was closed, its door locked for the night, and he found no sign of his sister on the road. He went immediately to a neighbor's, whose two small children also attended the school and often played with Anne.

Tom Beardsley, a planter, met the young militia officer at the front door, his expression grave. "I was just coming over to your house," he said. "I heard some terribly disturbing news from my children a few minutes ago." He made an effort to compose himself, then turned and called. "Billy, Edna—come here, please."

The little boy and girl, both of whom had been weeping, made an appearance.

"Tell Mr. Ridley what you just told me," their father directed.

Edna tried to speak, but dissolved into tears.

Billy struggled to get the words out. "We were walking home from school," he said. "Edna and Annie and I. When we came to the patch of woods where the road curves after you pass Mr. Allen's general store— you know the place I mean?—three Indians came out of the woods."

Ned stiffened.

"The Indians grabbed Annie, Mr. Ridley. They didn't do anything to Edna and me. One of them put a hand over her mouth so she couldn't scream, and they ran off into the woods with her."

"What did the Indians look like, Billy? This is important."

The boy thought hard. "Like—like Indians, Mr. Ridley."

25

"They were warriors," his sister added. "They had scalp locks. They were naked to the waist. And—and they all looked greasy and disgusting."

"Were they wearing any war paint?" Ned demanded.

Both children nodded. "It was blue," Billy said. "Bright blue, and it was smeared all over their faces and bodies."

Ned looked at Tom. "Pimlico," he said with quiet emphasis.

"No doubt about it," the planter replied. "You don't know how sorry I am. One thing is sure. There's going to be hell to pay for this."

Ned made an immediate decision. "Call up your militia company, Tom. I'll alert the other commanders, and maybe we can muster the whole battalion by tomorrow afternoon."

"My God! Are you thinking of attacking the Pimlico with a—single battalion?"

"I don't see that we have any choice," Ned said. "Not when my little sister's life is at stake."

Ned mounted his horse, then galloped home and gave his family the grim news. Tears came to Mary's eyes, but she bravely brushed them away. Betsy looked as though she had been struck across the face. Color rose in her cheeks, and her green eyes blazed with anger.

A tight, white line formed around Austin Ridley's mouth. "One of our sloops is due to put into port tomorrow. I'll send it after the brig that's taking the Wilsons back to Massachusetts Bay in the hope that they can be intercepted at sea. If not, the sloop will reach Boston even before they land there."

Ned told him he had called up the local militia.

"I'll have to think about that," his father said. "According to our estimates the Pimlico have at least a thousand warriors on hand, and at best we can muster three hundred men in these parts. We've got to save Annie, God knows, but I don't want the battalion to suffer needless casualties and lose a battle in the bargain."

They were still discussing the situation when a servant came into the room, highly agitated, to announce that a band of Indians had just come to the house.

Austin and Ned hurried out, cocked pistols in their hands, and were delighted when they saw that the newcomers were Seneca.

"Renno!" Ned cried, clasping his friend's hand.

"You've arrived just in time to join us on an expedition that I wish we could have avoided," Austin declared.

The Seneca escort was given a bivouac area on the Ridley property, and servants brought them food.

Renno, who listened in grave silence to the news of Anne Ridley's abduction, was invited to dine with the family. He said very little as he was taken into the house, where a servant brought him water for a bath and a suit and shirt of Ned's. He continued to wear his own moccasins.

Renno found that he enjoyed doing things in the English manner—though of course he would never do them in the land of the Seneca. His months in London and his long association with Jeffrey and the other colonists had finally made him feel at ease in the white man's society. He no longer feared that an easy command of the colonials' language and customs would endanger his secure sense of himself as a Seneca, faithful to the ways of his people.

Mary and her elder daughter had been told in detail about Renno, but they were nevertheless startled by the appearance of the white Indian, a tanned man with pale eyes, his head shaved on either side of his scalp lock, who could wear the clothes of an English colonial as though he had never known any other form of attire.

Sensitive to the family's distress, Renno was nevertheless stunned when he saw Betsy. He had heard Ned speak with amused affection of the sister who consistently rejected the many suitors who had asked for her hand in marriage. But he hadn't realized she was such a dazzling beauty or that she had such obvious strength of character. It was difficult for him to focus his attention on anyone else.

Aware of his interest, Betsy found him equally fascinating. She had been unable to form a mental picture of a white man who was at the same time a complete savage. Certainly she hadn't expected him to be ruggedly handsome, with a personality that immediately appealed to her, and when he held her chair for her at the dinner table she was startled by his familiarity with English manners.

A further surprise was in store for her. The young Seneca handled a knife and fork with aplomb, and he spoke a fairly fluent English, with an almost imperceptible accent.

Renno did far more listening than talking as Austin and Ned discussed their plans to attack the Pimlico. The colonel was in favor of waiting until reinforcements arrived from Massachusetts Bay, but Ned insisted that the local militia battalion conduct an immediate assault to release Anne from captivity.

At last Austin realized that Renno had said very little. "What are your thoughts? You understand the mentality of Indians far better than we do."

Renno ate some of his roasted beef and baked potato as he pondered. "As I understand it, sir," he said, "the Pimlico have been calling in their warriors from their outlying towns in preparation for a major campaign against the Virginia settlers. Is that correct?"

"It is," the colonel replied. "We estimate they have at least one thousand warriors already mustered in their main town."

Renno turned to Ned. "You've told me that only your sister was abducted. The two children who were accompanying her weren't harmed in any way."

Ned nodded.

"Then I feel certain the kidnapping was a deliberate

act intended to provoke you," Renno declared. "Most Indian nations prefer to fight a defensive battle when they face white men armed with rifles."

Betsy leaned forward. "You're saying that Annie was abducted in the hope that my father would retaliate by attacking the Pimlico?"

"Precisely," Renno said crisply.

"You sound as though you disapprove of an attack!" Ned became belligerent.

"Indeed I do," Renno replied. "In the first place, the Pimlico undoubtedly know your strength and realize you can't send more than three hundred riflemen against them. You understand the principles of wilderness warfare, Ned. Warriors will lie in wait for your column as you march through the forest to their town, and you'll lose at least one-third of your force before you can open your assault."

In spite of his anxiety, his burning zeal to rescue little Anne, Ned had to admit that his Seneca friend was right.

"What of my daughter, Renno?" Mary asked.

He hesitated. "May I be blunt, Mrs. Ridley?"

"Please. My little girl's life is at stake, and for all I know she has already been killed."

Renno shook his head. "Few Indian nations wage war against children, and nothing I've ever heard about the Pimlico indicates that they're barbarians. On the other hand, they won't hesitate to take swift action—brutal action, perhaps—if it becomes necessary."

"Spell that out for us, if you will," Austin said.

"Very well, sir." Renno spoke reluctantly. "If you conduct this attack, the Pimlico might try to take your daughter off to one of their more remote villages, where it would be impossible for you ever to find her. There she would either be brought up as a member of the tribe or would be given to the local sachem and his family as a slave."

Mary found it difficult to hold back her tears.

"If they couldn't spirit her away before the battle started," Renno continued, "I'm afraid they would regard her as too much of a nuisance, too much of a hindrance." He stopped short.

Betsy looked at him solemnly. "Are you saying what I think you're trying to tell us?"

"Yes, ma'am. They wouldn't hesitate to kill her."

There was a long, depressed silence as two serving maids cleared away the remains of the main course.

For the visitor's sake Mary ordered that dessert be brought to the table.

"If Renno is right," Colonel Ridley said to his son, "and I can't dispute him, our hands are tied. There's no way our frontier battalion can attack the Pimlico without placing Anne in even greater danger."

Ned pounded the table with a clenched fist. "What are we to do, then? Suffer the humiliation of opening negotiations with them and begging them to let us ransom Annie? All of us know how important it is to save face with an Indian nation if we hope to keep their respect!"

Betsy reached out and put a hand on her brother's arm to steady him.

He muttered a half-meant apology.

Only Renno was eating dessert. "If this unhappy incident had not taken place, how were you intending to use my services?"

"We had hoped you could persuade the Pimlico to make peace with us," the colonel said.

The young Seneca war chief turned to Ned. "Were you planning to go into the land of the Pimlico with me?"

"If you thought it appropriate. I was going to leave all that up to your discretion."

Renno spoke decisively. "Early tomorrow morning," he said, "my Seneca and I will march to the town of the Pimlico. You will come with us, Ned, as proof to them that we are friends and allies. But I alone will be the spokesman for our party. You will say nothing to them about your sister."

"You're asking a great deal of me, Renno."

Betsy was the first to grasp the import of what

Renno had in mind. "You think you can persuade or cajole them into setting Anne free?" she asked.

Renno measured his words. "In one way or another," he said, "I give you my pledge that I will return to Norfolk with your little sister, and I promise you she will remain unharmed."

All four of the Ridleys stared at him, wondering how he dared to make such a sweeping promise.

Austin started to ask another question, but thought better of it. Experience had taught him that it was unwise to quiz an Indian too closely.

Betsy was less cautious than her father. "How can you be so certain?" she demanded.

Renno's smile was tight. "I know my people," he said, and turned to Mary. "I know you're concerned, Mrs. Ridley, but try not to worry too much about your little girl. I'm sure she hasn't been harmed because she would be of no use to them as a hostage if she were dead. And you may rest assured the Pimlico will heed what I say to them. When a Seneca speaks, the warriors of other Indian nations listen."

Betsy realized he was not boasting or showing off. He meant what he said, and his self-confidence inspired confidence in others. All in all he was a remarkable young man. "You must be tired after your long journey," she said, "but perhaps you'd like a glass of port with Papa and Ned before you go to bed."

Renno grinned at her and shook his head. "It has been said that Indians become ill when they drink fermented juices. I know that my skin is the color of your skin, but I am nevertheless a Seneca, and I learned in England that I cannot drink the wine and liquor of the white man."

"Then perhaps you'll have a cup of tea with all of us." Betsy couldn't help returning his smile.

His bow was as courtly as that of the most polished gentleman in the entourage of King William. "Nothing would give me greater pleasure, ma'am."

As she led him toward the parlor Betsy knew she had never encountered anyone even remotely like him.

He was an Indian in every imaginable way, but at the same time his grace, his speech, and his manners were those of the English upper class. No wonder Papa and Ned had been singing his praises ever since the Louisburg campaign.

Before everyone retired, Renno further astonished Betsy and her mother by discussing the plays he had seen in London. "At first," he said, "I found the theater confusing because my knowledge of your language was so limited. Now I owe a great debt to your playwright, Shakespeare. *Hamlet* and *Macbeth* inspired me to gain a greater understanding of English, and by the time I saw *Julius Caesar* and *Othello,* I was able to grasp the meaning of most of what the actors said."

Betsy could not contain her curiosity. "Do you read and write our language?"

He shook his head, but was unwilling to reveal to her that he lost his teacher when Deborah Alwin had married the Reverend Obadiah Jenkins. "I can make out a few passages in the Bible," he said, "but that is all. Someday I hope to read."

She was tempted to offer her services as his instructor, but didn't want him to think her overly bold.

Ned showed the visitor to a guest chamber.

Renno grinned when he saw the four-poster that dominated the room. "When I first went to England," he said, "I spent a long time sleeping on the floor. Now I have learned to appreciate beds, even though I fear they make a warrior too soft." All at once he sobered. "Do not wear your militia uniform when we leave," he said, "and be ready to go very early in the morning."

Shortly after daybreak the next morning Ned, attired in buckskins, found Renno squatting at the campfire of his warriors in their bivouac area behind the house. He had quietly reverted to his Indian ways and was eating a slab of cooked, dripping meat with his fingers.

Before the Seneca departed, they carefully applied their war paint, smearing a broad streak of green on one cheek and yellow on the other.

"We use the paint on our faces for identification, so the Pimlico will know us," Renno explained to Ned. "But we put no paint on our bodies. If we did, that would mean we are on the warpath and that we think of the Pimlico as our enemies. This way they will know our mission is friendly."

Austin Ridley came out of the house a short time before the band was ready to depart. "We'll agree to any reasonable peace terms with the Pimlico," he said. "I just hope you won't have to include my daughter's release in your negotiations."

"I hope to bargain separately for her," Renno said.

"May the Lord God march with you," Austin declared fervently.

The company left and Ned, who was thoroughly familiar with the terrain, took the lead with Renno. To the Seneca's surprise he was untiring and managed to maintain their leader's swift, grueling pace.

By nightfall, when Renno called a halt, they had covered more than thirty miles, a far greater distance than a platoon of militiamen could have marched in the same period of time.

Several junior warriors went off in search of game, two others repaired to a small lake to fish, and Renno ordered a campfire lighted.

Ned protested. "Do you think that's wise? We're already deep into the territory that the Pimlico claim."

Renno remained cheerful. "Their sentries have been following our movements since this afternoon. You may be sure that their sachem and his war chiefs know we are making a journey to their town."

Regarding himself as an expert in wilderness travel, Ned was surprised. "I saw no Pimlico scouts!"

"I counted five of them," Renno replied. "But I knew of no reason to let them know I saw them. I know of no such reason right now, when two of their sentries are keeping watch on us."

Ned could catch no glimpse of the Pimlico in the dark forest that lay beyond the light cast by the campfire. "You don't think they'll attack us tonight?"

"We are as safe as we would be in our own land. Perhaps only their leaders can identify warriors who wear green and yellow paint, but that is enough. Their sachem and his chiefs know the Seneca would go to war against them if they attacked us. They have no claim or grudge against us, so we will not be disturbed."

His prophecy proved accurate. The Seneca roasted the game and fish they caught, then slept peacefully. In the morning they ate the remains of their food before putting out their fire and resuming their journey.

Before noon they could see the pointed tops of the poles on the stockade that surrounded the Pimlico town, and Renno donned his bonnet of hawk feathers. "Ned," he said, "I know this won't be easy for you, but say nothing on any subject, and don't even mention your little sister. I alone will act as our spokesman."

As he had anticipated, a delegation of Pimlico warriors led by a man wearing a cloak of dyed bright blue feathers left the town and marched across the cornfields toward the visitors, who were just emerging from the forest.

Renno promptly halted, waited until the Pimlico came close enough for conversation, and then raised his left hand, palm upward. "Ghonka, the Great Sachem of the Iroquois, sends his greetings of peace to his brothers of the Pimlico through his son, Renno, war chief of the Seneca."

The man in the blue cloak, who had also halted, raised his arm in a similar salute. "Moy-na-ho, sachem of the Pimlico, welcomes his brothers of the Seneca in peace."

Now the members of both parties saluted each other, and Ned controlled himself sufficiently to give the sign of peace, too. But the middle-aged warrior who stood behind Moy-na-ho, wearing headgear that indicated he was his nation's principal medicine man, kept his arms at his sides.

Renno was aware of the anger in the man's eyes. He

knew El-i-chi was conscious of the medicine man's hostility, too, so for the moment he was content.

The Pimlico fell in beside the Seneca, and the double file moved toward the town, where huge crowds emerged from longhouses and a few smaller buildings to stare at the strangers. There were more warriors than old men, women, and children, proof that the Pimlico indeed were mobilizing, and they were especially curious about the legendary Seneca, who reputedly had never lost a war for eleven generations.

The individual visitors were taken, one by one, to the homes of their hosts, and Renno, after a final warning glance at Ned, went with Moy-na-ho to his hut.

There the sachem's pretty wife awaited them and extended ceremonial gourds of parched corn and water to the Seneca war chief. Renno accepted a few kernels of corn and a swallow of water.

Moy-na-ho then offered his wife to the visitor. Renno refused, a quick look at the woman conveying that the Seneca followed a different custom and that he hoped she wouldn't be offended by his refusal. Her smile indicated that she understood, and she quickly left.

Moy-na-ho and Renno seated themselves on opposite sides of a small cooking fire outside the hut, the sachem of the Pimlico lighted a clay pipe, and the pair passed it back and forth in silence until its contents had burned to ashes. Then they began to converse, strictly observing the amenities of the universal Indian code of conduct. Renno spoke in the Mohawk dialect and Moy-na-ho used the tongue of the Potomac. Each spoke in his own language, which the other understood.

They discussed the prospects for the hunting season in their respective lands, speculated on the size of their grain crops, and quietly boasted about the corn and beans both nations had accumulated in their storehouses. Renno exaggerated politely, and Moy-na-ho did the same; the ritual had long outgrown whatever useful purpose it might have had over earlier centuries, but had to be observed.

In spite of the formality of the discussion, Renno concluded that he liked the Pimlico sachem, who appeared to be about thirty-five summers. A scar on his forehead and another on his chin indicated he had been valorous in battle, and his manner was pleasant and straightforward. Renno judged him to be a man who did not give his word lightly, but one who would keep any pledge he had made.

They talked for more than two hours, and then they adjourned to a natural amphitheater in the hills just outside the town. The other members of Renno's party were already on hand, with Ned Ridley having obvious difficulty controlling his impatience. Pimlico warriors by the hundreds had gathered, and several sides of venison were roasting over fires.

Moy-na-ho and Renno sat apart from all the others, near the fire, and the sachem's wife served them large chunks of smoking venison, a gourd of vegetables unfamiliar to the Seneca, and a corn pudding sweetened with maple syrup. They ate in polite silence, then wiped their hands on their bare torsos.

The demands of protocol observed, the fire was extinguished, and the two leaders took places opposite each other. The Seneca and Ned sat cross-legged behind Renno, and members of the Pimlico council filed in behind Moy-na-ho.

El-i-chi spoke quickly in an undertone to his brother. "I have learned much," he said. "The medicine man, Si-de-lo, is the troublemaker. He is ambitious for his son, Ra-san-ur. He is the tall warrior with the broad shoulders."

Renno, seemingly paying no attention to the Pimlico, studied a scowling young giant of a warrior.

"Si-de-lo," El-i-chi continued, "wants to make war against the colonists because his son will lead the Pimlico in battle. Regardless of whether they win or lose, he believes his son will succeed Moy-na-ho as sachem."

Renno addressed his brother softly. "What does the sachem want?"

"He leads the peace party."

The young war chief nodded. "What have you learned about the sister of Ned?"

"Only that she is alive and safe," El-i-chi said. "The Pimlico are not eager to speak about her, so I could find out no details."

There was no time for further private conversation. Moy-na-ho placed a tomahawk decorated with wild turkey feathers on the ground before him. Renno did the same with his own, unadorned tomahawk, and the parley began.

Moy-na-ho delivered a long, rambling speech of welcome expressing his pleasure that a delegation of the mighty Seneca had traveled so far to pay a visit to the people of the Pimlico. The only jarring note was his mild wonder over the presence of a white colonist in the ranks of the Seneca delegation.

Most Indian speeches were interminable, but Renno had learned from his father that it was almost always best to speak concisely and forcefully. "Renno, the son of Ghonka, the Great Sachem of the Iroquois, a war chief of the Seneca, thanks the Pimlico for their welcome to him and his brothers. Renno comes to the Pimlico in peace. But his heart is heavy. The six nations of the Iroquois League have made a treaty of peace with the sachems of the English colonies. Now they have learned that their brothers of the Pimlico prepare for war against the colonists who called themselves men of Virginia. Is this true?"

"It is true," Moy-na-ho said. "But my heart also is heavy. It is not my wish to lead my people to war. But my warriors clamor for this war."

Si-de-lo looked smug and Ra-san-ur grinned openly.

Renno disliked the pair and realized he had to take

37

a blunt approach. "Let it be known to the men of all lands," he said, speaking loudly so that all of the warriors of the Pimlico could hear every word, "that the nations of the Iroquois—the Seneca and the Mohawk, the Oneida and the Onondaga, the Tuscarora and the Cayuga—want peace with every Indian nation. We, who in my own time have conquered the Huron and the Ottawa, the great Algonquian and the Erie, seek war with no one. Let it also be known that the warriors of the Iroquois keep their sworn word. The English colonists are our friends and brothers. Ghonka, the Great Sachem, will throw the tomahawk of war at any nation that makes war on our English brothers."

Slowly, his gestures deliberately theatrical, he drew the strips of white and black wampum from his belt.

El-i-chi rose to his feet with easy grace, carried the two strips across the open space that separated the Seneca from their hosts, and placed the wampum strips side by side in front of Moy-na-ho. Then, not glancing at the Pimlico, he returned to his place.

A tense silence pervaded the amphitheater.

"Let the warriors of the Pimlico think about the words that Renno, the son of Ghonka, has spoken," the young Seneca war chief said. "Renno will wait until the god of the sun sleeps and the god of the moon appears for the answer of the Pimlico." It was clear that he was throwing down the gauntlet and was placing a time limit on the Pimlico deliberations.

There was a stir in the ranks of the warriors. Renno could see that only the young remained defiant. The senior warriors knew better, and Renno could detect that they had no desire for a war with the most powerful nations in all of America.

"The Pimlico will give their answer when the god of the moon rises," Moy-na-ho said.

Ordinarily that would have ended the parley, but Renno did not change his cross-legged position. "The Seneca have also heard," he said, "that the girl-child of the sachem of the Virginians has been taken as a captive of the Pimlico. Is this true?"

Moy-na-ho looked uneasy as he searched for a reply.

Ra-san-ur could not keep silent. "It is true," he shouted. "It is not the fault of the Pimlico that the sachem of Virginia did not guard his girl-child. She is fair booty!"

El-i-chi had to restrain Ned, who would have jumped to his feet.

Renno well realized that, according to the universal Indian point of view, the capture of Anne Ridley had been just and fair. The standards of the English were different, of course, but he could not place his major mission in jeopardy. At the same time he had to keep his word to the Ridleys that he would return Anne to them safely.

He stared hard at Ra-san-ur, his eyes lidded. "Is this warrior of the Pimlico the captor of the girl-child?"

"I am!" The burly warrior was belligerent, defiant.

"Is he a man who takes risks for sport?" Renno did not raise his voice, but there was a metallic ring in his tone.

Ra-san-ur knew what was coming. Rising, he drew his knife and, thrusting it forward, made a circle with it.

"Renno makes the warrior an offer for sport. Will you fight me, here and now, with each of us armed only with a knife? Will you agree that the girl-child will become the slave of the winner?"

"I will fight," Ra-san-ur shouted. "And I agree to the wager."

The huge crowd roared in delight. Only the small band of Seneca remained calm.

"My God," Ned said, "you can't do this, Renno. There must be some other way we can get hold of Anne. That brute might kill you."

Renno merely smiled as he stood, removed his bonnet, then divested himself of his pistols.

El-i-chi addressed Ned in the best English he could muster. "Renno is Seneca. All warriors afraid of Seneca. This help Renno win."

Ned understood what the young warrior was telling

39

him, but was still aghast. "Let me fight him, Renno. Anne is my sister, and I demand the right to take the chance for her sake. I—"

"Only an Indian," Renno said, interrupting him quietly, "knows the ways that other Indians fight."

Stripped to his loincloth, Renno moved into the clearing. The Pimlico warriors pressed forward, jostling each other for places that would afford the best view.

The Seneca remained seated on the ground in a double file, and although they made no move, they kept their rifles close at hand. Their weapons, as everyone in the amphitheater knew, were a guarantee that no ardent Pimlico would intervene and try to join in the fight.

Ned Ridley tried to console himself with the knowledge that the Seneca warriors were completely unflustered. Their confidence in Renno appeared boundless.

Moy-na-ho picked up the strips of white and black wampum and thrust them into his belt. For the moment the issue of war or peace was forgotten; his people were consumed with the lust of witnessing individual combat.

Si-de-lo was speaking earnestly to his son, and it was not difficult for Renno to guess what the medicine man was saying. Ra-san-ur had a rare opportunity. If he could defeat a war chief of the dreaded Seneca, he would be a hero and it would be far easier to dethrone Moy-na-ho and become sachem of the tribe.

His arms folded, Renno studied his foe. Ra-san-ur was taller and heavier. His chest was thick, his arms massive, and there was no doubt he would be a formidable opponent. Renno would need to rely on speed and intelligence rather than brute strength.

Ra-san-ur accepted his father's words in silence, and as he moved toward the open area at the base of the amphitheater, the Pimlico warriors roared their approval. Like his opponent, he wore only his loincloth, and in one hand he clutched a razor-sharp dagger of stone.

Renno braced himself, but made no attempt to draw his own weapon. His principal concern now was that of judging his foe's speed and agility. Dexterity would be the key to the outcome of the fight.

All at once Ra-san-ur raced toward him, the knife poised, and he brought his arm down in a vicious arc, intending to dispatch the Seneca with a single blow.

Renno waited until the last possible moment, then sidestepped neatly. The blade cut nothing but air. His original guess was confirmed. The Pimlico had great power, but he was relatively slow on his feet and slow to react to unexpected situations.

The giant turned, snarled, and gathered himself for another rush.

This time Renno moved inside the intended stab, the knife missing him only by inches. The Pimlico was forced to stop short. Renno promptly delivered two blows, the first to his foe's middle, doubling him over, followed by a stinging punch to the left side of his face.

Two bearlike arms reached out to embrace Renno and throw him to the ground. But Renno had already determined that under no circumstances would he allow Ra-san-ur to use his greater strength in a wrestling match. Putting his entire weight behind his next blow, his fist crashed into the heavier man's right eye, sending him reeling backward. The warriors shouted wildly, trying to encourage their champion.

Ignoring the commotion, Renno moved forward, raining punches on the Pimlico's face and body, then dancing out of reach when Ra-san-ur tried to use his knife or hurl him to the ground. So far he was untouched and unscathed.

The disciplined Seneca warriors continued to sit stolidly, their arms folded across their chests as they watched the fight with seeming passivity.

Ned Ridley was unable to match their calm. His fists

were clenched, perspiration drenched his buckskin shirt. "Finish him, Renno!" he yelled.

The duel was much like a fight with swords, an art that Renno had learned in London. The Pimlico was expecting him to use only Indian techniques and was confused when the Seneca relied on speed and balance.

As they drew nearer again Ra-san-ur kicked hard at his foe's groin. Renno jumped backward a short distance, caught hold of the Pimlico's ankle with both hands, and flipped him over. Ra-san-ur landed hard on his back, and his supporters groaned in disappointment.

Renno was expected to leap on the larger man and knife him, but Ra-san-ur, although momentarily dazed, was still far too strong for his lighter foe to take such a risk. The Seneca stood immobile, his face expressionless, and waited for Ra-san-ur to stand again.

His cool, almost detached manner aroused the reluctant admiration of the crowd, and some of the warriors applauded him. But Renno shut out the sounds of the commotion and continued to concentrate his complete attention on his enemy. Ghonka had taught him early in his boyhood that the warrior who allowed himself to become distracted from his goal for even an instant was sure to lose his life.

The humiliated Ra-san-ur dragged himself to his feet and took a fresh grip on his knife. He, the most powerful of all the Pimlico, was being disgraced by a Seneca whom he could tear apart with his bare hands. He was outraged.

Renno saw the violent anger in the man's eyes and was further encouraged. The warrior who lost his temper in combat lacked the ability to think clearly.

Once again the dogged Ra-san-ur ran forward, his knife raised. This time Renno misjudged his movements, and the knife slashed him above his left eye, inflicting a bleeding cut.

The sight of that blood threw the spectators into a frenzy. The warriors screamed in delight as they urged their champion to kill a member of the dreaded Seneca.

Renno's band remained motionless, accepting his injury calmly. Renno himself knew he could not afford to make another mistake. Brushing away the blood so it wouldn't drip into his eye, he moved backward in a circle, avoiding the giant who was now stalking him, ready for the kill.

Twice Ra-san-ur swiped at him with the knife, and twice Renno dodged and retreated. The Pimlico's face contorted by hate and anger, he struck yet again. Renno ducked successfully. Aware that he had caught the giant off balance, he unleashed a flurry of driving punches, each delivered with all the force he could command.

Ra-san-ur could not escape, and as he pawed the air with his knife he was rocked by blow after blow. Any one of these punches would have sent a smaller man sprawling, but the Pimlico's stamina was extraordinary. Although he staggered he did not fall.

Ultimately, however, he could no longer tolerate the barrage, and the crowd became hushed as he sank to the hard, bare ground, crumpling in slow motion.

He was not yet beaten, however, and still had one last chance. As he collapsed he threw his knife.

Renno saw him raise his arm and threw himself to the ground. His opponent's blade whistled harmlessly over his head and fell at the far end of the clearing.

Enough was enough. Springing to his feet again, Renno drew his own knife for the first time, leaned over Ra-san-ur, and coldly drove his steel blade deep into the Pimlico's heart. This was a fight to the death, and no warrior, regardless of his tribe, would have respected the combatant who showed mercy to his foe.

Ra-san-ur died instantly, and when Renno withdrew his knife the giant's inert body fell backward onto the ground. Renno swiftly and expertly cut away his scalp lock, the trophy of victory.

The grieving Si-de-lo stared at the body of his son for a moment and then turned to look at his Seneca conqueror.

Never had Renno seen such blazing hatred in any man's eyes. He called on the manitous of the Seneca to protect him from the evil spell the medicine man might try to cast over him.

The Pimlico were chanting Renno's name, saluting his triumph. He had been so masterful they did not resent the defeat of their own champion. All they had heard about the prowess of the renowned Seneca had proved to be true, and they hailed the winner. It occurred to Renno that his victory would help insure that the Pimlico would support their sachem in his bid for peace.

But there was a more immediate issue to settle. Holding Ra-san-ur's scalp lock high above his head to silence the crowd, Renno said in a clear, loud voice, "Let the girl-child be brought to me." Then he placed the scalp lock in his belt and turned to his own band.

El-i-chi reached into a small pouch he carried and shook a handful of a reddish powder into his hand. Then he smeared a quantity of the substance on the cut over Renno's eye.

The pain caused by the powder was excruciating, but Renno tolerated the agony in silence without flinching. In a few moments the pain began to subside, and his forehead throbbed dully.

A group of women in ankle-length doeskin dresses came into the arena, one of them leading Anne Ridley by a leather thong looped around her neck.

Ned would have started toward his sister, but Renno took hold of his arm.

"The Pimlico wouldn't understand," the young Seneca war chief said as he donned his bonnet of hawk feathers. "It was I who won her in combat."

The crowd fell silent again as Renno walked slowly across the clearing. The woman offered him the loose end of the leather thong.

Instead of taking it, he slashed it with his knife,

setting the little girl free. "You'll be safe now," he told her in English, and lifted her into his arms.

She clung to him and became ecstatic when she saw her brother. Ned told her what had happened, and she rewarded Renno with a fierce hug.

Several warriors removed the body of Ra-san-ur to a burial platform, where it would lie until vultures reduced it to a skeleton. Then Moy-na-ho led his war chiefs, medicine men, elders, and senior warriors to their council lodge, where they would debate the issue of peace and war.

The Seneca were conducted to a large hut. On the way Anne Ridley clung to the hands of her brother and Renno.

Women brought the visitors another hot meal of venison and vegetables, and the warriors quickly began to eat. But Anne was so excited she refused food.

"Eat," Renno told her. "We don't know when we'll have another meal of anything but parched corn and dried strips of meat."

Had her brother given her the order the little girl might have rebelled, but she obeyed Renno instantly and without question, her eyes wide with admiration for him. He had made a conquest.

Dusk came as the Seneca were finishing their meal, and when the moon appeared beyond the cornfields a senior warrior of the Pimlico came to the hut.

Renno took his senior warriors and Ned with him. "Stay close to my people and don't be afraid," Renno told Anne. "They'll make certain that no one harms you. We'll soon return."

The visitors were conducted to the council lodge, where the Pimlico were seated five and six deep in a semicircle behind their leader at one side of a fire.

Renno lowered himself to a cross-legged position on the opposite side of the fire, his followers ranging themselves behind him.

Moy-na-ho made a long, rambling speech in which he extolled the virtues of the Pimlico. Renno only half-listened and was conscious of the hatred in the eyes of the ashen-faced Si-de-lo. The medicine man had lost his bid for ultimate power as well as his son. It was well to keep in mind that he might try to make yet another move.

When the sachem of the Pimlico finished speaking, Renno replied briefly. It wasn't the way of the Seneca to praise themselves, and he gently but firmly reminded the sachem that the issue of war or peace had not yet been decided.

Moy-na-ho picked up the strip of black wampum and cast it into the fire. "The warriors of the Pimlico choose peace," he said, and offered a strip of his own wampum.

Instead of taking it himself, Renno gestured to Ned, who went to the sachem and accepted a piece of rawhide to which white beads had been sewn. The peace was now binding.

The ceremony ended with the lighting of a pipe, which was then passed back and forth. Renno noted, however, that Si-de-lo did not raise the stem to his lips and merely handed it to the elder who sat next to him. The young Seneca's eyes narrowed. There was no longer any doubt in his mind that the Pimlico medicine man had no intention of abiding by the decision of his sachem and the will of his people.

Moy-na-ho offered the visitors lodging for the night, but Renno politely declined the offer without explanation. Within a short time he and his party departed.

"We're going to leave the land of the Pimlico as rapidly as we can," he told Ned. "So keep up with us as best you're able. If you start to lag we'll adjust our pace to yours." Not waiting for a reply, he slung the sleepy Anne across his back.

Ned protested. "It isn't right for you to carry my sister," he said.

Renno smiled. "I doubt if she weighs more than sixty pounds, but you would soon find her a burden."

"So will you!"

"I think not," Renno replied, his grin broadening.

"Seneca are taught from boyhood to travel rapidly for long distances with fellow warriors on their backs. We never leave our wounded behind after a battle. But if you think you can carry your sister, try it for a time, and if you falter, don't hesitate to give her to me."

El-i-chi took the lead on the beginning of the return journey, and Renno stationed himself in the center of the column directly behind Ned, who held the dozing Anne in his arms.

"Beware of the sting of hornets," Renno called cryptically to his warriors. The Seneca needed no explanation. Their leader was warning them of possible danger from Pimlico unwilling to accept the peace treaty.

They jogged for an hour, and Renno was not surprised to note that Ned, burdened by Anne's weight, was beginning to tire. Rather than offer to relieve his friend, however, he preferred to wait until the Virginian asked for help.

Suddenly an arrow whistled through the air, passing close to Renno's head. He reacted instantly. Emitting a two-toned bird call, he simultaneously pushed Ned Ridley to the ground. "Cover your sister's body with your own," Renno told him tersely, "and don't use your musket or pistol without my permission. We don't want the sound of gunfire to arouse the entire Pimlico tribe."

The Seneca needed no instructions. Swiftly forming a circle, all of them dropped to the ground and fitted arrows into their bows. Renno drew his bow taut and waited. He was certain that Si-de-lo and his followers were responsible for this attack. He intended to retaliate without mercy, but it was imperative to judge the enemy's strength as soon as possible.

All at once his remarkable, hawklike eyesight made out a dark figure. He took careful aim, then released his arrow. Even as the Pimlico warrior fell, Renno was notching another arrow into his bow.

More arrows passed overhead, and there was no sound but the voice of Ned trying to calm and soothe the terrified Anne.

The Seneca were like carved statues, but they soon demonstrated the reason they were feared by other nations. Tracing the flying arrows to their sources, they reacted swiftly.

El-i-chi accounted for one of the enemy, and another senior warrior felled a second. The juniors were not to be outdone, and two of them brought down another pair of Pimlico. Then the remaining Seneca senior warrior killed yet another.

The battle lasted for no more than a few minutes. Then the Pimlico lost their appetite for combat with warriors whose reputation had not been exaggerated. They fled from the scene, making no attempt to maintain quiet.

Renno judged that their company had consisted of thirty to forty men and was pleased. Seneca were able to more than hold their own when they faced odds of only two to one against them.

The killers of the Pimlico quickly scalped their victims, but did not bother to remove the inferior Pimlico weapons from the dead warriors. Then the line of march reformed.

Renno decided to abandon diplomacy. "We'll stay on the trail all night," he said, "so I'll carry the child."

Ned gave him no further argument.

They did not halt until almost noon of the following day. Renno granted the band a respite only when he was reasonably sure they had left the Pimlico hunting grounds behind them. Camp was made in a well-protected hollow, and Renno and El-i-chi again went off on a short, successful hunting expedition.

For the sake of the tired little girl they remained at the site for the rest of the day and the night that followed, and the march was not resumed until the following morning. A rejuvenated Anne elected to straddle Renno's shoulders.

When they approached Norfolk, Renno moved to the head of the column. Anne's jubilant shouts brought her parents and older sister hurrying out of the house.

Renno lowered her to the ground, and she raced to her mother and father.

A happy Ned started to explain to his family what Renno had done. The young Seneca war chief was embarrassed and tried in vain to silence his friend. All at once Betsy Ridley realized that this self-confident white Indian was actually shy! Grateful to him without measure, she impulsively kissed him full on the lips.

Her touch jarred Renno like a bolt of lightning. Betsy felt the same, and for a timeless moment they stared at one another, looking deep into each other's eyes. This was no ordinary, polite kiss. Their mutual attraction had already developed strong roots. Then Austin Ridley was pumping Renno's hand and Mary was hugging him.

A side of beef was cooked in an outdoor pit for the Seneca, and the entire Ridley family ate with them, Anne remaining close at her benefactor's side.

"For however long the peace may last," Austin said to Renno, "you've saved us from fighting a war we couldn't win. I just hope we'll have enough new immigrants in the next year or two to build up our militia strength."

"As long as Moy-na-ho remains as sachem of the Pimlico there will be no war," Renno told him. "But the attack on us after we left their town proves that Si-de-lo will not rest until he gains control of the tribe and destroys Norfolk. Beware of him."

Mary waited until the discussion of military affairs ended before she asked, "Renno, can we persuade you to stay with us for a time?"

He declined with regret. "My warriors are eager to return to our own land," he said. "The season of hunting and fishing has started, and it would be unfair to deny them the sport they deserve."

"Well," Austin said, "I'm sending Ned on a business journey to Charles Town in South Carolina, and Betsy will go with him to visit her cousin there."

He explained that he maintained an office and warehouse in rapidly growing Charles Town and that it was operated by his niece, Lucinda Ridley Watson, an exceptionally competent young woman who had taken charge after an attack of the pox had killed her husband.

"It occurs to me," Austin said, "that you might enjoy seeing another of our English colonies, assuming that your warriors are competent enough to return to the land of the Seneca without you."

"El-i-chi has had more than enough experience to lead them," Renno said, and was tempted. He could not allow himself to look again at Betsy, but he well realized she was the reason he wanted to stay behind. He knew he would regret a failure to become better acquainted with her.

"None of our ships are available at the moment," Ned said, "so we'd travel overland and could take our time. I think you'd enjoy it, Renno."

It was true, the young Seneca war chief reflected, that no pressing business at home necessitated his prompt return to the land of the Seneca. He had accomplished the mission his father had given him, for however long it might last. If he went home now he would spend the rest of the spring and summer hunting and fishing, and he could engage in these sports on a march to Charles Town.

"I wish you'd reconsider," Betsy said to him.

Renno warned himself not to read too much into her invitation. The Ridleys were grateful to him for returning Anne to them, so perhaps she spoke only out of gratitude. He turned to face her.

Betsy's smile was shy, but there was eager anticipation in her eyes. Her hope was genuine.

That was all he needed to know. "I will join you," he said.

Chapter III

On the first day of the overland journey Betsy Ridley, born and reared on the edge of the wilderness, proved to the startled Renno that she was unlike any girl he had ever known. Dressed in a fringed, open-throated shirt and trousers of doeskin, she maintained his rapid pace, easily following him as he marched twenty miles through the wilderness. She was as adept as a woman of the Seneca in observing signs of game in the vicinity.

Renno had assumed that the light musket made for her in England was just an ornament, but Betsy demonstrated that he was mistaken. In mid-afternoon they came to a pond where a number of wild ducks were resting. At the approach of the humans the birds took flight.

Renno reached for an arrow from his quiver, but hesitated when he saw Betsy aim her musket. To his astonishment she felled a duck with a single shot, reloaded with practiced speed, and managed to bring down another before the flock vanished from sight.

He congratulated her on her expertise.

Ned Ridley laughed. "The children in our family have had little choice. Papa started taking us out into the wilderness before we were Annie's age, and he spanked the daylights out of us anytime we missed a shot."

That evening, when they made camp near a small stream, Betsy used her own knife to prepare the birds, then cooked them Indian-style over a spit of forked sticks that she improvised. She accomplished the task effortlessly and even found some wild herbs to sprinkle over the ducks a short time before the meal was ready. Renno had to admit that his mother had never done better.

When they retired, Betsy rolled herself in a blanket between her brother and Renno and slept on the hard ground without complaint. She obviously was completely at home in the forest.

The next day, when they stopped at noon for a light meal of parched corn and smoked venison strips, she ate the standard Seneca fare with seeming relish. Not even Deborah had shown such aplomb, Renno thought.

They were traveling through sparsely settled North Carolina now, and that afternoon they came to territory under control of the southern branch of the Tuscarora. Like their cousins in the north, these Indians were full-fledged members of the Iroquois League.

Renno sensed the proximity of a sentry before his companions from Virginia even realized anyone was nearby. He called out to the brave, identifying himself, and the warrior joined them.

Drums echoed through the forest, and a delegation of warriors appeared to conduct the travelers into the town of the Tuscarora. Renno's presence created a considerable stir; cooking fires were lighted in an open field outside the town's palisades, and the entire population of the town gathered for a banquet in the young Seneca's honor.

Betsy, required by Indian custom to sit with the

women, was fascinated by Renno's conduct and couldn't take her eyes from him. He was in his natural element with these Indians, and as he squatted near the fire he enjoyed exchanging jokes with the sachem, war chiefs, medicine men, and senior warriors. He had proved himself adept with a knife and fork in Norfolk, but here he ate with his bare hands, and his natural grace impressed the girl.

She didn't know it, but Renno was watching her, too. He admired the way she scooped food out of a gourd with her fingers without embarrassment. She established a rapport with the Tuscarora women despite the language barrier.

The sachem made a dignified speech of welcome to the son of the Great Sachem and his friends. Then Renno, dignified in his war bonnet, made a brief, eloquent reply. His listeners laughed and cheered, their faces glowing, and Betsy wished she could understand what he was saying.

When he stopped speaking, a drum began to throb softly, and all of the warriors rose to their feet, the elders quickly retiring to the rear of the throng. A second drum picked up the beat, then a third and fourth, and the sound became livelier as it grew louder.

The women began to chant. Betsy had no idea what they were saying, but the words were repetitious and she soon joined them, her enthusiasm compensating for her ignorance.

The sachem and his war chiefs looked at Renno. As the guest of honor, he made his way slowly across the open space that separated the men and women. Some of the younger women began to flirt with him, several of them smiling and two or three brazenly beckoning him. Instead, to her surprise, he came straight to Betsy.

"You will dance with me," he said, and helped her to her feet.

She followed him to the open space, but had literally no idea what to do.

He faced her and began to stamp his feet. She did the same.

Renno pranced, leaped in the air, and pirouetted. Beginning to enjoy herself, Betsy followed his lead.

A number of the Tuscarora cheered, and then other dancers, including the sachem and the war chiefs, took their partners into the clearing.

Betsy quickly lost her self-consciousness and within a short time no longer required Renno's guidance. Sometimes they danced far apart, then moved close together, their faces and bodies not quite touching.

The drums beat more rapidly.

Ned had found an Indian girl as a partner and was dancing, too. But Betsy was enjoying herself too much to be more than vaguely aware of him. Her dancing, like Renno's, became more abandoned, and for long moments at a time she was so breathless she could not chant.

Older couples soon found the pace too swift and moved back to watch.

The dancers followed no set pattern. Instead the warriors improvised, and their partners tried to antici-pate what they would do next. Betsy discovered she had an instinct that told her what Renno's next gyra-tion would be, and they moved around the clearing in perfect harmony. Other couples stopped dancing to watch them.

The drummers playfully continued to increase their rhythm.

Renno and Betsy flew back and forth across the open area, their legs moving in unison, their bodies swaying.

At last the drummers halted.

Betsy laughed breathlessly and clapped her hands together, indifferent to the fact that she was drenched with perspiration.

A number of the Tuscarora applauded her and her partner.

"If I didn't know better," Renno said, his own torso

glistening with sweat, "I would have sworn that you had been born an Iroquois."

As Betsy went off with the women for the night, she reflected that no one had ever paid her a greater compliment.

The travelers resumed their march the next morning soon after daybreak, and Betsy showed no signs of weariness. She had something on her mind, but not until Renno paused at noon for a light Indian meal did she have the chance to reveal it.

"I felt so foolish last night," she said. "I couldn't understand your speech or the sachem's, and I couldn't talk with even one of the Tuscarora. Will you teach me the language of the Seneca, Renno?"

Ned started to laugh, but checked himself when he saw his sister was sincere.

Renno smiled slightly. "I'll make a bargain with you," he replied. "I'll teach you the tongue of the Seneca if you'll give me lessons in reading and writing English."

"Wonderful!" Betsy exclaimed. "I accept the deal!"

They started their lessons at the campfire after supper that same evening. Ned, already familiar with the language to some extent, became intrigued and joined in. After a while he stopped and went to sleep, but Renno and Betsy continued late into the night.

That first night established a pattern, and every evening thereafter Betsy and Renno exchanged lessons, with Ned sometimes joining in. All were quick to learn, and they were excited with their progress.

Heading toward the southwest at Ned's suggestion to avoid Albemarle Sound and the broad rivers that emptied into Pimlico Sound, they saw few villages of English settlers. Most of the immigrants to North Carolina clustered in small communities on or near the Atlantic coast. The forest seemed endless, but Betsy continued to show that she was completely at home in the wilderness.

More often than not Renno or her brother brought

down game, but they made no objection when she demanded her share of sport. One day she showed courage as well as skill when a wild boar started to charge toward her. Renno raised his own musket, but quickly Betsy put a perfectly-placed shot between the beast's eyes.

She could butcher an animal's carcass without flinching and insisted on keeping the hide of a doe. Rather than lose time on the trail, she said she would cure it after they reached Charles Town.

She proved adept at fishing, too, and Renno was not surprised when she caught a fish twice the size of any that he and Ned caught in a large river. Quickly learning the Seneca technique of packing fish in clay, she searched for edible roots while the main course was baking, and in all produced a delectable meal, more savory than Renno had ever eaten on the trail.

Her talents made a deep impression on him. "Your father was wise to teach you how to make yourself at home in the wilderness," he said. "Not even the women of the Seneca know more than you," he added, paying her the supreme compliment.

Betsy glowed. "My father has always said I seem to have an instinct for forest living. That's because I feel so at home in the open. Not that I don't enjoy town life, too."

It was plain to him that she had a relish for life itself. She was extraordinary, as practical and down to earth as Deborah, and simultaneously as sophisticated as Adrienne.

But Renno warned himself not to become too involved with her. Although her family treated him with respect and gave him their unstinting friendship, their standards were not his. In their eyes he was a savage, even though his skin was white. They would be deeply disturbed if he offered marriage to her, and he had to admit he found it difficult to imagine her becoming acclimated to a day-to-day existence in the town of the Seneca.

It was wrong of him to think in such terms. Granted that he was at ease in the civilization of the English settlers, he was still an Indian. It was accidental that he belonged to the same race as the Ridleys. His inner core was that of a Seneca, and he would always be loyal to his people, just as he would always act, think, and react like the warriors he commanded in battle. It was a futile daydream to allow himself to dwell on the possibility that Betsy might consent to marry him. She had far too much to offer someone in her own world. Although she had not yet found a suitor she deemed acceptable, it was inevitable that some fellow colonist would win her heart and hand.

The travelers were able to increase their pace when they reached South Carolina and followed the Atlantic coastline southward. When possible they walked for many miles at a time on the flat, hard sand of the beaches, subsisting in the main on shellfish. Only occasionally did Renno or Ned venture into the forest for game.

A few days later they came to civilization, the rice-growing plantations established by colonists within the past two decades. The soil and climate were perfect for the cultivation of rice, and the plantations were flourishing. Ned refused to call a prolonged halt when they were so close to their destination, so they pushed on to the new, rapidly growing city of Charles Town, whose local residents were shortening its name to Charleston.

The community, founded in 1670, had one of the best natural ports on the Atlantic seaboard. As a consequence the city was already the center of growing trade with the islands of the West Indies, particularly Barbados. Trade was extensive, too, with the large Indian tribes of the interior, and the more prosperous of the community's citizens lived in large homes they had built several blocks from the waterfront.

One of the more impressive was the handsome brick dwelling of Lucinda Ridley Watson. Several years older than Betsy, with similar blond hair and green eyes, the young woman enjoyed a wide and deserved popularity. Ravishingly beautiful, she was serious-minded, exceptionally competent, and devoted the better part of her time to the operation of the local branch of her uncle's shipping business.

"Whenever I see you," Betsy said as they arrived, "I always expect to find that you've remarried."

Lucinda laughed. "My dear," she said, "I'm as particular as you are. It's an old family trait, you know. I've loved only one man in my life, and I very much doubt that I shall ever find another like him."

The local bachelors, she explained, accepted her independence, and having won the respect of the city's traders and shippers, she encountered few problems. "I've had my hands full warding off Sir Frederick Babcock, who just arrived from England a short time ago," she declared, "but now that you're here, hopefully he'll turn his attentions to you."

Betsy made a wry face.

Lucinda was intrigued by Renno.

"If you don't object," she told him, "I shall be happy to lend you some of my late husband's clothes and one of his wigs while you're here. Ned will be wearing them, too. Fortunately Betsy and I wear the same size clothes, because she'll use some of my gowns. Charleston society is taking itself seriously, and there will be fewer explanations necessary if I simply present you as a colonist from Virginia."

Renno shrugged and accepted the suggestion. Just when he thought he was gaining a thorough understanding of the English colonists, they presented him with another facet of their complicated way of life. He preferred the simplicity and direct approach of the Seneca.

That afternoon Ned went off to Lucinda's office with her for a review of her current business situation.

Renno, attired in a lawn shirt and knee breeches, a silk waistcoat and satin coat with pewter buttons, grinned at his reflection in a pier glass. His powdered wig was hot and uncomfortable, and he couldn't understand why any man would wear such a cumbersome headgear willingly.

His grin fading, he wandered down the broad, curving central staircase to the drawing room, where all of the massive furniture had been imported from England. He was reminded of great houses he had seen in London and couldn't understand why these people burdened themselves with divans of leather and chairs with padded, embroidered seats when it was so much easier to sit cross-legged on the floor. The weather here was warm, and he opened several windows as he perspired in his borrowed clothes. He had agreed to wear this white man's attire in order to humor his hostess, but he was comforted by the knowledge that he would be required to maintain the masquerade for only a few days.

Someone came into the room behind him, and he turned, then caught his breath.

Betsy looked lovelier than ever in a gown of a lightweight, pale lilac silk, with an off-the-shoulder, low-cut neckline. Her wheat-colored hair tumbled down her back, and she walked in her high-heeled slippers as easily as she made her way through the wilderness in her moccasins.

"You're more beautiful than any lady I saw at the court of King William," Renno blurted.

She smiled in appreciation, showing the dimples in her cheeks. "Well, sir," she said, "you're remarkably handsome in those clothes. In fact, I scarcely knew you. I thought you were a stranger until I came into the room."

He grimaced and addressed her in Seneca. "He who wears the skin of a lion does not become a lion. He is still a warrior."

"That is so," she replied in Seneca, then added in English, "Thank goodness! I'd hate to think of you turning into one of those impossible fops!"

"That will not happen," he assured her. "I do this only to please your cousin."

"Oh, Lucinda doesn't care for herself. She doesn't

know the forests as Ned and I do, of course. But it isn't easy for her, doing business every day in a man's world, so she tries to be discreet."

They wandered together in the extensive gardens behind the house, and although Renno was tempted to remove his confining wig, he refrained. The thought occurred to him that he was trying to impress Betsy with his ability to simulate the manners of someone from her own world.

Ned and Lucinda returned in the late afternoon, and the attractive hostess immediately hurried to the kitchen outbuilding to supervise the evening meal.

"I'm afraid we're going to have to tolerate one of those evenings we hate," Ned said gloomily. "We've arrived here just in time for one of Lucinda's supper parties."

"Oh, dear." Betsy drew in her breath. "Let me guess. There will be a warehouse owner or two, at least one gentleman who buys rice from the planters, and someone who owns a company that sells cooking utensils, blankets, and the like to the Indian tribes of the interior."

"You do not like these people?" Renno asked.

"We're being unfair to them," Ned said. "Actually, most of them are pleasant people, and so are their wives."

"Quite true," Betsy declared. "No one who has lived in the colonies for any length of time puts on airs. People here have to work too hard for a living. I daresay the only unpleasant person at the party will be Sir Frederick Babcock, who sounds dreadful from Lucinda's description of him."

"What bothers us, Renno," Ned said, "is that the gentlemen of Charleston—and even the ladies—discuss almost nothing but business. At home our father has always refused to allow trade and commerce to be more than mentioned at the table. Not that it will be all that bad, of course, and you really can't blame people for talking about the things that are uppermost in their minds."

At dusk the servants lighted bundles of rushes tied to long poles that were placed in the ground in the extensive garden, which produced a pleasing illumination.

Lucinda greeted her guests in the garden, where the men were served cups of rum and fruit juice. Renno took one taste from his silver cup, then quietly exchanged it for a cup similar to that being served the ladies, which contained only fruit juices. He made little attempt to join in the general conversation, although it amused him that the Charlestonians unquestioningly accepted him as a Virginia colonist who happened to have made the journey with Ned and Betsy.

Without exception these men and women from South Carolina, all of them born in England, were modest and calm, their eyes reflecting the serenity of life on the fringe of the wilderness. Renno found them very much like his good friends at Fort Springfield in Massachusetts Bay. It dawned on him that just as these people were changing the very nature of life in America, they were equally influenced in return by the great forests. No one could exist so close to the wilderness, which was both bountiful and dangerous, without being affected by it.

Sir Frederick Babcock was even more obnoxious than Lucinda had indicated. He was a tall, well-built man in his late twenties, but was the type of English aristocrat Renno had come to despise during his sojourn in London. His manners as exquisite as his lace cuffs, silver-buckled shoes, and superbly tailored clothes, he listened to the talk of the colonials with a mocking smile playing at the corners of his mouth, and his occasional comments dripped with sarcasm.

As Lucinda had predicted, he quickly devoted his attention to Betsy, inspiring an unprecedented surge of jealousy in Renno. The young Seneca soon realized, however, that she was only tolerating Sir Frederick.

Lucinda led her guests from the garden to the dining room, where candles burned on the table and in wall holders, contributing to the heat. Renno forgot his discomfort, however, when they were served a local delicacy known as she-crab soup. It was followed by quail, roasted and browned over a hot fire, and, as Ned had predicted, the talk soon turned to local matters.

"Governor Moore assures me he's planning on building an auxiliary fort on one of the offshore islands to provide better protection from an unexpected attack by the Spaniards," one of the warehouse owners said.

The rice trader nodded. "It's about time," he declared. "At the very least we'll force Spanish warships to stop disguising themselves as coastal pirates."

The drift of the continuing conversation made it clear to Renno that the South Carolinians were as uneasy about their proximity to the aggressive Spaniards, who had established towns and forts in Florida, which lay to the south, as New Englanders and New Yorkers were about their French neighbors in Canada. The revelation astonished him. He knew the French were enemies of the English colonists, and now it appeared that he had to add the residents of New Spain to his list of their foes.

Lucinda contributed her fair share to the conversation. "What bothers me most," she said, "is that our trade with the Huguenots is so uncertain."

"Are the Spanish troops still attacking their settlements?" one of the ladies wanted to know.

"So it appears," Lucinda replied. "The Huguenots are good customers, but whenever they hear a rumor that Spanish regiments are approaching, they flee into the interior."

Listening carefully, Renno was able to piece together the facts. Refugees from religious persecutions by King Louis XIV of France had established a number of small settlements in the otherwise unoccupied and unclaimed area that lay between English South Carolina and Spanish Florida. On friendly terms with the English colonists and the Indian tribes of the interior, they were subjected to frequent harassment by the Spaniards, who were vying with England for control of the territory in which neither had established colonies of their own.

"It strikes me," Sir Frederick sneered, "that half a battalion of British troops could put an end to the Spanish menace."

He was so uninformed that the others stared at him.

"Spain maintains a large garrison at a fort and town called St. Augustine," Ned said. "As for driving them out, British troops need the help of colonists and Indians—men who understand the principles of wilderness fighting. That was made very plain when we took Fortress Louisburg from the French. For all the good it did us, now that they've occupied it again."

"What more could be expected of colonials and savages?" Sir Frederick demanded with a contemptuous laugh. "Really!"

His rudeness was inexcusable, but the members of the party remained polite to him, principally because his father, a high-ranking marquess, was thinking of investing heavily in South Carolina and had sent him to the New World to investigate the prospects.

Ignoring the man, Renno concentrated on the important issue, the danger to the English colonies posed by Spain.

Aware of his interest, Ned explained that Spain had established a vast empire in the islands of the West Indies as well as in South and Central America. "Our one advantage," he said, "is that France and Spain haven't joined hands in a campaign against us. If they did, it might be the end for the English colonies in the New World."

Renno was gaining new insights that he was eager to pass on to Ghonka and the members of the Iroquois Council.

"I still say that one or two Royal Navy warships and a handful of King William's troops could utterly destroy the French and Spaniards," Sir Frederick said.

His arrogance was such that, although several of the

ladies smiled politely, none of the men deigned to reply to him.

"Does South Carolina have alliances with any of the Indian nations in the area?" Renno asked.

Lucinda, knowing the reason for his question, elected to reply herself. "We have a lively and mutually profitable trade with the Choctaw, some of whose towns lie in the region that England and Spain both covet. So far they've been reluctant to enter into a full treaty of alliance with us, even though the Spaniards hate them as much as they hate us."

"Why anyone should want a treaty with barbarians is beyond my comprehension," Sir Frederick interjected.

Renno shut out the man's voice, and as he enjoyed his dinner he considered his new information. The Choctaw, he knew, were a powerful people who had achieved an understanding with the southern branch of the Tuscarora, each tribe carefully avoiding the other's hunting grounds.

Perhaps he could be instrumental, through Ghonka, in persuading the Choctaw to cast their lot with the English settlers. Such an alliance would be mutually advantageous in the face of Spanish threats, just as the treaty of the Iroquois with the English colonies of the north protected both from the French.

Lucinda invoked her widow's prerogative and did not observe the custom of retiring with the ladies while the men stayed at the table over glasses of port. Instead the whole company went to the drawing room, with a few wandering out into the garden.

Betsy escaped to the cool garden, but Renno chose to remain behind with Ned, who continued to discuss the Spanish menace with several of the local businessmen and Lucinda. Twice within recent years Spanish warships had appeared in Charleston harbor, bombarded the town, and then hastily sailed away again. The threat of an overland invasion from the south was constant. The young Seneca was glad he had made this journey with Ned and Betsy; he was acquiring a new perspective on the problems the English colonies faced. Certainly he needed no one to tell him how acute the danger would become, from the Maine District of Massachusetts Bay to South Carolina, if France and Spain joined forces.

Only Renno's wilderness training made it possible for him to hear a faint, muffled scream from the far end of the garden. Certain he recognized Betsy Ridley's voice, he leaped to his feet and dashed out into the open. His gesture startled the others, but with one accord they followed him.

Beyond the circle of light cast by the flares Renno caught sight of Betsy struggling in the grasp of Sir Frederick Babcock. Rarely had the disciplined young war chief allowed himself the luxury of giving into a feeling of violent anger, but at this moment his temper exploded.

He raced to the couple, punched Sir Frederick so hard that a welt was raised on the nobleman's cheekbone, and then wrenched him away from the disheveled, frightened, and embarrassed girl.

Sir Frederick was outraged. "This is too much!" he exclaimed as the others arrived on the scene. "First this doxie rejects me, and now this—this boor has assaulted me!"

Renno paid no attention to him. "Are you all right?" he asked Betsy.

She blinked away the tears that had come to her eyes. "Yes, thanks to you."

Sir Frederick drew his gloves from his belt and slapped Renno across the face with them. "I demand immediate satisfaction," he said.

Renno turned to him, his expression icy. "You shall have it," he replied.

"As the injured party, I elect to fight with swords," Sir Frederick announced haughtily.

One of the warehouse owners hurried off to his own nearby house for a pair of suitable dueling blades.

A badly worried Lucinda drew Betsy and Ned aside. "I don't like this," she said. "When Sir Frederick first came here I was told he was a deadly swordsman. It's been said he's killed two men in duels in England."

The ordinarily self-contained Betsy gasped and clapped a hand over her mouth. Then she turned to her brother. "Stop the duel before it's too late," she begged. "I'd never forgive myself if something frightful happened to Renno."

It appeared too late for Ned to intervene, however. To the amazement of the entire company Renno pulled off his wig, revealing his scalp lock, and then he quickly discarded his English clothes until he was attired only in his buckskin loincloth.

"What sort of travesty is this?" Sir Frederick demanded, and laughed contemptuously. "It seems this colonial clod is an Indian, perhaps. Are you a white Indian or is this one of your crude games?"

"I am Renno, the son of Ghonka, war chief of the Seneca," was the calm reply.

The warehouse owner returned with a case containing the dueling swords.

"I shall take double pleasure in destroying you," Sir Frederick said, removing his coat and rolling up his sleeves. "If you have a god, savage, start praying to him."

"Please, Ned," the horrified Betsy whispered, "stop them!"

Shaking his head dubiously, Ned moved forward as Renno began to test the balance of the blade he had been handed. "I'm sure you could more than hold your own with a tomahawk or knife," the Virginian murmured. "But you're facing an expert with a reputation as a killer."

Renno smiled faintly. There was no time to explain that he had spent hours each day practicing his swordsmanship during the months he had spent in London, or that he had won a duel there. "I believe I can look after myself," he said. "Besides, this fellow dared to assault Betsy, so he needs to be taught a lesson."

There was nothing more that Ned could do.

The men gathered under several of the flares, and the ladies shrank into the shadows, although none of them went off to the house.

Betsy clung to Lucinda. "There must be something we can do to stop a murder!"

"You know men when they believe their honor is at stake," her cousin replied. "Renno would feel disgraced and would never forgive us if we intervened."

"Better that than lose his life!" Betsy fought to control the sense of hysteria that welled up in her.

The warehouse owner, appointing himself referee, moved to the center of the circle, the light of the burning rushes flickering on his face. He beckoned to the two principals, then asked, "Renno, do you know the rules of a duel?"

Even this colonist was treating him as though he were an ignorant savage! The young Seneca nodded curtly.

The warehouse owner sighed. "Very well. Honor will be satisfied when one of you draws blood."

"Indeed," Sir Frederick said. "I give fair notice here and now that I shall skewer this barbarian."

Betsy's fingernails dug into the palms of her hands. She was to blame for Renno's predicament. Although she appreciated his gallantry, she knew she would be haunted for the rest of her days by his death.

The referee stepped back, holding his own sword at arm's length to separate the combatants.

Sir Frederick mockingly went through the pre-duel ritual of saluting his opponent.

Renno did the same. His gesture surprised some members of the company, who assumed he was merely imitating what he saw.

"Colonist or Indian or whoever you are," Sir Frederick said in a soft voice that nevertheless could be heard by all of the spectators, "prepare to die!"

"On guard!" the referee cried as he withdrew his own blade and moved backward into the shadows.

Renno balanced on the balls of his feet in the classic pose of the duelist, his sword raised. He realized his foe's contempt was making him careless and decided to feign ineptitude for a moment longer. As the nobleman began to advance, Renno retreated. Not only was he quicker on his feet, but he knew that his extraordinary eyesight gave him another advantage in an arena where the flares were casting an ever-changing light.

All at once Sir Frederick lunged, the point of his blade aimed at his opponent's throat. To his astonishment Renno parried neatly, easily deflecting the strike.

The Englishman lost none of his confidence. Apparently someone had taught this buffoon the fundamentals of dueling, but he was no match for a blue blood who had known the art of swordplay since early childhood.

Renno continued to retreat slowly around the circle. Again Sir Frederick lunged. For the second time steel touched steel, and the Englishman's blade slid harmlessly past his opponent's throat.

Ned put an arm around his sister's shoulders. "We should have known that Renno is no novice," he murmured.

Betsy nodded, but was finding it so difficult to catch her breath that she could not reply. Her concern for Renno overwhelmed her, and all at once she knew the truth: attracted to him from the outset, she had fallen in love with him. She could only beg the Almighty to spare him so she could let him know.

Sir Frederick was still supremely confident, believing that mere luck was on his opponent's side.

Suddenly Renno changed his tactics. Subtly assuming the offensive, he feinted. The startled nobleman hastily raised his sword to protect his face.

But Renno's blade had moved. His touch featherlight, the young Seneca gently pricked the English aristocrat's shirt front with the point of his sword, indicating to all that he could have killed had he wished.

Sir Frederick realized he was being mocked. His face darkening, he determined to make short work of this upstart, and aimed thrust after thrust at his opponent. But Renno had no difficulty in warding off blow after blow.

There was no sound now but the clashing of metal against metal. Betsy, who knew nothing about sword-play, soon realized the Renno was more than holding his own. He actually appeared to be in command of the situation!

The dinner guests were muttering to each other, scarcely able to believe their eyes.

Grinning slightly, Renno demonstrated to them, to Betsy, and above all to Sir Frederick that he had truly taken charge. Abruptly, he reversed the procedure he had followed the first time. His blade seemed to be aimed at the Englishman's chest, and when Sir Frederick raised his sword to deflect the blow, the Seneca's blade hovered in front of his face, teasing him.

Humiliated in the presence of the colonists he despised, the aristocrat decided to bring the duel to an end. But Renno refused to yield the initiative, thrusting repeatedly while cleverly making it plain to the onlookers that he was toying with the Englishman.

Then, his grin fading, Renno struck a smart blow, and the sword flew out of Sir Frederick's hand. Aware that he had lost, the Englishman stood proudly erect, unmoving as he awaited the death thrust. Instead Renno touched him lightly on one cheek with his blade, the tiny scratch causing only a few drops of blood to appear.

The referee came forward instantly, his own sword raised as he shouted that blood had been shed and that Renno was the winner.

Lowering his sword, Renno bowed coldly to the man he had defeated. "I am only a savage," he said, "so I do not kill for sport." Handing the blade to the referee, he turned on his bare heel and, not glancing back, he walked toward the shadows.

Betsy raced to him. Unmindful of the stares of Lucinda and her guests, she embraced Renno and kissed him. In spite of his surprise he reacted at once, hungrily, and for long moments they were locked in an intimate, tender embrace.

When they drew apart Renno had eyes only for Betsy. The warmth of their kiss made it impossible for him to think clearly, but even now he knew that, no matter what, they had made an unspoken commitment to each other.

But there was no opportunity to talk now. Ned clapped his friend on the shoulder and wrung his hand, Lucinda and the guests surrounded him to congratulate him on his victory, and everyone seemed to be talking at once.

In the excitement Sir Frederick recovered his coat and slipped away in the dark. His humiliation was complete, and he had no desire to face any of the jubilant South Carolinians. He would return to England on the first available ship, and he would urge his father not to invest a ha'penny in this barbaric land, where even supposedly civilized men and women behaved like savages.

Renno climbed into his borrowed clothes again before returning to the house to accept the toasts of the company, but he refrained from donning the stifling wig again.

He was eager to speak privately with Betsy, but no chance arose. Flustered by her own gesture, she withdrew before the guests departed.

Renno grew tired of explaining his background to everyone, but when the time came for him to retire he was not sleepy. Betsy's kiss filled his being. Ignoring the bed and chairs so he could think clearly, he sat cross-legged on the floor, pondering the future.

Did he dare to ask Betsy to share his life in the town of the Seneca? That didn't seem fair to her. On the other hand, not even the great love he felt for her could compel him to desert his own people. His duty to his nation, to Ghonka, and to Ena came before his own desires.

Obviously nothing could be resolved until he and

Betsy talked. He stretched out on the hooked rug that covered the floor, and for a few hours he slept.

Renno was awake again when the first streaks of dawn appeared in the sky. He washed and shaved, and forcing himself to wear the borrowed clothes, he went downstairs.

A few moments later Ned joined him for an early breakfast. "Renno," he said, "I'm borrowing one of our company's coastal sloops, and I'm sailing as soon as we've eaten to visit one or two of the French Huguenot communities to the south of us. Come with me, why don't you?"

Renno hesitated.

"We can reach their nearest village in a couple of days, and we'll only stay for a day or two. I want to find out for myself, so I can give my father a direct report, just how seriously they're being threatened by the Spaniards in Florida."

"Why do you seek my company on this journey?"

"For one thing," Ned replied, "I don't know how well they speak English, and I know you can make yourself understood in French. But I have another reason, too." He placed his hand on his friend's shoulder. "It isn't hard for me to guess what you and Betsy are feeling. I saw it all happening to both of you on the trail. Mind you, I'm all in favor of it, but the decisions are up to you and Betsy, not me. And I figure both of you will appreciate a breathing spell for a few days."

The advice made good sense. "I will go with you," Renno said.

They departed before Betsy and Lucinda came down to breakfast, and Ned left them a brief note of explanation. Then he and Renno hurried to the waterfront, the latter happily wearing Seneca attire and carrying his Indian weapons in addition to his musket. They paused at the open air market long enough to buy food for their voyage, and then they went to the Ridley wharf, where the night watchman was still on duty.

Ned identified himself, then led his companion to a

boat tied at the end of the wharf. "Isn't she a beauty?" he asked as they climbed on board.

Renno saw that the craft had one main mast and another, much smaller, that jutted from her prow. He knew virtually nothing about boats other than canoes and the huge brigs that had carried him to England and back to America.

Ned stashed the food in the small cabin, then began to untie the sail on the smaller mast. "This is the jib," he said. "We'll use it alone to carry us through the harbor. I'll appreciate it if you'll cast off."

"Cast off?" Renno was puzzled.

Ned laughed. "You know so much about so many things that I failed to realize you have no knowledge of the sea. Never mind. You'll learn." He untied the line that held the boat to the pier, then took the tiller and, as the jib filled, expertly threaded a path between merchant ships until he reached the open Atlantic.

Renno, following his directions, unfurled the mainsail and Ned set a southward course.

"In the event that you and Betsy decide to marry," he said, "this voyage will be instructive for you. We earn our living in shipping, and my father will expect you to know and understand nautical terms, you can be sure."

Not awaiting a reply, he began to sing.

Renno relaxed as best he could on the small deck and made no comment. It would be unseemly to say anything about the future until he and Betsy spoke in private. In fact, his peace of mind demanded that he dismiss the problem from his mind, if he could, until this trip came to an end and a solution was reached.

At noon Ned pointed toward the shore. "Someday," he said, "you and I will have to go hunting there. Those are the swamps that mark the southern border of South Carolina, more or less, and they're teeming with wildlife. The best hunting I've ever known anywhere."

Renno's grin indicated that he relished the idea.

By the time they turned toward the shore near the

mouth of a small river they had put the swamps behind them. All they saw was a mass of forest. They dropped anchor in shallow water and waded ashore to spend the night. While Ned made a fire, Renno went inland to search for game. The wilderness here was unlike the forests he knew. The evergreens were smaller, he saw many palmetto trees, and as he made his way inland, he saw numerous live oak trees draped with a thick, pretty growth that later generations would call Spanish moss.

In spite of the differences in the foliage, he felt at home in the forest, and within a short time he brought down two rabbits with his bow and arrows, ample fare for the evening meal.

When he returned to the beach he found that Ned had caught a turtle, which he was already stewing. The two young men feasted, and there was no need for them to use the food supplies they had purchased that morning in Charleston.

At daybreak the next day they resumed their voyage, eating a breakfast of bread and cracked corn after they put out to sea. Occasionally, as they sailed down the coast, they saw small beaches, but what impressed Renno was the omnipresence of the forest. Ghonka, who had not visited this portion of the continent, nevertheless had been right when he had informed his son that the wilderness hunting grounds of America were endless.

Ned navigated with skill, and late in the afternoon he headed toward the shore at the mouth of a small river. Again the sloop was anchored near the beach, and the pair started inland. They had gone only a short distance when a young man in buckskins, bearded and carrying an old-fashioned blunderbuss, blocked their path and, speaking in French, demanded their identity.

Renno replied as best he could in his own halting French, and the visitors were escorted to a clearing where sixty or seventy small log houses had been built on stilts about ten feet above the ground. This was the largest Huguenot settlement in the unclaimed territory and had a total population of approximately two hundred and fifty men, women, and children.

The entire community appeared to greet the newcomers, who were received with friendship when it became clear that they were friendly. All wore clothes of animal hides and appeared to be ruggedly self-sufficient.

They ate together at a cooking pit in the center of the village, and over a meal of shellfish, venison, and rice an elderly man who spoke fluent English explained their situation to the visitors. "We live as the Indian tribes of the area do, on hunting, fishing, and whatever food we can produce in our own fields. We sell furs to the English colonial traders from Charleston, and in return we receive blankets, cooking pots, and medicines. We do better than that. We make progress, a little at a time. We have only two enemies. The snakes that have forced us to build our houses on stilts. And the Spaniards, who will not allow us and others like us to live our lives in peace.

"Three times in the past two years," the old man said, "Spanish warships from St. Augustine have dropped anchor off our coast. Each time they sent soldiers ashore, hundreds of them, to kill us. We have been fortunate because we fled farther inland, into the land of the Choctaw, who are our friends. The Spaniards are afraid of the Choctaw, so they have not followed us. They have looted our houses and then withdrawn."

"Why are they your enemies?" Renno wanted to know.

"Their king, in Madrid, and their viceroy, in Cuba, hope to claim all of this territory and annex it. They are waiting only long enough to bring settlers here from Spain."

Ned frowned. "You think, then, that they intend to creep up the coast?"

"There can be no doubt of it," the old man declared. "In five years they hope to capture Charleston. Little by little they will drive out the English settlers and make the entire seaboard a part of New Spain. They are not like the French, who try to conquer your colonies in a major war. They prefer to nibble. They bite off a small piece, digest it, and then go on to the next. But their long-range policies are very clear."

Renno began to recognize the gravity of the Spanish threat. The Seneca and other Iroquois had been concentrating on the French in Canada, but here was an insidious, equally dangerous foe.

"What I can't understand," Ned said, "is why your people and those of the other Huguenot villages continue to live in the wilderness under such harsh, dangerous conditions. Surely you know you'd be welcome in the English colonies, where you'd be free to worship as you please."

"Many Huguenots have come to Massachusetts Bay and are happy there," Renno added.

"I will let our people answer for themselves," the old man declared with a weary smile.

A middle-aged woman was the first to speak, and it was obvious that her feelings ran deep.

"Madame Brunot says that she and her family suffered greatly in France, where they lost their home, their shop, everything they owned. She prefers to dwell here, in spite of the snakes and the threats from the Spaniards, because we have our own community, our own way of life."

A burly man added something.

"Monsieur Charveaux believes it is important that we live apart," the old man declared. "Here we continue to speak our own language. If we move to South Carolina or another of your colonies, our children will soon learn English. They will be absorbed by the majority and will forget their own customs."

Renno nodded soberly, sympathizing with these courageous people. As a white Indian he had been subjected to many alien influences. He was able to cling to his basic identity only because the manitous had given him the strength always to remember his duty and primary loyalty.

He and Ned talked with the Huguenot villagers far into the night, finally retiring to one of the stilt-houses. "I've learned what I came here to find out," Ned said. "I wish these people would have the sense to move to a safer location, but I'm afraid they won't budge."

"They think of themselves as being truly free here," Renno said. "And man will suffer any hardship for the sake of liberty."

Their mission completed, the pair left the tiny settlement early the following morning and set out on their return voyage to Charleston. Traveling at the same leisurely pace, they reached their destination late the following afternoon. Ned went first to the Ridley office to report to Lucinda at the same time giving his friend an opportunity to meet his sister in private.

Renno went directly to Lucinda's house and found Betsy alone, reading in the garden. She was wearing a gown of a pale orchid, and she looked so pretty that his throat ached.

She rose slowly to her feet when she saw him, absently marking her place in the leather-bound volume. Renno crossed the garden, but stopped short and made no attempt to touch her. "During these days of our separation, I have thought constantly of you," he said.

"You've been on my mind day and night, too," Betsy replied.

"I think it will be best for you," he declared, "if I leave this place at once and return to the land of the Seneca without delay."

The girl was stunned.

He hadn't intended to explain, but now felt compelled to. "I love you more, far more, than any woman I have ever known," he said, "and I will carry your memory in my heart for the rest of my days."

Color burned in Betsy's cheeks. "I find it hard to believe you love me, not if you're intending to move out of my life forever!" she cried.

"I have no choice," he said. "You are a lady. You are the daughter of a prominent, wealthy citizen of Virginia. I can offer you nothing."

"You seem to forget you've already achieved a high rank in your nation," Betsy said. "And I'm sure that someday you'll succeed your father as Great Sachem."

Renno shrugged. "If that is the will of the manitous, I will do their bidding. If it is not, I will continue to serve my people as best I can. My place is with them."

The girl took a step toward him, her green eyes blazing. "You're leaving one very important element out of your neat calculations. My place is with you!"

It was his turn to stare.

"I've been thinking hard, weighing my own feelings," Betsy said, "and I know that I love you, too."

His mouth and throat felt dry, and he moistened his lips. "You would willingly live with me in a small house—in the land of the Seneca? Rather than a lovely home like the mansion of your mother and father?"

"Things like houses and furniture don't matter. Neither do clothes like this dress of Lucinda's. I've turned away more suitors than I can count because none of them interested me. I've lost my heart to you, Renno, and there's no way I can recover it. Leave me now, and I swear to you that I'll never marry anyone else as long as I live."

He studied her in silence for a long moment.

She expected him to step forward and take her into his arms. But he was still a Seneca and reacted in the manner of his people, folding his sinewy arms across his bare chest. "I will return to Norfolk with you," he said stolidly, "and I will have words with your father. If he gives his consent, we will marry. If he refuses, I will go alone."

In spite of the tension, Betsy had to laugh. This man, whom others might call a savage, was endowed with a more sensitive, highly developed sense of honor than anyone she had ever known. Even knowing that she loved him, just as he loved her, he would not touch her until her father approved of their union.

She was still in high spirits when Lucinda and Ned came home for supper. Both were curious, but politely asked no questions. All they realized was that Renno and Betsy had arrived at some sort of understanding that satisfied them.

"One of the Ridley brigs put into port here today and will be returning to Norfolk in a few days," Ned said. "So I think we'll go back to Virginia by ship. It will be much faster than traveling overland through the forest."

Betsy was agreeable, and Renno inclined his head. He was afraid Colonel Ridley would reject his request for Betsy's hand, but it was best to know as soon as possible. He tried to harden himself, anticipating the refusal.

Two days later, just as Lucinda was sitting down to noon dinner with her house guests, a messenger arrived at her home from the office of Governor James Moore, King William's recently appointed head of the Crown Colony of South Carolina. "Ma'am," the young man said breathlessly, "His Excellency knows there's an Indian staying here and wants him to come to Government House. There's an Indian who just got here from the interior somewhere. He speaks no English, and it makes him hopping mad. He appears to have something he wants to tell the governor, but nobody can make out a word he says."

It was typical of Moore, Lucinda thought, that he had surrounded himself with incompetents. Arrogantly aristocratic, the governor accepted no local invitations, even from Charleston's most prominent citizens, and seemed intent on creating a miniature version of the royal court at Whitehall.

In spite of his rudeness, however, Lucinda was gracious. "I suppose you'd better go," she said to Renno and Ned. "We'll hold dinner until you return."

The pair accompanied the young official on the short walk to Government House, a sprawling building of yellow brick located directly behind the fort overlooking the harbor.

James Moore, wearing a shoulder-length wig, with a broad sash of silk across his chest, sat behind a huge, highly polished desk, listening blankly to a torrent of words that a voluble Indian brave was shouting. Several aides, as overdressed as the governor, huddled on one side of the chamber and were equally at a loss.

Ned bowed to King William's representative. Renno, however, paid no attention to anyone but the Indian, whom he identified by the feathers in his scalp lock and his purple war paint as a senior warrior of the Choctaw.

The brave fell silent when he saw Renno, and they exchanged formal greetings, each identifying himself. Then, speaking with quiet dignity, the Choctaw revealed his reason for coming to Charleston.

Renno translated for him as he spoke. "Weh-no-su, senior warrior of the Choctaw, brings the greetings of his sachem and his brothers to their friends of this town. He grieves because the news he carries is filled with sorrow."

The others gave him their full attention.

"Weh-no-su brings news of the men with white skins who live near the Great Salt Sea in the town that is built high in the air."

Ned interrupted hastily. "Obviously he means the village of the Huguenots that we visited this week."

Renno listened as the Choctaw renewed his recital. Ned knew instantly from his friend's fixed expression that the word the warrior brought was indeed bad.

"All who lived in that town are dead," Renno said. "The men, the women, and the children have gone to join their ancestors. Their town has been burned to the ground."

The governor grew red-faced. "If the Choctaw were responsible for this outrage—"

"No." Renno, unimpressed by Moore, cut him off sharply, then listened again. "Warriors came in two ships. The ships were very large and looked like huge birds. They flew flags that were yellow and red, and in the center of each flag was a bird that looked like an eagle."

"The flag of Spain," Ned said curtly.

"The warriors landed, carrying many firesticks. They attacked the town before those who lived there could run away into the forest. The people who lived high in the air fought hard. But their enemies outnumbered them, and the noise of the firesticks was very loud. The warriors made fire appear from their firesticks until all the people of the town were dead."

"My God!" Ned said in a shocked voice. "The Spaniards from St. Augustine slaughtered innocent people whose only crime was that they were Protestants occupying land that Spain covets!"

Renno gravely thanked the Choctaw and, acting on his own initiative, invited him to Lucinda's house for a meal before he returned to the wilderness. These inept officials apparently had no idea how to treat a messenger who had traveled a long distance for their sakes, and if necessary the Seneca was prepared to give this warrior his own food.

Ned turned to the governor. "Your Excellency," he said, "what the Spaniards have just done is barbaric. It's a virtual declaration of war against all of the English colonies. I trust you'll send an expedition to teach them a lesson!"

Moore smiled faintly and shook his head. "You're mistaken," he said. "As much as I deplore the wanton bloodshed, it was French Huguenots the Spaniards attacked, not His Britannic Majesty's subjects."

Ned was furious. "Will you wait, sir, until they send their warships and troops sailing into Charleston's harbor before you act?"

"They've given me no cause to take up arms against them," Governor Moore replied. "Great Britain and Spain are at peace."

Thoroughly disgusted, Ned and Renno departed, taking the Choctaw with them. "Moore," Renno said, "is a man who does nothing until enemy warriors enter his town with burning torches."

"May the Lord have mercy on South Carolina," Ned said bitterly. "At least Virginia will be prepared!"

Chapter IV

Austin Ridley met the brig at the Norfolk dock, and on the road home, Ned and Renno gave him a full report on the mounting Spanish threat to the English colonies.

The colonel shook his head grimly. "I'm never surprised by the Spaniards' lack of humanity," he said. "According to what my captains who visit the islands of their West Indies empire tell me, they're nowhere near ready to attack us, but all of us here—and in New England, New York, and the other colonies as well—will have to keep our eyes and ears open from now on. The Spaniards are mean devils, as greedy as they're lacking mercy to the people they overpower and conquer."

Betsy said very little on the ride home, but as soon as she greeted her mother and sister she insisted on having an immediate, private conversation with her parents. Her request was so unusual that they took her without delay to the small sitting room that adjoined their bedchamber. "What can be so important that it couldn't wait?" Austin asked with a smile.

Betsy was too agitated to sit, and her attitude defensively defiant, she looked first at her mother, then at her father. "I don't know how to say this diplomatically, but Renno and I want to marry. He's going to ask you for my hand, Papa. Today."

The colonel remained calm. "I'm not in the least surprised," he said. "Renno is as fine a young man as any I've encountered. You show good judgment, Betsy."

Mary Ridley did not raise her voice, either. "We're permanently indebted to him for restoring Anne to us and risking his own life in the process. But marriage is a terribly important step. Just be sure this is what you want."

Betsy had expected violent opposition and could not conceal her amazement as she sank into a chair. "Then you have no objections?"

Her mother didn't reply directly. "He was reared as an Indian, to be sure, but it's plain he was the son of colonists, whoever they might have been, poor souls. Papa's shipping interests are so extensive that I'm sure he can find a position for Renno in the company."

The solution wasn't that simple, and the girl clenched her fists, her nails cutting into her palms. "Renno is the youngest war chief of the most powerful nation in the Iroquois League. I couldn't ask him to give up that position. And I'm quite positive he wouldn't."

Mary swallowed hard. "You mean you'd go to live with him in an Indian town?"

"That will be my first duty as his wife," Betsy replied.

Her mother stared at her for a long time. "I never knew you were such a romantic, dear. You know nothing about life in a Seneca community, and I'm afraid you'd find it far different from what you may expect."

82

The colonel was conspicuous by his continuing silence.

"I have no false expectations, Mama," Betsy said. "Renno has told me a great deal about Seneca life, more than even he realizes. And he's been teaching me their language, just as I've been teaching him to read and write English."

"Love is a potent persuader," Mary said, "and I have no doubt that both of you are sincere. But all the same. . . ." Her voice trailed away.

"I intend to visit you here as often as I can," Betsy said. "And when we have children we want to give them the best of both worlds, that of the Seneca and that of the settlers."

For the first time Mary looked openly disturbed.

"Everyone here speaks glibly of the New World," Betsy said. "Well, it really is a new world, Mama. You can see for yourself how important and valuable a link Renno is, joining the Indians and the people who come here from the British Isles. Think of how much more our children can accomplish."

Mary turned to her husband.

Austin broke his silence. "If I didn't know Renno," he said, "I'd be apprehensive. I'm sure he'll love and cherish and protect you, Betsy. That isn't my worry. You have the greater problem, that of fitting into his society."

"I'll do it!" the girl declared in a ringing voice.

"Then Mama and I won't stand in the way of your happiness," he said. "We've watched you send one suitor after another away from here empty-handed, and we've wondered if you preferred to remain a spinster. You've never been giddy. In fact, you've been levelheaded and mature for your years ever since you were little. I credit our trips into the wilderness for that. So, if you're sure you want a life with Renno, we'll give our consent. Tell him I'll join him in the library shortly."

Betsy hugged and kissed her parents, then raced down the stairs, her face radiant.

Officers and men who had served with Renno in the Louisburg campaign heartily approved of him as a husband for Betsy Ridley, but there were others in Norfolk who felt less certain. They were willing to grant that he was white, but at the same time he was a savage, and they couldn't picture him as the husband of the elder daughter of Virginia's most prominent citizen.

It was Mary Ridley, after a struggle with her own conscience, who silenced the doubters. "There's no more prominent family in the colony than the Rolfes," she said. "Remember, it was the first John Rolfe who introduced tobacco to Virginia, and our whole economy is based on that plant. I do hope you aren't forgetting that John Rolfe's wife was a Chickahominy princess named Pocahontas."

Betsy and Renno were married in Norfolk's Anglican church, the bride exquisite in a white gown and veil, her groom actually dashing in a suit of black broadcloth, boots, and a wig that had been made to his measure. There were many in the crowded church who wept when the rector intoned the familiar opening words of the service.

Ned proudly acted as best man, and Anne, the flower girl in the procession, behaved with unaccustomed dignity. She had been forbidden by her mother to ask Betsy and Renno to take her with them to the land of the Seneca, but she was determined, all the same, to raise the question with them before the day ended.

Virtually everyone in the community and its environs attended the reception at the Ridley estate, where sides of beef and venison were roasting over open fires. Betsy and Renno accepted the congratulations and good wishes of the guests, and then Ned spirited them away, before some of the younger men could play the customary post-wedding pranks on the bridal pair. As Ned later explained, Renno had grown familiar with the customs of the settlers but wouldn't look with favor on any man who had the temerity to tease his wife.

The last place anyone would have thought of looking for the bridal couple was the Ridley sloop that Ned had sailed to the village of the Huguenots. It was peacefully at anchor in a small, otherwise deserted cove, and Renno, still in his wedding finery, rowed his bride out to the boat in a small dinghy. Betsy, who had changed into a peach-colored gown, was jittery.

Her apprehensions soon proved groundless. Renno was even more gentle, more tender than she had dared to hope. He carefully brought her to the heights of pleasure, and their passions exploded in ecstatic release. It was joyful beyond their wildest expectations, truly bringing them together as man and wife.

They made love repeatedly through the night, and in the morning they went ashore again, dressed in buckskins. Renno caught a fish in the cove, Betsy cooked it for breakfast, along with some herbs that she brewed for tea, and both swore it was the finest meal they had ever eaten.

Late in the morning a grinning Ned appeared with horses, and all three rode back to the Ridley estate for dinner before the bridal pair departed on their long march through the wilderness to the land of the Seneca.

To Mary's dismay Betsy decided to leave all of their many wedding gifts at her parents' home. "We'll use them whenever we visit here," she said. "But there won't be any proper place for them where we're going. Renno is going to add a second room to our house, but we'll live quite simply. Besides, it isn't practical to carry packages when we're going on foot."

"I wish you'd take two of Papa's horses," her mother said.

It was useless to explain that the Seneca had spent many generations traveling through the wilderness on foot. "We prefer to walk, Mama," was all that Betsy replied.

Little Anne laid siege to her new brother-in-law. "Take me with you, too, Renno," she begged. "Why won't you take me?"

He regarded her solemnly, his lifetime of training enabling him to hold back his smile. "First you must go with your father and Ned into the forest and learn how to live comfortably there," he replied. "Then you will visit us."

To the surprise of her parents the child became silent. It was obvious Renno's word was law.

Colonel Ridley drew his new son-in-law aside before the couple departed. "I've already written the latest news of the Spaniards to General Wilson in Massachusetts Bay and the commanders of the other colonies' militia. Make certain you bring Ghonka up to date on all that's been happening."

"I will tell him," Renno promised. "The Iroquois will be surprised, I know. No one has ever told them that Spain is a threat to the English colonies."

"How do you think they'll react?"

"I cannot speak for the Great Sachem or the members of the Iroquois Council," Renno replied. "But we will keep the pledges we made in our treaty. If Spain makes war against you, we will join you in battle against them. And I do not believe it will be difficult to persuade the Choctaw to stand beside us. I learned from the warrior who visited us in Charleston that the Choctaw hate the Spaniards, who make slaves of any unfortunate warriors and women they capture."

"What is the best way to keep you informed of developments?" Austin wanted to know.

"Write to General Wilson, who will send a courier to the land of the Seneca. That is how Betsy will keep in touch with you and her mother. I will send junior warriors to Fort Springfield with her letters to you, and they will bring your letters to her."

Mary became tearful when the time for parting came. "You have such a long journey ahead of you," she said. "I just hope that all goes well with you."

"No harm will come to Betsy," Renno assured her.

The bride smiled. "Mama," she said, as she hugged and kissed her mother in farewell, "I'll be even safer with Renno than I'd be right here in this house, with a battalion of Papa's militia standing guard over me!"

Ned gripped his brother-in-law's hand. "We'll meet again soon, either here or in Seneca country," he said.

The colonel's farewell to Renno was brief. "Take care of my girl," he said.

There were moments when silence was preferable to words, and Renno solemnly inclined his head, his simple gesture speaking more loudly than he could have done had he delivered a long speech.

The Ridley family stood together on the lawn, and the bridal couple turned to wave for a last time before they moved on into the deep woods.

The long trek northward to the land of the Seneca was the most pleasant interlude that Renno had ever known. Ever mindful of Betsy's comfort, he deliberately set a leisurely pace. She carried her own musket, but he taught her to use a bow and arrow. At first she was clumsy, missing repeatedly, but after two weeks of repeated practice she shot a rabbit and was delighted.

They swam in rivers and lakes, hunted and fished when they were hungry, and they made love every night before they fell asleep. The ever-alert Renno made certain they encountered no Indian parties in the wilderness, and Betsy trusted him implicitly. What she had told her mother was the truth. No harm could come to her when Renno was shielding her.

They continued to exchange language lessons every evening, but Renno postponed them for a time after he shot a doe. He cured several strips of the animal's hide, and thereafter he busied himself for several evenings burning intricate designs into the leather with small coals from their campfire.

When he offered no explanation Betsy became increasingly curious, and after watching him for a time one evening she asked, "Whatever are you doing?"

He continued to burn a series of regular patterns on the surface of the leather, but made no reply. He did not even look up from his work.

The incident remained vivid in her mind for a long time. It had taught her something that she knew it would be wise never to forget. The wife of a Seneca war chief did not ask frivolous or unnecessary questions. He would tell her whatever he deemed appropriate for her to hear.

Spring became summer, and Betsy's skin grew almost as dark as Renno's. "Now," she told him one morning when they emerged naked from a small lake and dried themselves in the sun before resuming their journey, "I'm as dark as any other Seneca."

He could not resist the temptation to tease her. "No other woman of the Seneca has hair your color or eyes your color."

She laughed, refusing to back down. "Well, no warrior has hair or eyes like yours, either. But make no mistake about it. I am a Seneca now!"

Renno's proud grin reflected his pleasure. He had married the right woman.

After they had spent uncounted weeks on the trail, Renno called a prolonged halt. He brought down a buck, foraged for wild corn, and then spent several more days slowly drying strips of venison and kernels of corn at their campfire, which burned day and night.

By now Betsy knew better than to question him. When he was ready, he would reveal his reasons for accumulating the supplies.

When he was satisfied that the food would not spoil, he gave her the larger portion and told her to store it in a special rawhide pouch he had fashioned for her.

"Tomorrow," he said, "we will march again, and the next day we will come to the land of the Erie."

She looked blank.

"The Erie," he explained, "are the most ancient enemies of the Seneca. They do not have the courage to attack our towns, but they try very hard to capture Seneca in their territory. Our warriors are put to the trial and are killed. Our women are kept as slaves as long as they live."

Betsy tried not to shudder.

"We will be careful," Renno said. "We will make no cooking fires, and we will eat only the food I have prepared. We will rest only in protected places. But we will travel swiftly, as rapidly as you can walk. And at night, when you sleep, I will keep special watch over you."

"When will you sleep?"

"When there is danger," he said, "a Seneca sleeps very little."

In spite of her attempt to remain calm, Betsy felt increasingly apprehensive.

Renno raised his head proudly. "A Seneca need have no fears. You are a Seneca, and you will wear these."

He handed her the strips of leather into which he had burned the designs. She didn't know what to do with them. He placed the largest around her forehead. Then he bound the others around her wrists.

"You will wear these in the land of the Erie," he said, "and you will wear them always when we join our own people. Then everyone who sees you will know you are the wife of a Seneca war chief."

It occurred to her that the headband and bracelets were a Seneca version of a wedding ring, but were even more explicit as a means of identification. The dangers that lay directly ahead would be acute, but she comforted herself with the knowledge that her husband would allow no harm to come to her.

When they resumed their journey they spent their first day on the trail walking at a leisurely pace, but in mid-morning the following day Renno suddenly, without warning, began to move rapidly.

Betsy kept up with him, taking great care not to step on dead twigs or branches, much less make a rustling sound when she passed through mounds of dried leaves. Her father had taught her the rudiments of being quiet in the forest, and she had practiced the art on this long trip, with Renno frequently advising her. Now her efforts paid dividends, although she couldn't hope to match Renno's ability to glide noiselessly through the forest.

He maintained the grueling pace for long periods at a time, occasionally glancing at her to make certain she was not faltering. Betsy called upon her reserves of strength and energy and made a supreme effort not to let her husband become aware of her discomfort.

But Renno seemed to sense the moments when she reached the limits of her endurance. Then he found concealed hollows or clusters of boulders that made adequate hiding places, and there he allowed her to rest.

Occasionally, silently, he urged her to eat, and she obeyed him without question, even when she had no appetite. She marveled at his ability to survive on a few strips of venison and a handful of dried corn morning and night. Even when they came to a fresh stream and she drank eagerly, he contented himself with a few sips of water. Yet he seemed never to tire.

Renno had not indicated specifically that there was to be no conversation while they were in the land of the Erie. But he did not speak, and Betsy was quick to follow his example.

She was exhausted when he finally called a halt long after sundown, and they camped for the night in a narrow, flat area surrounded by thick, almost impenetrable bushes, with a huge boulder also shielding them. Renno indicated that the time had come to sleep, and when he stretched out on the ground she did the same. To her surprise he appeared to doze off within moments.

The forest was alive with sounds. The chirping of crickets, the buzzing of insects, the occasional, faint rustle of small animals kept Betsy awake. She realized she was tense, but it was impossible for her to sleep. In exasperation she sat upright.

Renno instantly bounded to his feet, his tomahawk in one hand, his knife in the other. He remained motionless for a long time, listening intently for any alien sound, and only when he satisfied himself that it was safe did he rest again. Aware now that he was not really sleeping, Betsy was content and dropped off.

Her husband's touch on her arm awakened her at daybreak, and after she had eaten they started off again.

As the sun was rising, they came to the edge of a small clearing and Renno halted, shielding his eyes as he peered up at the sky. By now Betsy knew him well enough to realize that, although his expression had not changed, he was pleased.

He pointed upward.

She, too, looked up at the brightening sky, but it took her some moments to see a bird that was circling overhead. It swooped lower, and she recognized it as a hawk.

He had told her in detail about occasions when hawks had appeared to guide and protect him as emissaries of the manitous. She had not revealed that she regarded his attitude as mere superstitious rubbish.

On the other hand, was she really so certain there were no manitous and that they did not utilize the services of hawks to guard those whom they favored? She could dismiss the presence of the hawk overhead at this moment as coincidence, but the fact remained that they were passing through the land of an enemy nation and were in great danger. Perhaps the manitous were real and the hawks truly were their representatives.

Never again, Betsy told herself, would she scoff at her husband's beliefs. Indians lived close to nature and understood it intimately. In spite of her background she had to admit it was comforting to see the hawk and at least to hope that supernatural forces were at work, shielding her and Renno from the Erie.

Each day blended into the next, and no untoward incidents marred the journey. The couple hiked interminably, pausing only when Betsy became too weary to continue, and at night she slept soundly, no longer apprehensive. She couldn't be certain whether her faith in Renno or the appearance of the hawk was responsible.

One day at noon after they had been in the land of the Erie so long that Betsy could no longer count the passage of time, they heard a drum throbbing in the distance. Renno halted at once and emitted a shrill, bird-like whistle. An answering whistle sounded from the depths of the forest.

He turned to Betsy, embraced her and kissed her. "Now we are home," he said in a loud, clear voice.

They were able to reduce their pace again, but Renno was so eager to reach the main town of the Seneca that he did not tarry. Drums continued to beat, evidently passing along word of their progress.

Now a new worry assailed Betsy. Soon she would meet Renno's family. She would meet his colleagues on the council, the warriors he commanded in battle, and the young women whom he had known since childhood. It was all well and good to call herself a Seneca, but she didn't know whether any of these people, his mother and father in particular, would accept a blond, green-eyed Virginia settler as one of their own.

Stealing a glance at her husband, Betsy saw that he seemed unconcerned by the impending crisis, and for once his Indian phlegm was too much for her. She wanted to scream, but he was tranquil and unflustered.

Several braves appeared unexpectedly on the trail ahead, led by a senior warrior, and Betsy instantly recognized El-i-chi, whom she had known slightly in Norfolk. He greeted his brother in an elaborate ritual, then turned to her.

She lowered her head to him, as Renno had taught her to do when greeting a senior warrior. To her surprise he grinned at her, then hugged her.

She thanked him with a smile, grateful for his warmth and bolstered by it, but she did not speak. Not until she met Ghonka and Ena would she reveal that she could make herself understood in the language of the Seneca.

Surrounded by their escort, the couple went on, and late in the afternoon they came to a large, cleared area where vegetables and corn were growing. Scores of women working in the fields stood and watched the procession.

Betsy knew she was the center of attention and told herself that soon she would be laboring beside the women in these same fields. Perhaps, when they saw her zeal, they would accept her.

Directly ahead stood the stockade of the Seneca town, and with several drums now beating rhythmically, the popular war chief and his bride went through the gate, with Betsy walking behind Renno in the appropriate Seneca manner.

The size of the crowd startled the girl. War chiefs and their families came out of small, private dwellings, as did medicine men and elders. Senior warriors stood together in a body, while junior warriors and young women poured out of longhouses. Barking dogs frisked, and several very small children fell into line behind Betsy in a single file, making her feel like a freak.

Everyone in the community was staring at her, measuring her. She steeled herself for the ordeal.

At the far side of the town, sitting cross-legged on the ground outside a dwelling somewhat larger than the others, sat an imposing man and a quiet, gray-haired woman with a sweet, dignified face. The man, his strong features looking as though they had been carved out of hardwood, wore a grand bonnet of feathers. In spite of the heat a buffalo robe decorated with dyed porcupine quills was draped over his shoulders. The woman, attired in an unornamented doeskin dress, seemed equally stern.

For a moment Betsy's heart stopped.

Renno paused and raised a hand in salute to his parents. They responded with brief, almost mechanical gestures.

Then he stepped aside, and Betsy knew it was her turn to move forward. She bowed to Ghonka, her hands folded across her breasts, then extended both arms to Ena in the symbolic gesture Renno had taught her. Taking a deep breath, she intoned the words that she had rehearsed so frequently. "The new daughter of the Great Sachem and his woman greets them," she said.

For an instant Ghonka's eyes widened, but he gave no other sign that he had even heard her. A fleeting smile appeared on Ena's lips, and then she, too, looked straight ahead impassively. The ceremony was ended, and Renno beckoned.

Betsy knew he would lead her to their own hut. They had gone only a few paces, however, when the solemnity of the occasion was shattered. An adolescent girl hurled herself at Betsy, and a boy who was a little older also came forward and hugged her.

"You are my new sister!" Ba-lin-ta cried exuberantly. Walter Alwin also appeared estatic.

Betsy was reminded of her own little sister, and her tension was eased. "The woman of Renno has heard much of Ba-lin-ta and Wal-ter," she said. "She already holds them in her heart."

Ba-lin-ta was so overjoyed she clapped her hands together before she hugged Renno. Walter tried in vain to emulate a warrior by displaying his indifference, but he was delighted, too, and continued to grin as he and Renno clasped each other's forearms.

"I'm so happy that Renno will marry you," Ba-lin-ta said after her brother had disengaged himself and she was on the verge of darting away.

Betsy waited until the children were out of earshot before she spoke. "Doesn't she know we're already married?"

Renno's eyes twinkled. "We have been married in your church," he said. "Tonight we will be married according to the Seneca custom."

Saying nothing more, he led her into a small hut which had two window openings, several wall pegs for clothes, and two wooden ledges, raised slightly from the floor, that were covered with mats of rushes. The floor was the hard ground, and for a moment Betsy's heart sank.

"Tomorrow," Renno told her, "El-i-chi and some of the junior warriors will build another room for us. We will sleep here, and in the other room we will sit."

She nodded and was already making plans. She knew of no reason they couldn't have at least a rough-hewn table, and she fully intended to cover the bare ground with a rug of rushes.

Renno carefully placed their muskets and his other weapons in one corner, then hung the rawhide bags containing their belongings on pegs. That brief chore completed, he seemed impatient. "Come," he said.

"Where are we going now?"

"Back to the house of my parents. I must report what I have learned to the Great Sachem, and you may watch my mother as she prepares supper."

Betsy followed him, developing ideas of her own.

Ghonka had shed his ceremonial headdress and cloak, but continued to sit in front of his dwelling. When he saw his son, he picked up a clay pipe and began to fill it with tobacco, but he did not even glance in the direction of his new daughter-in-law.

Renno sat beside his father, and Betsy knew that, in due time, they would converse.

Left to her own devices, she walked around the building. Ena was standing at a crude table, preparing filets of fish, and did not as much as look up at the girl. Betsy watched her in silence for a moment, then took another fish from a basket, picked up a knife, and went to work. Scaling it expertly, she gutted it and removed the bones swiftly.

Ena grunted, apparently indicating her approval. Then she gestured toward a slab of meat and mounds of vegetables, making a chopping gesture.

Betsy went to work with a vengeance. She had made venison stew on many occasions, and she cut up the meat into small pieces, adding sliced onions, corn which she removed from the cob, and chopped beans. Then, conscious of Ena's surreptitious attention, she sniffed several herbs, selected what she wanted, and threw them into an iron pot along with the other ingredients. Adding water from a bucket, she walked around the house to a cooking pit, where a silent Ba-lin-ta and Walter were building a fire. Ghonka and Renno sat nearby, talking earnestly in low tones, and it was plain they were not to be disturbed.

Betsy saw there was no place to hang the pot, so she looked around until she saw a number of forked sticks. Driving two into the ground, one at either end of the fire, she suspended the pot over the flames on a pole she placed between them.

Aware that Ena was watching her from a corner of the house, the girl returned to the table, under which she saw several clay pots filled with edible roots. Again she chose those that most nearly matched her own recipe for venison stew, scrubbed them with a stone, and washed them with water. Then she cut the roots into small pieces and, making several trips, threw them into the pot, which was already beginning to simmer.

Renno had told her it was impolite for a younger person to speak before being addressed by an elder, so Betsy asked her new mother-in-law no questions. Various containers of woven vines stood at one side of the table, and she examined them, one by one. First she discovered a large chunk of salt, obviously taken from a lick. Making a careful estimate, she cut off enough for the stew, then swiftly chopped several buds of wild garlic into small bits.

After throwing the seasonings into the pot she returned to the table and cleaned her knife.

Ena broke the silence. "The ways of the wilderness are not strange to the woman of Renno," she said.

"She has much to learn," Betsy replied.

Ena's eyes brightened. "She already knows much," she said, and to the girl's astonishment embraced her.

Betsy clung to her, overwhelmed by the sudden gesture of acceptance. Renno's mother was as sweet and warm as he had claimed, and when they smiled at each other, Betsy knew they had established a rapport.

"Ghonka and Renno will talk for a long time, until the stew is ready to eat," Ena said. "We will swim."

Betsy accompanied her to a lake that was located outside the palisade, knowing that Ba-lin-ta and Walter were following quietly. The young woman from Virginia knew she was still creating a stir, but the presence of Renno's mother comforted her, and her embarrassment was diminishing.

A number of Seneca of all ages were swimming and cavorting in the lake, all of them nude.

Ena, Ba-lin-ta, and Walter divested themselves of their clothes and waded into the water. Betsy hesitated for a moment, then undressed and followed them.

Ba-lin-ta promptly challenged her to a race, and Walter's gesture indicated that he intended to compete, too. Both were completely at home in the water, but Betsy had been swimming since earliest childhood and quickly accepted. "Where will the contest take place?" she asked.

"We will swim to the far end of the lake," Ba-lin-ta said. "We will touch the old tree that has fallen into the water there, and then we will return to the side of my mother."

Ena glanced at Betsy, warning her not to race these two youngsters. Betsy shook her head, eager to demonstrate her own competence. Ena struck her hands together, indicating that the race was under way.

By the time Betsy started, the youngsters had already gained a commanding lead, and both swam like fish. She plunged in, her strokes powerful as she struggled to catch up with them. Other Seneca silently stopped swimming and watched the race.

Concentrating on the task, Betsy swam smoothly, her arms digging through the water, her legs thrashing. Not until she touched the fallen tree, made her turn, and started back did she realize she had gained the lead. She improved on it stroke by stroke and quickly found that the Seneca did not always refrain from showing their emotions. Grizzled elders, white-haired women, husky warriors, and even young girls, all naked, were shouting and screaming, urging her to win.

She reached Ena's side and stood in the neck-high water, gulping welcome air. They had a considerable wait before Ba-lin-ta and Walter reached the finish line.

Ba-lin-ta was deeply impressed. "Only Renno and El-i-chi are better swimmers than Ba-lin-ta and Walter," she said.

Ena smiled serenely. "The woman of Renno is worthy of him," she said.

The compliment made Betsy glow. Her mother-in-law had become her friend and ally.

When they left the water they let the warm air dry them before they dressed again, and Betsy, no longer self-conscious, gave in to Ba-lin-ta's insistent plea and allowed the girl to arrange her hair in two braids. It occurred to her that, like the other women of the Seneca, she would wear her hair in this style most of the time.

They returned to the town, and Ena stood aside to let her new daughter-in-law taste the stew. Betsy added more salt, then threw in several pinches of a dried, pungent herb, slightly stronger than a similar one she had used at home. Then she put bear grease into a frying pan and quickly cooked the fish.

El-i-chi seemed to have an instinct for knowing when a meal was ready. He arrived just as the others were sitting, and after inclining his head respectfully to his parents, he lowered one eyelid slightly in a suggestion of a wink as he glanced at his new sister-in-law for an instant.

Inasmuch as Betsy had been responsible for the meal, Ena stood aside to let her serve it. This, as the girl learned later from Renno, was a special honor.

They ate the fried fish, then the stew, and no one spoke. Betsy had anticipated the silence, but was still disturbed because the all-powerful Great Sachem had not acknowledged her. She had won his mother, El-i-chi had made it plain that he approved of her, and Ba-lin-ta and Walter had become her admirers. But Ghonka appeared not to know she existed.

When he finished his bowl of stew he held his gourd over his head.

Ena nudged Betsy, who realized he wanted more, so she refilled the bowl.

Again he ate heartily, and then he emitted a long, satisfying belch. "She who was my sister and has gone to join our ancestors," he announced, "was the only woman who ever made this good a venison stew."

Renno's quick smile told Betsy she had been awarded Ghonka's supreme accolade.

As soon as the meal was finished, it was time for the Seneca wedding ceremony. Ena applied smears of white paint to Betsy's cheeks, forehead, chin, and nose, then draped a heavy cloak of buffalo hide over her shoulders.

Feeling stifled, Betsy thought Renno was fortunate. Other than his feather bonnet and his war paint, he wore only his loincloth.

The entire family walked together to a large lodge where a fierce fire was burning, adding to the heat. So many people were already crowded into the building, chanting, that Betsy was afraid she would suffocate.

Three men wearing hideous masks carved out of wood and decorated with feathers and animal hair were standing immobile near the fire. Remembering what Renno had told her, she knew these were the principal medicine men of the town. Their masks, one the head of a human, another that of a bear, and the third that of a huge hawk, were the Great Faces, the sacred representations of the manitous who guided the destinies of every Seneca. The bear, she realized, indicated that Renno was a member of the Bear Clan, into which she was being inducted. And she wondered whether the hawk head meant that hawks who were emissaries of the manitous would extend their protection to her, too.

She was led to the fire, and the medicine men

instructed her to prostrate herself on the ground, lying on her back. Then they chanted interminably, shaking wooden rattles over her, and finally they sprinkled her with a powdered herb.

The entire assemblage began to chant in unison, joining the medicine men.

Renno was handed two buckets of water, and Betsy judged that vinegar or some other sharp-smelling substance had been added to it. He soaked two cloths of soft, inner tree bark in the water, then commanding Betsy to rise, scrubbed her face until it was clean. "Now you must do the same to me," he whispered.

Controlling a desire to giggle, Betsy removed his feathered bonnet, then scrubbed away his war paint. Both were sopping by the time she was done.

To her infinite relief, this act ended the formal ceremony. The men of the Great Sachem's family formed around her, with Ghonka in front, Renno on her right, El-i-chi on her left, and Walter behind her. The men of Ghonka's family were taking her into their fold, offering her their protection.

They led her out of the lodge, and then everyone trooped out to an open field beyond the palisade, where the drums were already throbbing.

One final surprise was in store for Betsy. The Great Sachem led her into the clearing and, with the entire population of the town watching, began to dance with her. His movements were stately, but gradually became livelier, and the girl threw herself into the spirit of the occasion. Laughing happily, she danced with abandon, and Ghonka matched every movement.

Then Renno came into the clearing with his mother, and after they joined in the dance for a short time he and his father changed partners.

Betsy looked at her husband with shining eyes. Now, as she had hoped, she had won the acceptance of his family and his people and at last was a full-fledged member of his nation.

Scores of warriors took turns dancing with the bride. First came the war chiefs, led by Sun-ai-yee, and the drums did not stop beating until the youngest of the junior warriors had circled the clearing with Betsy.

She was exhausted as Renno scooped her up into his arms and carried her to their dwelling. They had not been intimate since they had entered the land of the Erie, and the bride soon discovered she was not too tired for a repeat of the night of their first wedding.

The changes in the house of Renno and Betsy were startling, so dramatic that other Seneca women began to copy them. Rugs of woven rushes covered the dirt floors of both rooms, candles and crude but effective oil lamps provided illumination after dark, and strips of beaded wampum, squares of leather decorated with dyed porcupine quills, and several bunches of multi-colored wild corn enlivened the walls. Several chairs and two tables were placed in the living room, a few stools were scattered in the sleeping chamber, and a cabinet with shelves contained their clothes. Perhaps the most significant change was the conversion of the two sleeping ledges into one.

Quickly acclimating herself to Seneca life, Betsy was supremely happy. When Renno went hunting or fishing, which he did almost daily, she worked with the other women in the fields. She prepared breakfast and supper, sometimes entertaining the entire family, and on other occasions she and Renno went to his parents' house for a meal. El-i-chi was a frequent visitor, and Ba-lin-ta and Walter were constantly underfoot.

Before long Betsy found herself gossiping with the other women, curing animal skins and making clothing, experimenting with unfamiliar herbs, and washing clothes in a brook that ran nearby.

The entire town participated in frequent games. Betsy surprised herself by beating El-i-chi in a swimming contest, but she took great care not to compete against Renno. Although it was unlikely that she could defeat him in a race, she didn't want to take the risk. Under no circumstances could she cause him to lose face.

One day, when the warriors were engaging in a competition, shooting at targets with their muskets, she cast a sidelong glance at Renno. He nodded, so she hurried home for her own musket. To the astonishment of every man present, except her husband, she proved to be an expert shot. Even Ghonka shook his head slowly from side to side, and thereafter, at family gatherings, he abandoned all formality with her. In fact, one evening, when he was discussing the Pimlico, southern Tuscarora, Choctaw, and other major tribes to the south, he paid his daughter-in-law the rare compliment of inviting her to join in the discussion. Her attitudes, he reasoned, were those of the Virginia settlers, so he was eager to listen to her.

Betsy wrote regularly to her own family, although couriers went off to Fort Springfield no more than once a month. They always returned with letters for her from her parents and Ned, with Anne contributing scribbled drawings.

Ena was her daughter-in-law's mentor and guide, advising her, explaining unfamiliar customs, and helping her settle into the routines of tribal life. She advised Betsy which of the young women were jealous of her, which had wanted to marry Renno, and which would prove reliable friends.

Betsy's relationship with Renno, which formed the core of her existence, was perfect. He was always gentle and considerate, placing her well-being, happiness, and comfort ahead of his own. When representatives of the other Iroquois nations came to the town for a conclave, a number of warriors embarrassed her by ogling her. Quickly aware of her feelings, Renno acted. She had no idea what he did, but the atmosphere changed immediately, the visiting warriors treating her with the profound respect that was due the wife of a war chief.

Renno was beginning to read and write English reasonably well. Betsy, in return, was becoming fluent in her command of the Seneca language and quickly learned many of the nation's songs, myths, and traditions.

Their lovemaking left nothing to be desired.

Betsy talked so much about Renno that one day, when Ena was helping her cut a cured doeskin for a new dress, the older woman laughed. "My daughter," she said, "you sound as though you and Renno have never had harsh words with each other."

"We have no reason to fight," Betsy replied. Curiosity impelled her to ask, "Do you quarrel with the Great Sachem?"

"Often," Ena admitted cheerfully.

It was difficult for the girl to imagine anyone disputing the word of Ghonka. "Do you win?" she asked incredulously.

Ena lowered her voice, even though they were alone. "Always I allow him to think he has won. But very soon he does what I have wished him to do."

Her mother-in-law sounded like her own mother, and Betsy reflected that women everywhere, regardless of their civilization, were required to handle their husbands without allowing the men to know they were being manipulated. Soon she had an unexpected opportunity to exert her influence over Renno.

The summer was warm, with ample rainfall, and when the first hint of autumn appeared in the air the pace of life in the Seneca town quickened. The harvesting season was at hand, so the women became busier. This was the best time of year for hunting, and the warriors went out into the forest at daybreak, not returning until nightfall, as they accumulated enough supplies of meat to see the community through the long winter.

Betsy did her fair share, and one day when she and some of the other younger women had gone swimming after completing their day's work, they strolled back to the town. Suddenly the girl from Virginia stopped short.

A group of ten boys, clad only in loincloths, were

trotting toward the wilderness, and she saw that they were looped together with rawhide thongs. One of them was Walter Alwin. She tried to attract his attention. The grim-faced Walter paid no heed to her.

Ba-lin-ta was standing just inside the palisade, obviously having watched the procession, and as usual she was showing her feelings.

"Is Walter being punished for something?" Betsy demanded. "Why were he and the other boys tied to each other?"

The child plainly was upset. "They are being taken to the forest for their manhood tests," she replied. "They will spend three nights and four days in the forest."

Betsy returned to her own dwelling deeply disturbed. All she knew about the tests was that they were exceptionally rugged, with each boy being tried to the limits of his endurance and courage. It was wrong to expect Walter to suffer through these trials when he could neither speak nor hear. She waited with growing impatience for Renno to return home.

He did not appear until long after nightfall. "My group shot three bucks and two does today," he told her. "And Sun-ai-yee's warriors brought down two buffalo. We are doing well, and tomorrow's hunting promises to be even better. All of us are going to an area where a large herd of buffalo is grazing."

Betsy served him a platter of smoking venison, along with a gourd of corn and beans, then waited until he started to eat before she expressed her own thoughts. "I saw the young boys going out for their manhood trials," she said. "One of them was Walter."

Renno nodded complacently. "On the last day of the trials it will be my duty to join the test master and judge them. I feel sure all of them will become junior warriors."

Here was the opening she was seeking. "Including Walter?"

He nodded and continued to eat.

"How can you expect so much of a mere youth who is deaf and dumb?"

Renno became aware of the shocked incredulity in her voice. "For five years," he said, "Walter has lived with the Seneca. He has learned our ways. He is at home in the wilderness. He knows how to take care of himself."

"But it's cruel to subject him to torment!"

"Life is cruel," Renno said. "He who becomes a warrior must be strong and brave. He must know how to survive in the wilderness. He must protect himself and others from their enemies. The Seneca have become a great nation only because our warriors are men of courage and cunning and strength."

"Walter is handicapped!" His continuing calm infuriated her, and she forgot her own meal. "I suppose it's fair enough to put boys who are in sound physical condition through harsh trials. But it's barbaric to torture someone who can't speak or hear."

"Warriors who cannot fight or hunt are soon killed by our enemies," Renno said, speaking slowly. "Since the time of our ancestors we have taught them to be brave. There is no other way."

"I've been hoping," Betsy said, "that you'd intervene and bring Walter back here."

He shook his head. "It is Walter's time to take the tests. I cannot interfere. I will not interfere. He would be shamed if I brought him here. He would think he was being treated like a woman."

"Better that than to torture him!" she cried.

"My father was tortured when he made his trials. I was tortured. Today we are men. My sons also will be tortured when their time comes. A warrior knows what is best for those who will join them in the hunt and on the warpath."

"How can you be so unfeeling? I thought you were civilized!" This was their first quarrel, and she knew it was a mistake to insult him, but she was so angry she did not care.

Renno folded his arms across his chest. "I am a Seneca," he said. "If my people are savages, I am a savage. I do what a warrior must. Walter, too, will do what is necessary." He spoke with finality.

Betsy knew she had hurt him, but she wasn't sorry. The very thought of the deaf and dumb boy being subjected to cruel torment devastated her.

They ate their meal in silence, and Renno did not speak again before he went off to confer with the other war chiefs and plan the next day's hunting expedition.

Betsy cleaned the gourds, platters, and cooking pots, fed the scraps to a pair of dogs, and promptly went to bed. She pretended to be asleep when Renno returned.

He turned his back to her when he joined her on the sleeping ledge.

For the next three days their relations remained strained. They seldom addressed each other, confining their talk to essentials. Ena soon realized they were quarreling, but wisely refrained from asking questions. She well knew that every married couple went through difficult periods and had to work out their differences in their own way.

On the last day of the trials Betsy steeled herself, deathly afraid that Walter would be crippled or maimed for life. Even worse, he would feel disgraced because he had failed tests far too severe for someone suffering from his handicaps.

Shortly after noon Renno returned home from a morning's hunting, donned his full war paint, and settled his war chief's bonnet on his head. Armed with his tomahawk, bow, and quivers of arrows as well as the knife he carried in his belt, he neither looked at Betsy nor spoke to her as he went off to the forest to make the final judgment of the candidates for admission to the ranks of junior warrior.

Although his wife did not realize it, he was less sanguine than he appeared and was entertaining serious doubts about Walter's endurance and strength. Perhaps Betsy was right. It was possible that he and the other leaders of the nation were expecting too much of a boy who was handicapped and, unlike the born Seneca, had enjoyed only five years of training.

Trotting effortlessly, Renno moved far into the forest until he came to the site of the trials. The senior warrior who was conducting the tests exchanged formal greetings with him.

"How do the youths fare?" Renno asked.

"They are very tired," the senior warrior replied. "But so far not one has collapsed."

Renno concealed his relief.

"Now they are making their last trial-by-water. If none fail, I recommend that all become junior warriors."

They walked together to a deep pool at the base of a small waterfall. Each of the candidates was standing alone in the neck-high, icy water, his hands folded across his chest. Not one moved or made a sound.

Renno well remembered the living hell of this final test. Their nerves ragged and their bodies exhausted after the unending trials, the boys were being subjected to the most severe of their tests. Occasionally a candidate wept, moaned, or fainted and was disqualified, forced to wait a full half-year before being allowed to take the trials again. Those who fell short were marked for the rest of their lives.

All ten of the youths were in agony, but Renno, after scanning the faces of the others, concentrated on Walter. The veins at his temples were bulging, and the expression in his glazed, hollow eyes was an indication of the torture he endured. Like the others, he had been standing immobile in the cold water for more than three hours.

Renno was tempted to beckon Walter and bring him out of the water. The other youths were silent because they were exercising what was left of their will power. But it was possible that Walter wanted to groan aloud. Unfortunately, he had never made a sound in his entire life. So there was great validity to Betsy's arguments. Uncertain what to do, Renno hesitated.

Walter Alwin looked toward him and thought he saw Renno standing on the bank at the side of the pool, but couldn't be certain. For the past night and all of this day he had been hallucinating frequently, an experience that was common in the last phases of the trials. His body felt numb, but at the same time every bone, every joint ached. He was alternately cold and on fire, and although it didn't seem possible in the icy water, he was certain that his forehead was bathed in perspiration.

He had no idea how much longer he could last. From time to time he felt consciousness slipping away, and only by marshaling what little remained of his strength and endurance was he able to haul himself back from the brink.

Averting his face from the war chief he believed to be Renno, Walter looked up at the sky. Far above him, circling slowly, he saw a tiny, dark speck that seemed to be growing larger. He thought he was dreaming again, but nevertheless continued to watch.

All at once he recognized it! A hawk! Surely he was imagining things again.

Following the direction of the youth's gaze, Renno looked up and instantly identified the hawk, too. A cold chill moved up his spine. Not only did the manitous send hawks to guard and watch over him, but now they were showing their favor to Walter, too. Under no circumstances could he remove the boy from the water. Walter was one of the elect.

The hawk moved still lower until it hovered no more than one hundred feet overhead.

All at once Walter knew he was not hallucinating. The hawk was real, and he was truly seeing it.

The significance was not lost on him. He had learned from Ba-lin-ta that Renno owed his extraordinary eyesight to the hawks who kept watch over him, that he was one of a very small handful of warriors who stood high in the esteem of the omnipotent, ever-present manitous.

The hawk dipped still lower, directly over his head,

before soaring again, gathering speed, and vanishing from sight. A feeling of overwhelming power and joy surged through Walter. All at once he opened his mouth and shouted exuberantly.

All of the others, also aware of the hawk, were stunned. Renno's whole body tingled.

No one was more astonished than Walter himself. For the first time in his life he had actually made a genuine sound! Though he could not hear the sound, he felt the vibration in his throat—and saw the shocked reaction on the faces of the others.

Renno instantly halted the trial, and the boys were ordered out of the water. Their ordeal had come to an end. Staggering up to the bank one by one, each raised his arm in a salute to the war chief. When it was Walter's turn and he knew it was really Renno, he shouted again, the triumphant cry echoing through the wilderness.

Everyone knew that a miracle had taken place. Walter had become a member of the tiny band on whom the manitous showered their blessings.

Everything that happened thereafter was anticlimactic. The boys donned their loincloths, then lighted a cooking fire for their first real meal since the trials had started. While several wild turkeys were roasting, they took quantities of green and yellow war paint from gourds that Renno held for them and daubed themselves with the nation's colors. Then each was awarded a single feather to affix to his scalp lock.

Renno took a hawk feather from his own bonnet and handed it to the overjoyed Walter.

By the time the turkeys were cooked the boys were ravenous, but carefully accepted the advice of Renno and the senior warrior, who warned them that, after fasting for days, they would become ill if they ate too much. Exerting the self-discipline expected of their new rank, they obeyed. No one was happier than Walter, and even those who were his closest friends regarded him with awe.

The party jogged back through the forest to the

Seneca town, then slowed to a stately pace. The families of the candidates were gathered to welcome them, parents finding it difficult to conceal their apprehensions, and as they saw the war paint and feathers they rejoiced loudly.

Betsy stood with Renno's family, dreading the sight of Walter, but when she saw that he, too, had a feather in his scalp lock and was smeared with green and yellow paint, she felt relieved.

Walter marched up to Ghonka, raising his arm in salute, then turned to the girl who had been his voice and ears. He struggled for the power of speech and slowly mouthed each syllable. By listening carefully, the others could make out what he said: "Ba-linta."

Even Ghonka gaped at him.

Renno, looking directly at Betsy but speaking to the whole, elated family, related what had happened.

Ba-lin-ta hugged her good friend, and Betsy wept openly as she embraced him. There were tears in Ena's eyes, too, when she kissed him.

There was no opportunity for further conversation. The time had come for the formal induction of the new junior warriors. Ghonka donned his bonnet and buffalo robe and, flanked by Renno and El-i-chi, went to the main lodge for the ceremonies.

The lodge was so crowded that Betsy preferred not to push her way in. Instead she returned to her own dwelling in a daze, unable to think clearly. The significance of what she had just seen and heard staggered her.

She sat for a long time and did not stir until people began to return to their homes and longhouses after the ceremony. She listened for Renno's approach, and when she heard him she rose and met him at the entrance.

"I owe you an apology," she said abruptly. "I was wrong about Walter, and you were right."

Renno took her hand and led her into their living room, then seated himself opposite her. "It is you who had the right feelings," he declared. "I was in the wrong."

Betsy stared at him.

"When I saw Walter standing still in the cold water, where he had been for a very long time," Renno continued, "I suddenly realized how different he was from the others. They were silent by choice. He was silent because he could not speak. I was ready to take him out of the pond when the hawk appeared. Then I waited. I have already explained how the hawk gave him the power to speak."

"Are such things possible?" Betsy asked. "How could a hawk grant a person the power of speech?"

"All I know," Renno said, "is that Walter was mute. The hawk flew close to him. All at once he could speak. So I am pleased that I did not remove him from the trial."

"I've never believed in miracles," she said in a low tone. "All that's happened today is too good to be true."

"You heard Walter yourself," he said. "With the help of Ba-lin-ta he will learn many words. I do not ask you to believe in the manitous. I can tell you only that they do many wonderful things for those who have faith in them."

Betsy pondered, shaking her head, and then she smiled. "Perhaps it was the manitou who brought us together again," she said, and laughed aloud. "I never expected both of us to insist we were wrong."

Renno grinned, rose, and went to her, lifting her into his arms and carrying her to their sleeping room. As he well knew, there were times it was wise not to scrutinize the acts of the manitou too closely. It was far better just to accept and enjoy the favors they bestowed.

Chapter V

Ned Ridley returned from a voyage to Boston and New York on one of his father's brigs, and after greeting his mother and little sister, he went directly to the library, which the colonel used as his office.

Austin Ridley looked up from the document he was reading, stood, and grasped his son's hand. "Welcome home," he said.

Ned handed him a sheaf of papers. "We turned a substantial profit in New York, and we did even better in Boston, as you'll see when you read these. Mama tells me you've had several more letters from Betsy."

The colonel gave him a small packet. "Read these when you have the time, and then return them to your mother. Betsy and Renno are both well. She's made herself a long cloak of buffalo hide, and she's lined a pair of leggings with fox fur, so she's ready for the cold weather."

"It's winter up there now," Ned replied. "I was strongly tempted to visit her and Renno. But when General Wilson came to Boston to meet me he said they've already had snow at Fort Springfield and that a

112

great deal has fallen farther to the west, in Mohawk and Seneca country. I was anxious to come home with the cargo of tea and English kitchenware I picked up in Boston, so I didn't go. The journey into the interior would have taken too long."

"Betsy hopes to visit us in the spring," Austin said.

The younger man leaned forward. "Is she having a baby?"

His father shrugged. "That's what she hinted, or so your mother thinks. If so, she was being too subtle for me. I read the passage a number of times. Make your own judgment and draw your own conclusions."

"I shall. What news do you have, Papa?"

The colonel's smile faded. "Two of our ships have just come back from the West Indies, and both our captains tell the same story. Don Pedro de Rivera—the Spanish Viceroy for the Americas, who makes his headquarters at Havana—seems determined to create trouble."

Ned immediately grew tense.

"He's going out of his way to be thoroughly unpleasant to trading vessels from the English colonies. First he wouldn't allow them to land in Havana. Then he changed his mind, provided they paid a double port fee and lowered their British flags. And Spanish customs men hounded them, forcing them to leave before they could sell their cargoes or buy anything. One of them went on to Guadeloupe, where the French weren't particularly cordial, but at least did business with them. The other sailed to our own crown colony of Jamaica and made a fair enough deal at Port Royal."

"Are you saying, sir, that Viceroy de Rivera is deliberately trying to discourage trade with English colonies?"

"After two of our ships were given the same cavalier treatment over a ten-day period, I can only conclude that he's being downright hostile to us. When the French behave that way toward us it's always a clear indication that a declaration of war against Britain and her colonies is pending. But—as you know—that isn't the way the Spaniards operate."

"They prefer undeclared wars, at least on this side of the Atlantic," his son replied. "Don Pedro can cut our colonies to ribbons without alarming London and causing King William and Parliament to declare war on Madrid."

"That's my analysis," Austin said. "First they starve us, then they attack us, and by the time Whitehall wakes up to what's happening in the New World, the Spanish flag will be flying over Charleston and Norfolk, perhaps even New York and Boston."

Ned hooked his thumbs in his waistcoat pockets. "They'll have one hell of a fight on their hands if they invade any of our colonies. General Wilson took great pains to assure me that Massachusetts Bay—and the other New England colonies to a lesser extent—will join forces with us at once if we go to war with Spain."

"I've been reasonably certain they would," the colonel said, "but that's the least of our problems. Lucinda sent me word from Charleston saying that Governor Moore is reluctant to join forces with any of our other colonies. He's one of those independent men who like to do things strictly on their own."

"Then he's even more stupid than I thought, sir," Ned said emphatically. "South Carolina is so sparsely settled that I don't believe Moore could raise more than two battalions of militia there."

"Our greatest headache," Austin declared, "is that of persuading our English colonies to cooperate with each other. All of them are jealous of their petty powers and prerogatives, which they're unwilling to put aside for the common good. I'm afraid that only Virginia and Massachusetts Bay are being unselfish. Don Pedro de Rivera must be aware of our situation, and it wouldn't surprise me if he attacks one colony at a time, conquers it, and digests his victory before he goes on to the next."

"That would be a catastrophe, sir!"

"Try to convince some of the shortsighted. Many weeks ago I wrote to the commander of South Carolina's only full battalion, a Major Strickling. I've just received an indifferent reply from him. He speaks of false alarms and says in so many words that he has no interest in joint ventures."

"There are people in Charleston who don't agree with that approach, Papa. Renno and I met some of them, and they're prominent citizens."

"To be sure. But this Major Strickling is echoing Governor Moore's attitude."

"Then what can we do, sir?"

"Several things. I intend to keep as close a watch as I can on Don Pedro de Rivera. Every ship I send to the West Indies will visit Cuba. I'll go to Boston myself for a meeting with General Wilson and as many of the other colonial militia commanders as we can drag to a conference there. And—more than anything else—we'll keep our powder dry."

When Ena learned that Betsy was pregnant and planned to have her baby in the land of the Seneca she made no comment. She spoke privately and at length with her husband, and only then was she ready for the next step.

The evening meal was cooked out of doors, as usual, but it was too cold to eat in the open. That night the family gathered around the fire inside the Great Sachem's dwelling, where the smoke escaped through a hole in the ceiling. As always, supper was consumed in silence.

A glance from Ena told El-i-chi to take himself elsewhere, and he departed at once.

It was more difficult to get rid of Ba-lin-ta and Walter. The latter now lived in a longhouse of the junior warriors and thoroughly enjoyed his occasional meals with the family.

Finally Ena had to be blunt. "Ba-lin-ta," she said, "the time has come for you and Wal-ter to go somewhere. You will want to teach him to speak more words."

Only then did the youngsters go.

Renno and Betsy exchanged a swift glance, both of them realizing that his parents wanted to speak with them in private.

Ghonka responded to his wife's subtle nudge. "It is said," he declared, "that the woman of Renno will have a child. That is good."

The young couple had known he would be pleased by their news and smiled at him.

"It is also said," he went on, "that the child will be born in the town of the Seneca. What is the reason for this?"

Renno and Betsy were startled by the question. It would have been inappropriate for her to reply, so he spoke for both of them.

"I am a war chief of the Seneca," he said with dignity. "Betsy is my woman. Now she also is a Seneca. Our child will be a member of this nation. It is right that he should enter the world in the home of his father and his mother."

Ghonka's look told Ena that he wanted her to speak. "It is true that Betsy is a Seneca," she said. "But she has been a Seneca only for a short time. When Ba-lin-ta marries and has a child, he will be born here. Ba-lin-ta has lived here since she herself was born. She knows our ways. She knows what the medicine men will do. I have given birth here. It was not easy or simple, even though I have been a Seneca all of my life."

Renno wanted to say something, but his father's slight frown warned him to wait until his mother finished.

"The child of Betsy," Ena went on, "should enter the world in the house of her own father. Her mother will be there to help her. The medicine men of her people will be there to help her."

Betsy could remain silent no longer. "But Renno

and I have talked about all this!" she cried. "We want our baby to be born in the land of the Seneca."

Ena silently appealed to her husband.

His expression unchanging, the Great Sachem folded his hands across the buckskin shirt he now consented to wear during the winter. "It is good that Renno and the woman of Renno are loyal to the Seneca. Their son—or their daughter—truly will be a member of this nation. Ghonka will rejoice and make offerings to the manitous in thanks for the birth of a child to the woman of Renno. Ghonka will carry the child in his own arms to the lodge of the Bear Clan when prayers are offered to the manitous and they are told the name of the child."

Betsy opened her mouth to speak, but Renno touched her arm and shook his head vehemently.

Ghonka did not raise his voice, but he spoke with the authority of one long accustomed to unquestioning obedience. "The child of Renno and his woman," he said, "will be born in the home of Betsy's father." He reached for a coal to light his pipe, indicating that a decision had been made and that the subject was closed.

To Betsy's astonishment, Renno accepted his father's verdict in silence. Shaken by his seemingly docile acquiescence, she helped Ena clear away and scrub the platters, gourds, cooking pots, and utensils. By that time Renno was ready to return to their own dwelling.

Not until they entered the place, lighted a candle, and lowered the flap of buffalo skin over the entrance did Betsy speak. Then she exploded. "How could you be so meek? You know how much we want the baby to be born here. But you didn't say a single word to defend our position!"

"You don't understand," Renno told her soothingly. "You heard my mother's reasons for wanting you to go to Virginia. What she said makes sense, although I could have argued with her. Then my father issued his decree, so I didn't protest. Not because he is the Great Sachem, but because he is the head of our family."

"You'll dictate to your children after they're grown and leading their own lives?"

"Yes, if it should be necessary," Renno said. "That is the way of the Seneca."

Betsy recognized the futility of further discussion. "I'll write to my parents tonight," she said.

Early the following morning El-i-chi went off to Fort Springfield with the letter. General Wilson speeded it to Boston, and it was dispatched without delay on board a brig whose captain agreed to put into Norfolk with it on his way to Charleston.

Colonel Ridley replied immediately and made specific suggestions. He was coming to Boston to a meeting of colonial militia commanders the following month and would be accompanied by Mary. So he proposed that Betsy return to Norfolk with them.

Enclosed with the letter was another, a formal invitation to Ghonka to take part in the conference. Renno, Colonel Ridley added, was being asked to join in the latter portion of the meeting, as was Ned. There was no indication of the colonel's reasons for including them.

The Great Sachem was well aware of the dangers of a confrontation with Spain, so he immediately consented to attend the conference. Fifty warriors under the command of Sun-ai-yee were assigned to escort him. Renno was given no escort responsibilities because he and Betsy would remain in Fort Springfield for several days before going to Boston. Members of Ghonka's family also agreed that Walter Alwin, accompanied by Ba-lin-ta, would go as far as Fort Springfield so he could surprise his mother. Ba-lin-ta promptly began to teach him words in English.

The snows were melting by the time the party set out from the land of the Seneca. Ena put her arms around her daughter-in-law and held her tightly. "May the manitous watch over you when the child is born," she said, "and may you return safely to your home."

Tears came to Betsy's eyes when she realized that the Seneca town truly had become her town.

The party traveled at a leisurely pace through their own country and that of the Mohawk, and the warriors knew that Ghonka was being considerate of his daughter-in-law's health. They knew that, although he would have admitted it to no one, he wanted to take no chances that might endanger her or his first grandchild.

Renno offered to have a chair made for Betsy, with warriors in teams of four carrying her, but she refused. The women of the Seneca did not indulge themselves, she said, and never had he been more proud of her. All the same, she and Ba-lin-ta were not allowed to do any of the cooking on the march. The junior warriors not only made camp every night but also prepared all of the meals.

The day before they were due to reach Fort Springfield, Renno sent a courier ahead, writing a letter to General Wilson in his own hand. In it he emphasized that Walter was a member of the Seneca party and that he hoped the boy's mother, Ida Carswell, would be on hand to greet him.

At noon the next day the Seneca crossed the Connecticut River. The guns at the sturdy fort boomed a salute to Massachusetts Bay's allies, and a short time later the company reached the Wilsons' large farmhouse.

Andrew Wilson came to the gate to greet the newcomers, accompanied by his son, Jeffrey, one of Renno's closest friends. In the background, clustered at the entrance to the main building, were Renno's other friends, among them Jeffrey's red-haired wife, Adrienne, as well as Deborah and the Reverend Obadiah Jenkins and Tom and Nettie Hibbard.

Renno and the tall, lean Jeffrey, now a major serving on his father's militia staff, greeted each other joyfully, and Betsy, suddenly self-conscious in her Indian attire, met her husband's old comrade-in-arms. Everyone suddenly fell silent as the front door of the Wilson house opened, and a spare, gray-haired woman came timidly into the open.

Ida Carswell, her face toil-lined, still wore plain linsey-woolsey dresses, although her husband, Leverett, well could afford silk. She glanced back at him for support, then moved forward a few paces and waited, controlling her impatient desire to see the son whom she had seen so seldom during his years with the Seneca.

Walter detached himself from the group of junior warriors and proudly advanced toward his mother, his hawk feather in his scalp lock, green and yellow paint smeared on his face.

Ba-lin-ta caught her breath and clenched her fists. Ever since Walter had regained his voice and, miraculously, had called her by name, she had been painstakingly teaching him to speak. The task had been difficult since he had never heard the sound of a voice, but he was able to make himself understood now, and she had rehearsed him repeatedly in what he intended to say at this moment.

Ida blinked, then stared at the young warrior, for a moment scarcely recognizing her son.

Walter approached her, stopped short, and drew a deep breath. When he spoke his voice was very loud, and all of the English colonists could hear him clearly.

"Mama," he said, "I . . . love . . . you."

A bolt of lightning could not have had a more devastating effect on the entire assemblage.

Ida Carswell stared at her son in stunned disbelief. For the first time since she had brought him into the world she had heard the sound of his voice, and his expression of love staggered her. She continued to stand unmoving, and then tears trickled slowly down her weathered cheeks.

Neither Walter nor her niece, Deborah Jenkins, had ever known her to weep. Tears came to Deborah's eyes, too, and Mildred Wilson dabbed at her face with a handkerchief.

Walter stepped forward, smiling, and took his mother into his strong arms to embrace and kiss her. Then Ba-lin-ta, still acting as the youth's interpreter, went to Ida and explained the circumstances that had enabled Walter to gain the use of his voice. Reverend Jenkins offered a prayer of thanksgiving, and at least a dozen of the colonists joined in a fervent "Amen."

Andrew and Mildred Wilson showed Ghonka where his warriors could pitch their tents behind the house, and meanwhile Renno presented his own friends to his wife.

Betsy was uneasy. Not only was her body ungainly, but her Indian pigtails and doeskin dress seemed out of place, particularly in the presence of handsome young women who seemed to know Renno so well. She guessed that he and Deborah once had been intimate, and her instinct told her, too, that he and Adrienne had been lovers.

Then Adrienne moved apart from the crowd, and it was evident that she, too, was carrying a baby. "Come with me," she told Betsy, taking charge, and led her into the house.

"Forgive me if I appear too bold, my dear," she said, "but you seem uneasy, and I think we can correct that situation very easily. I have a maternity wardrobe far larger than I need." They entered a bedchamber and she opened a closet door. "Help yourself."

"I'm overwhelmed," Betsy said, and found it strange to be speaking in English for the first time in months. Ultimately she selected some clothes, changed, and then combed out her hair at a dressing table pier glass.

Adrienne sat on the foot of a four-poster bed, watching her. "In many ways I envy you," she said. "Your courage is greater than mine."

Betsy turned to look at her for a moment.

"Jeffrey and I have a wonderful marriage, and our life together is good, so don't misunderstand me. I still think there's no man in all the world like Renno. And any girl from the colonies who could marry him and live with him in the land of the Seneca must be extraordinary."

There was no longer any question in Betsy's mind that Renno and this girl had slept together, but that was past, and her own life with him filled the present. "I enjoy life in the Seneca town," she said, "but that shouldn't be surprising. I love Renno and I'd willingly live anywhere with him."

Adrienne impulsively embraced her. "We hope your child and our child will be as close as Jeffrey and Renno have been."

They walked down the stairs together arm in arm, and Betsy felt infinitely more at ease. Certainly she wasn't ashamed of having become a Seneca, but she felt more comfortable in this company wearing attire like theirs.

Ghonka disliked sitting at a formal dining table and eating in the European manner, which his host and hostess well knew. So, even though the weather was still raw, they arranged an outdoor barbecue in his honor, with the warriors and colonists sitting around fires where beef, lamb, and pork were roasted.

Ida Carswell was still in a daze and was so excited she ate very little, instead watching every move that Walter made and listening intently as he spoke to her. Whenever she could not understand what he was saying, Ba-lin-ta continued to interpret for him, and Ida insisted that the girl accompany Walter to her house as a guest. Ghonka readily granted his permission, and it was arranged that the Seneca who would accompany the Great Sachem to Boston would stop at Fort Springfield for Walter and Ba-lin-ta when they returned home.

Andrew Wilson had a brief, private word with Betsy before she was surrounded by Renno's Fort Springfield friends. "Your father is due to arrive any day now in Boston for our meeting with Ghonka," he said, "and I'm sure your mother is coming with him."

"So I understand," she said. "I'm planning on going to Norfolk with them and having my baby there."

"Your parents must be very pleased," Andrew said as he went off to join the Great Sachem.

The guests were given their choice of meats, which were served with roasted potatoes and a variety of vegetables. Betsy was amused to be using a knife and fork again. Deborah Jenkins and Nettie Hibbard tried in vain to prevent the men from discussing military matters.

"Renno," Tom Hibbard said, "I wonder if you've heard that—after all we went through to conquer Fortress Louisburg—the French have reoccupied it."

Renno nodded gravely. "The British Government," he said, "can't seem to understand the problems that the colonies face."

"Eventually," Jeffrey Wilson said, "I'm afraid we'll have to face the French in another war."

"I'm sure of it," Renno replied. "The Ottawa—and the Huron, above all—are feeling disgraced because we beat them so badly, and they're certain to be prodding the French, wanting revenge."

"What do you think the Algonquian will do?" Obadiah Jenkins wanted to know.

Renno shrugged. "They are the largest Indian nation in this part of America. But they were at peace for so long they forgot how to fight, as we proved to them. If they're wise they'll stay neutral in the next war. It's my guess their position will depend on the size of the bribes the French offer them."

"We'll know better in a few years," Jeffrey said. "It will take the French a long time to regain their strength, and in the meantime we don't need to worry too much about them. Our frontier here is a measuring stick, and neither the French nor their Indian allies have conducted raids on any of our wilderness outposts for many months."

Renno nodded. "From what I've seen in South Carolina and the unclaimed territory between there and Florida, Spain is the real menace to the English colonies these days."

The women were unable to stem the talk of war, so

they conversed separately. Deborah, obviously well acquainted with the land of the Seneca, asked if Betsy had ever known Renno's aunt.

"Sah-nee-wah? They speak of her often, but she died before Renno and I were married."

"She was a remarkable old lady," Deborah said with a smile. "Even Ghonka deferred to her."

"I can't imagine him deferring to anyone," Betsy said with a laugh.

"Well," Deborah said, "he listened to his sister, and he treated Ja-gonh with respect."

"Did you actually know the great bear?"

Deborah lowered her voice. "I don't speak about him here because no one believes me. I saw him just once, and he was a huge, lumbering creature who weighed hundreds of pounds. But he and Renno truly had a rapport and seemed to understand each other. It was an extraordinary relationship."

"I've often wondered if he was a myth," Betsy said.

"Indeed not! We came upon him in the forest one day, and I almost died of fright. But he and Renno faced each other for a long time and somehow managed to communicate silently."

"The more I learn about the Seneca the more I realize they're unique," Betsy said.

Ghonka and his entourage left for Boston the following morning, with General Wilson and a half battalion of militiamen accompanying them. It was arranged that Renno and Betsy would follow in three or four days, and that Jeffrey would go with them.

That same afternoon, when a group of old friends gathered at the Jenkins's rectory for a dinner party in honor of the Seneca war chief and his wife, Renno found an opportunity to take Jeffrey aside. "Why have I been asked to join the latter part of the conference?"

"I could guess, but I'd rather not," Jeffrey replied. "My father hasn't taken me into his confidence, so I don't really know for certain."

"I suspect it has something to do with Spain."

"That's my own hunch, Renno. Spain has established the headquarters of a powerful empire in the West Indian Islands. That empire is spread through South and Central America, and if the stories that her garrisons in Florida are being strengthened happen to be true, she has designs on North America."

"Then you'll have to fight them, and so will the Iroquois. The French may not be trustworthy, but at least they try to make peace with Indian nations when they invade a territory. But the Spaniards make slaves of Indians and send them off to work hundreds and even thousands of miles from their homes."

"I know. It's a deliberate policy. Viciously cruel, as only Spaniards can be, but also highly effective. There are few uprisings and rebellions in lands that they conquer."

Adrienne came to the parlor entrance and peered out into the corridor. "Come in here, you two," she called, "and stop plotting more bloodshed. Wait until you hear the plans Betsy and I are making."

Betsy waited until the men rejoined them before she said with a laugh, "Adrienne and I have the future neatly arranged. If I have a daughter and she a son, or vice versa, we hope to see to it that they'll marry someday."

Renno looked at her and blinked.

Jeffrey roared with laughter. "Now that's what I call planning. Settling the destinies of children who aren't yet born." He turned to Renno. "Just think of it! In another generation we can be the grandfathers of someone who won't come into the world for at least another twenty to twenty-five years."

Adrienne flushed, but Betsy held her ground. "Far stranger things have happened, you know."

Renno smiled, then became serious. "It would give me great joy if your child and my child should marry," he said to Jeffrey. "But I think we have many things that will keep us busy before we attend their wedding!"

Betsy was paying her first visit to Boston, and when she arrived in the largest city in the English colonies of North America, she was impressed by its bustle and size. Scores of ships rode at anchor in the port, the Governor's House occupied a prominent place, not far from the buildings of the colonial legislature, law courts, and provincial offices. The officers and crews of merchantmen, sailors who spoke at least a dozen different languages, spent much of their shore leave in numerous taverns, and the community boasted many large churches, a huge meeting house, a hospital, and a library. Riders and coaches, horse-drawn carts and more pedestrians than the girl had ever seen in any one place filled the winding, cobbled streets. Vendors were selling meat pies, oysters, fried fish, and roasted chestnuts. Attorneys in long robes and wigs gathered outside the law courts to chat, and even though the weather remained chilly, housewives thronged to open air markets.

Renno and Betsy went direct to the Common, where sheep and cattle were gazing. A portion of the grassy area had been set aside for the visiting Seneca, and Renno learned from El-i-chi that Ghonka had just gone off to a conference with General Wilson and other leaders. He was also told that Betsy's family had arrived several days earlier.

The young couple hurried to the town's one inn of quality and were delighted to discover that Austin and Mary Ridley were accompanied by Ned and little Anne. The family reunion was joyous but brief.

"Renno," Colonel Ridley said, "you've arrived just in time. I'd like you and Ned to come with me right away."

The trio walked the short distance to the armory that was the headquarters of the Massachusetts Bay militia, and there the military commanders from Connecticut, Rhode Island, New Hampshire, and New York were seated with their host around a large table. Ghonka held the place at the right of General Wilson, who had been acting as his interpreter, and Renno first saluted his father, then greeted the other commanders, all of whom he had known at the siege of Louisburg.

General Wilson wasted no time. "We welcome Renno, war chief of the Seneca, and Captain Ned Ridley of Virginia to our deliberations. With your permission, gentlemen, I'll bring them up to date." He faced the pair. "For the past four days we've been discussing the Spanish threat to the English colonies and our Indian allies. As both of you well know, that threat has been severe and is growing worse. More than fifty percent of the merchant ships we send to the West Indian Islands have been refused permission to land at Havana, where Don Pedro de Rivera grants or withholds his permission according to his caprice of the moment. New troop reinforcements are arriving in Havana from Spain, and the garrisons in Florida are being strengthened. We have no accurate information on details, so I can cite no actual figures. Also, we've been informed on good authority that the Spanish viceroy has made a new alliance with the Seminole nation in Florida."

Renno instinctively turned to his father.

The Great Sachem addressed him in their own tongue, which only General Wilson, Colonel Ridley, and Ned also understood. "The Seminole are mighty warriors. Three summers ago they fought against the Choctaw, who are not only fierce but outnumber them. The Seminole won that war."

Ghonka's face showed no feeling, but Renno knew him well enough to realize he was troubled. "It cannot be, my father," he replied, "that the Seminole are stronger than the Seneca and the other nations of the Iroquois."

"The warriors of no nation have the strength and courage of the Seneca." The Great Sachem was uncompromising. "But how can we fight against them? An army of the Iroquois would spend two moons on the trail before they reached the land of the Seminole. By then they would be very hungry and very tired."

Andrew Wilson interrupted, first repeating Ghonka's question in English. "I believe it is premature to think in terms of waging war with the Seminole," he said.

Renno interpreted the comment to his father, speaking in a low tone.

"I'm afraid I'm forced to agree," Colonel Ridley said. "I can't deny the possibility that someday we may be compelled to send transports of militiamen from all of our colonies and many warriors of the Iroquois to Florida to confront the Spaniards and the Seminole. That is how we beat the French at Louisburg. But there, thanks to Renno's scouting expedition, we knew a great deal about the strengths of the French regiments and the number of warriors their Indian allies were putting into the field with them."

"That's correct," General Wilson said succinctly. "We have already sent three of our best espionage agents to Havana and two others to Florida. All have vanished, and we believe they've been killed. We cannot measure the dangers we face and take steps to protect ourselves until we know more about our enemies. We must learn how many of their regiments they can put in the field against us, how many are infantry, how many are artillery and cavalry. We need to know their naval strengths and dispositions. We need to find out much more about the Seminole, who are something of a mystery tribe. Not even the Great Sachem of the Iroquois has much information about them."

"That's a tall order," Ned Ridley muttered.

"My colleagues and I," his father said dryly, "have already reached an identical conclusion."

"Tell them our plan, Colonel," the commander of the New York militia urged.

Several of the others agreed.

"We have decided," Austin Ridley said, "to send an innocent merchant ship to Havana and then on to St. Augustine. She will be carrying a full load of genuine, legitimate cargo and ostensibly will be engaging in a normal trading mission. But the men we judge to be our very best scouts will be on board that ship, which I intend to provide out of my own fleet. Our scouts will report back to us with as much specific information as they can gather."

"It is our hope," General Wilson said, "that Captain Ridley of Virginia and Renno of the Seneca will volunteer for this difficult and hazardous mission."

Everyone present looked at the two young men.

Renno was startled and stared at his father, whose face was wooden. "I am a warrior," he said. "I am not a trader. Why do they ask me to perform this task when there are others who can do it better?"

"There are no others," Ghonka replied. "For two days the sachems of the English colonies and I have talked about many scouts. Only Renno went to Quebec and Louisburg and brought back the information we needed to win that war."

Colonel Ridley translated his remarks, which brought nods of emphatic confirmation from the others, then added, "It is with a heavy heart that I have suggested my son and my son-in-law for this task. Both may lose their lives. My daughter will want her husband close at hand when their baby is born. But this mission is more important than any one woman, even my daughter. If the Spaniards conquer us, many babies in our colonies will die. Many babies of the Iroquois will be sold into slavery."

Ned Ridley spoke for the first time. "If Renno will take the assignment, I agree to go with him. I do speak Spanish, after all, even though my accent isn't very good. If you've got to find someone else to replace him, I'll want to know much more about him before I'll accept."

Renno's bewilderment was real. "I am a warrior, not a trader," he repeated, speaking this time in English.

"We've given a great deal of thought to your situation," Colonel Ridley declared. "If you allow your hair to grow longer, no Spaniard would even guess you're a Seneca."

The very idea of no longer having a scalp lock was appalling, and again Renno turned to his father.

The Great Sachem folded his arms across his chest and stared straight ahead. "It was Ghonka," he said, "who suggested his son's disguise."

The humiliation would have been unbearable had his father opposed the idea, but his sponsorship of it put a far different light on the matter.

He had not enjoyed being a spy in Quebec and Louisburg, but he had done what had been required of him. And he was forced to admit that, by virtue of his heritage, his training, and his experiences, he was uniquely qualified. If he were a member of the Iroquois-colonial high command, he would select someone like himself for the task.

General Wilson, Colonel Ridley, and the other colonial commanders made it plain that they sympathized with his dilemma, and he knew that no one would blame him if he turned the mission down. Only the ever-present protection of the manitous had saved him from destruction in French Canada, and it would be tempting fate to go off on another such venture. Even more important, he was a family man now, and had a wife who needed him.

The unmoving Ghonka continued to stare straight ahead, revealing his thoughts to no one. But his son knew what was going through his mind: a war chief of the Seneca sacrificed his comfort and that of his family when duty called.

Taking a deep breath, the white Indian folded his arms across his chest. "Renno, war chief of the Seneca," he said, "will do what he must."

The militia commanders were elated, but Ghonka revealed neither joy nor sorrow as the meeting came to an end.

The Seneca would depart the following morning for home, stopping at Fort Springfield for Ba-lin-ta and Walter, so Renno went to the camp in the Common for a final meal with his father. He asked Ned to tell Betsy he would join her later, and at his request Ned and Colonel Ridley readily agreed not to mention his mission.

Sun-ai-yee, the other war chiefs, and El-i-chi joined Ghonka and Renno for the meal around the campfire, which they ate in the customary silence. Then, knowing the Great Sachem and his elder son wanted to talk in private, they withdrew.

Ghonka gave Renno the privilege of filling and lighting their pipe. Rarely had any warrior been granted such an honor.

"Ena, the mother of Renno, will not be surprised when she learns where he will go," Ghonka said at last. "She guessed the truth when her son was invited to the conclave."

"My mother is wiser than I am," Renno said.

Ghonka drew on the pipe, then handed it to him. "When the warriors of the Seneca are boys," he said, "they are taught to fight with fairness against enemies who are also fair. That is the honorable way. But a Seneca does not lose his honor when he fights an evil enemy in that enemy's own way. It is said by Wilson and Ridley that no warriors are more evil than the warriors of Spain." The Great Sachem spoke softly, but with emphasis. "The son of Ghonka will do what he must to win in combat with the warriors of Spain."

"The son of Ghonka," Renno assured him, "has heard his father's words and will remember them. He will be as cunning as the wolf and as sly as the serpent. But his enemies will not know it."

The pledge satisfied Ghonka, and he grunted his approval.

But Renno was still disturbed. "If the son of Ghonka dies and goes to join our ancestors in the eternal forests of the Seneca," he said, "it is his hope that Ghonka will give his protection to the child of Betsy and Renno."

The farsighted Iroquois leader well understood what his son had failed to consider. If Renno was killed, it was possible that Betsy might prefer to remain with her own family in Norfolk rather than return to the land of the Seneca and live there without her husband. As much as Ghonka wanted his first grandchild to be reared a Seneca, his sense of honor made it impossible for him to make a promise that circumstances could compel him to break. "The manitous will keep watch over Betsy and her child," he said, "and they will direct her feet on the right path."

Renno had to be content with that answer. He drew on the pipe, then silently handed it back to his father. Suddenly, in an unexpected hint of emotion Ghonka said harshly, "The hawks who are the special messengers of the Seneca manitous also will guard the son of Ghonka, as they have guarded him in the past."

Renno bowed his head in silent prayer, his spirits revived.

Ghonka emptied the ashes from the pipe, a sign the discussion had come to an end. Renno rose, as did his father. Neither spoke again as they gripped each other's forearm and looked directly into each other's eyes.

As Renno went off to bid farewell to El-i-chi, Sun-ai-yee, and some of his friends, Ghonka continued to watch him with searching eyes that still concealed the love he had for his son.

Night had fallen by the time Renno joined the Ridley family, who had just finished their own supper.

"Papa says you're sailing to Norfolk with us." Betsy's pleasure was obvious.

Renno nodded but made no reply. Betsy immediately sensed something was amiss. She looked at him for a moment, then demanded, "What's wrong?"

Reassuring her that everything was all right, he told her about his forthcoming mission, carefully explaining that no details had been settled as yet.

Maintaining a surface calm, Betsy asked quietly, "Why have they chosen you?"

Renno shrugged. "I have succeeded as a scout in the past, so the Great Sachem and General Wilson had confidence in me."

"I have no doubt you'll succeed again," she told him.

He grinned at her, reflecting that no other woman he

knew would have accepted this situation with such tranquility. He just hoped he would return to Norfolk in time for their child's birth.

At breakfast the next morning Mary Ridley was far less accepting than her daughter. "Ned and Renno are being sent on a hazardous mission," she complained, "and I think it's too much to ask one family to assume all of the risks." She looked at her husband and demanded, "Why couldn't you have given the assignment to General Wilson's son, for instance?"

Renno intervened before his father-in-law could reply. "Jeffrey is a good officer," he said, "but he knows nothing about scouting. He could not survive by himself in the wilderness. And he could not pretend to be other than what he is."

"That's right," Ned added. "Renno and I have the ability to adopt disguises when it's necessary."

There was nothing more that Mary could say.

The other militia leaders had gone off to their respective homes, so there was no reason to linger in Boston. Betsy had seen very little of the city, but Renno promised to return with her at some future date, and before noon the family sailed on one of the Norfolk brigs. Ned volunteered his services as a mate and stood regular watches, wanting to keep in practice.

The others had little to do on the week-long voyage, so Renno and Betsy spent most of their time with her parents. Even when they wanted to be alone, however, they were constantly shadowed by little Anne.

"When will you take me to visit you in the Seneca town?" she asked repeatedly.

Renno tried to mollify her by saying a visit would be arranged at an appropriate time. But Betsy finally silenced her sister. "The Seneca appreciate quiet," she said. "We'll invite you as soon as you learn to stop talking so much!"

The Atlantic was rough, but they were all good sailors, and the voyage was not marred by any unpleasantness. When the brig landed at Norfolk, Renno went ashore in his Indian attire and war paint, and he and Ned departed at once to pay a brief visit to the Pimlico.

"We want to make certain they're abiding by our treaty with them," Ned explained, "and we've got to go now, before Renno's hair grows out."

Moy-na-ho greeted his visitors cordially. The war chiefs, elders, and senior warriors of the tribe were hospitable, too, but Si-de-lo made it his business to avoid the visitors. They saw him only at a distance and caught no more than brief glimpses of him.

Traveling swiftly home in order to avoid a possible attack by the medicine man and his followers, Renno and Ned agreed that the peace with the Pimlico was still precarious. "The day will come," Renno said, "when the Pimlico will be sorry they elected Moy-na-ho as their sachem. He is too gentle. A true sachem would send Si-de-lo into the wilderness with no food or weapons and let him die there."

"I'm afraid that if Si-de-lo ever deposes him," Ned said, "the treaty with Virginia will be broken instantly. The medicine man couldn't have made it plainer to us that he hates us. If he becomes sachem he'll use any flimsy excuse to go to war against us."

They explained the situation to Colonel Ridley, recommending that the settlers send emissaries to the Pimlico at frequent intervals, and then settled down to prepare for their coming mission. A tailor was engaged to make a full wardrobe of European clothes for Renno, and no longer shaving his head on either side of his scalp lock, he allowed his hair to grow.

In many ways he enjoyed this peaceful interlude because he could spend more of his time each day with Betsy. But he and Ned were restless and spent at least two hours fencing every morning, then practiced their marksmanship with muskets and pistols every afternoon. As an English colonist Renno would not be able to carry his tomahawk or his bow and arrows. At best he would be able to use his steel-shafted knife and had to content himself with throwing it at a variety of targets. At Ned's suggestion he also practiced with other knives, and his extraordinary eyesight, combined with his sense of balance, enabled him to hurl any blade with deadly accuracy.

Austin Ridley made careful preparations for the special voyage, setting aside quantities of his finest broadleaf tobacco, which the Spaniards in Cuba prized. His son-in-law would travel on board his newest brig, which he had named after Mary, and would be carrying letters of introduction identifying them as traders from a majority of the governors of the English colonies.

Exercising great caution, the colonel refrained from telling even the master of the brig, Captain Cavanaugh, the true nature of the mission. In fact, he knew only that they would sail to Havana. Ned would carry a letter to give the master after they left Cuba, and only then would he know they also would visit St. Augustine.

Renno's hair was still short, but his scalp lock vanished, and when he wore his new clothes he no longer resembled a Seneca. Several visitors to the Ridley estate, including a pair of traders from North Carolina, assumed that the colonel's son-in-law was a Virginia settler, and no one told them otherwise.

Austin's final instructions to the scouts were succinct. "There's no way of telling in advance whether the Spaniards will allow you to dock at Havana, even though your letters of introduction should help. Don Pedro de Rivera adopts a different policy every few days. If he keeps you at arm's length from Havana, I'm afraid you'll have to go ashore somewhere on the uninhabited coast of Cuba and go on to Havana. You'll be on your own there, of course, and you'll have to find some way to get back to the mainland."

"We've been discussing every possibility we can imagine, sir," Ned replied, "and that's the only one that really concerns us. My Spanish is passable, although I speak it with an accent that obviously identifies me as a foreigner."

"And I know only a few words," Renno added, but did not appear concerned.

"You two were chosen for this task because you're resourceful," Austin said. "If there's an emergency, you'll have to rely on your ingenuity."

The colonel placed his hands on their shoulders. "I'm not going to make any farewell speeches to you," he said. "You know your places in this family, and you know how much all of the colonies are depending on the information you'll bring back to us."

When a Seneca went off to battle he frequently left his home without saying goodbye to members of his family, and Renno was inclined to follow that tradition. But he knew Betsy would be hurt, so at dawn on the day of sailing he kissed her tenderly. "If all goes well," he said, "I'll be back before the baby comes. But don't worry or fret if we're delayed. Ned and I are not easy to destroy, and you know I'll return to you."

"I'm sure of it," Betsy replied, and although she had a hollow feeling in the pit of her stomach she smiled steadily at him.

His farewells to Mary and Anne were equally brief. "If I can," he told the little girl, "I'll bring you a souvenir from Havana."

Colonel Ridley rode with his son and son-in-law to the Norfolk dock. Shaking hands before they went on board, he spoke in a husky voice. "May the Almighty and the manitous of the Seneca watch over you and protect you."

They grinned at him and moved up the gangplank. The bluff Captain Cavanaugh, who had spent ten years commanding Ridley merchantmen, promptly gave the order to cast off.

Renno and Ned stood at the rail for a time as the *Mary* moved under reduced sail toward the open Atlantic, and then went down to the cramped wardroom for breakfast.

The first officer took the watch, and Captain Cavanaugh joined his passengers. "If the winds are fair," he said, "I hope to have you in Havana in no more than a week's time. I could shave a day or two off our schedule, but I prefer not to sail too close to the coast of Florida."

"Why is that?" Ned asked.

The ship's master frowned. "I'm no more superstitious than most," he said, "but strange things have been happening off Florida. I've heard tales of sea monsters that swallow ships and their crews whole. Not that I believe such stories."

Renno grinned, and Ned laughed aloud. "It's far more likely," he said, "that ships are vanishing because they're attacked by pirates who are encouraged by the authorities of New Spain to capture or sink merchantmen from the English colonies."

Cavanaugh shifted his bulk in his chair. "I've had some mighty cold receptions in Havana in the past half-year. But egging pirates into attacking ships that fly the Union Jack—that's serious!"

"The problem may be even more serious than you realize," Ned replied. "It wouldn't surprise me if some attacks on our shipping are actually made by Spanish men-of-war. When there are no survivors, nobody in London or in our colonies on this side of the Atlantic will ever learn the truth." Aware that Cavanaugh was increasingly troubled, he added, "In any event, Captain, I think you're wise not to stay too close to the Florida coast. There's no need to ask for trouble."

The *Mary* rode through a squall, and then the spring weather became fair. The passengers paced the main deck and fenced, to the amusement of the crew. And Ned tried to teach his brother-in-law the principles of navigation.

But Renno was not interested. "It's enough," he said, "that I can find my way through an uncharted wilderness without losing my sense of direction. I know very little about the sea, and I don't want to fill my mind with useless information."

"You already know how to use the stars to guide you," Ned said. "It would be so easy for you to learn the rest."

Renno merely shrugged. He had acquired a vast knowledge of his brother-in-law's civilization, but at no time did he feel completely comfortable on board a large ship. It was enough that he could build a canoe and paddle it for hours.

Day by day the weather grew warmer, and one morning, after breakfast, Captain Cavanaugh called to his passengers from his quarterdeck. "I estimate that we're standing due east of the southern tip of Florida," he said. "We'll sail no more than another one hundred miles before we reach Havana."

The morning passed uneventfully. The sky was cloudless, so Renno and Ned fenced before the sun became too hot and then paced the main deck briskly before donning the waistcoats and swallowtailed coats that gentlemen were obliged to wear when they dined. It was necessary, even in the presence of no one but the brig's crew, to maintain the fiction that they were traders.

Shortly before noon the lookout in the crow's nest called, "A ship off our starboard bow, sir!"

The master was only mildly interested. Traffic between the mainland and the West Indies was heavy and most merchantmen followed the same routes.

The stranger grew larger on the horizon, and the lookout raised his voice again. "She 'pears to be a warship, Cap'n. Leastwise she's carrying cannon a-plenty."

Renno and Ned drifted to the starboard rail, and studied the approaching vessel. "She's larger than a sloop-of-war and smaller than a frigate," Ned said. "I've never seen anything quite like her. But there's no doubt she's heavily armed." He counted four nine-pounder cannon on her forward deck.

"Could it be a pirate ship?" Renno asked.

"Possibly, but I think not. All the sailors I can see are wearing uniforms."

Everyone on the *Mary* watched as the stranger hoisted a flag. It was red and yellow, and Ned recognized it at once. "Captain," he called, "she's a Spanish warship!"

Cavanaugh ordered his own identifying pennant unfurled, and the Union Jack rose to the brig's yardarm. He did not alter his course, even though the Spaniard was bearing down on him.

The brig's company froze when they saw a flash, followed by the roar of a gun, and smoke curled from the barrel. The shot fell more than a hundred yards short.

"Good Lord!" the stunned Cavanaugh cried. "She's firing on us! That's an act of war!"

Renno remembered Ned's prophecy. The Spanish navy were attacking English and colonial merchantmen. "We must fight," he said quietly.

"Impossible," Ned told him. "We carry only a pair of six-pounders, useful to ward off pirates, but that ship can smash us to kindling without coming within our range. We'll have to make a run for it."

Cavanaugh was already bawling the necessary orders, and the brig tacked, then tried to flee in the direction from which she had come. But the warship advanced at the same steady pace, and her cannon continued to roar.

"Her gunners could take lessons from us," Ned said with contempt as shot after shot fell short.

All at once the cannoneers found the range. A lucky shot sliced the *Mary*'s mainmast, crippling her badly, and another cannonball, dropping only seconds later, crashed onto the quarterdeck, instantly killing Captain Cavanaugh and the helmsman.

The mate immediately took command.

"We need our muskets!" Renno shouted above the uproar, and started toward the cabin.

Ned caught hold of his arm. "Muskets will do us no good when we can't even come close with six-pounders."

The barrage continued unabated. Renno soon lost

count of the shots that cut deep furrows in the wallow-ing brig's deck, slashing what was left of her mainsail and jib to ribbons. Men were dying or already dead, and several of the wounded were screaming.

Never had Renno felt so helpless. It was a new expe-rience. So far he and Ned were unscathed, but they were unable to retaliate against the constant barrage of cannonfire. Now he knew why he disliked the sea. On land a warrior always could strike back against an enemy, then lose himself in the wilderness, but at sea there was no place to hide.

The mate was weeping, so great was his rage. "We've got to strike our colors before we're sent to the bottom," he said in anguish.

The bo's'n, apparently the only able-bodied seaman still able to function, lowered the British flag and hoisted a white pennant of surrender.

The cannon continued to boom, however, and two more shots landed on the *Mary*. One killed the mate, and the second toppled the bo's'n overboard.

Within moments the water churned around the strug-gling man, and Renno caught a glimpse of several long, silvery shapes.

"Sharks," Ned said, sickened.

The water boiled even harder, spreading out a pool of red. Then, suddenly, all was still.

The Spanish warship bore down on the shattered hulk of the *Mary,* her guns at last silent.

"She's going to send boarders," the grim-faced Ned said. "But they won't find many of us alive. You and I are the only men on board who haven't been killed or injured."

"We'll have a surprise waiting for them," Renno said, and again started toward the cabin.

"No!" Ned said firmly. "Think, Renno! I'll grant you that we're good enough shots to take a number of them with us. But there are fifty to one hundred sailors on board the warship, and we're badly outnumbered. Remember our mission! If we have an opportunity to show them our credentials they may not kill us. It's a chance we've got to take. Our only chance!"

The self-discipline Renno had been taught since earliest childhood gave him the strength to stand motionless at the remains of the shattered rail, in plain view of the Spaniards, who had dropped anchor and lowered a longboat into the sea. They could see he was carrying only a short dress sword. Perhaps, if they intended to murder him and Ned, he would have the chance to draw his knife from its place of concealment at the small of his back. No Seneca ever allowed himself to be killed without drawing the blood of his enemies.

Ned was right, of course. As long as they stayed alive, there was always a possibility they could complete their mission. It was far better to suffer temporary disgrace than to jeopardize their chances.

As the longboat came alongside the battered merchant ship, Ned slowly raised his hands above his head. "Do as I'm doing," he muttered.

Meek surrender was against every principle Renno held dear, but he forced himself to follow his brother-in-law's example. Spanish sailors poured onto the shattered deck of the *Mary,* followed by three officers, two of them very young. The third, older and wearing a silver epaulette on one shoulder, obviously was in command.

The commander studied the expensively dressed pair. It was plain they were civilians, not members of the merchantman's crew. Turning to several sailors behind him, he gave an order in a low tone.

Renno was forced to endure yet another humiliation when, wrists tied behind his back with a length of rope, he was subjected to a search. His dress sword was removed, and one of the sailors, finding his knife, calmly appropriated it and slid it into his own belt.

Ned was subjected to the same treatment. Then both of the prisoners were lowered to the longboat, where a grizzled, toothless sailor pointed a pair of cocked pistols at them. His eager expression made it clear that there was nothing he would enjoy more than killing them on the spot if they tried to escape.

Renno, alongside Ned, lay unmoving at the sailor's feet. Pistol shots sounded above, and it dawned on him that the Spaniards were murdering the injured members of the *Mary*'s crew.

The hulk of the *Mary* was taken in tow, and rowed back to the warship.

It soon became evident that the officer in charge of the boarding party was leaving the fate of Renno and Ned in the hands of his captain, a bearded, elegantly uniformed man with a thin face, the eaglelike nose of an Andalusian patrician, and dark, cold eyes. He sat in a comfortable chair beneath a canopy on his aft deck, smoking a *segaro*. He looked the prisoners up and down.

Renno's stonelike face could have been carved out of a block of granite. Ned started to address the officer in Spanish, but the captain cut him short. "Who are you?" he demanded in English.

"You'll find documents identifying us inside the pockets of our coats," Ned replied, trying to sound civil.

A sailor removed the letters, and the captain read them carefully. He pondered at length, chewing on his *segaro* as he stared up at the canopy that shielded him from the tropical sun.

"It is unfortunate," he said at last, "that you who bear credentials from the governors of the English colonies witnessed the capture of the ship on which you were sailing. We have taken great pains to conceal the activities of Spain's navy from the very governors you represent. So, if I had my way, I would have you thrown overboard at once and allow the sharks to finish you. But I don't wish to exceed my authority, so I shall refer the problem to Don Pedro."

Ned could restrain himself no longer. "Sir," he said, "I want to protest your unwarranted attack on a peaceful merchantman and your murder of her entire crew.

You have committed an act of war, sir, against subjects of His Britannic Majesty!"

"His Britannic Majesty may go to the devil." The captain rose and drew a small, jewel-hilted poniard from his belt. "As for you, learn to keep silent until you're told to speak."

The blade flashed in a sudden, downward sweep, and a thin line that spurted blood appeared on Ned's face. Renno strained against his bonds, wanting to hurl himself at the Spanish officer, but he managed to hold back.

He and Ned were herded into the depths of the warship. At last they halted in a windowless area where, by the light of an oil lamp, two sailors affixed heavy shackles and chains to their ankles. The ropes binding their wrists were cut and replaced by even heavier shackles and chains.

They were shoved through a hidden opening and a hatch was closed and bolted above them. It was an airless section of the hold, the heat so intense it was difficult to breathe.

Ned broke the tense silence. "Maybe we should have used our muskets," he said. "I'd give almost anything to have that damned captain in my sights for just one shot!"

"How is the cut on your face?"

"It will soon stop bleeding, I think. It's nothing. But I'm afraid it's an indication we aren't going to remain in this world for long."

Chapter VI

Renno's eyes soon became acclimated to the dark. He and Ned were in an area with barely enough space for them to lie side by side. The weight of their chains was so great that it was difficult for them to stand. Renno guessed that it was something after daybreak.

"The ship has stopped," Ned said. "We're at anchor."

Time dragged. The hatch opened once just enough for a sailor to lower two slices of stale, moldy bread and two gourds of lukewarm water.

At Renno's suggestion they ate and drank very slowly. "We will become ill if we eat too quickly," he said. "How's your face?"

"It's stiff now, and the blood has caked. Not that it matters." Ned was glum. "The only question in my mind is whether we'll be hanged, shot, or strangled with these confounded chains."

"We are still alive." Renno was surprisingly calm. "And until the last of our breath is squeezed from us, we cannot give up hope. I could tell you the stories of many Seneca warriors who have been in worse situations and have survived."

"They weren't prisoners of the Spaniards, who don't know the meaning of mercy or decency."

Renno fell silent, relaxing as best he could.

It was at least late morning before the hatch opened and they were dragged up into the bright sunlight, momentarily blinded. Strong hands shoved them down a gangplank onto a wharf. Renno caught a glimpse of a crowded harbor and, at its outer rim, a large stone fort on a hill that commanded the entrance.

A bo's'n's mate, stripped to the waist and carrying a long rawhide whip, pointed inland.

The two prisoners moved forward. Their chains, dragging behind them on the ground, were so heavy it was an agony to place one foot in front of the other. Soon both were panting for breath as they made their way up a cobbled street under a blazing tropical sun.

In spite of the tremendous difficulty, Renno took note of their surroundings. They were in a city far larger than any in the English colonies of North America, larger any he had ever seen other than London. Houses, some of stone and others of wood, lined both sides of a tree-shaded street. A number were three or four stories high, and some of the smaller buildings had signs above their doors, printed in Spanish. They had to be in Havana.

They passed a very large church adjacent to a park. A crowd of worshipers was emerging as the two captives were driven past. The well-dressed men and the women in black with black shawls covering their heads halted and averted their faces.

So did other pedestrians, some expensively attired, some in rags. The only people who stared were soldiers wearing the canary-yellow uniforms of the Spanish infantry, who patrolled the city in fours and fives, muskets on their shoulders. But even they showed only faint curiosity, and Renno guessed that captives were a common sight.

Ned stumbled and sprawled on the cobblestones. The bo's'n's mate cursed, and the whip sang out, cracking viciously as it landed on Ned's back, slicing through his clothes. The shock of the blow caused him to groan. He struggled hard in an attempt to rise, but the expertly wielded whip struck him again and again.

Renno deliberately dropped to one knee. The bo's'n's mate transferred his attention to the second captive, giving Ned time to summon his strength and haul himself upright again.

The whip landed on Renno's back, and although he knew it raised an ugly welt, he gave no indication that he felt the agonizing sting of the rawhide. He suffered a second blow in stoical silence. Only when he was certain that Ned was standing again, able to move on, did he rise to his feet.

Soon they heard the clatter of horses' hooves on the cobblestones. A troop of Spanish cavalry swept past in formation. These soldiers looked magnificent in brightly burnished helmets, yellow tunics, and red breeches tucked into highly polished black boots. Not one cavalryman deigned to look at them.

Ned was right, Renno thought. Spaniards were a cruel, hardhearted people.

All at once the young Seneca saw his companion waver unsteadily. The combination of the heat, lack of food and water, the weight of his chains, and the beating were taking their toll. Afraid Ned would collapse and be beaten senseless, Renno addressed him in Seneca.

"Have courage, my brother! Even the worst ordeal must come to an end."

Ned slowly straightened as best he could and started forward again, his gait somewhat improved. Renno silently begged the manitous to help his companion. He could endure the torment himself, he told them, but

Ned had not been trained as a Seneca warrior. There were limits to his stamina.

The cuts on their backs smarting, perspiration drenching them, mingling with blood, the captives staggered on. After a seemingly endless march, Renno saw a high wall ahead and, behind it, a building that looked like an old palace. Rusting metal bars covered the windows, and yellow-clad soldiers armed with muskets were stationed at intervals on the wall, most of them dozing in the hot sun.

Renno sensed the ordeal was coming to an end. He was right. A gate creaked open, the bo's'n's mate produced a paper that an arrogant young officer signed, and the prisoners were half carried, half pushed into the building.

They found themselves in a large room, and at least it was cooler here. But their relief was short-lived. Seated behind a large desk was the most repulsive-looking man Renno had ever seen. He was so badly overweight that he seemed to have a succession of chins, all of them unshaven, each melting into the one below it. His corpulent body bulged beneath his soiled uniform, the open collar of his tunic was drenched with sweat and he exuded an offensive odor. Picking his yellowed teeth with the point of a dagger, he paused to scrutinize the captives, then cleaned his filthy fingernails with the blade.

To their surprise he addressed them in strongly accented English. "Welcome to your last home on this earth, North American merchants," he said in a deep, grating voice. "How long you will be my guests no one can predict. Some die in a few days, others linger for weeks, but no matter what your stay, the day will come when your bodies will be given to the vultures who wait for you in the courtyard."

He raised a fat, hamlike hand to have them removed from his presence, then decided he had something more to say to them. "His Excellency, Don Pedro de Rivera, is a most compassionate man. He could have handed you over to my hangman or my torturers. But you have committed no crime other than that of witnessing events you should not have seen. So you are being confined here while your cases are under investigation." His high-pitched giggle echoed through the chamber. "It is a pity for you that those investigations will not end until your souls have left your bodies."

His giggle followed them down a stone-lined corridor. They were hauled down one flight of steps after another. Renno managed to count four flights, twenty steps each. At the bottom they came to an area where a candle flickered, and a guard in a dirty uniform hauled himself to his feet.

"I bring company for you and your rats, Miguel," the man in charge said to the guard. "The warden orders you to place them in the large cell."

The guard was startled. "But I cannot, Francisco. You know very well that—"

"I know enough to obey the warden's orders so I'm not put in chains myself. Hurry, will you? This place makes my flesh crawl!"

The guard yawned, stretched, and produced a key to a metal door, which creaked open. The prisoners were dragged inside and their chains affixed to large support posts placed about ten feet apart.

"I'll feed you now," Miguel said, "and then I won't have to bother again until tomorrow." He left the cell, returning with chunks of stale bread and bowls that contained what appeared to be a watery soup.

When he retreated again, the cell was plunged into darkness. The heavy door creaked shut, the key grating harshly in the lock.

Ned was the first to break the silence. "I was told that Spanish cuisine was excellent, but I'm afraid the reports were a trifle exaggerated."

"I have tasted worse," Renno said as he slowly ate.

After a time Ned said, "I've figured out something that should have been apparent to us as soon as the Spanish warship started to move against our brig. I had a hunch, and the confiscation of our cargo proved I'm right. The tobacco we were carrying was valuable. Who do you suppose gets it? I'm convinced that the viceroy himself takes a large portion and shares the profits with his naval captains."

The greed of so-called civilized men continued to shock Renno, who saw at once that his brother-in-law was right. "That must be his real reason for making certain that you and I die."

"Exactly. I can't believe the government of Spain has authorized sneak attacks on our merchant shipping. Oh, Madrid undoubtedly regards London as an enemy, and there well may be a direct confrontation soon that will determine whether our colonies remain English or are incorporated into New Spain. But this confiscation of expensive cargoes couldn't be officially inspired. The viceroy simply has his own sources of private income."

"Don't give up hope!" Renno was emphatic. "We're still alive. And strong. Somehow we'll find a way to get out of this dungeon."

Ned's only reply was a deep sigh. Exhausted by his ordeal, he stretched out on the floor, his chains rattling, and soon dropped off to sleep.

Left to his own devices, Renno began to experiment. He found he could walk, with difficulty, for a distance of about five paces, and he made up his mind to exercise frequently so his physical strength would not diminish. As his eyes became accustomed to the gloom, he examined the surroundings with care. He and Ned each had a slop pail, and there were pails resting near the bases of two other columns, indicating that this cell could incarcerate additional prisoners.

In the distant corner he saw a rat. He stood motionless and watched it. The creature began to advance cautiously, and Renno waited until it was only a few yards away before he rattled his chains. The rat retreated instantly and vanished through a small hole in the corner.

If a rat can find a way to leave this place, the young Seneca told himself, so can I.

He lowered himself to the floor to conserve his energy, and managed to arrange his heavy chains so he could sit cross-legged. In no other position was he as comfortable when he wanted to think. He forced himself to recall every detail of the descent into the dungeon, the number of steps, the length of the corridors, and the number of guards he had seen. Many troops were stationed on the ground floor, but he had seen only one on each of the lower levels. Apparently the Spaniards believed it was impossible for their prisoners to free themselves. It was a fact worth remembering.

Renno's thoughts were interrupted by the sound of a key turning in the lock. Then the door opened noisily, and Miguel entered, carrying a candle. Preceding him, to Renno's astonishment, was a slender, short woman dressed in a gown, suitable for the court of King William. She was young, with black hair that fell down her back, and her delicate features were exquisite. Her wrists and ankles were chained. In spite of his surprise the young Seneca noted that at least her chains were much lighter than the links of heavy metal that he and Ned wore.

Paying no attention to the other prisoners, the guard addressed the woman in Spanish, which Renno could not understand. "Señorita Mirador," he said as he chained her to a post, "I did not expect to have the pleasure of your company again."

She held herself haughtily, making no reply.

"You are not a stupid woman," he told her. "Surely you know you are fighting a battle you cannot win. It is madness to oppose Don Pedro."

"Then I am mad," she replied.

Renno knew only that her voice, in spite of her scornful tone, was high and sweet.

"When His Excellency loses patience, you'll die here."

150

"If it is God's will, I shall die," she said.

The guard shrugged, turned, and left the cell, locking the door behind him. Renno remained silent until the young woman's eyes became acclimated to the gloom. She did not seem surprised when she saw him and Ned. She said something in Spanish that he couldn't understand.

"I am afraid I do not speak your language," he said.

"Ah! You are English?" When she spoke English, her accent was light.

"We come from the colonies, I from New York and my companion from Virginia." He had no wish, at present, to reveal his true identity.

The sounds of voices awakened Ned, and he gaped when he made out the beautifully gowned young woman in the dark,. Scarcely able to believe that a woman was being jailed here, he joined in the conversation, and soon he and Renno explained how they had been captured.

The woman was emphatic when they told her their feelings about the viceroy. "You are right," she said. "Don Pedro is a despicable beast, the greediest and most unscrupulous man on earth!"

Little by little she told them her own story. She was Consuelo Mirador of Madrid and Toledo, the only child of Cristoforo Mirador, for more than a generation Spain's leading firearms manufacturer and merchant.

"Two years ago," she said, "My father bought a galleon and filled it with muskets, pistols, and cannon. He came here to Havana, hoping to sell arms to the viceroy and to the governors of other Spanish colonies in the New World. I came with him, and when we arrived here we bought a house, intending to remain for a reasonable time. At first all went well. Don Pedro bought many guns. Then, when some of the governors wanted them, too, he suddenly changed. . . ." Her voice trailed away.

"Perhaps you'd prefer to wait until another time to tell us the rest," Ned suggested. "We have a great deal of time on our hands here."

She shook her head and composed herself. "The viceroy suggested to my father that they become partners. He renewed that suggestion frequently, but my father always refused, saying he saw no reason he should give away half of his profits. Then he learned what happens to those who oppose Don Pedro. My father was arrested on charges of treason." Her voice broke. "He died in this very cell."

Renno and Ned could say nothing.

"Then it was my turn," Consuelo went on, her voice hardening. "Don Pedro paid court to me, wanting to take me under his protection, even though he already has a wife and an official mistress. For many months I refused. He confiscated our galleon and most of our supplies of arms, thinking he could force me to weaken. But still I refused him. His pride is so great that one month ago he sent me to this place, believing he would break my spirit. But he has not broken it."

Renno was revolted. "You have committed the crime of refusing to accept this—this scum as your lover?"

"That is my crime," Consuelo replied. "So far I have been given special treatment. I am fed decent meals so I do not become too scrawny for the viceroy's taste. Each week I am taken upstairs, allowed to bathe and change into clean clothes that are brought from my home. Each week I am asked if I have changed my mind." Her voice rose slightly and became even firmer. "Each week I have said I shall never change my mind!"

"How is it possible," Renno asked in wonder, "that one man could have such great power?"

"Obviously you do not know Spain and her government," the girl said. "At home the Crown has great powers, but in the New World those of the imperial viceroy are even greater. As long as he sends gold regularly to the royal treasury, no one interferes with him and he does as he pleases. He has the power of life and death over everyone, even the governors of colonies, the generals who command his armies, and the admirals who command his navy. No man—and certainly no woman—dares to defy him."

"But you have defied him," Ned said.

"Yes, and I know what my fate will be. I have watched two fellow prisoners die in this cell, just as both of you will die because each day you will be given less and less food. My turn will come when Don Pedro loses all patience and no longer desires me. The flesh will fall away from my bones, too, and I shall become a skeleton—like all the rest who are sent to this accursed place!" She turned away from them.

They heard the muffled sounds of her weeping. Ned wanted to comfort her, but the outlook was so bleak that he felt tongue-tied.

Shedding tears was against Renno's training, and the manitous despised signs of human weakness. He could not remain silent. "Don't despair," he said. "We will find some way to leave this place, and we will take you with us."

Consuelo wanted to tell him not to hold out false hopes. All prisoners felt as he did when they first came to the underground cell, but as they lost their physical strength, their confidence ebbed and they gradually abandoned the desire to live. But there was a ring in this man's voice she had never before heard, and she took heart.

Consuelo Mirador's predictions about prisoner treatment proved accurate, much to their misfortune. Each day their meager supply of food was systematically reduced. It was only a matter of time until they were starved to death.

Renno knew that time was as great an enemy as his Spanish jailers. He knew that it wouldn't be long before he and Ned became so weak they would be incapable of even trying to escape. So he made his plans swiftly, watching every move made by the guard who came to the cell once each day with food and water.

Miguel was a husky Spanish peasant and apparently had held his present position for so long that he had grown careless. Instead of leaving his ring of keys at the cell entrance when he came in, he always carried the chain on his belt.

Renno explained his scheme to Ned and Consuelo, adding, "Sometimes the guard comes with food late in the day, sometimes early in the evening. We will act the first time he comes at night because escapes are always easier after dark."

"It isn't possible to tell day from night this far below the ground," Consuelo said.

"Renno knows," Ned said.

"I'm sure you realize that, if we fail, all of us will be hanged," she said.

"Would you prefer that we leave you behind?" Ned asked.

"Never!" Consuelo exclaimed. "I would rather die trying to escape than to stay here and suffocate a little at a time."

Renno approved of her. This woman was as courageous as Betsy, he decided, and he could pay her no greater compliment. She was worthy of sharing in their desperate adventure.

That evening he made a single, flat statement. "The guard is late," he said. "It is already night. When he comes we will strike."

They waited in a tense silence until they heard the key turning in the rusted lock. Renno immediately lowered himself to the floor and pretended to be asleep. Miguel came into the cell, and, as always, he brought Consuelo her food first.

"The prisoner at the far post may be ill," she told him in Spanish. "He seems to have lost consciousness."

The guard thought it strange that a captive who had spent less than a week in the cell could have collapsed so soon, but prisoners were unpredictable. Moving closer to the figure sprawled on the stone floor, he bent down to examine the man more closely in the light of his candle.

Renno moved with speed and precision that were all the more remarkable as he was hampered by his heavy chains. Knocking the candle from the startled Miguel's hand, he looped one length of his chain around the guard's neck and began to strangle him.

Miguel struggled wildly in an attempt to free himself, but had too little breath to cry aloud.

Showing no mercy, Renno did not relax his pressure until long moments after Miguel went limp and stopped breathing.

This was no time for talk. The young Seneca removed the key ring from the guard's belt, then tried several of the keys until he found those that released his wrists and ankles.

Next he unlocked Ned's chains, then handed the key ring to his brother-in-law. While Ned unlocked the girl's chains, Renno searched the guard's body. He had been carrying no knife or pistol, but in his hip pocket was a club about eight inches long, weighted with lead. It would suffice.

Consuelo fell in behind Renno and Ned as they headed toward the door. Suddenly Renno halted and removed his moldering boots and filthy stockings. Making no sound, he started up the first flight of stone steps, halting and raising a hand in warning after he had counted fifteen steps.

Ned and Consuelo waited obediently.

Still moving like a wraith, Renno climbed the last five steps, and on the landing he saw another guard, dozing in a chair beside an oil lamp. Approaching silently, Renno raised the club and brought it down with all his might on the Spaniard's head. The guard's brains and blood spattered the wall behind him.

Renno's only regret was that he carried no knife so he could scalp the dead man. But he had more urgent matters on his mind. An ancient musket stood propped against the wall, and the young Seneca seized it, saw it was not loaded, but nevertheless took it. The gun was so old it would require a long time to load, but it might prove useful in other ways. He returned to the stairs, beckoned, and handed the musket to Ned.

Employing the same technique, they climbed to the next landing. There a more difficult situation arose. The guard on duty outside the cell block was drinking from a bottle and looked up just in time to see the man in the dirty clothes creeping toward him. He tried to shout and raised the bottle to protect himself.

He didn't have a chance. Renno struck again with vicious accuracy, and the Spaniard slumped to the stone floor, the partly consumed bottle still clutched in his hand.

He, too, carried a lead club. Renno took it, and the climb was resumed.

At the next landing the door leading to the cell block was open with no guard in sight. It appeared he was giving his prisoners their evening meal. The trio moved swiftly toward the last flight of stairs. Consuelo lifted her skirt so she could run more easily.

Now, as all three knew, they were in the gravest danger. They were approaching the ground level, where it was likely they might encounter a number of guards and soldiers. Ned moved up beside Renno, and they advanced together, with Consuelo two steps behind.

As they approached the top of the stairs, Renno put a hand on his brother-in-law's arm and both halted. They could hear a murmur of several men's voices above them, but Renno heard something else, too, and listened intently. Ah! a heavy rain was falling, beating against windows. He was pleased. If the sentries stationed on the walls of the prison were as indolent as the guards, they would have sought shelter from the downpour.

Advancing two more steps, Renno saw four guards seated around a table, playing cards by the light of an oil lamp. The guard who sat facing them posed the greatest hazard because he would see them instantly if he happened to glance in their direction.

Retreating a step of two, Renno silently indicated his plan. Testing the leaded club he held in his right hand, he climbed boldly to the top of the steps, well aware he never had thrown such a weapon.

He had only one chance. He hurled the club at the oil lamp. Before the startled card players knew what was happening, the lamp shattered, its glow extinguished.

Leaping forward in the dark, Renno used his remaining leaded club to smash the head of one guard, then turned and accorded the same treatment to another.

Meanwhile, Ned, grasping the old musket by the barrel, brought the butt down with full force onto the head of the guard who faced the staircase.

Only one guard remained, but at that critical instant the blood-smeared, slippery club fell from Renno's hand. Not hesitating, Renno threw himself at the Spaniard, and they fell to the floor. The guard tried hard to protect himself, but he was no match for his foe in hand-to-hand combat. Before he knew what was happening, Renno snapped his neck, and the man was dead.

Consuelo stood at the top of the stairs, a hand pressed to her mouth as she watched the grisly, silent battle.

Renno quickly went to the outer door, and Ned shepherded Consuelo toward it. They emerged into the open and found they were standing outside the high wall. The tropical downpour was so heavy it was impossible to see more than a few feet in the dark, but that was all to the good. Ned quietly closed the door, Consuelo pointed toward the left, and all three began to walk rapidly.

Looking back, Renno could see no one stationed on the wall. The streets were deserted because of the rain, so the trio encountered no immediate difficulties. Consuelo led them up one winding, deserted street after another. She was breathless by the time they passed through an open, walled gate. They were in an overgrown garden, obviously untended for a long time, and ahead stood a dark, silent house.

The front door was locked.

Renno agilely climbed the stone wall to a small, second floor window, which he managed to open. He squeezed inside, and moments later he opened the front door.

Consuelo broke the long silence. "How much time do we have?"

"There's no way to guess," Ned told her. "The bodies of the guards might not be found until the watch is changed, which could be tomorrow morning, or they might have been discovered by now."

"When it is learned we have escaped," Consuelo said, "they will search for us here. This is my house. But we can go nowhere until we have cleaned ourselves and dressed in fresh clothes."

Lighting neither candles nor lamps, they went to the rear of the house, where Consuelo led them into a chamber with a floor made of handsome, Arabic tiles. In the center of the room was a tiled, sunken area, and Consuelo pointed to a water pump.

Renno was astonished. He had become accustomed to pumps in the English colonies and London, but never had he seen one indoors. The marvels of civilization were as endless as the cruelties of supposedly civilized men. He stripped off his rank, filthy clothes, stepped into the sunken area, and began to pump water.

Ned and Consuelo hesitated for only a moment before they followed his example. With their recapture possible at any time, they could not afford the luxury of modesty.

In spite of himself Ned could not help noticing Consuelo's body. Her waist was tiny, her breasts high and firm, her buttocks and thighs feminine, yet scarcely larger than those of an adolescent boy. And her stomach was flat.

They washed away the prison grime, and for the first

time Renno exulted. He was free! But it was far too soon to celebrate, he cautioned himself.

They emerged dripping from the sunken area, and Consuelo led them up a flight of stairs. Opening a door, she pointed inside. "My father was tall, so his clothes should fit both of you fairly well," she said. "Help yourselves to whatever you need." She disappeared down the corridor.

In a chest of drawers they found underclothes, shirts, and stockings. A dozen plumed hats filled several shelves, and a score of suits made of expensive fabrics hung in a wardrobe. Renno and Ned selected what they needed and grinned at each other when they discovered the girl had been right. Her father's clothes fitted both of them reasonably well.

Then, Ned found many pairs of shoes in a closet. Renno found some boots of stout leather that were a comfortable fit, and Ned did not fare too badly, either, although the shoes he selected were a trifle long.

Consuelo returned, and both men stared at her. She was wearing a jacket and skirt of fine-spun maroon wool, with frills of lace at her neckline. Her high-heeled shoes and narrow-brimmed, plumed hat matched the rest of her attire.

Ned couldn't help staring at a deep slash in her skirt, which revealed one leg above her knee.

"This was a riding costume," she told him apologetically. "I chose it because the opening in the skirt gives me the freedom to run, if we must."

Hurrying back to the main floor, she surprised her companions by moving a sliding panel in what appeared to be a salon. Inside it was a cabinet from which she began to remove swords, pistols, and knives. "This was my father's secret armory," she said. "Don Pedro's men did not find it when they removed everything of value except clothes from the house."

Renno felt far better able to face the uncertain future when he had buckled on a long sword, took two loaded pistols and additional ammunition, then slid a perfectly weighted knife of razor-sharp Toledo steel into his belt. He told himself that, should another fight develop, he would give a good account of himself before he was killed.

To the surprise of both men, Consuelo took two tiny, pearl-handled dueling pistols from the weapons horde before sliding the panel into place again. "I've been familiar with pistols since I was very small," she said. "You may take my word for it that I shall kill two of Don Pedro's soldiers before I'm captured."

Renno knew it was not an idle boast. "It seems to me," he said, "that we must go to the waterfront, steal a boat, and leave Havana before sunrise."

"I suppose so," Ned replied. "Although I hate to leave before we learn something about the size and makeup of the Spanish army here."

Consuelo wasted no time asking his reasons for his interest. "I can tell you much that you may want to know," she said. "Remember that the troops here have been armed with Mirador muskets. We can talk as we go to the harbor." She quickly outlined their route.

Ever conscious of the swift passage of time, they left the house, carefully closing the door behind them. Renno advanced first through the garden, his gaze penetrating as he searched for any signs of troops. The rain had stopped, and, as so often happened in the tropics, the sky overhead had cleared. There were stars everywhere, their position in the sky unfamiliar to the young Seneca war chief, and a half-moon was shining overhead.

When Ned and Consuelo joined him at the entrance to the property he saw by the light of the moon what he had not noted earlier. Consuelo's face was heavily plastered with cosmetics. She had lined her eyes with a black substance that also coated her lashes, her cheeks were rouged, and her lips were almost as deep a shade of red as her costume. She looked strikingly attractive, but something in her appearance puzzled him. Then he remembered: she looked very much like the harlots he had seen in London.

Consuelo was aware of his gaze and flushed. "It must be very late at night now," she said. "I thought that if we pass any military patrols in the streets we can pass ourselves off as a party of roisterers."

Ned laughed quietly. Here was a woman with an inventive mind as well as courage.

She linked her arms through those of her companions, and they walked boldly down the street. "If we're questioned, let me do the talking, please," she said. "Your accent will give you away as a foreigner, Ned, and you're even worse, Renno."

The streets of Havana were still deserted.

"We're making a detour around the principal garrison," Consuelo said. "We needn't ask for trouble."

"You indicated you can tell us something about that garrison," Ned prompted.

"Indeed I can," she replied briskly. "Until a few months ago there were four thousand Spanish troops here. They were joined by another two thousand, and the last I heard before I was thrown into prison, an additional two thousand are expected to arrive at any time."

Ned whistled softly under his breath. Eight thousand trained soldiers were far more than Spain needed to maintain order in Cuba, particularly when each of her colonies supported a garrison of its own to deal with possible local uprisings. "Are there insurrections or rebellions anywhere in Spain's New World empire?"

"None of consequence. All of the new troops are being held in barracks right here in Havana."

"Why should there be so many?" Ned asked.

She shrugged. "There have been many rumors, of course, but no one knows for certain. Don Pedro is a very secretive man." She glanced first at Ned, then at Renno, her violet eyes sparkling, and all at once she laughed. It was the first time Ned had ever heard her laugh, and the sound was melodious.

"I should have guessed," she said. "You aren't merchants. You're espionage agents from the English colonies."

"If we're captured, all of us may be tortured," Ned said. "So there are things it is best that you don't know."

"Have no worries about me," Consuelo replied firmly. "Spain is the land of my birth. But the murder of my father and my own fate have caused me to lose whatever loyalties I had. I honestly don't know if Don Pedro is planning an invasion of the English colonies, as some believe. If he is, I hope you destroy him and take his whole empire!"

Avoiding the issue, Ned continued to probe. "What percentage of the troops are foot soldiers, do you think?"

"Most of them. Only the cavalry use the expensive, newest muskets, and we had no more than two hundred in our arsenal. Don Pedro repeatedly wanted muskets for foot soldiers."

Renno suddenly interrupted the conversation. "Men are coming," he warned.

Consuelo loosened her grip on her companions' arms so all three could draw their weapons quickly if necessary.

Four Spanish infantrymen rounded a corner and, in no great hurry, strolled toward the approaching trio. Ned promptly began to pretend he was somewhat intoxicated and staggered slightly. Consuelo, obviously a talented actress, laughed foolishly.

Only Renno's gait remained purposeful. He saw the soldiers looking at Consuelo's legs and knew that she had convinced them she was a doxie. Apparently they were wondering if they could take her from her companions.

Both wore the attire of gentlemen, to be sure, and were armed. But it was Renno's alert, stone-faced expression that deterred the infantrymen. They had no desire to become injured in a brawl with this broad-shouldered man and then be subjected to punishment by their superiors. No woman was worth that.

The two groups passed each other, and Ned, realizing the soldiers were looking back over their shoulders, continued to stagger.

Renno had no need to turn his head as he said, "They are not stopping or following us. In a moment all will be well."

"You seem to have eyes in the back of your head," Consuelo said, "and you heard those men before we even saw them. How do you manage to do those things?"

He did not reply.

"Once we've left Cuba behind us," Ned said, "there is much we can tell you. But not now."

Consuelo had to curb her curiosity.

A short time later a colonel of Spanish infantry, flanked by two aides, rode on spirited horses past the three pedestrians, apparently returning home from a party. The officers did not deign to glance in their direction.

Farther on, as they drew nearer to the harbor, Renno again warned of others in the vicinity. "There are many men in the group. There is much laughter. It may be they have had too much to drink."

Consuelo could hear nothing, but took his word and made a detour. A little later she heard laughter in the distance, and about a city square away she saw a large party of sailors wearing the uniforms of the Spanish navy. Never, she thought, would she question Renno's hearing.

They passed several large warehouses, and all at once the harbor was spread out ahead of them. Three huge ships-of-the-line were riding at anchor, as were at least four frigates and many schooners and sloops-of-war. It was obvious that a potent armada was stationed here, a flotilla far larger than the colonies of New Spain needed for purposes of self-defense.

Thanks to Consuelo and good fortune, Ned reflected, he and Renno had acquired most of the information they needed in the capital of New Spain. But it would be useless unless they escaped.

"Where are the fishing boats docked?" he asked.

Consuelo knew little about the waterfront, and hesitated. Renno advanced a few more feet, stopped, and peered intently at the many ships that filled the great harbor. "We will find them to our left," he said.

Consuelo was beginning to rely on him and was only mildly surprised when she saw thirty or forty fishing boats tied up at the rickety civilian wharves.

Ned wasted no time selecting a boat he liked. The vessel he chose was about thirty feet long and had a jib as well as a stout mainmast. It also boasted a cabin that covered the better part of the deck area, an important item.

"Go below," he told Consuelo, "and stay there until I tell you it's safe to come up. Fashionably dressed ladies don't go for cruises on board fishing boats before daybreak."

He lifted her onto the deck, and she obediently vanished into the cabin as he and Renno leaped on board.

The whole area was deserted, but it wouldn't be long before fishermen began to appear. Ned lost no time unfurling the jib and, holding the line in one hand, seated himself at the tiller. His nod told Renno to cut the line that held the vessel to the pier, and he slashed it with a single stroke of his knife.

"We'll take off our hats, coats, and waistcoats," Ned said. "Gentlemen don't man fishing boats."

They removed a portion of their clothing, and Renno rolled up his shirtsleeves, too. When necessary he could wear European attire, but he strongly disliked the lace cuffs that fell around his hands.

Ned expertly guided the craft through the crowded harbor, twice passing so close to huge warships looming high above them that he and Renno could have reached out and touched the hulls.

Officers of the watch and armed sentries were stationed on the quarterdecks of every warship, Renno noted, but none paid any heed to the shabby fishing boat whose owner presumably was stealing a march on his colleagues. For an instant the young Seneca felt sorry for the proprietor of this boat, who undoubtedly would regard its loss as a catastrophe. But he put the thought out of his mind, just as he did not dwell on memories of the prison guards he had killed. He and his companions were still in great danger.

In the outer reaches of the harbor, Ned was able to maneuver more freely and gave every warship a far wider berth. He began to breathe a trifle more freely, but one major obstacle remained. The mammoth fort that guarded the approach to Havana loomed directly ahead. The flow of dark water beneath his hull told him he would find the entrance channel almost directly below the ugly guns that studded the fort. He was certain that sentries were stationed there day and night, and if they challenged him, demanding a password, he and his companions would be trapped. The guns could sink the fishing boat with a single well-placed shot.

"Unfurl the mains'l, Renno," he directed. "Slowly, if you please, so she doesn't make a cracking noise in the breeze. Feed the canvas with air gradually and gently."

Renno followed instructions, his natural agility compensating, at least in part, for his unfamiliarity with sails. He was sorry now that he had not accepted his brother-in-law's offer to teach him about ships.

Ned realized he was taking a risk using his mainsail before reaching open sea, but he had to be prepared to move as rapidly as possible if he should be challenged.

"Men in uniforms are looking down at us from the walls of the fort," Renno said quietly.

"I don't doubt it." Ned grew taut as he waited for a shout from above, but there was no sound except the gentle lapping of small waves against the wooden hull.

The fishing boat emerged from the shadow of the fort and entered open water. Her mainsail filled, and she leaped ahead. It was an omen, perhaps, that the first streaks of the coming day began to smear the velvetlike texture of the blue-black sky.

Not until the great fort began to dwindle in the

distance did Ned call, "Come up whenever you please, Consuelo!"

She appeared in triumph, carrying a round loaf of bread, a large chunk of cheese, a raw onion, and a dust-covered bottle of wine. "There is more food in the cabin," she announced. "The poor fisherman who owned this boat must be a man of great hunger."

Immediate danger behind them, they discovered they were ravenous and ate heartily. For the present, at least, they could relax. Ned set his course for the North American mainland as he and Consuelo chatted.

Renno, eating in his customary silence, observed his companions. Thanks to Consuelo, he and Ned had learned much of what they had gone to Havana to find out. But an equally difficult task lay ahead, that of finding out the extent of Spain's preparations for war in their colony of Florida.

It was plain to him that Consuelo would have to accompany them on that journey. They could not abandon her, even though her presence would be a handicap. They had been fortunate to have escaped unscathed from Havana, but their future threatened to be hazardous.

The mail pouch from Boston reached Fort Springfield at noon, and two letters were delivered to Andrew Wilson as he sat at dinner with his wife, son, and daughter-in-law. Both bore official seals. One had been sent by Governor William Shirley of Massachusetts Bay, and the other came from the War Ministry in London.

He frowned as he glanced through them, but made no comment. Finishing his meal quickly, he refused a final course and excused himself so he could go off to his library. Jeffrey joined him there a short time later and found him staring out at the rolling hills of the farm that descended gradually to the bank of the Connecticut River. "Bad news?" he asked.

The general waved him to a chair. "Potentially disturbing news," he replied. "Our relations with Spain are even worse than we thought and may become far more complicated."

His son waited.

"What do you know about Charles II of Spain?" his father asked.

"Only that he has been a weak ruler and has been strongly influenced by the ambitious nobles at his court. They, rather than Charles, are responsible for whatever efforts Spain may be making to expand her New World empire."

"Quite correct, as far as you've gone," Andrew said. "Even more important is the fact that Charles, who is in poor health, has no children. That means no one knows who will succeed him when he dies, and the settlement of that question will determine our own future, I'm afraid."

"How so, Father?"

The general toyed absently with a tinderbox that sat on his desk. "One candidate is the nephew of the Emperor of Austria, the ally of Great Britain and the Netherlands. If he wins the Spanish throne, Madrid's policies will be changed overnight. New Spain will engage in open and unlimited trade with the English colonies of North America. The threat of war will be removed, and the Spaniards will become our friends."

"But you don't think that's going to happen," Jeffrey said.

"The prospect appears far less likely than it did." Andrew tapped the two letters he had just received. "The other candidate is Philip, Duc d'Anjou, one of the grandsons of King Louis of France."

Jeffrey nodded somberly. Louis XIV not only was the implacable foe of Great Britain, but was determined to annex her New World colonies and subject them to the rule of his own governor-general in Quebec. He had been dealt a severe setback when an expedition of English colonies, Iroquois warriors under Ghonka, and a small contingent of British regulars had captured Louisburg. But everyone in America knew that Louis XIV, glory-seeking and vain, had not abandoned his goals.

"France," General Wilson said, "has just concluded a new treaty with Spain. The terms are so generous to Spain that London believes, as does Governor Shirley, that Charles has made a secret deal with Louis."

Jeffrey drew in his breath. "What you're saying, Father, is that Louis's grandson, Philip of Anjou, will become King of Spain when Charles dies."

"The odds are strongly in favor of it. And the situation here is even more dangerous than it is in Europe. If Louis and Charles have really made a deal, our colonies will face the combined might of France and Spain. We'll have enemies to our north, enemies to our south, and enemies to our west, on the Mississippi River. And at sea there will be two enemy fleets trying to cut our lifelines. We'll be subjected to attacks on every side."

Jeffrey weighed the problem. "Father," he said at last, "it seems to me we ought to act first, before France and Spain join forces."

"At present we can't," the general said bluntly. "King William and his ministers don't want to be the aggressors in a new European war, and they won't support us if we open hostilities here. They insist that we wait until Louis actually places his grandson on the throne in Madrid. Or, at the very least, until we can provide proof that Spain intends to conquer our colonies. If we can furnish that proof, London will allow us to take any steps we deem appropriate to defend ourselves."

"I see." A white line formed around Jeffrey's compressed lips. "This means our whole future—the decision of war or peace—depends on what Renno reports to us."

"Yes, his mission is now far more important to us than it was when he and Ned sailed off to Havana."

Chapter VII

The gale blew up quickly. Rolling, dark gray clouds obliterated the sun, and a sharp wind forced Ned off his course. Soon rain was falling in torrents, the wind became even stronger, and the sea grew mountainous. The little fishing boat dropped deep into the trough of one wave, only to soar perilously to the crest of the next.

Consuelo was sent below, and the hatch was closed tightly. Ned lashed himself to the tiller and fought the storm hard. Renno insisted on remaining on deck with him and for the sake of security tied one end of a line around his middle, affixing the other to the base of the mainmast.

At Ned's direction he lowered the jib, a dangerous task. Twice he lost his footing and would have been swept away if the rope around his middle, and his sheer physical strength, had not saved him. Then there was little for him to do, and he watched in fascinated awe as the gale battered the small craft. He felt no fear, however. His future lay in the will of the mani-

169

tous. He had no control over life or death and was content to leave his destiny to his gods.

Ned struggled unceasingly to remain on course. He tried to keep the boat headed into the wind, but the massive waves fought him every foot, and the gusts of wind were so treacherous that the problem of staying afloat became his main concern.

In spite of his efforts, the fishing boat was driven steadily toward the southeast. Occasionally Ned caught a glimpse of land, but had no idea whether he was seeing Cuba or some other island. He recognized the constant danger of being driven ashore, but the hazard of capsizing or foundering was even greater.

For more than twenty-four hours he remained at his post with Renno. When the storm began to subside somewhat Ned had no idea of their location. There were no charts or maps on board the boat, but he was grateful, for the present, that they survived. The craft was sturdy, and in spite of the beating she had taken, she was still intact.

As the wind began to subside appreciably Ned summoned Consuelo from the cabin. She appeared, white-faced.

"There are two buckets below," he said. "Bring them up here. Quickly."

Consuelo didn't understand the order, but she obeyed it.

He smiled at her wearily. "We may be in for a long haul. The rain is still falling, and we'll need as much water for drinking as we can gather."

The buckets were better than half-filled by the time the sun broke through the clouds and the last of the wind dissipated. Consuelo took the water below so it wouldn't evaporate too quickly.

The two men untied themselves, and Ned surveyed the damage. The tiller still operated, but the mainsail had been ripped to shreds and could not be patched or repaired. He would have to use only the jib, which was intact.

Consuelo returned with bread, cheese, and the last of the wine. "There's less food than I first thought," she said. "This is the end of it."

Ned nodded, his face grim. "I don't want to fool anyone. Our situation isn't good. The mains'l is useless, and even if we had ample supplies I can't imagine us sailing all the way to the North American mainland using only the jib even if I knew our present location, which I don't. All I can tell you is that we're much farther from the mainland than we were when we left Havana."

"Are we near Cuba or Puerto Rico?" Consuelo referred to the two principal Spanish colonies of the West Indies, islands they were anxious to avoid.

"I think it unlikely," Ned said, "but I don't really know for certain. I'm afraid that sooner or later we'll have to take our chances and put in at some island for water and any wild fruit we can find. Our alternative is to die of hunger and thirst in the Caribbean Sea."

Renno made no comment and went below. He returned in a short time with a thin line and a hook he had found in the fisherman's tackle box, and affixing a lure of burnished copper to the base of the hook, he moved to the stern and dropped the line overboard. His practical nature was asserting itself with a vengeance. Rather than waste time speculating on what might happen, he was taking positive steps.

Mary Ridley tried to conquer her apprehensions, but her fears mounted as the days became weeks. At breakfast, after Anne had gone off to school and only her husband and Betsy were still present, she could remain silent no longer.

"We should have heard something by now!" she said.

Betsy knew what her mother meant, but calmly sipped her tea. She frequently felt the movements of her baby inside her, and these reminders of Renno gave her greater strength.

Austin Ridley merely raised an eyebrow and buttered another slice of bread that had been baked less than an hour earlier.

"I was so sure," Mary said, "that Ned and Renno would be home by now."

Her husband shook his head. "Even if they encountered no hitches," he said, "there's been just enough time for them to visit Havana and St. Augustine and then return here. You need to make allowances for weather. The imperial viceroy in Havana might have kept them waiting for many days before seeing them. There could be hundreds of reasons for delay."

She glared at him. "Just last week you told me you had a letter from General Wilson telling you all sorts of political reasons why this mission is more important than ever. I can't for the life of me understand how you can remain so calm." She turned to her daughter and was equally explosive. "You're carrying Renno's baby, who will be born in several more weeks, but you act as though you don't have a care in the world."

"Now, now," Austin murmured.

Betsy smiled at her mother. "You're right, Mama," she said. "I have no cares. If Ned had gone off alone on this mission I'd be worried sick, and I admit it. But no harm can come to him when he's traveling with Renno."

"I'll grant you that the man you married is extraordinary," Mary replied. "But he's human, too, you know. He's hungry when he doesn't eat, and he bleeds when he's injured!"

"When it's necessary, Renno can go for many days without food, Mama!" Betsy retorted. "If he bleeds, I'm quite sure he knows all sorts of secret Seneca ways to stop the flow of blood. Please stop worrying."

"Betsy is quite right, my dear," Austin said. "Renno and Ned were chosen for this mission because there's no one more resourceful in all the English colonies. Their skills and talents complement each other. There's no doubt in my mind that they'll come home safely."

He refrained from adding that he also prayed they would be bringing the eagerly awaited information.

"I've had a premonition that they're in great danger! I know it sounds ridiculous, but I can't rid myself of the feeling that awful things are happening to them!" Mary burst into tears and, unable to control herself, hurriedly left the dining room.

Betsy would have followed, but her father's gesture kept her at the table.

"You have a right to know something," he said. "Your mother's fears aren't as exaggerated as they may seem."

She looked at him and his solemn expression threatened to crack her tranquil facade.

"I wasn't going to mention this until I obtained further information," Austin said, "and I believe it will be best to say nothing at present to your mother."

Betsy clasped her hands tightly over her bulging middle.

"Yesterday," her father said, "one of my brigs that was long overdue from the West Indies finally put into port. Her master was delayed at Havana for six weeks by port authorities who harassed him by inventing new laws and regulations every day and refusing to let him sail until he complied with them." He drained the last of his tea, even though it had cooled. "At no time in the past month has Captain Cavanaugh put into Havana in the *Mary*."

Betsy's head swam.

"I questioned the master for a long time and then had separate conversations with his mates, both of them reliable officers. All of them told the same story. The *Mary* never showed up while they were docked in Havana, and they saw no sign of Cavanaugh. Much less Renno and Ned. Mind you, they had nothing to do but hang around the waterfront all day, every day for weeks on end, and they were aware of every merchantman that sailed in or out of the port."

"What could have happened, Papa?"

Austin shrugged. "In all this time there's been only

one storm, a nasty gale that broke soon after our brig left Cuba. But that was no more than a week ago."

"Then the *Mary* has disappeared?"

"Few ships vanish without a trace," he said, trying as best he could to soothe her. "Captain Cavanaugh is a first-rate sailor. For that matter, so is Ned. For all we know, he and Renno may have decided to go ashore in some uninhabited part of Cuba and then travel overland to Havana. We discussed that possibility before they left."

A real Seneca wife would have assumed that the best had happened until she learned otherwise, Betsy told herself angrily as she tried to banish the sense of dread that engulfed her.

Austin stood and patted her shoulder. "It wasn't fair to keep the news from you. But as you've said yourself, Renno is unique. And Ned is well able to look after himself, too. Whatever may have happened, they'll come through it."

Alone at the table, Betsy refused to emulate her mother's hysteria. She sat motionless for a time, then spoke aloud in Seneca. "I am the woman of a war chief," she said. Pushing back her chair, she walked out of the dining room slowly, composed and dignified.

Renno caught a large fish with firm, white flesh. Consuelo cooked it on the tiny stove in the cabin, using the last of the wood supply, and for two days the fish provided the trio with their only sustenance. Renno deliberately ate smaller portions than the others because his lifelong training made it possible for him to subsist on very little.

The fish refused to bite again, although all three tried their luck, and the meager water supply shrank at an alarming rate. The wind died away almost completely, with only the most gentle of breezes blowing occasionally to vary the monotony of drifting under a scorching sun that blazed in the cloudless West Indies sky.

"At least we're not becalmed," Ned said, "so that's all to the good."

Whenever there was a breeze he sailed doggedly westward, never mentioning their certain fate if they failed to find land. At no time did Renno show his feelings. Consuelo was consistently cheerful. Ned, who admired her courage, was impressed when she uttered no complaint.

One day in mid-morning he sat at the tiller, feeding the jib with faint puffs of breeze, when on the horizon to the west he saw land. Saying nothing until the fishing boat drifted closer, he was able to see mountains so high that their upper portions soared above the timberline.

"Renno," he called, "look yonder and tell me I'm not having an hallucination."

The young Seneca shielded his eyes from the glare of the sun. "There are many mountains," he said. "They are so tall their tops are hidden in white clouds."

The relieved Ned promptly answered Consuelo's unspoken question. "All I can tell you," he said, "is that the island isn't Cuba or Puerto Rico. Their mountains are smaller."

She moved to the prow and sat there, watching the island grow larger and larger. The wind freshened when they were two or three miles from the shore, and the jib filled, enabling the boat to pick up speed.

When they sailed still closer they were able to make out a vast, seemingly impenetrable jungle of deep green, and Renno was pleased. "In that wilderness," he said, "we will find animals that will give us food and rivers that will give us water."

The coastline was rocky, and the possible presence of coral reefs made Ned cautious, so he sailed parallel to the shore for a time.

"Ahead," Renno said, "there is an opening."

They came to an inlet. Ned sailed through its mouth, where tall trees, thickets of bamboo, and tangles of bushes grew almost to the water's edge. The foliage became less dense as they sailed on, and after a time they saw bluffs of sand, studded with spiked cactus plants. Directly ahead was an expanse of white beach.

Ned sailed as close as possible to the beach. Renno stripped off his clothes and jumped into the water. Ned threw him a line and he swam ashore, hauling the boat. Consuelo was surprised by his strength as he dragged the prow up onto the beach.

The others waited for him as he dressed again, and then all three went ashore, carrying their weapons. The cove was deserted. They heard no sound, although several pelicans swooped and glided overhead, unafraid of the presence of humans.

The trio walked a short distance and Renno suddenly stopped. He sniffed several times, then ran toward the jungle. The others followed him, and he grinned as he pointed toward a small stream of clear water that flowed down from the mountains and apparently had its outlet to the sea farther up the coast.

They drank their fill, and Consuelo was curious. "How did you know where to find this brook, Renno?"

"He smelled it," Ned said with a laugh.

"That is true," Renno said seriously. "The smell of fresh water is not like the smell of salt water."

They returned to the water's edge, where shellfish were plentiful, and nearby Renno found several nests of gull's eggs. He built a fire, and they ate their first meal in almost seventy-two hours. Never had any of them tasted more delicious food.

They relaxed somewhat after they had eaten. "With ample food and water," Ned said, "we can stay here as long as necessary. We—"

Renno gestured suddenly, urgently for silence and leaped to his feet.

A few moments later a heavily tanned man emerged from the jungle at the inner side of the beach. Bearded and wearing a broad-brimmed hat, he was dressed in an open-throated shirt, breeches, and high boots. In one hand he carried a musket and in his belt was a long knife, but it was significant that he made no menacing gestures with his weapons. He studied the trio in silence, then said something in a language they did not understand.

He repeated the statement in a guttural English. "Welcome to Hispaniola, the home of the *boucanier*," he said.

Renno responded at once, raising his hand in the Seneca salute. "We greet you in friendship," he said.

At last Ned knew where they were. On the southern coast Spain had a colony, the city of Santo Domingo and land they had cultivated around it. But the better part of the island was a wilderness. For more than one hundred years, Ned knew, the pirates of the Caribbean had made their headquarters on Hispaniola, which was ideal for their purposes. There were many harbors and coves on the uncharted north and east coasts where they could hide their ships from the navies of the civilized nations that searched for them. Firewood, timber to repair their ships, and water were plentiful. They lived on the vast herds of wild cattle that roamed the islands and on the fruits and vegetables that grew in profusion.

They were known as *boucanier*, Ned had been told, because the word was French slang for those who ate roasted meat.

"Come with me." The stranger was polite but firm and led them into the jungle. Apparently the thought did not occur to him that they might refuse.

Ned, speaking softly, explained their whereabouts and situation to his companions. Renno, who had removed his boots and stockings and was making his way with ease through the undergrowth, merely nodded. He did not appear concerned.

Consuelo, tired after their ordeal, became alarmed and stopped short. "Pirates!" she whispered. "They are cruel men who may kill us."

Ned grinned at her. "Trust Renno and me."

The brilliant smile she bestowed on him in return was warm. "I do, with all my heart," she said.

They made their way through the jungle for at least a half hour, and Renno slowed his pace from time to time in order to draw his sword and cut away vines that might hamper Consuelo's progress. They were climbing higher into the hills.

After they reached the pinnacle of a hill from which they could see much of the shoreline, including the cove where they had come ashore, they dipped into a hollow beyond it. There, in a clearing, was the camp of the buccaneers.

Renno made a quick, accurate estimate and saw that at least thirty tents of pure silk stood in the clearing. Later he learned that the silk came from bolts of cloth captured when a French merchantman had been taken and sunk.

A company of more than fifty men was gathered in the clearing, many of them playing cards. A few were at work, building a fire. Some continued to play, but most paused to look at the newcomers. Consuelo's discomfort increased when she realized that she was the center of attention. Ned, too, was aware of the interest she aroused.

The man who had led the trio conducted them to the far side of the clearing where a tall man, clean-shaven and about forty years old, was seated in a magnificent tapestried chair. He was dozing and held an unlighted *segaro* in one limp but brawny hand.

Renno was quick to note that, although he wore a boot on one foot, the other was encased in what looked like a large leather bag.

The messenger cleared his throat. "Cap'n," he said. "Cap'n van der Kuyt! I brought them."

The sleeping man opened his eyes, was surprised to see that an attractive young woman was one of the visitors, and struggled to his feet. Suddenly he winced. "Damn all Spanish jailers," he muttered. Recovering his poise, he bowed. "Host van der Kuyt at your service," he said pleasantly, but his eyes remained cold as he took the measure of the new arrivals.

Ned stepped forward, introduced his companions

and himself, then asked politely, "You're Dutch, Captain?"

"My father was Dutch, my mother was a whore in New York, and I have no nationality," Van der Kuyt growled. "Who are you and why have you come to Hispaniola?"

Ned related their story, taking care not to mention the secret mission that had taken him and Renno to Havana.

The captain's eyes glittered when he heard of the treatment they endured while imprisoned by the authorities of New Spain. It was clear that he hated Spaniards. Ned continued with his recital, but broke off when a high-pitched scream of pain echoed across the clearing.

"Pay no attention," Captain van der Kuyt said. "I have two Carib Indian braves in my company who aren't the easiest lads to keep pacified. They captured an Arawak warrior in Jamaica recently, and they amuse themselves with him. They do no real harm, and it keeps them docile, so they don't quarrel with my other men."

A tall, very slender young warrior, far darker than most Indians and clad only in a loincloth, was lashed to the trunk of a thick tree. His wrists and ankles were bound by a single length of rope that was knotted between his feet.

Standing on either side of him were two shorter, husky Carib, who were taking turns tormenting him with their knives, deftly slicing small patches of flesh from his body. His torso, shoulders, neck, and arms already were covered with sores and scabs.

Renno was outraged. His own people tortured their enemies, to be sure, but only for the purpose of testing the courage of a warrior already condemned to death. If he absorbed such punishment in dignified silence, his soul was certain to join those of his ancestors in an eternal hunting ground.

This, however, was a shameful and savage pastime that sullied the stature of all Indians. A cold anger

179

rising within him, he could not tolerate such disgusting behavior.

Instinctively reverting to his own language, he addressed the torturers in a metallic voice that rang across the clearing. "Renno, war chief of the Seneca and son of Ghonka, the Great Sachem, orders that this trial stop!"

The buccaneers, hearing the strange tongue, began to drift toward him to see what was happening. The Carib braves could not speak his language, but they understood his meaning and gaped. Even the victim momentarily forgot his pain and blinked in astonishment.

Ned was afraid trouble might develop and moved closer to his companion. But Consuelo, still unaware of Renno's background, was too stunned to follow him.

Renno was indifferent to the stir he was creating. He knew only that he had to act quickly to convince the two Carib to obey his commands. Whipping his knife from his belt, he weighed it in his hand for an instant, then hurled it.

The blade appeared to be aimed straight at the helpless Arawak, but it sank lower and miraculously severed the knot in the rope between the captive's feet. Although he was as dazed by his sudden good fortune as he was by the pain he was suffering, he quickly struggled to free himself from his bonds. The knife continued to quiver in the ground between his feet.

Renno pointed toward a high branch of a tree at the edge of the clearing, where inedible yellow berries about the size of cherries were clustered. "The oil of the fruit of that tree," he said, still speaking in his own tongue, "will heal the body of the Arawak." Stepping forward swiftly, he drew a tomahawk from the belt of one of the Carib and threw it with deadly accuracy. The sheared branch fell to the ground.

Only the other Indians and Ned had understood what he had said, but his meaning had been plain to the entire company, and the buccaneers could scarcely believe what they had just seen. Consuelo continued to gape, too.

Snatching the tomahawk of the second Carib, his eyes glittering, Renno caught hold of the brave's scalp lock. "Rub the body of the Arawak with the oil of the fruit," he directed.

The brave hastened to obey, and the other Carib followed. The Arawak submitted to the treatment, then moved slowly toward the man who had saved him. "Linnick," he said, "thanks him who has become his friend."

The language was strange, but Renno could understand it. He returned the other's greeting and then they clasped forearms.

Seeing a white man behaving like an Indian fascinated most members of the pirate crew. But one of their number, who apparently had been drinking heavily, was far more interested in Consuelo. He removed his hat, bowed to her, and said something to her in an undertone. Her face grew scarlet beneath her sun-bronzed skin.

Ned noticed her outrage and did not stop to weigh the consequences, but drew his pistol and fired. The sound of the unexpected shot echoed through the silent jungle. The buccaneer, still holding his hat in his hand, stared at the bullet hole that had punctured the center of the crown.

Ned strode toward Consuelo and placed an arm around her shoulders. "This lady," he said succinctly, "is under my protection."

The pirates had no desire to argue with him or with his extraordinary friend. These newcomers were too adept with their weapons. They had to be treated with respect.

The offending buccaneer staggered away to the far side of the clearing.

Host van der Kuyt broke the spell. "Go about your business, lads," he said harshly. "I want to have words with these gentlemen."

The buccaneers promptly dispersed, slowly followed by the awed Carib. Only the Arawak made no move and continued to stand near Renno.

"You, whoever you are," the buccaneer leader said to Renno, adding to Ned, "and you, sir, have just given us an exhibition unlike any I've ever seen. What's more, you must know navigation to have reached our shores in that dilapidated boat. So, if you'll join my band, I'll happily make you my lieutenants. There's nobody I'd rather have fighting beside me in battle than you two."

Renno and Ned exchanged a quick glance. They had no desire to join a company of cutthroats, but at the same time they didn't want to anger Van der Kuyt. So far they had survived against heavy odds and somehow they intended to carry out the rest of their mission.

"We appreciate your offer, Captain, and we hope you'll give us time to think about it. We have other work that needs to be done, and we can't let anything interfere with it. At the present we're too weary to make any decisions, as you can imagine."

"Stay with us," Van der Kuyt replied, certain they would succumb to the lure, "and take all the time you need. Part of my band is off making a raid at sea, and I won't ask for your answer until they return."

Renno went off through the jungle, accompanied by Linnick, who followed him everywhere, and in a grassy pasture on a Hispaniola hillside he shot a wild calf. Returning to the buccaneer camp with it, he gave the meat to Captain van der Kuyt, keeping only the hide for himself. Then he went off with Linnick for several days. He did not even confide in Ned.

When he returned, the silent Linnick still at his side, he was transformed. He had cured the hide and made a loincloth, moccasins, and a cape for himself. He had shaved the sides of his head to restore his scalp lock and had somewhere found berries that made green and yellow stains like Seneca warpaint. Using strong wood that he found in the jungle, he also had fashioned a new bow and a quiver of arrows.

Linnick was carrying a bow and many arrows, too, but they did not resemble the heavy weapons that Renno had made. Instead, after the fashion of the Arawak nation, he had made a bow of light wood and small arrows, about one-third the size of those preferred by the Seneca. He had already proved his expertise to his mentor, who was well satisfied with his efforts.

"I have worn the clothes of your people long enough," Renno told Ned. "Now I must become myself again."

By now Consuelo had learned the truth about Renno from Ned, but she nevertheless was fascinated by the change in his appearance.

"I am the same inside," he assured her with a grin as he went with Linnick to rummage in a hollow, overgrown with vines and weeds that stood behind the buccaneer's camp. This was the place where unwanted items were thrown after a raid, and it was here that Renno found a battered metal strongbox. He used portions of it to make himself two new tomahawks, which he sharpened on hard stones.

The Arawak did not use tomahawks, but Linnick utilized a part of the metal box, too, and painstakingly made himself a pair of light knives, which he was able to throw with great dexterity.

Ned and Consuelo occupied tents of pure silk similar to those of the buccaneers. Consuelo also acquired an extensive wardrobe, the sea robbers having no use for the chests of women's clothes they had taken in various raids.

Ned expected his brother-in-law to move into his tent with him, but Renno politely refused. Linnick spent several days weaving two curious contraptions of vines. Called hammocks by the people of his nation, they were strung between two trees and provided full-length reclining platforms in which an occupant could sleep comfortably. The two hammocks were placed between trees a short distance from Ned's tent.

The buccaneers, astonished by Renno's transformation, continued to regard him with respect, but kept their distance. The majority of them deserters from the navies of Great Britain, France, and Spain, while others had come from the merchant marine fleets of the Netherlands and the English colonies, they were hard-bitten men who recognized that he had qualities even harder. They were strong, but he was stronger, and they didn't want to put him to the test, knowing their own wanton cruelties paled beside his total disregard for the feelings of his enemies.

They felt somewhat closer to Ned, who spent virtually all of his time with Consuelo, but he held himself apart, too, and made no attempt to encourage their friendship. Although deliberately rude to no one, Ned treated only Host van der Kuyt as an equal, and the captain, who kept to himself, made it plain he was biding his time, waiting for these new arrivals to tell him whether they would accept his offer to join his band.

Renno enjoyed himself hunting and fishing, and nowhere had he found game and fish so plentiful. Ned, however was reluctant to leave Consuelo behind in the camp. One day he mentioned the problem to Renno.

"I keep wishing there were some way we could sail ourselves to the mainland," he said. "This atmosphere is explosive, and it grows more dangerous from day to day. There are more than fifty men here, all of them desperadoes, ready and willing to slit the throat of anyone who stands in their path. They aren't like those two Carib braves who follow you around like a pair of tamed puppies. These buccaneers are dangerous."

"All men who earn their living as fighters are dangerous," was the matter-of-fact reply. Heavily tanned by the tropical sun, with several feathers in his scalp lock, Renno was again the complete warrior, with only his pale eyes and light hair giving him a somewhat incongruous appearance.

"You don't seem to grasp what I mean. It's Consuelo. She's the only woman here, and no matter where she goes or what she does, they keep watching her!"

Renno nodded. "That is natural. She is pretty."

Ned exploded. "Pretty, you say? She's downright beautiful, the loveliest girl I've ever seen!"

Renno refrained from smiling. Ned, like so many colonists and Englishmen, was too civilized for his own good and sometimes failed to understand basic truths. It was evident that he was in love with Consuelo, but didn't realize it.

"I'm afraid one of them will assault her when I'm not around. That's why I hate to let her out of my sight."

"On the day we came to this place," Renno said, "you told the buccaneers Consuelo was under your protection. But you sleep in different places, so everyone knows she is not your woman. To make her safe you must sleep with her."

His candor shocked and embarrassed Ned. "Just like that? It isn't so simple. Consuelo is a lady."

"Betsy is a lady. But she is not ashamed to sleep with me."

"You're married to her. That's very different!"

Their discussion was interrupted by a member of the band who told them that Captain van der Kuyt wanted to see them. Postponing their talk, they went to his tent and found him sitting outside his dwelling in his easy chair. He was reading a leather-bound book, but put it aside when he saw them.

"I'm not a patient man," he said, looking first at Ned, then at Renno, "but I've tried to give you ample time, gentlemen. By now you must know whether you intend to accept my offer. Oh, I realize that there's been no need for anyone else to go out for food since you came here and took charge of our Indians, Renno. But I have a right to know where you stand, both of you."

"It was understood," Ned replied quietly, "that we would be required to make no decision until the rest of your band returns from sea."

"God only knows when they'll get back!" the captain said, irritated.

Ned saw an opportunity to delay further. "Not that it's any of our business," he said, "but I've been wondering why you'd send only a portion of your company out to sea."

"It's no secret." Van der Kuyt glowered. "We had two ships, both of them small. Far too small. We tried to raid the French at Guadeloupe, where a huge schooner that would have been perfect for us was riding at anchor. That was a mistake. Their shore batteries tore one of my ships apart, and I was lucky to transfer the bulk of her crew to the other ship before she sank."

Ned became thoughtful. "So you need a larger ship. Something fast and agile and seaworthy."

The captain's temper flared. "Are you mocking me?"

"Not at all. Just thinking out loud." Ned pondered for a time. "I'll need a chance to work out the details, but I'm wondering if you'd be amenable to a deal."

"What sort of a deal?" Van der Kuyt demanded suspiciously.

"As I've already indicated to you, Renno and I came to the islands of the West Indies on a mission of our own. The greed of Don Pedro de Rivera almost destroyed us, and now we're responsible for the safety and well-being of Senorita Mirador, which further handicaps us. But what I'm wondering is this. Suppose we were to find you a way to obtain the kind of ship you need. A graceful ship capable of sailing swiftly. Heavily armed. And large enough to accommodate your entire company—"

"I don't believe such a ship exists. Anywhere!"

"Let me finish, Captain. If we made it possible for you to commandeer such a ship, would you be willing to help us in our own private venture?"

"Hellfire, Ridley! In return for such a ship I'd raid the British New World treasury at Port Royal, even though the whole of the Royal Navy's West Indian squadron was lying in wait for me in Jamaican waters!"

"I make no promises," Ned said, "but I'll see what I can work out."

He and Renno left the captain and wandered back across the compound. It was apparent that Ned wasn't yet ready to discuss his scheme. Renno forced himself to be patient even though he was anxious to complete their mission. He was eager to return to Norfolk before Betsy gave birth to their baby, but he knew better than to hope for the impossible. They had been extremely fortunate so far, and he didn't want to ask too much of the manitous. He would not call on them for further assistance until necessary.

Linnick awaited him outside Ned's tent, and Renno knew at a glance that, in spite of his seeming impassivity, he was excited.

"Linnick," he said, "has found the tracks of two wild pigs in the jungle. They are very large."

"Where did you see the tracks?" Renno wanted to know.

The slender Arawak's gesture indicated that he had located the signs some distance from the pirates' camp.

"It may be they cannot be found this day," Linnick said. "It may be the search will last until another day."

The succulent, roasted meat of wild pig was a delicacy, and Renno looked forward to the hunt. "Get the Carib," he said. "Let them bring their weapons. We will carry enough food for three days and nights in the jungle."

A short time later he led the party into the thick, almost forbidding wilderness, and the buccaneers who watched them depart shook their heads. Neither the Arawak nor the astonishing white Seneca seemed to bear any grudge against the pair who had captured and tortured Linnick. And the Carib, in return, unquestioningly accepted Renno's leadership. The buccaneers told each other, as they had on other occasions in recent days, that no civilized man could possibly understand the mentality of savage Indians.

That afternoon, when the company gathered to eat,

Ned and Consuelo sat apart, as usual, and Ned questioned her gently. "On the night we escaped from Havana, I wonder if you remember the large party of drunken Spanish navy sailors we almost encountered near the harbor."

"I shall never forget them," Consuelo assured him, wondering why he was thinking about their narrow escape now.

"Was it unusual for so many sailors to be ashore, do you think?"

Anyone who had lived in Havana would have regarded his question as naive, and she laughed. "Indeed not! Every night they fill the waterfront taverns and the houses of the harlots. At sea they lead mean, hard lives, so in Havana they use rum and women to forget." Realizing he was not simply making idle conversation, she added, "I do not know this for certain, but I believe the officers of the Spanish navy give them much free time in Havana on purpose. Then the sailors do not mutiny when they go back to sea."

"But surely they keep some crew members on board," Ned said.

Again she laughed. "This is something I do know. Twice, when my father was still alive, we were invited to dine by captains, one who commanded a ship-of-the-line and the other a frigate. Except for their cooks and those who waited on them—and their staffs, of course—the warships seemed deserted. I remember very clearly that my father and I talked about it at the time." Consuelo became curious. "Why do you ask?"

Ned shrugged. "I just wondered."

She knew he was not telling her the complete truth, but she didn't care. Ned was wonderful to her, and never could she repay her debt to him. Not only did she owe her freedom to him and Renno, but since they had come to Hispaniola he had been devoting all of his time and attention to her. She thought it likely that he would have preferred to go hunting for wild boar with Renno today, but instead he was remaining close beside her.

Consuelo was grateful for his unflagging protection. No, grateful was far too mild a word to express what she felt. She had come to realize that she loved this gentle, strong English settler. But she was careful to hide her feelings because she didn't know whether he felt the same for her. Unlike ardent young Spaniards, who had to be fended off, Ned was always calm, always in control of himself, and never made advances to her. Perhaps he was just shy, or maybe he didn't care for her, staying beside her because he regarded it as his duty. She was unaware that she, too, was circumspect in her actions.

In any event, he seemed to lose interest in the habits of the Spanish navy's sailors in Havana. That afternoon they went down to swim in the cove where they had left the fishing boat. Although they were still embarrassed when they saw each other in the nude, they enjoyed themselves thoroughly.

They returned to the camp at dusk, and Captain van der Kuyt, making a gallant gesture, loaned Consuelo the leather-bound book he had been reading, a volume taken from the luggage of a passenger on board a schooner whose ship the buccaneers had sunk. The author was an English poet named John Milton, who, Van der Kuyt said, had died only in recent years. Neither Consuelo nor Ned had ever heard of him or the book, which was called *Paradise Lost,* but she thanked the captain for it and promised she would start reading it that very night.

A full moon was rising overhead by the time they sat down to supper. After dark Consuelo was always comforted by Ned's proximity, and this evening was no exception. A half-dozen or more of the company were drinking heavily, helping themselves to quantities of rum and brandywine from captured cargoes. Captain van der Kuyt never interfered when his men were excessive, and Consuelo reflected that he was wise. Like commanders of the Spanish navy he detested, he preferred intoxication to deadly brawls.

All the same, she was glad that Ned was nearby and

that they sat alone. "How much longer do you think we will remain in Hispaniola?" she asked him as she tried to shut out the sounds of raucous laughter from the far side of the fire.

"I hate to predict," he said. "But assuming that Captain van der Kuyt's ship hasn't been sunk and returns, we might be able to work out an arrangement with him. I'm hoping he'll land us on the coast of Florida."

"You and Renno will go on with your assignment, then."

"Of course, Consuelo. We must. The leaders of our colonies are waiting for the information we bring them."

She hesitated for an instant. "You will take me with you?"

"I'm afraid we have no choice," Ned replied with a frown. "The very thought of subjecting you to more dangers makes me ill, and I wish there were some way we could land you at Charleston and have you stay there with Cousin Lucinda. But we've already lost so much time that we can't afford to squander more by sailing that far north and then turning back toward St. Augustine."

"I will not be a burden on you," she said solemnly.

"You're never a burden," he assured her. "I have no more intention of leaving you with this crew than I have of dropping you off somewhere in New Spain. You'll come with me—with us—because there's no alternative."

"Then you must allow me to help you." Consuelo spoke quietly but emphatically.

"The Spaniards would execute you as a traitor if they captured you after you acted as an espionage agent."

She smiled broadly. "What do you think my life will be worth if I fall into Don Pedro's hands?"

"You're right, of course. I'm not sure what you can do to help, but I'll remember your offer."

Consuelo's eyes shone.

190

Ned resisted the urge to take her in his arms because they were in plain view of the drunken buccaneers at the opposite side of the campfire. Soon, he told himself, he would be compelled to tell her he loved her. Yet he wanted to wait until they were safe. He wanted her to respond to him truthfully, not because she felt obligated to him or felt she had no alternatives.

For a thrilling instant Consuelo thought he would embrace her, but all at once his eyes clouded. She suspected he was strongly drawn to her, but couldn't understand why he always pulled back. Well, it was improper for a lady to make advances, even under these bizarre living conditions. She would have to wait for him to make the first move.

The drinkers were becoming still noisier. Ned gave Consuelo his hand and helped her to her feet. The night air was balmy, a gentle breeze from the high mountains dispelled the sickly sweet smell of jungle rot that seemed to be ever-present in the tropics. Consuelo paused to pluck a gardenia from a bush and place the white flower in her dark hair.

Looking at her in the soft glow of the moonlight, Ned wished fervently that he could bring her to safety soon. She had already endured so much, and he was afraid that still more trials awaited her before their fearful journey came to an end.

"I think I shall read some of Captain van der Kuyt's book tonight," Consuelo said when they reached her tent, then bade him a demure good night.

The flap was lowered, and Ned, watching her shadow inside the thin fabric of the silk tent, saw her silhouette spring to life when she lighted her oil lamp. Then he turned away while she undressed and donned her nightgown and negligee. He was being neither prudish nor modest, he told himself. He simply didn't want to be taking unfair advantage of her. No, that wasn't true, either. He wanted her so much that he was afraid he wouldn't be able to trust himself if he continued to watch.

For the next quarter of an hour he walked briskly,

always keeping the girl's tent in sight. Then, when he finally retired to his own nearby tent, he grinned as he took one last look at her tent. She had propped herself up in bed and was reading.

Ned lighted a candle, then removed his shirt, stockings, and boots. Ever since their first night in this camp of cutthroats he had made it a practice to sleep in his breeches. Lowering his own tent flap, he placed his sword and a loaded pistol close beside his bed.

Knowing he would remain awake for a long time if he allowed himself to dwell on Consuelo, he contented himself with thinking, briefly, how well she would get along with the various members of his family. Then he resolutely shut her out of his mind, and after a time he dozed off.

A scream that lasted no more than a second or two jolted Ned awake. For an instant he thought he was dreaming, but then he was certain he had heard Consuelo cry out. He leaped to his feet, picking up his sword and pistol, and raced outside.

The light in Consuelo's tent was still burning, and through the thin silk he saw a sight that caused his blood to congeal. The burly figure of a man was looming over her, and she was struggling to ward him off. He had one hand clamped over her mouth, stifling her screams, and with the other he was tearing at her nightclothes. Ned had no idea who it was.

For an instant a hot, red blur blinded Ned. Then the sensation gave way to a colder, more calculating rage. Taking a firm grip on his sword, he thrust it through the thin silk, and the blade sank deep into the intruder's back.

Uncertain whether he had killed or merely wounded the man, Ned wrenched his sword free and raced into the tent. Consuelo was sobbing, gasping for breath, but it was clear she had not been harmed. He caught hold of the intruder's collar, and as he hauled the man backward onto the hard ground, a pair of sightless eyes stared up at him.

All at once the tent filled with other members of the

company. Consuelo tried to cover herself with her torn nightclothes.

Captain van der Kuyt pushed his way through the throng. The dead buccaneer on the ground, the weeping girl in the torn nightdress, and her protector looming over her facing the crowd, his bloodstained sword still in his hand, told the whole story.

The captain reacted swiftly. "So," he said, "Ference had one cup of rum too many. Ridley warned all of you to stay away from the woman." He jabbed a finger at several members of his crew. "Take Ference's body out of here and throw it into the gully at the rear of the mahogany grove. The vultures will make short work of him and save us the trouble of burying him."

The buccaneers carried away their dead comrade in silence, and the crowd dissipated.

Captain van der Kuyt bowed to Consuelo, then to Ned, and smiled ironically as he picked up the leather-bound *Paradise Lost* from the ground. "What appropriate reading matter," he murmured as he placed the book on the foot of the bed and took his leave.

Consuelo was beginning to regain her self-control.

Ned stared at her for an instant. "I'll wait outside while you compose yourself," he said. Not waiting for a reply, he went out into the open and cleaned the blade of his sword on the damp grass.

Soon the oil lamp was extinguished and Consuelo, who had changed into another nightgown and robe, made her appearance. Dry-eyed now, with her hair falling loosely down her back, she went straight to Ned's tent. He followed, then busied himself lighting the candle.

Consuelo looked at him in the candlelight. "I thought for certain that brute would rape me," she said. "I never dreamed anyone could act as quickly as you did."

Her praise disconcerted him, and to his own surprise he stammered. "I—I didn't stop to think," he murmured. "I—I thought I heard you scream, and I just reacted."

"I thank the Lord—and you—that you did," she said, and forced a laugh. "You've been making a habit of coming to my aid in distressing situations."

Ned could restrain himself no longer. He took her gently in his arms. "Consuelo," he said, "I want to take care of you as long as we live. I would have proposed to you before now, but it isn't fair or right to ask you to marry me when neither of us knows what lies ahead for us. We may never leave Hispaniola alive. There's no telling what may happen to us if we're able to reach St. Augustine. Then there's the danger of—"

"You're right, it is too soon," she said breathlessly, interrupting him.

The firm warmth of her body beneath her thin night attire overwhelmed him. Using all of the will power he could command, he released her and took a step backward.

Consuelo was surprised, but thought she understood. She smiled, then spoke slowly and distinctly. "I cannot go back to that blood-soaked bed in the other tent tonight."

"Of course not." Ned was annoyed with himself for being so thoughtless. "Take my bed."

"Where will you sleep?" she asked innocently.

He shrugged. "I'll find a place. Renno's hammock, maybe. He won't be coming back to camp before tomorrow."

"I accept your invitation on one condition," Consuelo said. "If I sleep here, so will you."

No power on earth could have prevented Ned from going to her again. She blew out the candle, then raised her arms to him.

The following morning the members of the buccaneer company, the memory of the night before still fresh in their minds, saw Consuelo and Ned emerge from the same tent and make their way together to the breakfast fire. Even the most dim-witted knew what had happened, and by unspoken consent the corsairs agreed not to offend him in the future.

Chapter VIII

Ida Carswell's husband, Leverett, was the most prosperous merchant in Fort Springfield and provided his wife with a well-furnished home, her own horse and carriage, and many other luxuries. But her memories of the years as a widow she had spent struggling for survival on her little farm were still fresh in her mind. Perhaps that was why she so frequently felt ill at ease at the elegant house of General Andrew Wilson and his wife. Mildred Wilson was her best friend in the area, but that didn't make Ida's situation any better; this house overwhelmed her.

Leverett understood and grinned at her as they sat in the parlor. He was listening to the general's current assessment of the military-political crisis the English colonies faced.

"I'm strongly inclined to agree with the opinion of the war office in London," Andrew said. "Charles of Spain is a sick man and can't live for more than a few years, at most. So Louis of France has ample time to build up an army on the Spanish border and gradually

195

increase the size of his fleet at Marseilles. The moment Charles is gone, Louis will send his troops and warships into action, and before Great Britain, Austria, and the Netherlands can do a thing, his grandson will be sitting on the Spanish throne. It's a foregone conclusion."

"Then you regard a war with Spain and France—with the New World a major theater of that war—as a certainty," Leverett said.

"There's no question of it," Andrew replied. "What we don't know is whether the grandees who currently hold the real reins of power in Spain—their high-ranking generals and admirals and men like Don Pedro de Rivera, their imperial viceroy for New Spain—will try to consolidate their own power before Louis strikes. It makes sense to think they will."

"Indeed it does, Andrew. The stronger they are when the French arrive, the better their chances will be of hanging onto their present positions."

"So we constantly come back to the starting point of the circle," Andrew said. "Every day we keep hoping that Renno and Ned will return with information. And every day they fail to show up, we become more apprehensive."

"Might it be wise to send another team of agents to New Spain?"

"We've thought of it, but we've rejected the idea," the general said. "The Spaniards have their own way of forcing foreign agents they capture to talk out of turn. They started the Inquisition, remember, and it still thrives there. We don't want to give Don Pedro a seemingly valid excuse for starting a war with us."

Mildred refilled their teacups and, much to Ida's relief, ended the discussion. "You men talk of nothing but wars," she said. "There's been quite enough for now. Besides, Ida has told me she and Leverett want our advice on something personal."

General Wilson turned to the lean woman with the lined face, gently raising an eyebrow.

"Go ahead, my dear," Leverett prompted.

"I feel real foolish coming to you with this," Ida said hesitantly. "But Leverett and I have been going round and round so much we've just confused ourselves."

"I'm not sure our advice is worth much," Andrew said, encouraging her, "but we'll try."

"It's about Walter," Ida said. "Hearing him talk was the biggest thrill of my life. Lord have mercy! I never thought I'd live to see the day."

"Nor did any of us," Mildred said.

"You don't know how many hours and hours I agonized," Ida went on, "wondering if I did the right thing when I allowed him to go to live with the Seneca. Well, Ba-lin-ta has been a wonderful help to him, as all of us know. And now that he can speak—all I can say is that I made the right decision at the time I did."

The Wilsons nodded emphatically.

"Now I can't help wondering whether it's right to let him stay on with the Seneca," Ida said. "You saw how he looked when he was here recently. Just like all of those other painted savages. It won't be long before he starts carrying scalps in his belt." The very thought made her shudder.

"Ida and I are torn," Leverett said. "We realize how much the Seneca have done for Walter. But maybe he can rejoin us now and become a highly useful member of our society. There's a place waiting for him in my business, and I'd think that with all he's learned about Indians, he'd be a great help to the militia."

"What does Walter want to do?" the general asked.

Ida looked pained. "I asked him. Through Ba-lin-ta. And both of them were shocked that I could even think about his coming back home to stay. His one ambition is to work his way up to the rank of a senior warrior. By then he'd be so much a barbarian that he'd be permanently lost to us."

"Not necessarily," Mildred said. "Look at Renno. He's as much at home with us as he is with the Seneca."

"Walter still has physical handicaps," Ida said. "He

isn't Renno. He and Ba-lin-ta are so close that I can see the time coming when they'll want to marry. They already spark to each other, although I don't think they realize it yet, thank the Lord."

"Your son could do far worse than to marry Ba-lin-ta," the general said calmly. "Thanks to her, he's become a whole person."

"I've grown fond of Ba-lin-ta, and I won't object if they want to marry one of these years. But I can't help wishing they'd settle here instead of in a hut of clay and reeds and logs out in the middle of a godforsaken wilderness!"

Leverett didn't want his wife to become too upset, so he became brisk. "In a nutshell, do we bring Walter back here or do we allow him to stay on with the Indians?"

"You've asked our thoughts, so I must be honest with you," Andrew said. "Walter was a helpless deaf-mute when he went to live with the Seneca more than five years ago. Through God's grace he's gained the powers of speech, and through his own efforts he's become a full-fledged junior warrior in a tribe that takes such things seriously. They didn't give Walter his new status because Ghonka or Renno felt sorry for him. He earned his place. In the most difficult of trials. And I'm not so sure that you have the right to take that standing away from him."

"Judging by what I saw of Walter during his visit here," Mildred said, "I'm not at all sure that he'd come back, even if you tell him you want him at home."

Ida laughed unhappily. "We've thought of that possibility, too."

"In my judgment," Andrew said, "you ought to leave well enough alone."

Leverett looked relieved. "That was my feeling until we started whirling so hard I no longer knew what I thought."

"Give the boy time to find himself and become a man in every sense of the word," Andrew said. "You'll never lose him completely. And don't forget he's being subjected to civilizing influences. Betsy and Renno, for example. His visits here. It wouldn't surprise me, after he's proved himself to his own satisfaction, if he'll be happy to settle in Fort Springfield. But you aren't in a position to make his choice for him. Only Walter himself will do that. With Ba-lin-ta's help."

"And in the meantime, Ida," Mildred added, "console yourself with the knowledge that a frightened, miserable little boy is turning into a happy, self-reliant young man. Walter can hold his head high now, so it really doesn't matter where he lives or whether he identifies himself with the Indians rather than with us."

Ida nodded slowly. She had made so many sacrifices for her son in the past that she was willing to curb her own desire to have him near her now. His contentment was all that really mattered.

One afternoon a medium-sized brig sailed into the Hispaniola cove, and a company of twenty-seven corsairs—two officers and twenty-five crew members—stormed ashore. Their mission, the disgruntled buccaneers reported to Captain van der Kuyt, had been a total failure. Twice they had almost captured ships large enough for the band's purposes, but on both occasions their quarry had slipped away because they had lacked the fire power and the speed to take their prizes.

That evening, as the returned pirates told their frustrating stories to their comrades, Renno accompanied Ned and Consuelo to the far side of the clearing, out of earshot of the entire band. "I think the time has come for us to act," he said.

"Yes," Ned replied, "we must take steps now, before the captain forces us to join his company." He placed a hand over Consuelo's. "We're aware of the terrible risks we're taking. Are you quite certain you want to go ahead?"

"I am," she said quietly. "We'll be together, so I don't really care what risks we take."

Renno thought of Betsy, as he so often did when he became aware of this couple's happiness, and a desire to be reunited with his wife almost overwhelmed him. "We will go to the captain now," he said.

Ned frowned. "It might be better to wait until morning. He may join some of the men who'll be drinking away their sorrow tonight."

"All the more reason to reach him first." Renno was resolute.

They walked together around the campfire, where some of the newly returned corsairs stared hungrily at Consuelo. But they were quickly warned by friends that the pair who flanked her were not ordinary men, that it was worth a buccaneer's life to make advances to her.

Captain van der Kuyt was just finishing a talk with the two lieutenants who had been in charge of the unsuccessful voyage. Picking up an unopened bottle of wine, he started toward his own quarters but stopped when Ned hailed him.

"We want a word with you in private," Ned said.

"I wouldn't blame you if you refuse to join us," the disgusted Van der Kuyt said.

Ned did not reply. They were silent until they reached the privacy of his tent.

"Captain," Ned said after two oil lamps were lighted, "you badly want a very large ship. There are things we want just as badly. We'll help you if you'll help us. But let it be understood that all of us will be taking enormous risks. Every last one of us will die if the venture fails."

"We take chances every time we go to sea," van der Kuyt said gruffly.

"We've concocted a daring scheme," Ned said. "And there's a bonus if it succeeds. We'll be dealing a severe blow to the rulers of New Spain. Don Pedro de Rivera in particular will become a laughingstock."

The captain's eyes narrowed, and he smiled grimly. "I am interested," he said.

"For several weeks," Renno told him, "we have spent most of our time refining our plan. Each of us has made contributions. Consuelo knows much about the habits and schedules of Spanish officials. Ned knows the sea. And I am not new at the business of attacking enemies who expect no attack."

Ned explained the plan in detail.

Captain van der Kuyt made no comment until he was done. "This scheme is more than daring," he said. "It is insane, so insane that it might be effective."

"We're reasonably certain it will work," Ned replied, "provided every last one of your men understands the part he will play and lives up to expectations. Renno will take charge of the two Carib and the Arawak. They'll play a key role, but I'm not concerned about them. Your men must be drilled until each of them acts instinctively. Consuelo will have her own important part. Do I understand correctly that one of your lieutenants who returned on your brig today is Spanish?"

"Yes. Escalero."

"Good. He'll be trained by me." Ned was firm. "I have just one overall condition. You and your entire company must place yourselves under my command during this operation. There can be no question about who will exercise authority."

"We are a band of brothers," the captain said, "so I cannot speak for my men. They will have to vote on your proposal."

"Very well. But this scheme will be placed in operation only on my terms."

"I'll tell them I'm willing to relinquish temporary command to you, Ridley. That's the best I can do."

"It will be enough."

"It is important, too," Renno said, "that each man will be told only what he himself will do in the operation. We will not disclose the entire plan to them until the day we sail."

"That's reasonable enough," the captain said with a

ragged grin. "I rarely trust those bastards myself. Now, what do you want from me in return, assuming we succeed?"

"Sail us to Florida," Ned replied, "and send us ashore as close as possible to the Spanish fort at St. Augustine."

Van der Kuyt was astonished. "That's all you want?"

"Nothing else," Renno assured him.

The following morning, when the drinkers were still recovering from the previous night, Captain van der Kuyt summoned his entire band to a meeting in the clearing. Their guests, he said, had developed an ingenious, dangerous scheme to gain possession of a ship that would enable the company to become the terror of the West Indian Sea. Only volunteers would be taken, he said, because the risks would be so great, and he concluded by saying that he would relinquish his command temporarily to the man he called "Captain Ridley."

Ned spoke briefly but persuasively, explaining the mission in general terms, deliberately omitting specific details.

Then Van der Kuyt called for a vote.

Only five of the corsairs refused to submit to Ned's authority.

"Then you'll stay behind," the captain told them.

The recalcitrants hastily changed their votes, and the issue was settled. The atmosphere in the lazy camp changed at once as everyone went to work, with the men first directed to spend several hours each day swimming and hiking. Ned called a meeting of the officers and bo's'ns and explained the entire project to them.

Lieutenant Escalero, a swarthy man in his late thirties, laughed until he wept. "Even if we die," he said, "think of the grand joke we are playing on the Spaniards."

Ned took him off for the first of a series of long, strictly private conferences.

Consuelo asked for bolts of various kinds of cloth that the corsairs had accumulated. She took the body measurements of the Arawak and the two Carib, much to their amusement, and then went to work herself behind the lowered flap of the tent she shared with Ned. No one questioned her.

Renno led the three Indians deep into the jungle and then addressed them in his own tongue. "Only the Arawak and the Carib can win the battle we will fight," he said. "Now we will prepare for that battle."

All four practiced shooting arrows, then throwing knives and tomahawks. Renno set a grueling pace, and the Carib, whose previous efforts had been uninspired, improved steadily under his tutelage. Linnick was already an expert with his own knives and proved an excellent marksman with his own light bow and arrows.

After several days of such steady practice, Renno deliberately lagged behind with him as they were returning one afternoon to the corsair camp. "When the work is done," he said, "the great bird will carry Linnick to his own home. To the island the white man calls Jamaica."

"When will Renno return to the land of the Seneca?"

Guessing what was in his mind, Renno became laconic. "When the manitous will it."

The Arawak was not fooled. "Then Renno will go first to other places. Where?"

Unwilling to lie, the Seneca decided to tell the complete truth. "I must go to the land that the men of Spain call Florida. There I must learn whether the men of Spain prepare to send war parties against the English colonists and my own people."

The Arawak halted abruptly. "So Renno may face new enemies."

"It may be so."

The slender warrior folded his arms across his chest and spoke firmly. "Linnick will not go to the land of

203

his people. Where Renno goes, there Linnick also will go."

Renno tried to dissuade him in terms that would make sense to any Indian. "The enemies of the Seneca are not the enemies of the Arawak. The Seneca fight their own battles."

But the young native of the Caribbean made it plain that he had already settled the issue in his own mind. "The enemies of Renno are the enemies of Linnick. Renno saved the life of Linnick. He stopped the tortures of those who mocked Linnick. Renno is the friend of Linnick. So Linnick will go with him and help him defeat those who would try to kill him."

As Renno well knew, that was the end of the discussion. The young brave had made a voluntary choice and would be deeply offended if his offer was rejected. Grateful for his loyalty, Renno reached out and clasped him by the forearm. Linnick returned the gesture, grinning at him. They did not speak again as they trotted back to camp.

The tempo of the special training program increased day by day, and the members of the band, long accustomed to indolence, began to grumble. But Ned held firm and was strongly supported by Captain van der Kuyt and Escalero. "Our operation," the leader of the company repeatedly told his subordinates, "will be like nothing we have ever done. No other corsairs have ever attempted such a feat, not even the great Henry Morgan, who led an army and captured a city!"

Little by little the plan began to take shape. Consuelo finished making the special clothes for the Indians, and the Carib protested when they were required to don loose-fitting shirts and trousers of solid black, with black, knitted stocking caps that completely concealed their scalp locks. "We must appear to be almost invisible," Renno told them. "At the place we will go, no one will know we are warriors when they see us at night. It may be they will not see us at all."

The Carib were satisfied, although they remained curious about the nature of the mission. Linnick, however, asked no questions, and was content to follow anywhere that Renno might lead him.

A few days before the venture was scheduled to take place a number of the men were sent into the interior for coconuts and wild fruits, which they were ordered to bring back in large quantities. To the surprise of the crew, these natural products were piled on the deck of their cramped ship. At the same time, under Escalero's direction, a new name was painted on either side of the prow. For the time being the vessel became *El Gato*. Only her oldest sails would be used on the forthcoming voyage, and she would carry none of her cannon.

Individual crew members, however, would be heavily armed. Ample food and water were taken on board, but rum and brandywine were left behind. "At the critical time," Ned said, "every man on board must be sober."

The members of the band were uneasy, and when they boarded *El Gato* at dawn one morning, the appearance of the ship did not reassure them. Her dilapidated sails, peeling paint, and the produce piled on her deck caused her to resemble "an interisland trading hulk," as one of the French members of the company remarked. When Ned and the captain heard the comment, they grinned at each other.

Consuelo came on board in doeskin trousers and shirt. The men were mystified because a large leather clothing box was placed in the cramped cabin that she and Ned would occupy, Lieutenant Escalero having relinquished his quarters to them. No explanation was offered.

Before the anchor was weighed, Ned gathered everyone on the aft deck. "Remember," he said, "anytime a ship is sighted, all but eleven of the Spanish members of the band will go below and stay there until the ship moves off. When we approach our destination only those eleven, along with Captain van der Kuyt, Lieutenant Escalero, and me, will be allowed above deck. Everyone else will stay below until you're told your next move. Many of you will have to sleep on deck because we're so cramped for space, but that can't be helped."

"Where in the devil are we going?" one of the buccaneers shouted.

Ned's smile was tight. "It's time you found out," he said. "Our immediate destination is Havana. We're sailing there for the purpose of stealing a Spanish warship."

The men were stunned into silence by his announcement.

Van der Kuyt broke the spell. "All sailing hands to sailing stations. Hoist your mains'l and weigh anchor!"

Leaving the immediate operations in the capable hands of the captain, Ned went to the cabin. He found Consuelo standing at the single square window, looking back at the beach and the fishing boat in which they had made their escape from Cuba. He came up behind her and slid his arms around her waist.

"I'm almost sorry to be leaving Hispaniola," she said. "I'll always remember this place because it was here that you and I really found each other."

"Are you quite sure you want to play a role in what lies ahead?" Ned asked her.

Consuelo twisted around in his grasp until she faced him. "I'm certain," she said, placing her hands on his shoulders. "If anything goes wrong, all of us will die, and I'd never forgive myself if I cowered here while others took all the risks. Don't forget that I have a score to settle with Don Pedro, too."

"Fair enough," Ned replied, "but I'm still reluctant to force you to take an active part once we reach Florida. Assuming we get there."

"I insist," Consuelo said. "It was chance that caused us to meet in Don Pedro's cell, but now we're partners in this enterprise." She raised her face and kissed him.

Ned remained troubled. "Well," he said, "we'll proceed one step at a time. All I really know is that if we survive whatever may lie ahead of us, I want you to marry me."

Consuelo became evasive. "As you've just said, we'll proceed one step at a time."

"Are you turning me down?"

She smiled up at him. "No. But our first task is to stay alive long enough to complete your mission." She didn't mention her fear that he might feel compelled to marry her simply because fate or circumstance had brought them together. Only when they were safely out of danger would he know whether he really loved her enough to want to make her his wife.

Ned didn't want to pressure her. For now, it was enough that they were together and that they faced risks far graver than any lady should be forced to take. Later, in safety, he would convince her that under no circumstances would he permit her to escape from him.

They left the cabin, and when Ned went up to the quarterdeck, Renno unobtrusively took his place beside Consuelo. She knew that he and Ned had arranged to keep her closely guarded at all times on the cramped ship, and she was relieved. She wouldn't put it past any of the men to assault her if they thought they might go unpunished.

The brig plowed her way slowly under fair skies. The sea was a tranquil green-blue, so clear that, from the aft deck, it was possible to see far below the surface. The sun was searing, and even the gentle breeze was hot, but Consuelo smilingly refused Renno's offer to take her back to the cabin. "My skin is almost as dark as yours," she told him, "so a little more sun can't hurt me. Besides, the cabin would be stifling."

Everyone felt as she did, and the men who were not members of the sailing crew lingered on deck, too. They took care, however, not to change the artfully arranged jumble of coconuts and fruit. At last they understood that the brig hoped to make her way through Havana harbor disguised as one of the scores of little merchant ships that brought produce from outer islands to the capital of New Spain.

The leisurely voyage took two full days, and late in the second afternoon word was passed from the quarterdeck that Cuba lay ahead. The buccaneers needed no urging to buckle on their swords and load their pistols.

Consuelo went into her cabin, and when she reappeared on deck for Ned's inspection the corsairs who saw her gaped, then began to cheer. Making good use of the clothes and cosmetics that had been taken on various buccaneer voyages, she was flamboyantly dazzling. The scooped neckline of her silk gown revealed more than it concealed of her bulging breasts, a girdle of thin silver seemed to shrink her already tiny waist, and a deep slit in her ankle-length skirt rose high on one thigh. Her heels were so high that she walked with difficulty. The paint on her lids emphasized the violet hue of her eyes beneath black-coated lashes, a beauty patch of black velvet was affixed high on one rouged cheek, and her mouth had become a slash of scarlet. She acknowledged the cheers with a wave and a saucy smile, secure in the knowledge that Ned faced her and Renno, now clad in black, was only a few feet behind.

The lust in the men's eyes attested to the spectacular success of her outfit. Ned was satisfied, and on the quarterdeck van der Kuyt and Escalero nodded in approval, too. Consuelo immediately returned to her cabin and took the precaution of bolting the door behind her.

Shortly before sundown the lookout announced that he could make out the great castle guarding the Havana harbor in the distance. The brig's speed was reduced so she would arrive after dark, and only her Spanish-speaking sailing crew remained on deck. The others, including Renno and his Indians, went below to an empty hold and sweltered there.

Night came, and a partial moon began to rise in a star-studded sky. As always in the tropics, the transition from daylight to darkness was sudden. Ned peered up at the sky, then nodded thoughtfully. He and the captain had worked out the date with great care: the night was dark, yet not too dark.

The castle loomed directly ahead now at the entrance to the harbor, and Van der Kuyt, posing as an ordinary seaman, lighted an oil lamp, then raised and lowered it three times as a signal.

"Who are you?" someone on the ramparts above called. Escalero replied in his flowing Spanish. *"El Gato,* out of Puerto Rico, Your Excellency, with a cargo of food so fine and such delicacies that the mouths of the highest-ranking grandees will water at their sight."

"Your cargo probably rots, and even a peasant would become ill if he ate it," was the bored reply from above. "You may go on."

"So far so good," Ned murmured.

Escalero sailed cautiously through the harbor, which was crowded with Spanish warships and at least a score of merchantmen, as always. Ned guided him by pointing silently, and the brig moved boldly toward the wharves that stood on either side of the customs station. Two members of the sailing crew leaped onto the shore and made the vessel fast, and after a silent, uncomfortable wait a customs officer in a soiled uniform made an appearance, yawning and stretching. As he came on board he took the precaution of holding a handkerchief soaked in strong scent under his nose.

Escalero, flanked by Van der Kuyt and Ned, both wearing dark, rough sailors' attire, called out as the man approached the quarterdeck. *"El Gato,* out of San Juan, Your Worship. I carry the best coconuts and plantains ever seen in the West Indies."

The customs man was amused. "What makes you think that no coconuts and plantains are grown in Cuba, Captain?"

Escalero contrived to look sorrowful. "Well do I know it, Your Worship, but San Juan is a sad little town that sleeps in the sun. In this great city my cargo will bring prices many times higher."

Joining him on the quarterdeck, the customs officer

could see the mounds of coconuts and bunches of plantains piled everywhere on the open deck. "If you can sell your cargo, you'll command higher prices," he admitted. "But there are many farmers here, you know."

Escalero ostentatiously fumbled in a purse hanging from his belt, deliberately jingling and removing several silver coins. "One in my position, with many children to feed, must take chances," he said confidentially. "It is my great hope that a warship planning to sail in the next day or two will buy my fine fruit." He extended a hand.

The customs officer took the coins, his lips moving as he counted them, and slipped them into his own purse. "You are less stupid than many who sail here from the provincial islands," he said. "And you may be in luck. The *Valencia* sails on the afternoon tide tomorrow, but I do not know if her quartermaster has already bought the produce he needs."

"The *Valencia*, Your Worship?" Escalero was giving a splendid performance.

Ned held a hand on the hilt of his knife and was ready to plunge the blade into the body of the official if it should become necessary.

The customs officer became scornful. "You Puerto Ricans! The *Valencia* is one of a new class of barques-of-war that make our navy the most powerful on the high seas."

The information gave Ned a feeling of grim satisfaction. It had been a barque-of-war that had battered the brig carrying him and Renno to Cuba. It was almost too much to hope that this was the same warship, but that was not important. What did matter was that it was perfect for a crew of ninety to one hundred men. If the maneuver succeeded, he would be keeping his end of the bargain by delivering a first-rate warship into the buccaneers' hands.

Still holding his scented handkerchief to his nose, the customs officer turned away.

"One moment, Your Worship. Where will I find the

Valencia? There must be thirty or forty ships in this harbor!"

Not pausing, the officer called over his shoulder, "Go to the far end of the east docks. You should find a slip open on the *Valencia*'s starboard side."

Escalero promptly ordered his sailing crew to cast off, and the little brig crept across the harbor. No one on the quarterdeck dared to speak because sound carried so clearly across water, but Ned knew what Van der Kuyt and Escalero were thinking. The potential prize that awaited them was almost too good to be true.

As they drew closer to the east docks, however, they could see for themselves that the customs official had told the truth. The barque's towering masts loomed ahead, and on her deck they could see any number of shrouded cannon. She was tied up at a wharf, and the slip on the far side of that dock was indeed empty.

While Escalero maneuvered his brig into the berth, Ned went down to the main deck, alerting Consuelo with a tap at her door, then rapping lightly on the cover of the forward hatch.

A few moments later the cover was raised partway, and four silent wraiths, led by Renno, appeared on deck and concealed themselves behind hillocks of coconuts.

"I see only the lieutenant of the watch on the barque's quarterdeck," Escalero murmured as Ned rejoined him. "The junior officer and the sailors of the watch must be below, while the rest of the crew are no doubt enjoying themselves ashore."

From what Consuelo had told them, they knew that the junior officer and sailors would be making a tour of the ship every half-hour, or thereabouts. The Spaniards were less punctual in adhering to schedules than were the officers and men of the British Navy.

The earlier docking procedure was repeated, with two seamen jumping onto the wharf and making the brig fast. The barque-of-war stood only fifteen feet away.

The door of the small cabin creaked open and Consuelo emerged, barefooted and carrying her absurdly high-heeled shoes in her hand. Ned went to her and silently squeezed her arm. They exchanged a long glance, and then she stepped onto the deck, where she donned her shoes.

Neither Ned nor the two corsair officers saw Renno and his three Indian companions slip ashore. Host van der Kuyt frowned, but Ned reassured him with a nod.

Consuelo swaggered up the wharf boldly, her hips swaying, and when she reached the far end, at the water's edge, she struck a provocative pose. She made no move until she was certain she had captured the attention of the officer of the watch on the barque's quarterdeck, and then she turned to him, smiling seductively.

"What brings you to this deserted wharf, little one?" the lieutenant called softly. "Surely you have no use for those who have just landed here in that tub filled with coconuts."

Consuelo's husky laugh was challenging. "I am here because I saw you, Captain. I do not associate with sailors and peasant scum."

"I am no captain," he replied.

"But you will become one." She was stalling for time now, praying that Renno and his companions were doing their part. A thousand things could have gone wrong. Perhaps they had been delayed in some way. Perhaps they had already encountered the other members of the watch and had been killed. Chills of apprehension raced up her spine, in spite of her confident stance, but she knew the risks she was taking. If an alarm was given, she might escape into the city, but she had no intention of abandoning Ned and taking the chance that she might be recaptured by Don Pedro de Rivera's men.

"Join me, little one, and we'll discuss it," the lieutenant said, and leaned on the quarterdeck rail as he peered hungrily at her.

"Civilians are not permitted on board warships, Captain, as you know even better than I! I might be fined or sent to prison." Or hanged, if I'm identified, she thought.

"I'll hide you when the men of the watch make their rounds, and then we'll have ample time to become acquainted. Well acquainted. I am not being relieved here for another two hours."

The tension on the quarterdeck of the little brig became even greater. Two hours was more than enough time to do all that was necessary and put out to sea, but unexpected emergencies might develop, and the first was already at hand. Where was Renno?

Consuelo's hesitation was genuine. "You are certain there will be no trouble for me?"

"Quite certain."

Consuelo had to stifle a relieved gasp when she saw a dark, hazy shape loom up silently behind the amorous officer. Renno had reached his appointed place, and all was well. Her confidence returning in a rush, she took two steps toward the barque, making sure that nothing obstructed the officer's view of her.

"I'll make a visit well worth your while, little one," the lieutenant said.

"I do not discuss matters of business at a distance," she replied with huffiness. "You are attractive, so that is enough for me. Surely we will reach an amicable agreement."

Her dazzling smile did not change when she saw Renno drop a length of rawhide over the officer's head and swiftly strangle him. It was imperative that the uniforms of the members of the watch not be torn or spotted with blood. But she could not continue to watch as Renno expertly choked the life out of the struggling lieutenant. Consuelo closed her eyes until the faint gurgling, choking sounds stopped and she could hear nothing but the quiet lapping of water against the hulls of the two ships.

When she opened her eyes again she saw Renno and Linnick removing the uniform of the dead officer while one of the Carib seemed to be attaching a heavy weight of some kind to the dead man's ankle. Then a knife flashed in Renno's hand. Consuelo gasped involuntarily when she saw him removing the top of the lieutenant's head with the blade. She felt ill when she realized he was actually scalping the Spaniard. Now she knew Renno truly was an Indian.

The stripped body of the lieutenant was heaved overboard and landed in the harbor a short distance from the place on the pier where Consuelo was standing. A few drops of water splashed her, and she averted her gaze for a moment. When she looked at the black water again, the body of the officer had vanished from sight. The quarterdeck of the barque was deserted now, too. Renno and his Indians had vanished again.

Consuelo wanted to run to the soothing security of Ned's embrace, but her job was not yet finished. She lingered on the wharf, searching the barque for possible signs of life, also keeping a lookout for a local constable or military patrol, which could cause trouble. A quarter of an hour passed and she felt as though she had been standing on the pier all night. It required all of her courage and stamina to stay at her post in the dark.

Suddenly, in the light of the half-moon, she saw a very young junior lieutenant climb the steps to the barque's quarterdeck, followed by three uniformed sailors.

"Martinez," the young officer demanded in an annoyed voice, "where in the names of all the saints do you suppose Lieutenant Dielgo has gone?"

One of the sailors laughed harshly. "Meaning no disrespect, sir, if he's been eating raw native vegetables again, all of us know where to find him."

The junior lieutenant nodded, then caught sight of the brazenly dressed girl at the end of the pier.

Consuelo struck a pose and smiled up at him.

"Martinez," the officer said, "see if Lieutenant

Dielgo is in the officers' toilet. You two continue your rounds. I'll wait here until the lieutenant returns."

The three sailors obediently climbed down the steps again, and Consuelo thought she heard the faint sounds of a scuffle. She could not be sure, however, and whatever was happening on board the warship was not her concern. She still had work of her own to do.

"I have been waiting a long time for you," she called in her huskiest voice. "You are very tardy making your rounds."

The young officer peered harder at her. "You have been waiting for me?" he asked incredulously.

Again a dark shape appeared at the far side of the *Valencia*'s quarterdeck.

Consuelo did her best to conceal her revulsion. "Of course," she replied, trying to sound both sultry and enthusiastic. "I asked some of your fellow officers where you were, and when they said you were on duty for this watch, I came here in search of you."

The rawhide loop fell over the junior lieutenant's head. Unable to force herself to see another man die, Consuelo turned away, her body rigid and her fists clenched.

She heard several splashes in the water behind her and knew the Indians had succeeded in disposing of the remaining members of the watch. Then the unfamiliar call of a bird sounded distinctly three times in succession.

All at once the brig came to life. Men leaped onto the wharf, racing the short distance to the warship, and jumping onto the deck. Lieutenant Escalero and the corsair bo's'n silently directed each of those who followed them to duty stations. The training proved successful. Not a movement was wasted.

Ned materialized beside Consuelo. "Come along," he told her gently, thrusting an unexpected bundle into her arms. "You were magnificent, but we don't want to linger in Havana." He led her to the barque, then lifted her onto the deck.

Renno awaited them, clad now only in his loincloth, and Consuelo shuddered when she saw two bloody scalps dangling from his belt.

"How long before we sail?" Renno wasted no words.

Ned shrugged. "We'll cast off as fast as we can, but it won't be all that easy. The men don't know this ship or her sails."

"Hurry," Renno said brusquely. "I climbed to the crow's nest just now, and a senior officer is coming down a street that leads to this ship. He has a half-dozen sailors as an escort."

For a moment Ned weighed the situation. "You'll have to allow all of them to come on board," he said. "There's no way we could fight our way out of this harbor if an alarm is given."

Consuelo saw Linnick and the two Carib appear seemingly out of nowhere behind Renno. Like him, they also were wearing only their loincloths now.

"I know what must be done," Renno said, and began to give crisp orders.

Ned quickly escorted Consuelo to the bottom of the steps that led to the quarterdeck. "Wait right here until I have the chance to find a more suitable place for you. At least you'll be out of harm's way, and I'll be nearby if you need me."

As he bolted up the stairs the bo's'ns mate hurried down and relayed orders to the corsairs in a low voice.

Consuelo peered up at the quarterdeck and saw Van der Kuyt and Escalero dressed in the uniforms of the two officers who had been killed. Ned told them Renno's news.

"We're acting as quickly as we can," Captain van der Kuyt said testily. "It takes time to man a ship of this size." He turned to the bo's'n and issued more orders.

Consuelo had to squeeze against the rail so the bo's'n wouldn't crash into her as he hurtled down the stairs and raced off down the deck. Lines creaked and pulleys squealed as the corsairs struggled to take the barque-of-war out to sea.

Watching the bustling, active scene, Consuelo noted that each of the men kept a pistol, sword, or musket close beside him. The danger was far from ended.

"Señora!" a man boomed in a deep baritone. "What are you doing on board my ship?"

The surprised Consuelo turned and was confronted by a middle-aged officer in a gold-trimmed uniform, a pair of silver epaulettes gleaming on his shoulders.

"And what's all this going on here?" the Spanish officer demanded. "These men aren't members of my crew!"

Consuelo turned on her charm. She quickly moved closer to the man, her violet eyes smoldering. She wanted to alert Ned and his companions on the quarterdeck above and behind her to the officer's arrival, but she could not create a disturbance. So she was obliged to capture and hold the commander's attention until the Indians disposed of the other Spaniards in their own way.

"Oh, you don't know how relieved I am that you've finally arrived, Captain," she said, her impeccable Castilian accent a match for his own aristocratic manner of speech.

She looked like a strumpet but spoke like a lady, and the officer was even more confused. "What are you talking about?" he demanded. "Speak quickly, before these vandals destroy my ship."

Running her hands up the front of the commander's tunic, Consuelo pressed close to him, murmuring something in a tone so low that he couldn't quite hear her.

"What's that you say? Speak up!" In spite of his irritation the man was excited by her, grasping her around the waist and drawing her still closer. Over his shoulder Consuelo saw Renno creeping down the deck, a knife in one upraised hand. Realizing she could not hold the officer's attention for more than a few seconds, at most, she lifted her face to his, her lips parting for his kiss. He responded and kissed her. Using all of her strength and willpower, Consuelo simulated overwhelming passion.

All at once his hands fell to his sides, his jaw became slack, and his body slumped. Consuelo took a single, faltering step backward, and turned away. Then, forced by her own curiosity, she looked back. Renno was squeezing the throat of the commander, finishing him off.

The Spaniard's eyes were open, bulging, and Consuelo saw an expression that would haunt her for a long time to come. The man knew he was dying and realized, too, that she had betrayed him. But he was already too far gone to fight. Feeling faint, Consuelo leaned against the base of the quarterdeck and closed her eyes.

"We have all of them, Ned," she heard Renno say.

"Good. I'll want the captain's uniform." Ned was equally cold and methodical. "Ready, Captain van der Kuyt!"

"Cast off!" Van der Kuyt was not wasting a precious moment. "Unfurl your jib and lower main. Step lively, lads, and we'll avoid the hangman's rope!"

For a long time Consuelo was so numb she couldn't move. Then a strong arm encircled her shoulders, and Ned was smiling at her. "That was magnificent," he said.

She was astonished to see that he was now wearing the gold-braided uniform. The body of the commander had vanished, but Renno, who stood nearby, now had three scalps hanging from his belt.

"We've got to get you out of sight until we're clear of the fort," Ned said, half-leading and half-carrying her to a door that led to the ship's interior.

Still too dazed to feel anything but horror, Consuelo allowed herself to be taken to a huge, well-furnished cabin at the rear of the ship. It was equipped with a full-sized bed, a table of carved oak, and a large, impressive desk. Apparently the barque's captain had made his quarters here, but she could not permit her mind to dwell on that. Through thirty or forty small, square windows set side by side in rows, she could look out at the dark waters of the quiet harbor, but she was afraid she might see bodies floating there, and she hastily wrenched her eyes away.

"You'll be safe here," Ned told her as he eased her into a cushioned armchair. "I'll lock you in and come for you after we reach the open sea. And never fear, I'll be here quickly if there should be anymore difficulties." He paused for an instant, looked at her in admiration, and shook his head. "No woman has ever shown greater courage or ingenuity than you've displayed tonight. Everyone in this company is indebted to you. Lord, what a sight that was—forcing the captain to kiss you when you knew Renno was approaching him from behind to do him in. You're a heroine if ever there was one, and I swear, there's no one quite like you."

Consuelo could only nod numbly. It was true that she felt no compassion for the Spanish officers. Certainly she had gained a measure of vengeance against official representatives of her native land, whose authorities had killed her father and treated her so shamefully. All the same, she had been a party to cold-blooded murder.

Ned knew she was still in a state of shock, so he said nothing more and left quietly. She heard the door close behind him and was comforted when the key turned in the lock.

Slowly, in spite of her efforts to blot the evening's horrors from her memory, she began to live through each phase of the awful experience again. Without quite realizing what she was doing, she raised the back of a hand to her lips and began to scrub them furiously.

Consuelo failed to realize that the barque was now in motion, but everyone else on board was well aware of it. Members of the crew crouched at their sailing stations so those on board other vessels in the harbor would not see that they wore civilian clothes.

Only the trio dressed as officers on the quarterdeck, along with the helmsman, who had changed into the uniform of a Spanish navy sailor, showed themselves openly.

Ned had relinquished the command to Host van der Kuyt, and the buccaneer chieftain performed admirably, threading his way slowly through the harbor while Ned stood beside him, occasionally offering a quiet word of advice. Escalero busied himself lighting an oil lamp and hanging it on the stern rail.

One final test awaited the band, and the barque slowed to a crawl as it drew closer to the mammoth fort that guarded the channel. Escalero stood close by Ned, ready to speak when necessary.

"Identify yourself!" someone shouted from the high ramparts.

"Barque-of-war *Valencia*!" Escalero replied promptly.

"Our colonel wants to know why you failed to make the appropriate signal with your lamp."

Escalero was at a loss for an answer.

"Tell them we're being dispatched on a secret mission," Ned murmured, watching as the ship edged closer and closer to open waters.

Escalero repeated his words. The officer on the rampart spoke to someone behind him, presumably the commander of the fort. Then he called, "What is your mission?"

The *Valencia* continued to inch forward, and Ned played for time, waiting several seconds before he whispered to the buccaneer lieutenant again.

"Our captain begs to inform you," Escalero called, "that we sail under sealed orders signed by Don Pedro de Rivera himself!"

The mention of the imperial viceroy's name was sufficient to stifle the curiosity of the fort's commander. "You may proceed," his spokesman shouted.

Host van der Kuyt, who had been holding his breath, exhaled slowly, but took care to wait until they were out of earshot of those in the fortress before he gave the order to crowd on all available sail. Aware that they could still be seen from the fort, he deliberately set a course to the east.

No one spoke until the fortress faded from sight and van der Kuyt changed course, directing that the *Valencia* sail northwest toward the North American mainland.

"By God, Ridley," he said, breaking the silence, "you kept your word. This barque can capture and sink any ship that enters West Indian waters. We'll soon be rich."

"There were times tonight when I was afraid we'd fail," Ned admitted.

Van der Kuyt shook his head. "I've never encountered anyone like Renno," he said, "and the girl was extraordinary, too. Throw in your lot with us, and you'll soon be wealthy beyond your dreams!"

"Thank you," Ned replied firmly, "but a bargain is a bargain. Sail as close to Fort Augustine as you can, and put us ashore there."

The corsair leader was unhappy. "I'll keep my word," he said, "but it won't be a simple matter. Before the night is out the Spaniards will know that a barque has been stolen from under their noses, and every sloop-of-war in Havana will be sent to find us. Remember that a sloop can sail half again as fast as we can. Once they locate us they'll send their entire New World fleet in pursuit to sink us."

"True enough," Ned said. "But—with luck—we'll be ashore and you'll be far out to sea again by mid-morning."

"We'll need that luck," van der Kuyt replied.

Chapter IX

Ferocious pains gripped Betsy in the middle of the night. Bathed in perspiration, she awakened out of a sound sleep in the bedroom that had been her own since she had been a child.

Her little sister heard her call, and a few moments later her parents came into the chamber, carrying candles. Mary Ridley took one look at her elder daughter. "Austin," she said, "her time has come. Fetch the doctor as quickly as you can."

Colonel Ridley dressed hastily while one of the sleepy servants saddled a horse for him, and then he rode at a breakneck pace to the home of Dr. Ward, who lived almost five miles away.

The physician, who answered the loud pounding on his door in a robe and slippers, was calm. "Betsy has fooled me," he said. "I wasn't expecting her delivery for another couple of weeks, at the earliest."

The fuming Austin paced the parlor while Dr.

222

Ward took his time dressing. Then the physician refused to gallop all the way to the Ridley estate.

"First babies," he said, "usually take a long time to come into the world. Relax, Austin. We have a long night ahead of us."

When they arrived at the house, Dr. Ward gave a few instructions to the waiting servants, then went in to see his patient.

Smiling down at Betsy, the doctor adopted his most soothing manner. "I'd ask how you feel," he said, "but I have a pretty fair idea."

Betsy kept her lips tightly compressed as he examined her. To her mother's astonishment she hadn't yet cried out in pain, and she was determined to suffer her ordeal in silence. Seneca women were able to endure agonies without making a sound. She reminded herself repeatedly that she was the wife of a Seneca war chief, and if he were here, beside her, she would want him to be proud of her.

After the physician completed his examination, he took the young woman's father out to the corridor. "It will be another hour or two," he said.

"What can you do for Betsy in the meantime?"

"Nothing, I'm afraid. If I give her laudanum to ease the pain, it will relax her muscles, and the baby's arrival will be delayed. All we can do is wait."

"It's just as well that Renno isn't here," Austin said. "If I'm as nervous as I am, I can imagine how he'd feel."

Dr. Ward laughed as he started back toward the bedchamber. "I've delivered more babies than I care to count," he said, "and I've never yet been able to decide which are worse, the fathers or the grandfathers."

The vigil went on. Betsy maintained her silence, occasionally gripping the hand of her anxious mother or apprehensive father. Then, suddenly, she spoke aloud in Seneca. "Manitous who guide and protect the Bear Clan," she said, her voice quiet, "help me and

223

present me with the baby of Renno, war chief of our nation."

Austin, who did not understand a word she said, was startled, but took care to ask no questions. His glance told Mary not to ask, either.

Betsy's agony became still worse, and at last she gasped, then said, "Renno."

A moment later her baby was born. Then her smiling mother was beside her, holding a bundle in her arms. Betsy reached up and took the infant.

"Here is your son," Mary said.

Betsy's smile was radiant. "He will be called Jagonh," she said.

Austin Ridley stared down at her.

"That was the name of Renno's brother, a great bear," she said. "And our son is already a member of the Bear Clan. But when we are here in the colonies, he will be known as James." Closing her eyes for a few moments, she thanked the manitous for the favor they had shown her. "I want Renno to know as soon as possible," she said, opening her eyes and addressing her father.

Austin Ridley smiled and nodded, and not until he left the room did he allow his concern to show. Renno and Ned were badly overdue. It was possible that Betsy might already be a widow.

Soon after sunrise a shout from the crow's nest indicated that a ship was on the horizon. Lieutenant Escalero, who had the watch, identified her as a small brig, without doubt a merchantman. He sent word to Captain van der Kuyt, who hurried to the quarterdeck. Soon they were joined by Ned, who had slept for a few hours with Consuelo in the luxurious commander's cabin. Renno had elected to spend the night on the open deck, and he, too, decided to take part in the conference.

Host van der Kuyt had already given orders that put the barque-of-war on a collision course with the brig.

"She's begging to be captured," Escalero said. "It would be a waste to let her escape."

"She won't escape, you can be sure of that," Van der Kuyt replied with a laugh.

Renno and Ned exchanged concerned glances. "We've driven hard all night so we could sail beyond the reach of Spanish sloops-of-war," the latter said. "They well may find us if we tarry."

"We won't tarry long," Van der Kuyt assured him. "Besides, my lads have taken no booty in a long time, and they deserve a reward."

Renno realized that the buccaneers had been cooperative when it had served their interest, but now their natural greed was asserting itself. Rather than argue and cause hard feelings, he and Ned had to stand aside and permit the corsairs to do as they pleased. The only real risk they were taking was that of possible discovery by a Spanish navy warship. He could not forget, nor could Ned, they needed the help of the buccaneers if they hoped to reach the coast of Florida.

Saying nothing, the young Seneca went below to the main deck. Ned followed him, and within moments they were joined by the silent Linnick. Together they watched the barque bear down on the little brig, which identified herself by hoisting the Spanish flag. Host van der Kuyt laughed savagely, then ordered his own Spanish pennant hoisted. Those on the brig obviously felt more secure and made no attempt to flee.

Several nine-pounder guns were unlimbered. Two were fired simultaneously, then the other two roared.

All four shots were wide of the mark, and the brig remained unscathed. Her alarmed officers and crew were confused, however, until Van der Kuyt ordered the Spanish ensign lowered and his own black pennant raised.

Now the men on board the little merchant ship knew the truth, but escape was no longer possible. Maneuvering expertly, Van der Kuyt bore down on the smaller vessel, tacked, and came up alongside her. Grappling hooks were thrown, lashing the two ships together, and eager buccaneers, all heavily armed, poured over the barque's rail and swarmed over the merchantman.

"They're going to slaughter those seamen," Ned said, raising his voice to make himself heard above the din.

Renno nodded, but made no comment. The cruelties perpetrated by so-called civilized men no longer surprised him.

The two officers and ten crew members of the merchant ship tried to defend themselves, but they were badly outnumbered and their resistance was feeble. The brig's master was cut down on his quarterdeck, and his mate crumpled with a bullet in his temple. One by one the others fell, too.

The battle was as brief as Van der Kuyt had promised. Within minutes the pistols of the corsairs fell silent, swords were sheathed, and buccaneers hurried below in search of loot. They returned with weapons, personal belongings, and sea chests. The better part of the cargo consisted of rugs, and they were transferred to the *Valencia* by grinning corsairs.

The last to return to the barque set fire to the smaller ship, and she was burning fiercely by the time the *Valencia* withdrew. Flames rose high in the air, sending black clouds toward the sky, and the brig became a funeral pyre for the twelve men who had died on her deck.

Linnick was shocked. "All who come from the far side of the Great Sea are wicked," he muttered.

"Not all, but many," Renno replied, and felt homesick for the land of the Seneca, where those who stole or killed for pleasure were subjected to severe punishment.

Consuelo came on deck in her doeskin shirt and trousers, part of the bundle that Ned had salvaged for her before they had boarded the schooner. She had scrubbed her face clean of cosmetics and looked very young, innocent, and frightened.

The buccaneers' celebration of their victory was

short-lived. No more than two hours after she left the burning brig, the lookout in the crow's nest sighted another ship. "Cap'n," he called after studying her through his glass, "she's a Spanish sloop-o'-war."

Van der Kuyt cursed volubly. The barque was far more powerful than the smaller warship, but his men were anything but proficient gunners. If he failed to sink her quickly, she could utilize her greater speed and escape with ease.

"She may suspect this is the stolen barque, but her captain can't be certain," he said. "We'll see if we can evade her." He shouted new orders, and to the dismay of Renno and Ned the *Valencia* tacked and sailed toward the southeast, away from the Florida coast.

For hour after hour the schooner followed a zigzag course as she headed back toward the Caribbean Sea, but the captain of the sloop-of-war had the tenacity of a bulldog, and Van der Kuyt could not shake off the smaller ship.

At nightfall, with the sloop-of-war still in pursuit, Renno went to the quarterdeck. His manner was grim, and he addressed Van der Kuyt bluntly. "We kept our promise to you," he said. "You wanted a big ship. You have that ship. You made us a pledge in return. We expect you to keep it."

"It isn't my fault that the sloop-of-war located us."

"It is your fault," Renno said quietly. "You took a brig and set fire to her. It was the smoke that caught the attention of the men on the sloop-of-war. Now you will keep your word to us."

Van der Kuyt eyed him uneasily. This white Indian meant what he said. The buccaneer leader knew that no excuse would suffice, that Renno would not hesitate to take his life if he failed to honor his word.

It would be simple enough to order the white Indian and his companions killed and thrown overboard, but the complications that might result would be dire. Every member of his band was aware of the debt the company owed to Renno, Ned, and the Spanish girl. Not only did the corsairs admire the trio, but they well might turn on a captain who went back on his word. Any man who led desperadoes of the sea kept his position only as long as his men had faith in him. If he proved untrustworthy they would not hesitate to murder him and elect someone else to take his place.

"I'll do what I can for you," Van der Kuyt said, and soon the *Valencia* was sailing toward the northwest again.

Afraid of the tricks he might play, Renno and Ned stayed on deck through the long night, with Consuelo sleeping as best she could a short distance away. Linnick had silently appointed himself to guard her and sat with his back to the bulkhead, watching her, his quiver of arrows over one shoulder and his light knives in his belt.

Captain van der Kuyt stayed on the quarterdeck himself, and in the small hours of the morning he summoned his lieutenants to a conference. They spoke in tones so low that even Renno's keen hearing couldn't hear a word.

Then Van der Kuyt came down to the main deck and spoke wearily. "Ridley," he said, "I've done my best to get rid of that damned sloop, but whenever there's a break in the clouds we can see she's still following us. You and Renno must know I can't sail you to St. Augustine. Part of Spain's New World fleet is stationed there, and I'd be flying straight into the lion's mouth. I have an alternative to suggest to you."

"We're listening," Ned said.

"The Florida coast lies directly ahead. It isn't the part of the colony where you want to go, but it still is Florida. When we get closer we can put you over the side in a boat without losing too much speed. You can make your way ashore from there without difficulty, and I'll do my damndest to lose that confounded sloop in the open Atlantic."

Renno and Ned looked at each other. Both knew it was the best they could expect under the circumstances, better than what they had anticipated.

"We accept," Renno said.

Relief made Van der Kuyt weak as he returned to his quarterdeck.

Lieutenant Escalero took charge. The smallest of the *Valencia*'s boats was lashed to the barque's side, and in it were placed a cask of water, quantities of rice and smoked fish from the ship's plentiful stores, and two sets of oars.

Consuelo was awakened, and Ned went with her to fetch their clothing bundle and spare weapons. "Are you sure you want to come with us?" he asked. "Only the Lord knows what lies ahead for us after we land in that wilderness."

She laughed without humor. "I know what would happen to me if I stayed on board," she said. "Before the sun rises and sets again I would be the buccaneers' whore. I'll go with you."

Captain van der Kuyt remained on his quarterdeck, his attitude indicating that he felt guilty because he had failed to keep his bargain. So it was Lieutenant Escalero who bid farewell to them. "I don't envy you," he said. "Spain has established no settlements or forts in this part of Florida, and for a good reason. Most of the land in this section of the colony is a swamp."

"How far do you estimate we are from St. Augustine?" Ned wanted to know.

Escalero hesitated, then knew he would be doing them a final favor if he told the truth. "More than three hundred miles," he said.

Renno was concerned, and so was Ned. If they were traveling by themselves they had few doubts they could survive in any terrain. But the presence of Consuelo would be a severe handicap, and they had no idea whether Linnick could survive, either, in a strange and possibly hostile land. But they had no alternative other than abandoning all they held dear and becoming permanent members of the corsair band.

Ned lifted Consuelo into the boat and Linnick followed her. Renno silently shook the hand of Escalero, climbed into the little boat and seated himself at the forward set of oars.

"May God go with you," Escalero said as he shook Ned's hand. "You've been good friends, and I just wish we could offer you better repayment than this." His regret sounded genuine.

Ned sat in the stern, and the boat was lowered slowly over the side until it touched the surface of the water. Then the lines were cut, and Ned began to row in order to swing clear.

Renno emulated him, but discovered that his efforts were clumsy. Every Seneca warrior could wield a canoe paddle, but he was unaccustomed to the two long oars. But his natural grace asserted itself, and he improved rapidly.

A number of the buccaneers lined the rail, and Consuelo raised a hand to them in farewell.

Linnick, who had stationed himself in the prow, said quietly, "Land is straight ahead."

Ned peered at the shore over his shoulder as he rowed. "We're about a mile off the coast," he said. "Perhaps a bit more. We should be there soon."

There was no sound but the creaking of the oarlocks as the little craft moved steadily toward land. The sky began to grow brighter as they approached it. Suddenly the first problem presented itself.

"There are many swamps," Linnick said.

Renno looked toward the shore, then nodded. "There is no place to land here."

"We'll have to follow the coast until we find a spot," Ned said.

The task was easier said than done, and they had to row for the better part of an hour before they came to a sand spit onto which they could haul the boat. It was about one hundred yards long, but they had no way of judging its depth.

Daylight had come, and after the three men had pulled the boat up onto the spit, Consuelo stepped ashore, peered out toward the sea, and smiled as she pointed. The *Valencia* was heading out into the Atlantic under full sail, but the Spanish sloop-of-war remained on her heels, just beyond the range of her guns.

"Van der Kuyt will be able to tolerate that shadow for just so long," Ned said with a chuckle. "And then he'll try to blast the sloop right out of the water. He may come to wish he hadn't wanted a warship."

The problems of the *Valencia* were no longer of interest to Renno. He and Linnick began to gather clams, crabs, and other shellfish, while Ned and Consuelo made a fire of dried driftwood and seaweed. All of them agreed with Renno that they would be wise to save their provisions for a later time, when they might be needed.

As they ate a hearty breakfast their spirits improved. They were free of the buccaneers. It was true that a long march to St. Augustine awaited them, but they had already overcome so many obstacles, they could not worry about the future.

Renno guessed they might spend as long as a month in the wilderness before they reached St. Augustine.

"If we can travel ten miles each day," he said, "we can reach the Spanish town of St. Augustine in just over four weeks."

Consuelo knew his comment was addressed to her. "I'll manage," she said.

Ned knew that, unlike Betsy, she had no knowledge of the wilderness. He squeezed her hand, smiled at her, and said, "Don't worry. We'll look after you."

When the meal was finished, Renno went off to explore the sand spit and was followed by Linnick. They exchanged no words as they walked, their faces impassive when they returned to the small beach.

"The insects here are ferocious," Ned said as they approached. "They're so tiny you can't see them, but they sting like hornets, and their bites itch like the devil."

"There are worse problems," Renno replied. "These

hills of sand go inland for about a mile. We seem to be on an island, with the sea on one side—and a swamp on the other three sides."

"How bad a swamp?" Ned asked.

Renno's expression did not change. "Very bad. It stretched as far as I could see. I tested it, and I sank in mud above my knees. The vines are so thick and there are so many exposed roots in the water that no boat can go there."

"Then I reckon we'll have to find another landing place where the earth is firm and dry."

"The swamp is everywhere," Renno said. "I looked from the top of a sand hill. But that way," he added, pointing toward the north, "about two miles from this place, there is a river that empties into the sea. There are swamps on both sides of the river. But it will carry us inland."

"The boat is not good," Linnick said, breaking his silence. "We need a canoe of the Arawak to travel on that river."

Renno shrugged. He, too, knew the blunt-nosed craft was not appropriate for travel through a swampy area, but they had nothing else.

"We'd best be on our way before the sun moves any higher," Ned said.

"Wait." Renno hastily began to collect more clams and crabs. He cooked them on the dying fire, then placed them inside the boat. "We do not know what may lie up the river," he said. "But this way we are certain we will eat again tonight without using the provisions of the buccaneers."

They launched the boat again, then rowed northward toward the mouth of the river. The task took longer than they had anticipated because the current was strong, and a sweating Ned removed his shirt, even though the insects attacked his torso with ferocious abandon. Consuelo slapped repeatedly at her arms and neck and finally found a square of gauzelike silk in her belongings that she draped over her head and face.

The river was more than one hundred feet wide at

its mouth, but it grew narrower as the party rowed inland, and by mid-afternoon it was no more than ten feet wide. The junglelike swamp became increasingly dense on both sides, and behind reeds that rose at least ten or fifteen feet from the muddy surface of the earth stood an impenetrable morass of thorny bushes and thick, tangled vines. Here and there were scrub trees no higher than the reeds, their branches imprisoned by vines.

The water that flowed gently toward the sea remained clear, however, and after Renno tested it he nodded, then handed the drinking container to each of the others. Finally he refilled the cask by immersing it in the stream, then hauling it on board again.

Consuelo, as she watched, became aware of the first law of survival in the wilderness: it was imperative to replenish supplies of food and water at every opportunity.

As the party moved farther inland the breeze died away, and although the sun frequently was obscured by foliage that drooped above the little river, the heat was intense, the dampness almost suffocating. "I can understand why the Spaniards haven't set up any forts or encouraged colonization in this part of Florida," Ned said. "I can't help wondering if there isn't some better route to the north."

Renno remained matter-of-fact. "If there is such a route," he replied, "we will find it."

Gradually the vines that extended across the narrow waterway became thicker, and ultimately the travelers were forced to halt, unable to proceed any farther.

Renno was puzzled. "The river does not become thinner ahead," he said, "but the growth becomes worse."

Linnick quickly lowered himself over the side into waist-deep water. "In the land of the Arawak," he declared, "there are many swamps. Linnick will learn what lies ahead." He waded forward slowly, one of his light knives in each hand, and cut a path for himself through the thick tangle of vegetation.

Forced to wait for his report, Renno and Ned refrained from speculation. Both knew they might be compelled to retrace their steps to the coast and find another, larger inlet that would enable them to travel toward the north. Consuelo was already tiring after the long day, and they didn't want to discourage her, even though both realized that many days of painful exploration might be needed before they found a suitable route.

Linnick at last returned with word that the thick vines spanned the river for a distance of somewhat more than one hundred feet. From that point forward, as nearly as he could judge, the river became clear again.

They decided to push onward. Ned stood at the stern, using one of his oars as a pole to propel the ungainly boat forward, while Renno and Linnick crouched at either side of the prow, slashing at the vines with their knives. Progress was almost maddeningly slow, and the day was far gone by the time they saw the expanse of the little stream stretching out ahead of them again.

The time had come, Renno knew, to search for a place where they could spend the night, but he could see no high ground anywhere. If necessary they could remain in the boat, with the men taking turns on sentry duty, but the little craft was so crowded it was only a last resort.

Dusk came with still no sign of a sanctuary. Only Ned was rowing now, Consuelo drooping and occasionally napping on the seat in front of him. Renno replaced Linnick in the prow, making full use of his superior eyesight as he peered ahead in the gloom. A long time elapsed before he was able to give his companions any encouragement.

"It looks as though the river parts ahead of us," he said. "There appears to be an island between the two forks."

Ned rowed more rapidly, and they came to the island, where trees somewhat taller than they had seen elsewhere were clustered. Renno and Linnick leaped ashore, then pulled the boat up onto the mossy bank. Ned and Consuelo waited while the two Indians made a tour of the island.

"The land is solid for several hundred feet," Renno said when he returned with an armload of firewood. "We should be safe and dry here."

Linnick came back to the campsite a short time later, grinning as he extended his cupped hands. He was carrying a number of delicate, speckled birds' eggs. "There are many more eggs," he said. "Birds make their home on this island."

Ned built a fire, and the Indians scoured the island, each returning repeatedly with handfuls of eggs.

Consuelo's spirits revived. The fire dried her damp clothes, and the prospect of the meal cheered her.

Then Linnick appeared again, this time carrying a large, white bird with a graceful, long neck. He had killed it with a single arrow, he explained. There was enough meat for supper and breakfast as well.

Renno showed Consuelo how to make a spit out of forked sticks. Her energy restored, she began to roast the bird after he had plucked the feathers and removed its interior organs. "This is better than life with the buccaneers," she said, obviously enjoying herself.

Linnick wove a little platform, and when the bird was cooked Renno split it and put half on the platform to keep it above the surface of the ground until morning. The eggs were placed in the coals, one by one, and the travelers began to eat the meat, which had a strong taste, surprisingly like that of a duck.

All at once Consuelo began to scream loudly, the terrified sound piercing the gloom.

The men were on their feet instantly, and Ned demanded, "What's wrong?"

Consuelo continued to scream and was so frightened she could not speak. She seemed frozen, unable to move, but at last, still hysterical, she pointed with a shaking finger.

Crawling slowly toward her was a large snake, perhaps three inches in diameter and four to five feet long, its scales gleaming a greenish-copper color in the light of the campfire. Its tongue flicked in and out ominously, and there seemed little doubt that it had selected her as its victim.

Renno reacted at once, drawing a tomahawk from his belt and hurling it at the serpent. His aim was deadly. The snake's head was separated from its body, which writhed convulsively.

Consuelo continued to scream until Ned took her in his arms and calmed her.

"I'm sorry," she said at last. "I know I shouldn't have made such a scene. But I've loathed snakes all of my life, and I can't help it."

Linnick deftly removed two small sacs of poison from the rear of the snake's head, then dipped the tips of his light arrows into the venom. Renno nodded in approval. He had regarded the Arawak's arrows as unfit for any purpose except that of bringing down birds and small game, but now Linnick was armed with a truly deadly weapon.

Ned had to soothe Consuelo for a long time before she grew calm enough to eat the rest of her meal. Even then she looked around repeatedly, searching the ground.

"Have no fear," Renno told her. "Now that we know snakes are nearby we will not let them harm you."

That night he and Linnick took turns keeping watch. Consuelo slept in Ned's protective embrace.

In the morning, while the fire was being built again, Renno quietly went to the center of the island, where he had seen a tree that stood fifteen to twenty feet tall. He climbed it with ease, then peered ahead. The right branch of the river, beyond the end of the island, was gradually reduced to a trickle, and no boat could navigate in those waters. But the branch on the left, which meandered slightly toward the northwest, remained wide and clear as far as the young Seneca could see.

Habit caused him to scan the horizon in other directions, too, and when he gazed toward the south he suddenly became motionless. A canoe made of several layers of bark sat in the river, beyond a bend which made it impossible for those at the campsite to see it. Seated in the craft, patiently waiting for the travelers to resume their journey, were two husky Indian warriors. Unaware that they were under observation, they neither moved nor spoke.

Renno studied them at length, taking in every detail of their appearance. Their skin was darker than that of the braves of most nations, double scalp locks were hanging down the backs of their necks, and instead of war paint they had daubed their faces and torsos with a black stain that appeared to be more or less indelible. They carried bows and quivers of arrows, and in their belts were stone knives.

Renno silently descended to the ground again and returned to his companions. First, speaking in English, he told them they would follow the left branch of the river when they left the island.

Then, not wanting to alarm Consuelo, he reverted to Seneca. "We are followed by two warriors," he said.

Ned frowned and replied in the same tongue. "Are they enemies?"

"They are the friends of no other nation," Renno replied. "They are Seminole."

His brother-in-law failed to grasp his meaning.

"The Seminole are not a true nation," Renno explained. "Many were Creek and Hitchiti. The laws of those nations are strict. Braves who did not want to obey the laws ran away. Together they formed the Seminole nation. They have been joined by black slaves of the Spaniards who ran into the swamps from the homes of their masters. The Seminole are a wicked people."

"Why are they wicked?" Linnick wanted to know.

"They raid the towns of other nations and steal women who will give them children. The Seminole," he

237

added, glancing for an instant at Consuelo, "will take many risks to capture a woman."

Consuelo knew she was being discussed, but she knew better than to probe. In the many weeks they had spent together she had learned that Renno told her only what he deemed it best for her to know.

"It is said in the councils of the Iroquois," he continued, "that the men of Spain wish to make the Seminole their allies. But they make their home far from the land of the Seneca. So no warrior knows if this is true."

"Do you think they will attack us?" Ned was very wary.

"Not for the present time," Renno replied. "First they will follow to see where we travel in these swamps and marshes. Only then will they try to kill us and take the woman from us."

Ned reverted to English. "I'm damned if I intend to wait for that to happen!"

Renno merely shrugged.

After breakfast the journey was resumed, the travelers taking many hard-cooked birds' eggs with them. Somewhat to Ned's surprise Renno made no attempt to maintain quiet, but conversed from time to time in a loud, clear voice. Obviously he was making no attempt to conceal their whereabouts from the Seminole braves; on the contrary, he appeared to be going out of his way to convince them he was unaware of their presence.

Twice that day tangled vines again impeded their progress, and both times Linnick went ahead on foot to investigate. Then he and Renno hacked at the heavy growth while the boat inched forward. It amused Renno that they were making the task easier for the Seminole who were following them, but he said nothing.

In mid-afternoon they came to another island, considerably larger than the previous one. Renno proposed they make their new camp there, but insisted they go to the north end of the island.

Ned did not argue, but raised an eyebrow. Renno offered no explanation, even though he knew it was probable, as Ned undoubtedly realized, that the Seminole would camp at the south end of the island.

Linnick went off to collect eggs and, if he could, bring down another bird. Renno announced that he had just discovered there were fish in the surrounding waters, so he made himself a line and hook with a thin vine and a long, barbed thorn. He remained within sight of the fire that Consuelo and Ned built and tended, and no one had to tell the latter that he was staying nearby so he would be prepared to act if the Seminole attacked.

The peace of the evening was not disturbed. Linnick came back with two plump birds slightly smaller than ducks, and Renno caught a large, bony fish that had a sweet taste. They enjoyed a feast, and Consuelo, knowing that Renno was keeping watch for snakes, was relaxed and voluble. Less tired than she had been the previous night, she continued to chat for a time after the meal, but eventually she became drowsy. Ned stretched out beside her, throwing a protective arm over her, and soon she dropped off to sleep. He started to doze, too, but was wide awake instantly when Renno touched him lightly on the shoulder. A quick gesture indicated that Renno and Linnick were taking themselves elsewhere, and they moved off into the thick underbrush before Ned could protest or question them.

Making no sound, Renno made his way to the south end of the island, noting with approval that the Arawak was equally silent. They halted, and peering out through the heavy foliage, they saw that the two Seminole braves were asleep, with their weapons on the mossy bank close beside them. The remains of a meal were scattered nearby, and it was evident that, unable to make a fire for fear of detection, they had eaten a raw fish and a raw bird.

Renno felt no pity for the braves and suffered no

sense of guilt for the steps he felt obliged to take. The world he had always known had been comprised of two groups, friends and enemies. No man was regarded as neutral, and in case of doubt he was branded as a foe. Certainly the Seminole were enemies: no warrior secretly trailed his friends through the wilderness.

Drawing one of his tomahawks, Renno balanced it in his hand. He had to throw it a distance of more than twenty feet, and on a night this dark even his exceptional eyesight could play tricks on him. He sucked in his breath, held it, and let fly with the weapon. The tomahawk crashed into the brave's head, and he moaned softly as he died.

That sound, however, was enough to awaken his comrade, who reached for his weapons as he leaped to his feet. Linnick strung his bow, but had no chance to release one of his light arrows.

Renno moved with the speed and grace of a panther, springing into the open area and racing across it, his knife in his hand. Seneca were taught from early boyhood never to hesitate in hand-to-hand combat. The warrior who struck the first blow almost always won the battle, provided his aim was true. That was the real secret, the only secret of Seneca success.

Aware that the Seminole was clutching his own stone knife, Renno concentrated his attention on his foe's throat. He could allow nothing to deflect him from that target. The Seminole tried to sidestep in the hope that his ferocious opponent would brush past him. But Renno knew every trick. His upraised hand shot downward in a swift arc. His steel blade penetrated the Seminole's throat, and the brave crumpled to the ground, blood spurting from his wound.

Linnick came up beside the Seneca and would have struck the fallen man again, but Renno shook his head. The Seminole was dying, and they watched impassively as he expired.

The bows and arrows the dead man had carried were so crude they were useless, and Renno broke them before dropping them back onto the ground. The stone knives could be dangerous, however, so he threw them into the swamp beyond the island.

Linnick broke the silence. "Many evil creatures of the swamp will eat the flesh of these warriors if we do not bury them," he said.

"They will not be buried," Renno replied firmly. "Their bodies will be left here to rot. It may be that other Seminole will follow these two. Let them be warned of the fate that awaits them."

Linnick could understand why the renown of the Seneca had spread as far as the remote islands of the West Indies. This young war chief was as merciless and cold-blooded in dealing with his enemies as he was compassionate and kind to his friends.

Renno examined the Seminole canoe, which had been hauled up onto dry ground, and found it to his liking. It was surprisingly sturdy, with a frame of hardwood, and both the inside and outside of the hull had been smeared with a thick coating of pine tar that made it watertight. It was far narrower than the boat from the *Valencia,* but all four of the travelers could squeeze into it, and by juggling their belongings they could find enough room to carry their water casket, the emergency food supplies Captain van der Kuyt had given them, and the bundle of clothing that Consuelo and Ned had brought with them.

A soft grunt indicated his approval. Linnick instantly understood and pushed the craft into the water. Renno joined him a few moments later, two fresh scalps hanging from his belt.

They paddled quietly up the river to the far end of the island, and Renno emitted a shrill bird call to tell Ned they were approaching. Ned required no explanation. The canoe, combined with the scalps, told him all he needed to know.

When morning came no one told Consuelo how they had acquired a craft far better suited for their purposes than the clumsy boat, but she noticed the fresh scalps. Obviously there were foes more dangerous than snakes in this forbidding, waterlogged land.

Renno broke up the ship's boat with a tomahawk, then fed the breakfast fire with the pieces. Although the vessel was no longer of use to him and his companions, he wanted to make certain that other Seminole did not obtain possession of it. Meanwhile, Ned packed away their various belongings in the canoe, distributing them evenly, and although he could envisage no immediate use for the boat's four oars, he took them, too.

Consuelo learned another rule of wilderness survival: nothing of potential value was ever thrown aside or wasted.

The quartet started off again after breakfast, and as Renno and Linnick were far more adept in the employment of paddles than Ned, he stationed himself in the prow, prepared to use his knife to cut away foliage. Renno, who guided the little craft from his seat in the stern, allowed himself the luxury of a slight smile. The canoe was far lighter than the boat had been and was infinitely easier to handle in these strange waters.

By that night they had penetrated deep into the interior of Florida, but found no indication they were drawing near the outer limits of the swamps. In fact, they were forced to spend the night on a muddy sandbar so small they had to crowd together. No food was available, so they had to eat some of the rice and smoked fish from the *Valencia*'s stores.

There appeared to be no fish in the vicinity, either, although Linnick tried his luck at dawn. Certain roots were edible, he said, presenting several to his companions. Renno and Ned chewed them dutifully, but Consuelo found their taste so bitter that her breakfast consisted of only a little rice.

As they repacked the canoe before starting out again, Renno, who had just loaded the muskets into the craft and was returning for the water cask, noted idly that a large log was floating a few feet away. It was of a different type of wood than any he had seen in the swamp country, but he paid scant attention to it.

Then the log was swept up onto the sandbar, and Consuelo gasped.

Renno was stunned. This was no log. Instead, it was the strangest, most menacing living creature he had ever seen. It was fifteen to twenty feet long, weighing hundreds of pounds, and it had a long, powerful tail that it switched from side to side. Renno recognized the danger at once: a single blow of that tail could knock a man unconscious and render him helpless. The beast was covered with a thick hide that resembled horned scales, its eyes were located on the top of its triangular-shaped head, and when it opened its huge mouth the Seneca saw two rows of yellow teeth so long and pointed they looked like a wolf's fangs.

Never had Renno encountered such a monster, and for a wild moment he imagined that the manitous had sent an evil spirit to punish him for some transgression that had displeased them.

"My God!" Ned cried. "An alligator!"

Renno was consoled by the realization that the creature was real rather than imagined. But he knew that he faced it alone, that the others were behind him, making it impossible for Ned to use his pistol or one of the rifles in the cramped space.

The alligator, moving with surprising speed, approached Renno by supporting itself on its paws. Reacting quickly and staying clear of the creature's tail, Renno fitted an arrow into his bow, which he drew taut.

Ned groaned in frustrated anguish. There was no time, he knew, for his brother-in-law to leap to one side and give him a chance to put a bullet into the beast.

The alligator opened its huge mouth again. Renno sent his arrow into the alligator's upper palate, which it penetrated. The heavy tail thrashed violently from one side to the other.

Renno saw that the strong, tropical wood of his arrow neither bent nor broke as the creature tried in vain to snap its powerful jaws closed again. He was uncertain that he could defeat the alligator. Reaching quickly for another arrow, he shot it into the beast's upper palate, then sent a third after it.

The pain-maddened alligator stopped advancing, but tried to turn sideways so it could avenge itself with its tail. Renno instantly leaped out of the way.

This gave Ned the chance he was seeking, and a pistol shot broke the quiet of the swamps. His bullet put out one of the alligator's eyes, penetrating its brain. The creature died slowly, its tail thrashing more and more feebly until it collapsed on the sandbar. Renno took a single forward step, intending to retrieve his arrows.

"No!" Linnick told him. "Often the great lizard only pretends he is dead."

With great regret Renno realized that even his steel blade might not cut through the incredibly tough hide. But the practical side of his nature forced him to ask, "Does man eat the meat of this beast?"

"I've never known anyone who has tried it," Ned said dryly.

Linnick was far more vehement. "When a warrior eats the flesh of the great lizard, the spirit of the lizard enters his soul."

Renno abandoned any thought of utilizing the meat and followed the others to the canoe.

Consuelo was badly shaken. But Renno put the incident out of his mind. His life had been spared, and henceforth he would be alert whenever he saw a log on or near the water's edge. This strange and eerie wilderness in no way resembled the forests in which he felt so completely at home. It was obvious that one could not relax for a moment here.

He and Linnick paddled steadily, and the vegetation that lined the banks of the little river became increasingly sparse as the morning wore on.

"Perhaps we're coming to the end of the swamp," Consuelo said, voicing the thought of all.

The hope appeared to be realized shortly after noon when they saw a long stretch of dry land directly ahead. The river grew so narrow they had to climb ashore. Renno and Linnick balanced the canoe on their shoulders, and the former also managed to carry what remained of the food supplies. Ned hoisted the water keg to one shoulder and, holding his musket in his free hand, walked beside Consuelo. They made their way through patches of knee-high scrub grass and saw that the landscape was dotted with drooping palmetto trees.

There appeared to be no other vegetation in the area, and after spending so much time in the swamp they were surprised to see that the ground under their feet was parched and cracked. They soon discovered why. The sun that beat down on them from a cloudless semitropical sky was blistering, and the lack of a breeze intensified the heat. Even the ground beneath the soles of Renno's moccasins felt hot. Neither in Hispaniola nor in Cuba had he been aware of such acute discomfort.

"I'm dizzy," Consuelo said.

They stopped long enough to give her a drink of precious water from the cask, but Renno refused to linger. "The sun here dries the bones of men and turns them white," he said. "We must find shelter."

They resumed their march, with Ned occasionally shifting the heavy water keg from one shoulder to the other. Linnick made no complaint, but it was plain that he, too, was encountering difficulty. From time to time he stumbled, and his shoulders sagged.

Renno, who was in the lead, quietly took more of the canoe's weight onto his own shoulder. He was slightly queasy, but his strength remained unimpaired. He knew he could continue indefinitely. He realized, however, that his companions were growing weaker, and that ultimately they would be forced to halt.

Heat waves danced before the young Seneca's eyes, and he marched methodically, sometimes wondering if his vision was impaired. He raised his head and looked up at the sky, blinking rapidly, and then he stopped short.

A bird was approaching at a great height. He wondered if he dared to hope. Then it came lower, and a feeling of great joy swept over him, overwhelming him. The manitous had not deserted him. The bird was a hawk.

It flew lower still, circled overhead, and flew off to the north in a straight, unwavering line, soon disappearing from sight.

"What we do is right," Renno told his companions in a hoarse voice. "Soon we will find food and shelter and water."

Linnick accepted anything his Seneca mentor said, and somehow found the inner strength to go on.

Ned Ridley wondered what had happened to make his brother-in-law so positive, but he knew better than to ask. On rare occasions in the past he had known Renno to be endowed with the ability to foretell the future, a trait he shared with the Great Sachem of the Iroquois. A civilized man presumably had the right to scoff, but Ned, like the Arawak, was inclined to accept the flat statement at face value. He, too, called on his inner reserves.

Consuelo was bewildered, convinced that the sun had deprived her companions of their senses. But she dragged on, planting one foot in front of the other and praying that the ordeal soon would come to an end.

In mid-afternoon Renno pointed his musket straight ahead. "There we will rest," he said.

The others were startled when they drew closer and saw a patch of deep woods.

The escape from the blazing sun was a relief, but Renno did not stop until he caught a glimpse of a pond directly ahead. Lowering his end of the canoe to the ground, he crept forward, beckoning Ned to follow him. Ned obeyed and he smiled quietly when he saw a number of wild ducks floating on the surface of the pond.

Renno fitted an arrow into his bow and shot one of the ducks. The other ducks rose at once, their wings flapping, but Ned brought down a second with his musket. "I reckon we'll eat a good supper tonight," he said.

They made their camp near the base of a sycamore tree a short distance from the pond. Renno discovered a spring of cold, clear water that fed into the pond, and they all drank until they could hold no more. Then they swam in the pond, and after they dressed again, Consuelo found a large patch of dark red berries in a spot where the sun filtered through the thick branches of the trees that formed a canopy overhead.

Linnick said the berries were edible, so he and Renno hacked away bushes studded with thorns that protected the patch. Linnick prepared the ducks while Renno made a fire, and Ned helped Consuelo gather enough berries to form a mound almost a foot high. That night they ate a delicious meal, and their difficulties were temporarily forgotten.

Long before daybreak Linnick was awake, and when the others arose he presented them with two dozen small fish that he had caught in the pond. While the fish cooked in the coals they ate more berries, and their spirits were high.

"What a curious insect," Consuelo said, pointing to a creature about half the size of her fist. It resembled a shellfish and was moving toward her.

Linnick was the first to react. Quickly removing a moccasin, he killed the insect with it.

"That was a scorpion," Ned said somberly. "It has a sting that might or might not kill you, but it sure would make you sick."

The joy drained out of Consuelo.

Renno, who had never before seen a scorpion, either, examined it with care. He had felt safe because these woods were similar to the forests he knew and loved, but he had been mistaken. There were countless dangers in this hot country with which he was unfamiliar, and he made it a point to remember each one.

Ned and Consuelo talked throughout the meal, which Renno found irritating although he did not show it. He ate quickly in his usual mealtime silence, then climbed the highest tree he could find to study the terrain ahead.

When he returned to the ground he was grave. "In another mile these woods will end," he said. "A sea of mud stretches ahead of it, and then the swamps begin again."

Consuelo covered her face with her hands for a moment, then forced her arms to her sides.

"What is the extent of this sea of mud, as you call it?" Ned asked.

Renno shrugged. "From here one cannot tell where the mud ends and the swamp begins. All I know is that the water, far off, looks deep enough for us to ride in the canoe."

"We'll have to go forward," Ned said. "We have no choice. We've already come at least a hundred miles, so we must be one-third of the way to St. Augustine, perhaps even more."

Consuelo's smile was stiff, but at least it was a smile, and she congratulated herself for not bursting into tears. This fear-laden journey seemed interminable.

They reached the edge of the woods in a short time, and then Linnick, with one end of the canoe balanced on a shoulder, took the lead as they waded into the ankle-deep mud. He appeared to have an instinct for knowing where to find dry patches, where the mud was the least deep, and only infrequently did he and his companions sink knee-high into the slime.

They made their way slowly, painstakingly, and eventually the mud gave way to water, which reached as high as their calves. Renno noted that this portion of the swamp was alive with eels, which could provide the party with food, but he refrained from calling attention to them, afraid that Consuelo's fear of snakes might cause her to become hysterical again.

Linnick halted, studying the morass that lay ahead, and after a long time he pointed toward the right, then started off in that direction. Renno was not surprised when they came to a small river, where they launched the canoe. He noted immediately that it flowed toward the north. Its movement was sluggish, but that did not matter. The waterway was taking them in the right direction.

He took his place in the stern, with Consuelo in front of him and the other two men crowded near the prow, ready to cut away vines and other obstacles. Gradually the river became wider, with foliage increasingly confined to its banks, so Linnick picked up the other paddle and Ned remained alone at the prow.

Consuelo was the first to comment. "This swamp isn't as bad as the one we've left behind us," she said.

Ned turned and grinned at her. "Perhaps the worst of our troubles are at an end."

Her quiet sigh was an expression of a fervent hope.

Renno continued to paddle steadily and without pause. Their progress was infinitely better than it had been at anytime since they had first come ashore, and there seemed to be good cause for optimism. But he refused to allow himself to feel pleased. One rule of the wilderness was inviolable, even in this strange and forbidding land that bore so little resemblance to the northern forests he knew and loved. The unexpected was commonplace, and a warrior had to be prepared to face any emergency.

After the thought struck him, he became uneasy, and after rounding a sharp bend in the river a sixth sense prompted him to look back over his shoulder.

The party was being trailed by another canoe. In it were three dark-skinned warriors wearing double scalp locks, their faces and torsos smeared with black dye. The Seminole were not abandoning the chase.

Chapter X

Adrienne Wilson sat in the sun at the edge of her mother-in-law's rose garden, gently rocking her infant daughter's cradle. Patience was sleeping peacefully, and after a time Adrienne put down the book she was reading and looked with delight at the baby. Little Pat already showed a strong resemblance to both of her parents, and Adrienne knew that all of her prayers had been answered.

From her vantage point she caught sight of the mounted postman, who came to the house three times each week, but she paid scant attention to him. Most mail that came to the house was addressed to General Wilson, and occasionally Jeffrey received a letter, but she herself knew so few people outside the Fort Springfield area that no one ever wrote to her.

So she was surprised, a short time later, when Jeffrey, who had just returned to the house after spending the morning in the fields, approached her with a square of parchment that bore a seal on the back.

She raised a finger to her lips.

Jeffrey laughed. "Pat sleeps through anything, including thunderstorms," he said, kissing his wife and handing her the letter. "This is from Virginia."

"It must be from Betsy. I wrote to her after Pat was born." Adrienne broke the seal, unfolded the parchment, and read hastily. "It is from Betsy," she said. "She's had a son. His Seneca name is Ja-gonh, and his English name is James. Isn't that wonderful? She says he looks more like Renno every day."

"That's grand."

"I was half-joking, you know, when I told her that someday our children might marry," the beaming Adrienne said. "But it really is possible. I wonder if they'd live in Virginia or the land of the Seneca."

Jeffrey abruptly ended her idle speculation. "What news does she send about Renno?"

His wife's smile faded. "She hasn't heard a direct word, and neither has Colonel Ridley. The only news —and it really is an absence of news—comes from a couple of Ridley shipmasters who swear that the brig carrying Renno and Ned never put into Havana."

"I was afraid of that," Jeffrey muttered.

Adrienne stared up at him, her expression grave. "Are you suggesting that something terrible may have happened to them?"

"I'm not suggesting anything, my dear. I'm trying to examine facts. I know that Ned can take care of himself in a crisis, and I doubt if any man on earth is more resilient than Renno. But they're mortal, after all. They knew the odds were against them when they went off on their mission."

Her concern deepened.

Jeffrey went to the far side of the garden for another straight-backed chair, returned with it, and sat beside Adrienne. "It's useless to guess whether Renno and Ned are alive or dead. All we know for certain is that they should have come home many weeks ago. My father and Colonel Ridley have been discussing the possibility of sending other scouts to learn the situation in New Spain. If and when they look into the matter seriously, I intend to volunteer."

Adrienne became alarmed. "I forbid it!" she exclaimed. "For the baby's sake. And because I'm selfish."

"Renno had a wife, too, you know," he replied firmly. "And he knew they were going to have a child. But that didn't prevent him from volunteering and going off to Havana."

She tried to blink away the tears.

"It's for your sake and Pat's that I'd be willing to go, my dear. You were actively persecuted by Louis of France because you were a Huguenot. Suppose he gains control of Spain, as we're afraid he will. I very much doubt that we could withstand a simultaneous attack from the French and Spanish colonies. And if we should lose a war, you and Pat wouldn't be safe anywhere. There would be no place you could go."

"I know you're right, Jeffrey," Adrienne said. "But I so dread the thought of losing you."

"Betsy must have felt the same way about Renno," he replied. "But she stood aside when he took an exceptionally dangerous assignment."

"I'm not sure," she murmured, "that I'm as strong as Betsy. I'd be lost without you, and so would Pat."

"Well," he said, stroking her shoulder and arm, "I haven't gone off quite yet. I haven't lost faith in Renno, and neither has the high command. I'm not saying he can perform miracles, but he'll come closer to it than any other man alive!"

Renno waited until they made camp on a patch of relatively high ground before breaking the news to his companions that they were being pursued again. Linnick was not surprised and nodded calmly. Ned made no comment, but grimly inspected his musket. Consuelo had learned to keep her emotions under control in the presence of these courageous men, so she managed to conceal her deep dismay.

"Our situation now is worse than it was," Renno said. "This time we are being followed by three braves, not two. That means they know we killed their comrades and seek vengeance."

"You think they found the bodies of the other Seminole, then?" Ned asked.

"I am certain of it. Not only that, but they must recognize our canoe as one of their own. They will not rest until they have killed you and Linnick and me, and can take Consuelo into captivity."

Consuelo's composure was badly shaken.

Ned's jaw jutted forward. "We should strike first," he declared. "Their bows and arrows are no match for our firepower."

Renno shook his head. "Ordinarily I would agree with you. If we faced only three warriors, I would advise that we attack them at once. The Seminole are ferocious fighters, but also canny. They would not send just three men to kill us. The warriors I saw today are only an advance party. There are many others who follow them. They intend to overwhelm us with great force. That is the way of inferior tribes."

"What can we do?" Ned demanded. "Just sit back and wait for a bloodbath?"

"Never," Renno replied. "I do not yet know what we should do. Tonight we will build our fire higher, much higher, and Linnick and I will take turns keeping watch. The Seminole will not come near us if we make a fire that throws much light. Tomorrow will come, and we will find a way to defeat them."

In spite of her fear, Consuelo was curious. "How can you be so confident, Renno?"

The young war chief stared into the fire. "One Seneca," he said quietly, "has the strength to stand alone against many Seminole. I am the son of Ghonka." Apparently he felt no other explanation was necessary.

Ned appreciated his self-confidence, but nevertheless was badly worried. If Renno was right and the Seminole had sent a large war party in pursuit of the travelers, the outlook was at best very discouraging.

The night passed without incident. The flames of the fire rose high above the little camp, fed frequently by Renno, then by Linnick. Consuelo and Ned slept fitfully, and both marveled that the two Indians could enjoy their rest when not on sentry duty.

Early in the morning Renno went off alone to catch and skin a number of eels. Chopping them into pieces, he wrapped the meat in large, wet leaves, which he cooked in the coals, and Consuelo thought she was eating fish. The meal was delicious, but she had little appetite.

Renno commanded her to eat. "It may be that many hours will pass before we can take food again," he said.

Ned studied him. "You have an idea," he said.

The young Seneca shrugged. "The manitous have been whispering to me," he said, "but I have not yet heard their voices clearly. When the right time comes, they will tell me what to do."

Consuelo became even more apprehensive. She did not doubt that Renno believed in the spirits that guided him, but she had no faith in what she regarded as mythical creatures.

Hoping to gain something of a head start on the Seminole, they left the fire burning as they returned to the water in the canoe. Renno and Linnick paddled hard and without respite for hours, and not until late morning did Renno find what he was seeking, another island that stood in the middle of the river, which was now much wider.

Scrub trees, bushes, and vines grew in profusion in the mud-caked soil, and Renno immediately sent the canoe up onto the bank. Then he insisted that they take the craft inland and conceal it. "Soon the Seminole will come," he said, and turned to Consuelo. "I have seen you shoot at targets with a musket and a pistol. Your aim is good. Will you shoot at a living target?"

She nodded, her lips compressed.

"Ned," Renno said, "make certain that all the firearms are loaded and ready for use. You will not have too many chances to reload." He handed his brother-in-law his own musket.

"Aren't you going to use it?"

"When my foes are many," Renno replied, "I use the weapons of my people. Linnick, you know what to do."

The Arawak inclined his head, and when he raised it again his eyes were shining. Like the Seneca, he was not disturbed by the prospect of facing overwhelming odds.

"We will hide in the brush," Renno said, arranging them in a single line facing toward the south. "No one will shoot until I give the signal. Consuelo, it will not be easy for you, but you must wait. All that I plan depends upon surprise."

Consuelo wasn't too sure what he meant, but assured him that she would obey. Ned, who began to figure out Renno's plan, was content to let him take the lead.

Flies buzzed overhead in the hot sunlight, and an occasional mosquito stung one or another of the party, but they had become so accustomed to the presence of insects they paid no attention.

Renno had positioned himself on their right side, a short distance from the gradual slope that was the only place a landing could be made on the island. He waited patiently, almost complacently, his bow and arrow on the ground beside him. He thought he detected a flicker of movement, and as he turned his head toward the water he saw a snake slithering through the mud toward him. It was small, no more than two feet in length and about as thick as his thumb, but long experience with snakes in his own part of the world made Renno realize that this creature, in spite of its size, was dangerous to humans.

Consuelo held the place to his left, and he was afraid that, if she saw the snake, she would not be able to curb her hysteria. The Seminole moving down the river would be sure to hear her screams, and the vital element of surprise on which his whole battle plan depended would be ruined. He had to kill the snake surreptitiously.

He drew his knife, tensed, and waited. When he judged that the snake had moved within arm's length, Renno slashed at it. But the snake was more agile than he had thought possible. Rearing back to avoid the blow, it started forward again, moving with surprising speed.

Knowing he could not afford to miss a second time, Renno utilized the same device he intended to employ in combat with the Seminole. He waited until the snake was no more than a foot from his leg, then brought his blade down in a swift, decisive cut. This time his aim was true, and he saw he had separated the creature's head from its body.

Not bothering to look at it again, he glanced at Consuelo. She was totally absorbed as she stared at the bend in the river above the island.

Their patience was rewarded when a canoe swept around the bend, manned by three warriors. Consuelo raised her musket. Renno touched her lightly on the shoulder and shook his head.

A moment later she understood. A host of other canoes followed the lead craft, with as many as five or six warriors crowded into each of them.

Renno estimated there were thirty to forty braves, and he was pleased. How Ghonka and El-i-chi would enjoy taking part in this fight with him. He strung his bow, then continued to wait.

Consuelo sucked in her breath. The warriors in the first canoe were so close now that she could actually count the number of shells they had strung on their crude necklaces.

"Fire!" Renno called softly, then waited to see how his companions reacted before letting fly with his arrow.

The fight beginning, Consuelo's nervousness vanished. She took careful aim at a point between the eyes of the brave who sat in the prow of the canoe and squeezed the trigger. The shot jolted him upright, then he toppled over the side of the canoe.

Linnick chose the warrior in the middle, and his light arrow soared into the air, then fell gently and imbedded itself in the man's cheek. The poison that impregnated the tip began to do its work, and the brave stiffened, unable to move, his eyes glazed.

Ned coolly dispatched him with his musket, then picked up Renno's musket and fired it at the third man, who pitched forward into the little craft. The canoe, with no one steering it, veered sharply and soon became entangled in the vines and reeds at the far side of the river.

The other warriors were in an uproar. Stunned by the unexpected attack, they slowed their canoes, uncertain how to proceed.

"Reload," Renno called. "We have a moment." He identified a senior warrior by the feathers he wore in his double scalp lock and sent an arrow into the man's throat.

The war chief in command of the Seminole repeatedly barked an order, and his subordinates became steadier. Three canoes advanced simultaneously, and the warriors in the front of the craft strung arrows in their own bows.

"Fire at will," Renno said, and put an arrow into the open mouth of another warrior. An arrow sang far overhead, and Consuelo, identifying the warrior who had shot it, killed him with her second bullet.

"Good," Renno told her.

His praise, rarely given, made her still calmer.

Ned and Linnick wisely concentrated on the braves paddling the canoes, and when the vessels went out of control it was not difficult to pick off the survivors.

Yet another wave of canoes came around the bend in the river, but Renno detected something unusual in the formation. Two of the additional canoes were crowding close behind three others that were exposed to the fire from the island. He guessed that an attempt would be made to land several braves on the island.

He said nothing, continuing to make each of his arrows count, and his shrewd estimate proved correct. The two canoes glided toward the landing place. Now!

"Look to your right," he called. "Forget the canoes in the river!" He sent a tomahawk sailing through the air to emphasize his words, and the first brave to set foot on the island was virtually decapitated.

Linnick began to throw his light knives, and his aim, too, was devastating. Consuelo and Ned, using pistols instead of muskets, brought down two more of the invaders. Linnick accounted for another, and Renno's second tomahawk smashed the skull of the last of the invaders.

Enemy arrows were being directed at the island in clusters now.

"Stay down," Renno directed. "Consuelo, don't raise your head."

Consuelo hugged the ground, reached for her musket again, and resumed firing, reloading with a skill and dexterity Renno admired.

A Seminole arrow grazed Linnick's cheek, but he ignored the slight wound and continued to send his light arrows at the enemy. Then an arrow lodged in Ned's shoulder, but he pulled it out instantly, cursed, and continued to fire, paying no attention to the blood that stained his shirt. The Seminole casualties were heavy, and Renno estimated that twenty or thirty of the braves had been killed or severely wounded. So far the injuries his little band had sustained had been light, but he knew that if the war chief in charge of the Seminole continued to send warriors against the island in successive waves, it would be only a matter of time before the Seminole could land and engage in hand-to-hand combat.

But the defenders kept up their steady fire, and the war chief became discouraged. He shouted an order to disengage and the remaining canoes turned and moved back up the river to the south.

With their retreat, Consuelo didn't know whether to laugh or cry. Then she caught sight of two rough logs drifting toward the far bank of the river, and she had to avert her face when two giant alligators began to feast on the bodies of the dead Seminole.

Renno paid no heed to the spectacle. Instead he and Linnick scalped the Seminole who had landed on the island, then retrieved their tomahawks and knives. Ned pressed a small square of cloth to his shoulder.

For the first time Consuelo noticed his wound. "Are you badly hurt?" she asked.

He shook his head. "The bleeding has stopped."

"Let me see." She pulled his hand away and inspected the wound. The bleeding indeed had stopped, but the arrow had penetrated a considerable depth into his shoulder, and the incision was ugly.

Renno approached and silently looked at the wound, too, prodding it with a finger until Ned winced. Then he opened a small leather pouch hanging on a rawhide thong around his neck.

Consuelo could not look at the fresh scalps hanging from his belt. "What are you doing?"

Renno took a pinch of a powdered substance and stuffed it into the wound. "This is the root of a plant I found in Hispaniola. It is like a plant that grows in the land of the Seneca. It will cause Ned much pain. He will dream strange dreams and say things he will not remember. But by tomorrow his shoulder will be healing well."

Ned was already rocking back and forth in agony, but made no sound.

"We will go now," Renno said. "Consuelo, hold Ned's head in your lap in the canoe, and do not be frightened by what he might say."

Her mind was still on the battle. "The Seminole—"

"They are gone and will not return. You fought with the courage of a Seneca. But now you have another task." Picking up Ned, Renno easily carried him to the canoe and deposited him in it, then dragged the craft back into the water.

In a few moments the journey was resumed, with Renno and Linnick paddling steadily, aided by an increasingly strong current as they moved downstream toward the north.

Ned was silent for about an hour. Then he began to perspire heavily and froth covered his lips. "Consuelo," he shouted in a strained voice, "if you refuse to marry me I'll follow you to the ends of the earth. You'll never get away from me."

"Do not answer him," Renno told her. "He is dreaming now, and he will hear nothing you say to him."

Ned's voice became still louder, and he babbled incoherently.

Consuelo looked down at him, cradling his head, badly worried. Yet she was aware of Renno's seeming lack of concern. The white Indian appeared to experience none of the emotions that were common in other people. Ned cursed at length, wept like a baby, and then laughed loudly and hoarsely.

Consuelo shivered.

Renno continued to paddle calmly for the better part of the afternoon, deaf to his brother-in-law's ranting. Late in the day he saw some high ground off to the right, and although the area was barren he decided to make camp there. Renno again carried Ned ashore.

Linnick began to gather what little firewood he could, and Renno again examined Ned's shoulder. There was no reaction when he prodded it, but for the second time he poked powdered plant root into the wound.

Consuelo was resentful. "He's been growing quiet," she said. "Why are you arousing him again?"

She was so worried that Renno smiled to reassure her. "He needed more of the medicine. This time he will dream in his sleep." He turned to more practical matters. "Tonight we must eat what remains of the food from the *Valencia*. We will find nothing else in this place. And tomorrow we will not eat until we find game or fish where they are more plentiful."

Consuelo had no idea how he knew they could find nothing to eat here, but she took his word. By now she realized that he knew what he was doing.

Mold had formed on the smoked fish, rendering it useless, and the remains of the rice had turned sour, so they had to throw it away, too. Renno and Linnick accepted the need to fast in phlegmatic silence, and Consuelo was glad she had little appetite.

The fire was small, doing nothing to ward off the dampness, and in the early hours of the morning it flickered fitfully and died. Renno and Linnick took turns keeping watch, as usual, and Consuelo, conscious of the deep breathing of Ned beside her, slept fitfully. At dawn Ned stirred for the first time, and she sat up.

He struggled to a sitting position, and when he looked at her his eyes were normal. "I'm famished," he said.

"How do you feel?"

He had forgotten his shoulder. Feeling it gently, he rotated it, then moved it up and down. "It's a trifle stiff, but otherwise it feels fine. Renno," he called, "anytime you want to leave the Seneca and make your home in Norfolk, you can easily establish a practice as a physician there. I just hope you're as good a cook."

"We have no food," Renno said quietly. "We had none last night, either. It is so empty in this place that not even insects come here."

"When do you suppose we'll find something to eat?" Consuelo asked, anxious to accommodate Ned.

Renno shrugged. "Florida is very large. Somewhere ahead there are fish and birds, game and fruit." Without further ado he launched the canoe.

The others were eager to leave, too. Ned was weak, but insisted on sitting in the craft rather than sprawling on the bottom. Consuelo knew his pride was at stake, so she made no objection.

The journey that day seemed endless. The swamps gradually vanished, and the land on either side of the river was dry and hard, the monotony of the brown landscape relieved only by a few tufts of spindly grass.

The bed of the river was more solid now, with gravel resting on rocks, and the water became increasingly clear, although the flow was still sluggish. As Renno and Linnick paddled, they spent long periods gazing into the water, their concentration complete, and ultimately they felt convinced there were no fish. Consuelo needed no one to tell her that there was no edible game or vegetation in the area. Apparently little rain fell in this arid region.

"The swamps were horrid," she said, "but at least we found food there."

Renno was thankful he had been reared as a Seneca. As long as he had water to drink he could survive for days without food. But his companions were less fortunate. Linnick had never encountered such problems in the land of the Arawak, food always having been plentiful in Jamaica and the other lush islands of the Caribbean. Consuelo and Ned required regular sustenance; the latter, as a hardened frontiersman, could do without in case of need, but in his present weakened condition he was far more vulnerable than he otherwise would have been.

A flock of geese appeared overhead, but Renno knew at a glance that the birds were flying far too high to bring down any with either firearms or arrows. Perhaps their luck would change for the better.

When they made camp for the night, it was impossible for them to build a fire for lack of wood. Linnick caught several eels in a small stream that fed into the river, but Consuelo balked at the idea of eating the meat raw. Ned had to persuade her to try, and she did her best, knowing her survival depended on it.

Soon after they resumed their journey the following morning, they encountered a sandbar in the river that impeded their progress. Linnick immediately climbed into the calf-high water, intending to pull the canoe over the shoal. To his astonishment, however, the ground under his feet proved to be very soft, and he began to sink lower.

"My God, he's stepped into quicksand," Ned cried.

Renno immediately made his way to the prow and, stretching out there, caught hold of the Arawak beneath his shoulders, clasping his hands behind the man's back. In spite of his considerable strength, however, Linnick sank deeper into the morass.

Ned could give him only limited help in his debilitated condition. "Linnick," Renno said, "don't try to pull yourself out. You'll just sink deeper. Ned, take hold of my left leg, and no matter what happens, don't let go. Consuelo, take hold of my right leg and do the same."

Linnick clung to Renno and obediently stopped struggling. This was his first experience with deadly quicksand, but he realized his mentor was right. He could do nothing for himself.

Renno held him in a viselike grip until his veins stood out at his temples, his face and torso were drenched with sweat, and he felt pains deep in his chest every time he sucked in breath. By now the Arawak had sunk to his waist in the quagmire, but his condition seemed to have stabilized. He was being drawn no deeper.

Aware that in time his own strength would ebb, Renno had to devise new tactics. "Consuelo," he said, "go now to the stern and try to paddle backward, away from the quicksand."

Consuelo obeyed, but the canoe did not move.

"Help her, Ned," Renno directed.

"But you'll be pulled overboard, too," Ned protested.

"Do as I tell you. Quickly. I can keep my balance here for a little longer."

With great reluctance Ned released his hold, went aft, and picked up the second paddle. Angry because he felt so helpless, his muscled, disciplined body responded, and somehow he overcame his weakness. His paddle dug into the water, and eventually he found a hold in the sandy bottom that was short of the patch of quicksand.

Little by little more of Linnick's torso appeared.

The panting Renno was near exhaustion, but didn't give in. He managed to stay in the little craft, and inch by inch they were able to release more and more of the victim's body.

"Do . . . not . . . move . . . yet," he gasped.

Linnick nodded.

Ned called on his last reserves of strength, plunging his paddle into the riverbed, then poling with all of his remaining might.

At last Linnick came free, his legs floating to the surface. Now, in spite of his numbness, he began to swim upstream.

Renno was able to release him, and for a few moments he sagged at the bottom of the canoe. Then he rallied, went overboard, and, swimming himself, pushed the craft up onto the bank of the river.

All four were so weary that they sprawled on the hard ground. None had the breath to speak. A feeling of relief caused Consuelo to weep, but she managed to check her tears. When Linnick recovered, he tried to thank his companions.

Renno cut him short. "Each of us helps the others," he said.

Eventually they all became steady again, and they proceeded on foot beside the river, with Renno and Linnick carrying the canoe. For a distance of several miles they saw a number of bars in the river and assumed that all were quicksand traps. Not until afternoon did the river narrow and the channel become deeper. They were hungry, tired, and dispirited, but Renno knew it would be useless to stop now.

"Where there is water," he said, "there must be plants and fish. This desert land is strange, but somewhere ahead there must be life."

"It's true we can't turn back to the swamps," Ned said. "We were fortunate to come through them alive, and next time we might not fare as well with the Seminole, either. We've got to go forward."

They launched the canoe again, and with Renno seated in the stern began to move northward once more, making better progress. At sundown the landscape was still bleak, and they had neither food nor a fire when they camped for the night.

Bone-weary, Ned and Consuelo soon dropped off to sleep. Renno signaled Linnick silently to keep watch over them and went forward himself along the bank to investigate conditions farther to the north. His keen sense of smell had told him that a change of some sort awaited the party, but he hadn't wanted to hold out false hopes until he learned more about the terrain.

He trotted easily, expending little effort, and although the night was dark he could nevertheless see a considerable distance ahead. The smell he had detected became stronger, and he felt encouraged. After he ran for several miles he knew that his hunch had been right. The ground became less parched, and with several small streams now flowing into the river, he saw more and more grass.

His pace unvarying, Renno ran until the grass became knee-high. Then he halted abruptly when he saw several cypress trees at the edge of the river, and beyond them made out the familiar silhouettes of yellow pines. Where there were trees there had to be food.

Running even more rapidly, he returned to the camp, where he immediately awakened Ned and Consuelo. When they learned of his discovery, they agreed that they start out again at once, even though it was now the middle of the night.

It was only a short distance by canoe to reach an area where trees were plentiful. Renno did not pause until the forest thickened and they could find ample quantities of firewood.

The exhausted Consuelo and Ned went to sleep again, lulled by the warmth of the fire. Renno found a pond nearby, and Linnick grinned when he heard the dismal croaking of frogs. At the very least they would eat breakfast.

Leaving the Arawak to catch as many frogs as he could, Renno pushed on into the pine forest, sensitive to every nuance of this wilderness that he understood so well. His self-confidence restored, he told himself their days of starvation were at an end.

His optimism was well-founded. He brought down a pair of large rabbits after hunting for only a short time, and in the morning, when Consuelo and Ned awakened, they were cheered immeasurably by the delicious scent of roasting meat. Linnick had done his part, too, and the party feasted on frog as well.

Refreshed and strengthened, they were in high spirits when they resumed their journey. But their hopes were dashed when the river became clogged by tree roots and other vegetation, making travel by canoe far more difficult. Then the river split into several smaller streams, all flowing northward, to be sure, but none navigable.

Once again Renno and Linnick uncomplainingly carried the canoe.

Late in the afternoon Renno studied the ground for some moments, and then instructed the others to make camp. Offering no explanation, he went off alone into the pine forest. The others made a fire, keeping their weapons close at hand as they waited for his return. He reappeared shortly before sundown, the carcass of a deer weighing almost one hundred pounds slung easily across his back. They ate venison for supper and again for breakfast the next morning, cooking the rest of the meat for future consumption.

Starting out on foot, with Renno in the lead, they noted that the soil was rich and black here, but they could not understand why the rivers continued to split and dwindle. They discussed the phenomenon when they stopped to eat at noon, and Renno shrugged.

"I think," he said, "that we may go by water no farther."

"I realize the canoe is becoming more difficult to

carry as the foliage grows thicker," Ned said. "Are you suggesting we leave it behind?"

"We must." Renno was emphatic. "Or we will spend much longer on the trail before we reach the Spanish fort. We had a need for the canoe, but that need is no more."

The men agreed to share the burden of carrying their various belongings, particularly the bundle of clothes that Ned and Consuelo would wear when they came within reach of St. Augustine. Consuelo was reluctant to leave their water cask behind, but Renno made it plain that it was too cumbersome to be carried overland.

"Where there is forest," he said, "there is also water."

Game was plentiful in the deep woods, so they suffered no hunger thereafter, and Consuelo was elated when they came across a patch of red, sweet berries that Renno pronounced edible. Occasionally they encountered a small brook trout, too, as Renno had predicted.

The Seneca was in his element again as he led the party through the wilderness, and even though he maintained a swift pace, Consuelo managed somehow to keep up with the men. She still felt rather ill at ease in the endless forest, but she was becoming acclimated to long marches and made no complaint. The moccasins that Renno fashioned for her out of the deer's hide made it far easier for her to stay on her feet for long periods, and her stamina surprised Ned.

Gradually, as the days passed, Renno became aware of something out of the ordinary about this forest. "Everywhere else in the wilderness," he said after supper one night, "there are Indians. Sometimes those of one nation, sometimes those of several nations. Here there are none."

Even Ned was incredulous. "Are you sure? What you're saying is that this is virgin territory."

Renno nodded solemnly. "No nation lives here. No warriors visit this wilderness."

"Not even the Seminole?" Consuelo wanted to know.

"I have found no signs of the Seminole," Renno assured her, although he could not explain why the members of the tribe did not hunt here.

Traveling conditions were much improved now, but Renno was privately concerned. Ned's wound had healed, but he had not yet regained his full strength and stamina. The fearful journey had harmed Consuelo, too. She gamely made each day's march, but her exhaustion was evident. Renno made up his mind to pause for some days of recuperation when he found the right place.

They came suddenly to just such a place one afternoon. They reached the shore of an inland lake so large that Consuelo at first thought they stood at the edge of the Atlantic Ocean. She would not believe otherwise until, at Renno's urging, she tasted the water and found it was fresh.

Renno called a prolonged halt. There were a half-dozen kinds of fish in the lake, and Linnick caught enough every morning for a huge breakfast. Renno brought down several wild ducks, in the process discovering nests filled with eggs. Ned, with Consuelo's help, dug up three different kinds of edible roots in the forest and also discovered a field of wild scallions. Game was plentiful, too, and for the first time since the party had landed on the North American mainland, there was not only more than anyone could eat but an actual choice of meals.

They swam in the lake before breakfast every morning, then swam again at sundown while their evening fire was building. The area was secure, so Consuelo slept soundly every night, and the smudges beneath her eyes gradually vanished. Ned was growing stronger, and little by little he regained the full use of his arm.

One afternoon, when Renno had gone hunting in the forest and Linnick was fishing in the lake, Ned and Consuelo lolled in the shade beneath a towering pine, resting on a thick, fragrant bed of needles that the tree had shed. Ned avoided discussing their difficult journey.

"First off, as soon as we get up to Norfolk," he said, "you and I are going to be married."

Consuelo gently but firmly shook her head.

He grinned at her. "After all we've gone through," he said, "don't tell me you're still going to turn down my proposal."

"I cannot marry you," she said.

"Damnation, woman, now you're just being stubborn. Who will prevent our marriage?"

Consuelo sat up, brushing pine needles from her doeskins, then locked her hands over one knee as she stared out at the blue, placid waters of the lake. "Too soon we would quarrel and part," she said at last.

"That's absurd!" he retorted.

"It is true," she replied. "You know I no longer have a family anywhere. You know also, after all that has happened, that I can never return to Spain or live in any Spanish colony in the New World. Whenever you and I might disagree, you would feel you had married me only because you were sorry for me and wanted to protect me."

"Of course I want to protect you!" Ned had no idea he was shouting. "As for feeling sorry for you, I never heard such nonsense! By now you ought to know I love you!"

He was so exasperated that he caught hold of her shoulders, intending to shake sense into her. But she looked so forlorn, so helpless that he kissed her instead.

Consuelo clung to him, and soon they made love in earnest, unmindful of their surroundings. Gradually their passion mounted, and not until both were satisfied did they move apart. Then they went for a swim.

When they returned to the shore and dressed, Ned was quietly pleased, convinced that he had won the argument.

Consuelo kept quiet. Certainly she did not deny the strong mutual attraction, and she had to admit she truly loved Ned Ridley. But she still believed his love for her was a result of a misplaced gallantry. She could not allow herself to become the wife of a man who felt obligated to marry her.

This was not the time to make an issue of the matter, however. The mission at St. Augustine still loomed ahead, and other dangers undoubtedly awaited them in the wilderness. Ned was far happier now that he thought he had persuaded her to become his bride, and she would await a more opportune moment to tell him otherwise.

Renno watched his companions being restored to robust health and knew the pause was a wise move. Each day he explored the forest and soon discovered that swamps lay to the southwest of the lake. Apparently the party had reached the lake by way of the only truly dry overland route.

Twice he killed snakes near the edge of the swamps, both of them venomous, but he made no mention of these to Consuelo. Instead he brought the poison sacs to the delighted Linnick, who soaked the tips of his arrows in them.

The Arawak also busied himself for at least a portion of each day whittling a number of short, light spears for himself. Consuelo and Ned were curious about his intended use of these weapons, but they knew better than to ask. It was best, they had learned, not to make unnecessary inquiries of an Indian. In due time, presumably, they would learn Linnick's purpose.

One day Renno brought down both a buck and a doe and took care to smoke the meat of the buck, a long, slow process that continued without pause for three days and nights. Then he rubbed the prepared meat with salt he had found at a lick, and finally divided it into four portions, saying that each would carry a parcel.

"Now we know," he said, "that we will not go hungry again."

The respite lasted for ten days. Then one night, at supper, Renno announced without preamble that they would march again the following morning. "In about ten more days," he said, "we will arrive at the great Florida fort of the Spaniards."

Later a puzzled Consuelo said privately to Ned, "I don't understand. None of us has ever been in Florida. So how is it possible for Renno to know when we'll reach St. Augustine?"

Ned shrugged. "I have no idea," he said. "But I can guarantee you that Renno knows."

They broke camp at dawn the next day. Renno led the group around the portion of the lake that curved toward the northeast. Soon they left the shore behind them and moved through uninhabited forests of varying density. At the end of the second day they could hear surf pounding in the distance, and after climbing over some high sand dunes they stood on the beach, looking out at the Atlantic Ocean.

They helped themselves to clams, mussels, crabs, and other shellfish. Linnick waded out into waist-high surf that night and surprised his companions by using his light spears to catch fish by moonlight. He proved adept at the art and returned to the camp nestled between two dunes with a large mess of fish.

They used driftwood to make their fire, and at Renno's insistence cooked enough fish for breakfast the next day as well as supper. Then, before they went to sleep, he kicked sand onto the fire, extinguishing it. There was no need for him to explain that he suspected there might be potential enemies in the vicinity.

The following day, shortly before noon, as they trudged northward on the hard sand, Renno suddenly called a halt. Then he climbed to the top of a high dune, crouching close to the ground as he drew near the summit. Flattening himself in the scrub grass at the top of the dune, he peered hard toward the north before rejoining his companions at the base.

"We will go inland for a time," he said. "About one mile ahead there is a Spanish fort."

Consuelo was startled. "Surely we haven't come to St. Augustine already!"

271

The Seneca shook his head. "It is a very small fort, made of wood, that sits near the water on a small bay. I think that no more than twenty or thirty soldiers live there."

Ned raised an eyebrow and looked at Consuelo.

"That is the Spanish system," she said. "At home, on the French border in the Pyrenees Mountains, the Spanish army has long kept small forts every few miles. My father told me they keep many such forts in the little islands of the West Indies, too."

Ned was puzzled. "Surely they have farms and orchards beyond the walls of the fort."

Renno shook his head. "The land has been cleared for a few hundred feet from the walls of the fort so no enemies can attack by surprise. But there are no farms and no orchards."

"That also is the Spanish way," Consuelo explained. "Warships and merchant vessels bring food and other supplies to the soldiers. The men always stay inside the garrison."

The practice was far different from that of the English and French, who established their colonies of settlers beyond the perimeters of their protective forts. The Spaniards, neither living off the land nor exploring the countryside, were deliberately cutting themselves off from their New World surroundings. This made their forts vulnerable to attacks by stronger forces, Ned realized, and his father and General Wilson would be delighted to hear it.

For the present Renno's advice made sense. They went inland more than a mile before turning north again, then proceeded cautiously until they knew they had left the little coastal fort far behind them. When they returned to the beach because their progress was more rapid there, Renno took the precaution of stationing himself at least a quarter of a mile ahead of the others. After hearing what Consuelo had said he was anxious not to run the risk of stumbling unexpectedly on another fort.

His best method of protection was to scout as far

ahead as he could. So, after supper that night, he went off down the beach alone, intending to climb a high dune that stood about a half-mile from the campsite.

The surf roared pleasantly, the strong moonlight gave the breakers an iridescent glow, and as Renno walked lightly up the beach he allowed himself the rare indulgence of thinking about Betsy. After being self-sufficient and relying exclusively on his own efforts ever since he had become an adult, he found it difficult to admit the truth. But he more than missed Betsy badly, which he already knew. He needed her, he depended on her, and only when she was beside him was he a whole man.

Whenever they were reunited, he would tell her how he felt. His understanding of women was very limited, but his instinct told him she would be pleased. Certainly he was not betraying his Seneca heritage by admitting his need for Betsy. No man on earth was stronger or more self-reliant than Ghonka, but his elder son well knew how much he leaned on Ena for comfort and warmth and advice.

Just thinking of his wife and parents made Renno glow inwardly, so he allowed himself the extreme luxury of speculating on the identity of his child. By now, he well knew, Betsy had given birth, and it was strange that he didn't yet know whether he had a son or a daughter. In all this time the manitous had shown him no sign.

His mind churning happily, he climbed to the top of the dune, then cursed himself for not lowering himself to the ground as he drew near the crest. Even a raw, junior warrior would have known better.

Directly ahead, around a bend in the beach, stood another small Spanish fort, located on a cove. The place was dark and silent, but a sentry in uniform stood on a raised walk that encircled the inside of the palisade. As Renno became aware of the man and froze, the Spanish soldier saw him, too.

There was no choice but to kill him. It was unlikely that the sentry could identify his war paint, but the man would know that he wasn't a Seminole, and all of the forts up and down the coast—including St. Augustine itself—would be placed on an alert.

The young Spaniard raised his musket to his shoulder and tried to sight this intruder down the length of the weapon's barrel.

The sound of the musket fire would awaken the entire garrison. Renno whipped an arrow from his quiver, fitting it into his bow, and letting fly. The arrow entered the young soldier's cheek and, penetrating upward, lodged in his brain, killing him instantly. The thrust of the blow propelled him sideways and, as he fell, he dangled for a few moments on the spiked tops of several logs before plummeting to the ground outside the fort.

To remove the arrow would be a long, difficult task that would force Renno to run the unnecessary risk of exposure, as he well knew. Nevertheless he had won the brief combat, and there was nothing to be gained by upbraiding himself with the reminder that, had he been concentrating as he should have been doing instead of mooning over Betsy and his parents, the sentry would not have become aware that he was nearby.

He raced down the dune, crouching low, then expertly scalped his victim. At the same time he noted the distinctive brass buttons on the soldier's tunic and cut off one of them before swiftly making his way around the bend in the beach and disappearing from the view of anyone at the fort.

Renno ran back to the campsite, where Consuelo was the first to see the fresh scalp hanging from his belt. Tersely explaining what had happened, Renno handed Ned the brass button.

"It looks like a regimental insignia to me," Ned said, turning it over in his hand before giving it to Consuelo. She did not flinch as she studied the highly polished brass button in the moonlight. "The man who wore this did not belong to one of the great regiments," she said. "He was a member of a regiment of conscripts."

Ned nodded thoughtfully. "That makes sense. No experienced troops would tolerate being stationed in a small wooden fort on the edge of the American wilderness, being cooped up there for weeks or even months at a time between the visits of supply ships. This is valuable information, Renno. My father will be pleased to learn that ordinary conscripts are manning the small coastal forts."

At least the killing had served some useful purpose, Renno reflected. "We will talk later," he said. "Now, because I was careless, we must march many miles out of our way."

They broke camp immediately, and the Seneca led the party deep into the interior before turning north again. He could only hope that the commander of the garrison would assume that the sentry had been killed by a Seminole warrior.

Only one thing was certain. Henceforth he would remain alert at all times until he succeeded in his mission and led his comrades to the safety of the English colonies.

Chapter XI

"**D**eep inside myself," Mary Ridley said to her husband in the privacy of their bedchamber, "I've been mourning for Ned and Renno for weeks. I'm convinced they've been killed by the Spaniards— or drowned—or that they've lost their lives in some way we'll never know."

Colonel Austin Ridley sighed and shrugged. "I can't argue with you, my dear," he replied. "I'm as much in the dark as you are. All I can say is that if I've learned one thing, it doesn't pay to speculate. Eventually we may learn something about them. Or we may never hear a word."

"They aren't the first who have gone off to New Spain and have vanished," Mary said, "and I'm afraid they won't be the last. As hard as it is to bear the loss of my son and my son-in-law, I've tried to reconcile myself to the facts we know. What worries me most now is Betsy's attitude."

Her husband raised an eyebrow.

"I've tried talking to her until I'm hoarse. But she refuses to accept even the possibility that Renno is dead. She keeps insisting he'll come back to her and the

276

baby. She simply won't admit there's a possibility that she may be a widow."

"If that's the way she's providing a cushion for herself, I don't think we have the right to blame her," Austin said gently.

She shook her head. "Betsy isn't being realistic, and when the truth finally dawns on her, I'm afraid she'll fall apart. I've tried to point out to her that without Renno she'd be wrong ever to go back to the land of the Seneca and try to bring up her son there. But she won't even listen to such talk. All she ever answers is that she and James—and she keeps calling him Jagonh—will return with Renno to the Seneca town."

Again the colonel sighed. The men of his militia regiment gave him instant, unquestioning obedience, but he found it impossible to shape, much less control, the subtleties of the feelings felt and expressed by the women of his family. "I don't see that there's anything we can do about it." He finished dressing and went to the door. "It may take a long time for Betsy to accept reality. I don't think it would be right for us to hound her. Let her come around in her own good time and in her own way. Are you coming down to breakfast?"

Mary nodded, and they descended the stairs together.

Anne was already seated at the breakfast table and had consumed two apples and several cookies that she had persuaded the cook to give her while she awaited her parents. A short time later Betsy appeared. She had already nursed her baby, and she was smiling slightly as she sat down at the table.

As Mary rang the bell for the first breakfast course, it occurred to her that her elder daughter looked positively radiant.

Betsy soon revealed the reason. "I saw Renno last night," she announced.

Her mother and father stared at her. Anne started to giggle, thought better of it, and managed to muffle her laugh.

"He came to me in a dream," Betsy said.

Colonel Ridley felt relieved and calmly began to eat. Mary continued to look at the young woman.

"He was no longer wearing the clothes of a colonist," Betsy continued. "He was dressed in a loincloth, his scalp lock had grown back, and he was carrying his Seneca weapons. The green and yellow of his war paint weren't true colors, but he explained that he had done the best he could with plant dyes that were strange to him."

Austin broke off a chunk of freshly baked bread and spread butter on it. Anne ate again, too, and although she was fascinated by her sister's story, her appetite remained unimpaired.

"Renno assured me that he and Ned are both well," Betsy went on. "They've had many strange adventures. Ned was wounded, but he has now recovered. They hope to be reunited with us soon. Within a couple of months, as nearly as I could gather. Renno spoke very quickly and softly, so I couldn't quite hear everything he said."

Anne saw that her sister was in dead earnest and could not help asking, "Where are Renno and Ned now?"

"He didn't say."

"And you didn't ask him?"

"You don't understand, Anne. When a vision comes to a Seneca in a dream, you don't ask questions. You just listen. Otherwise the apparition will fade immediately."

The dishes were removed, and they were served the next course.

Austin quietly sipped his light breakfast ale. Betsy seemed comforted by her dream, so it was best not to challenge her.

But Mary lacked her husband's patience. "You actually give credence to this dream?"

"Of course, Mama," Betsy said. "Since I've become a Seneca, I've learned many wonderful things. I never knew they existed in our world here, but they're true."

Ignoring her husband's warning glance, Mary bristled. "You mean to sit there and tell me that you believe Renno literally came to you in this dream and told you various things. Is that correct?"

Betsy nodded. "That's precisely what happened. When he returns here you'll find he's a Seneca again and that he's no longer disguised as a colonist. You'll also find that Ned was injured, but is now fully recovered. I can understand your skepticism, Mama. But the manitous can perform wonderful deeds for those who have faith in them. I've seen and heard enough to know they aren't imaginary beings. They're as real as Renno's appearance in my dream!" She spoke with conviction.

Mary fell silent, no longer able to carry on the conversation. Her heart ached for the daughter who had become too much of a Seneca for her own good. But nothing could be done for her. Ultimately Betsy's suffering would be all the more intense because she had accepted an Indian way of life.

St. Augustine was the oldest city in North America and was located near the spot where Ponce de Leon, the Spanish discoverer of Florida, had landed in 1513 in his search for the legendary Fountain of Youth. Founded in 1565 by Pedro Menéndez de Avilés, the original settlement had been burned and sacked two decades later by Sir Francis Drake. Doggedly rebuilt, it had suffered a similar fate in 1665 when it had been attacked by another Englishman, Captain John Davis.

Now the authorities of New Spain were taking no more unnecessary risks, and the community was heavily defended. Located on a peninsula between the Matanzas and San Sebastian rivers, it was protected from the open Atlantic by Anastasia Island, on which a small fort was located.

Renno and Ned stretched out on the beach facing St. Augustine opposite the point where the rivers converged, leaving Consuelo and Linnick behind the shelter of a sand dune, and the young Virginian pointed out the salient features. "I'm relieved to see that the

279

fort on the island isn't significant," he said, "even though it's made of stone. You'll note that it mounts only six cannon, and we can see—even from here—that they're antique relics." He laughed dryly. "I suspect they'd blow up if anyone actually tried to fire them. They're meant to frighten away attackers."

"It is the larger fort that interests me," Renno replied, indicating a massive structure of solid stone that stood near the outer end of the peninsula, a short distance from the river junction.

"Ah, that's the Castillo de San Marcos, which is far different," Ned said. "It isn't as big—by far—as the French fortress of Louisburg on Cape Breton Island. But it's infinitely larger than any fort in the English colonies. We've constructed nothing of this size and strength in Boston or New York, and our puny forts at Norfolk and Charleston are a joke."

"There must be a huge garrison stationed in the Castillo," Renno said.

"We'll never get inside the place, that's sure. But if I can just walk around it, I could at least count the cannon. And by strolling past the barracks behind it, which we can't really see from here, I could estimate the size of the garrison. Note the layout of the town, Renno. The docks are located at the end of the peninsula. Behind the Castillo and the outbuildings, which must include the military barracks, there's a high stone wall. The civilian community—including those two impressive churches with high spires—is located on the far side of the stone wall."

"The Spaniards," Renno said after studying the buildings at length, "protect only their soldiers and sailors, it appears. In case of an attack by land the civilian town has no walls or forts, no way to defend itself."

"That's because St. Augustine has sustained two nasty sea attacks that leveled the town. They've never had any reason to fear an overland invasion."

"That," Renno replied softly, "is something well worth remembering."

Ned grinned.

"How do you propose to get into St. Augustine and look around, Ned? I know some thoughts have been brewing in your mind."

"I've been thinking about it ever since we captured the warship and left Cuba," the Virginian declared. "I think it unlikely that there are many Indians here, other than a few Seminole and the poor devils the Spaniards have captured and enslaved. So you and Linnick will have to wait in the wilderness beyond those clearings where they appear to have built some farms and are actually raising crops."

Renno started to protest.

"Hear me out," Ned said. "You could never pass as a Seminole, and Linnick is too light-skinned, too. You'd be in trouble the minute the Spanish military saw you."

"I must admit their dungeons are not made for comfort."

"I've taken great care to bring one set of suitable clothes for Consuelo and me with us. I've planned all along for just the two of us to go into the town by the easiest route, mingle with the people, and see what we can learn. Keeping ourselves as inconspicuous as possible."

"I hate to see Consuelo being exposed to unnecessary dangers," Renno said.

"How do you think I feel?" Ned demanded. "But I know of no alternative. My Spanish is limited, and my accent would give me away the moment I'd start to speak. Consuelo, with her perfect Castilian accent, is indispensable, and I've got to take her with me. There's no other way."

"Tonight," Renno said, "I will go alone and find the easiest approach to St. Augustine for you."

They rejoined Consuelo and Linnick behind the dune, and Ned decided the time had come to determine Consuelo's reaction to his plan. He outlined it bluntly, mincing no words. "If we're caught and the Spanish authorities even suspect we're espionage agents," he said, "we'll be treated as harshly as we would have been in Havana. If we're fortunate they'll simply execute us without torturing us first."

Consuelo did not hesitate. "I will come with you," she said.

"You're quite sure it's what you want to do?" Ned demanded.

"Very sure," she replied with a smile. "There is no way you can pose as a Spanish subject if you are alone. You need me."

"I'm grateful," Ned said, "and I swear that this is the last time I'll ever ask you to expose yourself to danger."

"I want to do this not only because of you," she said, "but in memory of my father. I won't be at peace inside myself until I have obtained full vengeance against those who put him to death. Only then will I be able to think of the future rather than the past."

One major problem remained, and they had no solution as yet. Certainly total strangers to St. Augustine would be conspicuous. Basing an estimate on the number of houses that Ned and Renno had seen from the beach, the former guessed that the population of the town was approximately five thousand people, exclusive of the military garrison.

"The way I see it," he said, "five thousand people who are cooped up here and never go anywhere beyond the few farms on the outskirts of the town must know each other well. My mistake was thinking that St. Augustine might be as big as Boston, but it isn't even half of Boston's size. In a larger city we wouldn't be noticed. Here we'd stand out."

They talked about the matter at length, finally agreeing to defer a final decision. Unable to light a cooking fire for fear it would be seen from the ramparts of the huge Castillo, at sundown they ate some of their reserve supplies of smoked venison.

When night came Linnick was hurt because Renno intended to explore the approaches to the town alone.

Rather than insult him by saying it was far easier to

perform the task by himself, Renno found a convenient excuse. "You are needed here to stand guard with Ned and protect Consuelo," he told the Arawak.

Renno went off through the thick forest of pines. The farms of the Spaniards, he soon ascertained, extended no more than a half-mile from the houses that stood on the outskirts of the community. Oddly, there were no dwellings on these farms. There were barns and storage sheds at the side of each cultivated field, but no farmers actually lived on these properties.

Renno was puzzled until he figured out that these were communal farms. Apparently the residents of St. Augustine were required to spend some portion of their time working in the fields and then returned to the town. From all that he could see as he traveled in a half-circle, sometimes staying within the shelter provided by the trees and sometimes venturing boldly into the open, the rulers of St. Augustine were not even trying to make the town self-sufficient. The cultivated acreage was enough for the vegetables that were required, but it was plain that St. Augustine imported its meat, grain, and other staples.

This discovery was important. A naval blockade that could cut the colony off from the supply ships that were its lifeline could starve St. Augustine into submission. The short-sighted refusal of the Spaniards to make a colony self-sustaining made the place vulnerable.

Returning to his companions before midnight, he explained the situation to them.

Ned listened, then asked, "Did you locate a point of entry into the town for us?"

"There are many," Renno replied. "In some places the forest stands no more than one hundred feet from the dirt road where houses have been built. There are no sentries, no guards anywhere, so you are free to wander into the town where you please and come out again the same way. We will select a meeting place, but that is the least of our troubles."

Still uncertain how to spend time in St. Augustine

without creating undue attention, Ned drifted off to sleep again.

Shortly before dawn Renno awakened him and, placing a finger to his lips, led his brother-in-law to the top of the dune. There he pointed toward the harbor at the far tip of the town. The moon had vanished, and Ned could see nothing in the dark. "I don't have your eyesight," he said in irritation. "What are you trying to show me?"

"Three merchant ships have arrived at the wharves during the night."

"What of it?" Ned was still annoyed.

"We don't yet know." Renno's rebuke was gentle. "It may be, after day comes, that we shall find out."

They rejoined Consuelo and Linnick for a breakfast of the cold, smoked venison. Then, when the sun rose, they moved up the beach from the safety of the dune and, flattening themselves on the sand, watched the dock area come to life.

Fifty or more men, all of them hatless and wearing dark breeches and boots, with their shirts rolled above the elbows, began to unload barrels and casks from the hold of one of the ships.

The other two ships, one a large barque and the other a brig, remained quiet for a time. Then Renno's eyes widened when he saw people coming onto the open decks, where they lined the rails and stared toward the shore. There were women as well as men in these groups, and the Seneca felt the first stirring of excitement within him, but made no comment.

Ultimately there were seventy or eighty people standing at the rails of the two ships.

"What do you make of all this?" Ned murmured.

Renno's shrug was eloquent. Under the circumstances they could only wait in the hope of learning more.

Ned lacked the Seneca's patience, and ultimately he became restless. "Let me know if anything significant happens," he said, and went back down the beach to rejoin Consuelo and Linnick.

The sun stood directly overhead before Renno materialized beside his companions. He moved so stealthily that he was in their midst before they were even aware of his approach.

"The women and men are starting to come ashore now," he said. "Soldiers stand at the docks and allow a few at a time to land. Most are young, and many carry small clothing boxes or bundles."

Consuelo clasped her hands together. "They are immigrants sent from Spain," she said. "They come from poor families, and they are paid a few *dólares* to come to the New World. I saw many such immigrants arrive in Havana. They have been told many lies in Spain, and when they find it is not easy to live in the New World many become disillusioned and wish to return home. But that is not permitted. They are required to spend seven years here before they are allowed to go back to Spain."

Ned was ecstatic. "The Almighty couldn't have chosen a better time to help us!" he exclaimed. "No one will pay the slightest attention to us. We'll go into the town as fast as Renno can sneak us in."

He and Consuelo unpacked their clothing bundles, and she laughed when she saw the rumpled condition of the dress they had carried with them for so long. "I shall really look as though I've spent two months at sea, crossing the Atlantic."

Renno inspected the couple when they were ready, and Consuelo, wearing no cosmetics and allowing her hair to fall free down her back, well looked her part. She had made a new bundle of what was left of the clothing, and in it she placed a loaded pistol, taking the additional precaution of strapping a knife to one leg.

Something was wrong with Ned's appearance, and Renno could not figure it out. Consuelo spotted the problem without difficulty. "You cannot wear that elegant coat, no matter how crumpled it may be," she said. "You are a simple peasant who pruned olive trees in Castile."

"I've got to wear the coat," Ned replied. "I have a

pistol in one inner pocket and a knife in the other. There's no other place I can carry them without letting them be seen. I realize a sword would be out of place for a peasant, but I refuse to go into a Spanish garrison town unarmed."

Consuelo studied him for a few moments. "Help me, Renno," she said. "We must cut away the pewter buttons and the braid."

They worked diligently for a short time, and Ned asked with a smile, "Am I shabby enough yet?"

"Not quite," Consuelo told him. "You'll need a layer of dust on your boots. They're far too expensive for a peasant to wear."

"Renno," Ned demanded, "do you suppose you can sneak us into St. Augustine now, in broad daylight?"

"We will soon find out," Renno replied, and led them far inland, turning toward the north again after they had penetrated a considerable distance into the forest. Remembering the location of everything he had seen on his previous night's reconnaissance, he conducted them to a point where the forest stopped short only fifty yards from a row of houses with stone bases and pine walls.

Leaving the others behind, he scouted the immediate vicinity. "No one is working in the fields today," he announced when he returned to his companions, "and I see no activity in the houses."

Consuelo nodded. "I would guess that everyone in town has gone off to see the new immigrants come ashore."

"Mark this place well," Renno said, "and return to it. Linnick and I will wait for you here. How much time will you require, Ned?"

"No more than a few hours." Ned squinted up at the sunlight filtering through the trees so he could estimate the time of day. "Certainly we should rejoin you no later than nightfall. It might cause too many complications if we stay in town later than that."

"Then go." A Seneca was not one to waste time on elaborate farewells.

His brother-in-law hesitated. "I want to impress just one thing on you," he said. "If—for some reason—we don't appear and the Spaniards have taken us prisoner—don't stay here in the hope of rescuing us. Go up to Virginia as fast as you can travel and tell my father everything we've learned so far."

Renno nodded. Under no circumstances would he abandon Ned and Consuelo, but he didn't intend to argue. Folding his arms across his chest, he watched them, his face expressionless, as they crossed the open area, made their way up a rutted road, and disappeared behind the nearest row of crude dwellings.

Neither hurrying nor loitering, the couple tried to maintain a steady, even pace as they headed toward the heart of St. Augustine, guided by the spires of the two churches and the far taller bulk of the stone Castillo.

Consuelo stiffened when she saw a half-dozen men in shirtsleeves gathered in the road outside a cabin directly ahead. They were chatting animatedly and had not yet seen the approaching couple.

Ned's hand slipped inside his coat, and he grasped the butt of his loaded pistol. The conversation died away, and the men stared openly at the pair, most of them studying the girl and making it plain that until now few women had come to St. Augustine.

Consuelo's acting was superb. She murmured, *"Buenos tardes, caballeros,"* and in her tone was a perfect blend of timidity and respect for the established residents of the community. The men wished her a good afternoon in return and resumed their conversation.

Ned relaxed somewhat, his hand falling to his side as he grinned at the young woman beside him.

"When we next see people," she murmured to him, "don't glare at them and look ready to pounce."

She was right, and he nodded.

Soon they encountered more and more people, some of whom ignored them. Two middle-aged women stared at Consuelo in apparent distaste, but a number of residents smiled at the supposed immigrants. Consuelo smiled blandly in return, and Ned was quick to follow her example.

After a walk of less than a quarter of an hour they could see the stone wall directly ahead. A metal gate set in the masonry was guarded by two sentries in black uniforms with yellow sashes, both armed with bayonetted muskets. On the near side of the wall were a number of shops, the first the couple had seen, among them those of a tailor, a shoemaker, and a baker. Opposite these establishments was a place where bolts of cloth were sold and another that advertised its wares by placing two kegs of nails outside the door.

A scowling army sergeant hurried up to the couple. "Why aren't you in the church?" he demanded, pointing to the stone steps across the square. "You've already missed most of the Mass."

"A thousand pardons, Your Excellency," Consuelo said. "But we—we didn't know we were expected to attend church."

"You were told before you came ashore. You damned peasants are all alike—you're more stupid than swine!" The glowering sergeant gestured again in the direction of the church.

Ned thought the man would speed them on their way with his bayonet. In any event, there was no choice, and the couple entered the church.

The place was crowded, with scores of burning candles dispelling the gloom, and the scent of incense was thick in the air. Consuelo promptly covered her head with a travel-stained handkerchief and led her companion to a rear pew.

Ned had never before been inside a Roman Catholic church and was careful to follow Consuelo's example, kneeling on the stone floor beside her. The robed priest who stood at the altar had his back to the congregation and was intoning in Latin.

Although Ned had been forced to study the language as a boy, the Mass was conducted in liturgical Latin, and he understood little of what was said. It didn't matter. He was able to use this unexpected respite to good advantage.

Placing his lips close to Consuelo's ear, he whispered, "When we leave the church, we'll go straight to the military gate, where we'll tell the sentries we've got to return to our ship for belongings we accidentally left on board."

She nodded quickly.

At last the service came to an end and the doors were opened at the rear of the church. Consuelo and Ned were the first to emerge into the open.

A heavyset man in a black-braided tricorne, a yellow and red sash across his chest and bulging stomach, began to gesture toward the inner side of the square. "All new arrivals go to the town hall to register!" he bellowed.

Ignoring him, the couple went directly to the gate, where the sentries blocked their path.

Consuelo addressed the younger, a private with a bovine face. "If you please, Sergeant," she said, "we left our most valuable property on the ship. Allow us to go there for it before someone steals it from us, I beg you."

The soldier looked uncertain. "I was ordered not to let any of you new people go back through the gate."

"Please, Sergeant." Consuelo looked as though she would burst into tears.

The private looked around, saw that none of his superiors happened to be around, and relented. "All right, but be quick about it," he growled. "Don't loiter on board or the intendant for St. Augustine will nail both of you to the side of the town hall. He's a mean one."

Consuelo and Ned moved inside the wall and found themselves in the restricted military area, with the high walls and bastions of the Castillo looming ahead. Consuelo hesitated for an instant, and her companion inclined his head toward the road on their left, which, he hoped, would take them past the barracks.

His estimate proved correct, and he studied the

single-story stone buildings obliquely but intently while pretending to pay no attention to them. His rapid but precise arithmetical calculations led him to believe that the garrison probably consisted of a full brigade— approximately one thousand men. There were no stables anywhere in sight, so he assumed they were infantrymen. If he was right the garrison was strong, far stronger than he would have assumed. Later he would check with Consuelo and get her opinion.

Only one major task remained, that of learning how many modern cannon were emplaced in the Castillo. The black iron muzzles of a number of guns already projected from openings in the fortress walls, particularly on the side that faced the sea, and Ned counted rapidly, forcing himself to distinguish between the twelve-pounder and nine-pounder guns.

A horseman clattered to a halt, and a lieutenant, resplendent in a plumed helmet of brass, yellow tunic, and red breeches, with magnificently shined and spurred boots, dismounted. The sight of the couple annoyed him, and he scowled, stroking his thin mustache with one hand as he approached them. "What's this?" he demanded. "Don't you know this is a restricted area forbidden to civilians?"

"A thousand pardons, Colonel," Consuelo said. "We went back to the ship because I left my bundle behind." Hoping she was judging the man's nature, she deliberately flirted with him.

Now that the officer took note of the wench he discovered she was attractive, although he wouldn't have guessed it from her clothes. Her features were chiseled, and she was far prettier than either of the inmates of the bordello that commissioned officers patronized in this remote outpost of Spain's far-flung empire.

"Well," he said, "I suppose these things happen. But you and your husband must be more careful."

"Oh, he is not my husband, Colonel. He is my— ah—friend."

The officer's glowing eyes indicated that he was receptive to a woman's attentions.

Buttresses that supported the thick walls of the Castillo were located at regular intervals around the fort, and the lieutenant caught hold of Consuelo's arm and led her to the closest, almost out of Ned's sight. "I want a word with you in private," he said.

Consuelo continued to flirt with him, hoping she wasn't going too far. "Yes, Colonel," she said.

"Who are you?"

"Inez Hunfredo, Your Excellency, from a village that lies near Madrid."

"Ah. As you must know, Inez, everyone who comes to the New World is obliged to work. Have you registered and been given a place of work yet?"

"No, Your Excellency. We—we were just going to the town hall now, when you stopped us."

The lieutenant moved closer to her. "How would you like to keep house for my captain and me? The work would not be difficult, and you would enjoy many privileges." Reaching out casually, he began to fondle her breasts beneath the thin fabric of her gown.

"I—I would like it very much, Your Excellency," Consuelo forced herself to reply as she squirmed beneath his touch.

Ned was infuriated by the scene, but he commanded himself not to intervene. Consuelo was handling the situation well. He would only create complications if he meddled.

"Go to the town hall without delay, then," the lieutenant said. "I'll follow you there shortly and I'll put in a claim for you. If any other officer wants you, tell him that Lieutenant Gualterio has already hired you." He stroked her again, smirked, and went back to his waiting horse, his spurs clanking. He did not look back as he rode away.

Consuelo shuddered and quickly rejoined Ned. "That pig!" she exclaimed.

"I wanted to slit his throat, but let's waste no time

on him," Ned replied. "We've done well. We've learned about as much as we can, and we ought to leave at once, before our lies catch up with us and our luck runs out."

They returned to the wall that separated the fort and garrison from the town, and again Ned made a careful count of the barracks to assure himself that he had not made any errors.

A new pair of sentries stood on duty at the gate. Consuelo told her story for the third time, showing her clothing bundle.

The crowd in the square had thinned, but the portly civilian wearing the yellow and red sash still stood in front of the two-story town hall. "Have you two registered?" he bellowed.

"Oh, indeed, Your Worship," Consuelo replied promptly.

"Then don't linger here!" Like all minor Spanish officials, he was almost overcome by his sense of self-importance. "Go at once to the Plaza Mayor, where your new employers will claim you. And hurry! The gentry have better things to do than wait for tardy servants!" He gestured toward his right.

The couple started off in the direction he had indicated, but as soon as they left the square Ned nodded toward a narrow, winding street, scarcely broader than an alleyway. They walked more rapidly now, aware that their chances of escaping detection were lessening minute by minute.

Ned's sense of direction was unerring, and they took the shortest routes they could find, little by little working their way up and down narrow, totally unfamiliar roads and alleyways toward the opposite side of the surprisingly cramped town, which apparently had been built on as small an area as possible. Dusk was falling. Candles and oil lamps were being lighted in some of the drab little houses, and the odors of wood fires mingled with the pungent scents of cooking oil.

Here and there the fleeing couple heard snatches of conversation through open doors and windows, most of it in the deep baritones of men. Like so many of Spain's outposts, St. Augustine had an overwhelmingly masculine population. Relatively few women volunteered for expatriation to distant colonies, and those who did were not permitted to marry until their seven years of indenture came to an end. By that time many had died, while others, tired of the privations of living in tightly enclosed frontier towns, returned to Spain.

Consequently only a few of the women ever married and stayed in the New World. The result was that there were surprisingly few children in such communities as St. Augustine. The thought flicked through Ned's mind that he had seen no youngsters either playing in the streets or walking with parents in the center of the town.

Most of the residents had already retired to their little homes for the night, so only a few were abroad. These men paid no attention whatever to Ned, and although Consuelo continued to attract attention, the presence of her escort discouraged those who saw her from speaking to her. Apparently no one had yet realized their true identity.

Their tension increased as they drew nearer to the rendezvous with Renno, however, and without quite realizing what they were doing, they began to walk more rapidly.

Suddenly, when they were almost to the clearing that marked the outer limits of St. Augustine, a horseman loomed up ahead of them, blocking their path.

The dark-haired, gaudily uniformed lieutenant dismounted, looping his reins over his horse's head, and strolled slowly toward the couple. One hand rested lightly on the hilt of his sword.

"You have disappointed me, Inez." He smiled languidly. "I went to claim your services, but you were not there. So I took the trouble to check the register of the new arrivals, and I found that your name was not on the list. What is this game you are playing?"

Consuelo was nonplussed. She could think of nothing that would make sense to the officer.

The lieutenant stopped short of the pair. "I think," he said, "that you two decided you did not wish to live up to your obligations to Spain, even though you were required to swear an oath of obedience before you sailed. I think that perhaps you had foolish ideas of escaping into the interior and living as you please there." He laughed aloud. "You would not be the first. Others have gone off into the forest and have been killed by wild animals or consumed by the barbaric natives. Has no one ever told you that the Indians of this country are cannibals?"

Ned stalled for time, waiting to see if the lieutenant was alone or had been accompanied by others. If a number of Spaniards had set out in search of the fleeing refugees, he would have to fight his way out of the trap. If the lieutenant was alone, the task would be much simpler.

Amused by the silence of the escaping couple, the officer reached out suddenly, caught hold of Consuelo's wrist, and thrust her behind him. Caught off balance by his unexpected move, she staggered against a wall of stone and logs at one side of the road.

The lieutenant faced Ned, still smiling. "Now, my quiet friend," he said, "you and I will have a little discussion. I do not blame you in the least for lusting after this delectable damsel. No man in his right mind would reject her. Unfortunately for you, however, a lieutenant in His Majesty's royal corps of infantry takes precedence over a lump of a peasant. Return to the town, accept the work that has been assigned to you, and put the wench out of your mind forever. Do as I say, and I will not prosecute you. Refuse, and I guarantee that you will receive one hundred lashes across your bare back by sunrise tomorrow. So, my friend, what is your decision?"

Ned knew that if he tried to speak, his accent and broken Spanish would reveal instantly that he was a foreigner. He had no choice now: necessity compelled him to do away with this overbearing bully.

His problem, however, was that of trying to draw his

knife without arousing the officer's suspicions. To use his pistol was out of the question. Certainly the lieutenant could draw his sword and run the imposter through before Ned could attack him with the knife. Simulating a spasm of coughing, the Virginian reached slowly for the knife he carried in his inner coat pocket, his hand creeping upward.

The lieutenant became annoyed. "Are you deaf and dumb, my friend? Or are you too stupid to make a simple decision?"

Consuelo realized she was half-forgotten. Reacting swiftly, she raised her skirt and removed the knife that was strapped to her leg. She knew she had to kill the man before he aroused the entire neighborhood.

Out of the corner of an eye Ned saw her movements and, afraid of betraying her, did not as much as glance in her direction. He had to keep playing for time, however, and he hoped that she had the courage to go through with the grisly task. Pretending to stammer, he muttered something unintelligible.

The lieutenant totally lost patience. "You will not tell me your choice? Very well, idiot. I place you under arrest in the name of the Crown!"

Consuelo leaped toward him, her knife raised. She aimed at his back on the left side, but at the last instant before she struck, she inadvertently closed her eyes. Her momentum was so great, however, that her strike was true, and the sharp blade plunged to the hilt into the Spanish officer's back.

There was an expression of astonishment on the lieutenant's face as he pitched forward onto the road, the spreading red stain on his yellow uniform an almost perfect match for his scarlet breeches.

Ned didn't know whether the officer was dead or alive and had no intention of finding out. Grasping the hand of the petrified Consuelo, he squeezed past the lieutenant's horse and broke into a run, half-dragging her with him. The unmoving officer still was sprawled on the dirt road.

Neither then nor later did Ned and Consuelo ever

know why the occupants of the small houses on both sides of the narrow street remained indoors. Perhaps they were so afraid of those in authority in New Spain they had no desire to become involved. Whatever their reasons, the street remained deserted.

The neighing of the horse broke the silence.

Renno and Linnick, waiting behind the screen of pines, saw the couple running toward them. Uncertain whether Spaniards were in pursuit, the two Indians notched arrows into their bows and waited.

Consuelo was breathless when she reached Renno's side. A panting Ned explained what had happened in a few succinct words.

It wouldn't be long before the officer was discovered, and troops were sent in pursuit. Returning the arrow to its quiver, Renno picked up Consuelo, slung her across his back, and made his way silently into the deep forest, moving so swiftly that Linnick and Ned found it almost impossible to maintain his pace.

For their sakes he slowed his march slightly.

When Consuelo regained her breath she said quietly, "Put me down, Renno."

"No." He continued to move at a rapid trot.

"Please. I can walk."

"Your skirt will slow you, and there is no time for you to change. Do not speak again. If the Spaniards are already following us, they will hear us talk."

Consuelo fell silent, and as the hours passed she marveled at the strength and endurance of the Seneca war chief, who continued to carry her with no noticeable effort.

Making his way toward the north after going a considerable distance inland, Renno did not call a halt until long after midnight.

By that time Ned was exhausted, and Linnick felt the strain, too. Although both were in the best physical condition, neither was a match for his leader.

Renno dropped down, put an ear close to the ground, and listened intently for a long time. Then he moved to the bank of the small lake whose shores they had reached, and drank deeply. "No one comes after us," he said. "I do not think the soldiers of Spain would dare to go this far into the wilderness. So I believe we are safe. We will eat now. Then you will sleep, and I will keep watch."

No one had any intention of arguing with him.

Consuelo was so tired she dropped off almost immediately after eating the last of the smoked venison. But her sleep was troubled, and she saw herself, again and again, plunging her knife into the back of the unsuspecting Spanish officer. Perhaps, she thought, Renno was not as barbaric as she had thought. Now she, too, had blood on her hands.

Governor James Moore of the Royal Crown Colony of South Carolina knew all too well what the subjects of King William III under his jurisdiction thought of him. They claimed he owed his appointment to the influence exerted at Whitehall by his wealthy, noble relatives who were close to the King. Admitted. Governor Moore was not one to deny the truth.

The residents of Charleston and the plantations that were spreading inland also said, sometimes vehemently, that James Moore was intellectually and emotionally incapable of governing them—or anyone else. That accusation he denied with all of his unyielding, patrician vigor. Unfortunately, visitors from England sometimes carried the wrong impressions back to London with them, and some were men of high station. It was a well-known fact that King William refused to tolerate incompetence so the governor decided he would have to take decisive action to prove his worth before he was recalled and replaced.

His problem was that his background was exclusively that of a military man. He had fought with distinction in the Lowlands, on loan to the army of the Netherlands as a brigade commander, and later, in command of his own British troops, he had conceived and conducted a brilliant raid on the French fortress on the English Channel at Le Havre. That campaign, as much as the influence of his relatives and his wife's family, had called him to William's attention.

Consequently it was natural for Moore to conclude that the one certain way for him to demonstrate his efficiency was to conduct a dazzling military campaign. Contrary to popular belief, he was a man that considered every angle of an idea before he made up his mind. Once decided, he rarely changed his plans.

He pondered in self-imposed isolation for several weeks, pushing aside all other matters and keeping his aides busy as they searched for various documents that he demanded. Then, when he knew precisely what he wanted to do, the governor invited a very few of Charleston's most prominent citizens to an informal dinner at his palatial mansion that overlooked the growing city's harbor.

Two of the guests arrived together. Lieutenant Colonel Lindsay Pomfret, the commander of the South Carolina militia, his hair already silver at the age of forty, had grown wealthy in the cotton and tobacco trade. Clark Schofield, who spent at least a portion of his time at his extensive plantation outside Charleston, owned more land, most of it under cultivation, than anyone else in the colony. The governor greeted them so cordially that both were immediately suspicious.

The last of the guests to arrive was Lucinda Watson. Having managed the Charleston branch of the Ridley shipping interests, she was now a full partner in the firm, renamed Ridley and Watson. When James Moore had first come to the colony, his wife fortuitously remaining behind in England, he had been tempted to make advances to the lovely widow. Then he had discovered she was endowed with rare intelligence, a quality he despised in women, and thereafter he had been careful to treat her with the courtesy that her eminence in South Carolina demanded.

Sedate but almost girlishly attractive in a gown of dark silk with a modest neckline, Lucinda demurely refused a cup of the sack that all of the men were drinking. She and the other guests exchanged quick glances, and all three knew it was no accident that they alone had been asked to dine with the governor. Together they were the economic power elite of the colony.

James Moore outdid himself in his joviality. Escorting his visitors to the dinner table, he told ponderous jokes and indulged in gossip about the court at Whitehall. His guests laughed dutifully at the appropriate moments and, having already heard the stories from London, concealed their boredom.

Only after the meal came to an end did Governor Moore bring up the subject that weighed on his mind. "Colonel Pomfret," he asked abruptly, "how many troops can you provide for a military campaign?"

"Five hundred for the defense of the colony, Your Excellency, and three hundred and fifty for duty beyond South Carolina's borders."

"Mistress Watson, how many ships could you provide for purposes of transporting troops, and how many that could be converted temporarily into warships?"

Lucinda was as surprised as Colonel Pomfret and replied with equal care. "Ridley and Watson could provide at least three ships for use as transports, and I daresay others would willingly contribute two or three more. As for converting merchantmen into warships, the matter is quite complex, and I'd need to know more about the type of campaign you have in mind before I could answer your question."

For the moment Moore declined to reveal his thoughts. "Mr. Schofield, could you and other major plantation owners provide food supplies for an expeditionary force on no more than a month's notice?"

"Your Excellency, that would depend on the size of the force and the duration of the campaign."

"To be sure." The governor folded his hands across the velvet expanse of his embroidered waistcoat, then beamed at each of his guests in turn. "Mistress Watson and gentlemen," he declared. "I am about to make you privy to a state secret. I intend to launch an attack on the Spanish citadel of St. Augustine."

The guests were stunned.

The militia commander was the first to recover. "Your Excellency, as I'm sure you know, the more heavily populated colonies, led by Massachusetts Bay and Virginia, have been contemplating a campaign against New Spain for a long time. I assume you intend to act in concert with them."

The governor smiled, but made no reply.

For a moment Lucinda felt panicky, but her voice was calm. "As it happens, Your Excellency," she said, "my cousin, Captain Ned Ridley of Virginia, and our close ally, Renno of the Seneca, who is now related to me by marriage, have been conducting an extensive scouting expedition in New Spain. Surely you'll wait for their report before you launch a campaign against a strong Spanish fort!"

Moore's smile broadened. "That depends upon whether they return in time to submit their report before I'm ready to act. I intend to strike in one month, no more and no less."

Lucinda swallowed hard. "I have no way of knowing or even guessing when we may hear from Ned and Renno, or when we may see them," she said.

Moore's expansive gesture indicated that he didn't much care.

Colonel Pomfret could not hide his dismay. "Sir," he said, "I command a half-regiment of militiamen willing to leave their homes and wage war beyond South Carolina's borders. And to be blunt about it, Your Excellency, I cannot even contemplate an attack on St. Augustine with a force of only three hundred and fifty able-bodied men!"

The governor looked indulgent. "I've never been fond of suicide myself," he declared.

Clark Schofield was more emphatic than either of the other guests. "I'm not certain that I—or any other plantation owner I know—would be willing to contribute food or any other supplies to a campaign that's sure to fail!"

Lucinda became more courageous. "I think I can answer your question now, Your Excellency," she said. "Sloops, brigs, and barques can be outfitted as sea raiders and can function well in that role. But no converted merchantman would be capable of doing battle with Spanish ships-of-the-line and frigates, much less stand up to the pounding they'd receive from the guns of the Castillo at St. Augustine. Why, we don't know how many cannon the Spanish have available there, how large a fleet they could muster, or how strong a garrison they already have on hand."

Moore's smile faded. "Listen to me before you condemn me as mad," he said. "I didn't acquire my reputation as a soldier by accident, and I have no intention of losing a campaign. I do plan, however, to act without help from any other colony. The Spaniards have been terrorizing our merchant fleet long enough, and I want South Carolina to win full, exclusive credit for a victory!"

His listeners were shocked.

"I also have another reason for acting alone," he continued. "If we obtain the help of other colonies, London will have to approve of the campaign in advance. Naturally. Because King William doesn't want a war in Europe with Spain. But if South Carolina takes action alone, the campaign will have been fought and won before the King or his ministers can object."

"But how can we possibly win such a campaign, Your Excellency?" Schofield demanded.

"All of you have forgotten our greatest strength," the governor replied, not hiding his self-satisfaction. "Our Indian allies. The Choctaw hate Spaniards, and so do the Tuscarora. Surely they'll send their warriors into a campaign with us."

Colonel Pomfret became thoughtful. "So they will, Your Excellency, provided we supply them with muskets and ammunition, as well as blankets, iron cooking pots, and other objects they prize. At the moment I wouldn't want to guess how many warriors they'd actually be willing to send on an expedition. That would depend on their approval of our plans."

"I'm being elastic and intend to stay that way," Moore declared. "Now you know my biggest secret. I shall send one expedition by sea and another overland. I hope they'll be able to strike simultaneously and reduce St. Augustine together. In any event, as I see the situation, it isn't likely that both will fail."

Lucinda had to admit that his reasoning wasn't as insane as she had at first thought, although she knew that Austin Ridley and General Andrew Wilson would be upset when they learned that South Carolina would conduct her own, unaided campaign.

Pomfret and Schofield reluctantly conceded that it might be possible to deal St. Augustine a devastating blow. But the militia commander was thinking even farther ahead. "Let's suppose we win this victory you seek, Your Excellency. The leaders of New Spain will be furiously angry, naturally. And I wouldn't put it past the viceroy in Cuba to send a fleet and army to annihilate one of our ports. Charleston is the closest, an almost certain target."

Moore shook his head. "You're mistaken, Colonel. Rivera's hands are tied, just as Wilson's and Ridley's hands are tied. That's my whole point. An all-out attack on Charleston by Spanish warships and troops would be an invitation for Britain to declare war against Spain. Rivera doesn't want it, and neither does Madrid. That's why it is imperative that we act alone instead of making a campaign the joint responsibility of all the English colonies. Now, I hope, you see the beauty of my scheme!"

His guests nodded, but none were enthusiastic.

The governor stiffened, his manner severe. "Now that you know what I have in mind, I want you to act accordingly. Pomfret!"

"Sir?"

"Prepare your troops for an out-of-colony expedition. Send messengers immediately to the Choctaw and

Tuscarora, inviting their leaders to come to Charleston and confer with me."

"Yes, sir." Colonel Pomfret was resigned.

"Mr. Schofield, by the day after tomorrow I'll expect you to return with a detailed list of provisions you and the other plantation owners can provide our troops. I'll also want a detailed list of the merchandise you can make available to our Indian allies."

"Very well, Your Excellency." Unable to defy a direct order, Schofield knew he had no choice.

"Mistress Watson." Governor Moore turned to the young woman. "By the day after tomorrow I'll want a precise list of the maximum number of ships that can be made available as transports. And I shall also want, as soon as possible, the names of the vessels that can be converted into warships."

Lucinda agreed with a sigh. She would write to Austin at once, in the hope that he and the military leaders of the other colonies would be able to intervene in time to prevent the dispatch of a South Carolina expedition to Florida. And she would pray that Ned and Renno would return in time to provide information of value to a man who was determined to wage war in his own way.

Chapter XII

F our days after leaving St. Augustine behind, Renno
and his companions reached the vast area between Spanish Florida and British South Carolina.
"Both countries claim this territory," Ned said, "but
neither has settled it or established forts here as yet. So
we should be reasonably safe now, provided we don't
venture too near the coast, where we might encounter
parties of Spanish raiders."

Seventy-two hours later they reached the sentry outposts of a party of one hundred Choctaw warriors and
soon discovered that the braves were escorting the
sachem of their nation to Charleston for a conference
with Governor Moore. Renno was treated with the respect due him as a war chief of the Seneca, and the
leader of the Choctaw graciously invited him and his
companions to join the party.

No Choctaw had ever seen an Arawak, so the
braves regarded Linnick with great curiosity, but no
one challenged or molested him. He was the friend of a
Seneca leader, and consequently he was safe.

Consuelo was somewhat apprehensive, too, when she learned she would be surrounded by so many heavily armed, lioncloth-clad warriors, but Renno assured her.

"Any warrior who causes harm to Consuelo," he said, "would become the enemy of Renno. He would also become the enemy of all the Seneca, and no Choctaw would want that to happen."

His words soothed her, at least to a degree, and she began to realize that he was a far more important personage in the world of Indians than she had realized. Nevertheless, she remained close beside Ned at all times. He, too, told her repeatedly that the worst was behind them now and that the fearful journey was coming to an end.

They marched inland to avoid the swamps that marked South Carolina's southern border, and Renno was delighted when they met the vanguard of a company of Tuscarora. These warriors were bringing word that their sachem also was setting out for Charleston. It was obvious, Renno and Ned agreed, that something was in the air.

The augmented group reached Charleston at noon and immediately went their separate ways. Ned took his travel-weary companions to his cousin's spacious house. Lucinda was overjoyed to see Ned and Renno, instantly made Consuelo welcome, and extended her hospitality to Linnick, too.

"I'm surprised that we're still alive and have come this far," Ned said with a tired grin. "But I reckon our mission was successful. We've picked up a lot of information about Spain's military and naval forces in Cuba and St. Augustine."

"Then Governor Moore will want to see you, but I insist you have dinner first." Lucinda led them to the table, then told them in detail about the governor's plans.

Renno ate in silence, as usual, but listened intently. All at once Lucinda looked at the white Indian and gasped. "Oh, Renno!" she exclaimed. "I'm so sorry. It just occurs to me that you don't know."

He raised his head and looked at her.

"You and Betsy have a fine, healthy son. He's called James, and in your language he's known as Ja-gonh." She mispronounced the Seneca name.

Renno merely nodded, his expression unchanging, but he was filled with joy. Betsy's choice of the name Ja-gonh was proof not only of her love for him but of her continuing acceptance of her own status as the wife of a Seneca. Silently he thanked the manitous for keeping watch over her. "Before we see the governor," he said, "I will write to my wife."

"And I'll send a letter to my father," the grinning Ned added. "Moore will just have to wait."

By the time the two scouts walked to the governor's mansion, their letters were being rushed to the fastest sloop in the fleet that flew the banner of Ridley and Watson. Lucinda promised that it would sail for Norfolk on the afternoon tide.

Soon thereafter Ned and Renno were conducted into the office of James Moore by an aide who, offended by their earthy smell, held a scented handkerchief to his nose. The governor spent the rest of the afternoon questioning them. "You're quite sure the Spanish garrison at St. Augustine has one thousand men?" he asked with a frown.

Ned shrugged. "We didn't count them one by one, sir, but that's the approximate number. Just as I know the Castillo has eleven twelve-pounder cannon and at least fifteen nine-pounders, all of them facing the harbor."

Renno spoke with quiet emphasis. "Only a very strong fleet of powerful warships can attack St. Augustine by sea," he said.

"That's true," Ned declared. "But an inland attack by a land force well could succeed in destroying the town. The civilian portion of St. Augustine is undefended, and once the walls of the military compound are breached, attackers could create havoc there, too."

"Not so fast, if you please." Moore was grateful for their information, but would have to ponder for a long time before he made any changes in his initial plans. "I think a sea attack well might be useful. Especially if it's made in conjunction with a land attack by the Tuscarora and Choctaw."

Ned and Renno exchanged a quick glance, and the latter bristled. "The sachems of the Tuscarora and the Choctaw will hear the words that Renno of the Seneca will speak to them. Then it will be decided whether the warriors of the Tuscarora and the warriors of the Choctaw will join the men of South Carolina."

Moore stared at him incredulously. No one ever contradicted him to his face, but this white Indian seemed to be holding a threat over his head.

"Renno," Ned said, trying not to laugh, "happens to be a war chief of the most powerful tribe in North America. You may be quite sure, sir, that the sachems will not only listen to him, but will take any advice he chooses to give them."

The Tuscarora and Choctaw were vital to Moore's plan. His attitude changed at once. "I hope you two, having been in St. Augustine in recent days, will accompany our expedition. And I hope to have many more talks with you in the days to come. I'm always malleable, gentlemen, and I have no doubt that you can help me devise a campaign that will succeed."

Colonel Ridley was disgruntled, his temper badly frayed. For several days, ever since he had heard from his niece in Charleston telling him of Governor Moore's plans, he had found more and more reasons why the campaign should not be conducted. The problem, he had to admit as he walked through the broad tobacco fields of his estate, was a matter of time. If Moore held to his plan he would march in three weeks. In that short a time Virginia could do nothing to deter him. Nor could Massachusetts Bay, although Austin had sent Lucinda's letter to Andrew Wilson by sloop the same day it had arrived.

Seething and scarcely noticing the green leaves of the plants growing beneath the muslin canopies that protected them from the strong sunlight, Austin was so lost in the thought that he failed to hear his younger daughter calling until she raced across the fields toward him.

"Papa, Papa, come quickly!" Anne screamed. "You have a letter from Ned, and Betsy has a letter from Renno!"

For the first time since he led his Virginia militiamen in their final assault on Fortress Louisburg, the colonel began to run. Anne fell in beside him as they hurried toward the house. "The letters came on a sloop that Cousin Lucinda sent from Charleston, Papa," she said, so excited she couldn't stop speaking long enough to take a deep breath. "Renno says he's fine, and I don't know what Ned says because I came to get you right away!"

Betsy sat in the parlor, Renno's brief letter in one hand. She was smiling quietly, her eyes serene. There was no need for her to mention the dream in which Renno had appeared before her. It had now come true.

"This was addressed to you," a beaming Mary said as she handed her husband a thick letter on which the seal had already been broken. "I paid no attention to all the military things. What matters is that Ned is well, and so is Renno. Well and safe."

Her husband, ordinarily the most civil of men, snatched the communication from her, sank into a chair, and read it avidly. When he had finished he went over it a second time, far more slowly. The information on the state of Spain's military and naval forces in Cuba and St. Augustine was enormously valuable, and he was proud of his son, proud of his son-in-law. He would have copies of the letter made and would send them to the commanders of the militia in every English colony in North America. No longer would they be groping in the dark.

"What do you think of Ned's remarks about the girl?" Mary asked.

"What girl?" Her husband looked blank.

Betsy's laugh filled the room.

"He went on and on about her," Mary explained.

"Apparently I didn't pay too much attention to that part." Austin turned back to the letter, then smiled. "You don't need me to tell you that Ned is very much smitten. If she'll have him, I'd say he'll be coming home with a permanent memento of his expedition." Other thoughts intruded. "If Governor Moore is listening to our lads, it's just possible his campaign won't end in disaster. I can't prepare my regiment in time, but sure as shooting, I can get a better idea of what's being done. I believe I'll have the master of the sloop take on provisions for an immediate return voyage. I can be in Charleston before the end of the week."

Mary and Betsy looked at each other. Anne quickly read their minds and caught her breath.

"Are you trying to tell us you're going off to see Ned and Renno without us?" Mary demanded.

Austin smiled sheepishly. "The quarters on a sloop are terribly cramped," he said, trying to placate them.

"Papa," Betsy said firmly, "I'm coming with you, and I'm bringing the baby."

There was no need for Mary to say anything. Her expression spoke for itself.

Austin gave in. "All right," he said. "The whole family will go to Charleston. But you'll have to get ready in a hurry. We'll sail on the late tide today."

Consuelo was kept busy with fittings for the new wardrobe that Lucinda, in spite of her repeated protests, was having made for her. Linnick, ill at ease in this white men's town on a strange continent, spent most of his time in the extensive garden behind the Watson house, where he assiduously practiced his archery. Governor Moore continued to take full advantage of the information that Renno and Ned had obtained, and each day the two scouts spent hours at the governor's mansion, conferring with Moore and Lieutenant Colonel Pomfret, helping devise specific plans for the coming invasion.

Renno was satisfied that their advice was being

accepted, so the sachems of the Tuscarora and Choctaw agreed to provide warriors for the campaign. In all, the two tribes agreed to send a total of six hundred men. But the Seneca continued to resist the insistent offers of the governor and the militia commander to accompany the expedition.

"I do not know that we will be needed," he said to his brother-in-law one afternoon as they started to walk the short distance to the Watson house.

"Well, I believe we can be a big help to them," Ned replied. "You know the countryside around St. Augustine far better than anyone else, and I'm familiar with the town itself. Nobody else can do for the expedition what we can do."

"That may be so." Renno set his jaw. "But I have done what your father and General Wilson asked me to do. I have spent a long time far from the home of my people. And I long to see my wife and set eyes for the first time on my son."

"I sure can't blame you for that." Ned had made up his mind to take part in the expedition, but felt it would be wrong to press Renno.

As they drew nearer to the house Lucinda and Consuelo approached them in the carriage, the latter wearing one of her new silk gowns, her face apprehensive beneath a broad-brimmed hat.

"Thank goodness you're here," Lucinda said when the coach quickly halted. "I was afraid I was going to be forced to break up your meeting."

At her urging the men climbed into the carriage, both of them somewhat bewildered.

"We're going to the pier," Lucinda explained. "A runner just came to the house with word that our sloop has entered the harbor—and is flying the commodore's flag."

Ned grinned as he said to Renno, "My father is on board!"

They soon reached the Ridley and Watson docks. Lucinda was elated as she looked at the figures at the rail of the sloop that was approaching the pier with all of her sails except her jib lowered. "I knew it!" she cried. "He's brought the family with him!"

Renno stood apart from the others, his hands folded across his chest, his expression solemn. He was jolted by the realization that he would be reunited with Betsy in a few minutes and would meet his son. But no one looking at him would have suspected the excitement seething within him.

The first to leave the sloop was the irrepressible Anne, who threw herself at Renno, then fiercely hugged her brother. She was followed by her parents, Colonel Ridley having deemed it wise to wear his militia uniform.

The last to appear was Betsy, dressed in her Seneca doeskins and headband, with her baby strapped to her back. She paused for a moment on the deck, and her eyes met Renno's.

Not until that instant did he allow himself to realize how much he had missed her. Now he was alive again, a whole man. Betsy walked to her husband, stopped short, and lowered her head in the prescribed Seneca form of greeting.

It would have been unthinkable for him to address her in any language but his own. "The heart of Renno becomes light at the sight of his woman."

"The manitous have answered the prayers of Betsy," she replied. Then, suddenly, her own lifelong background asserted itself. Abandoning her self-control, she took a single step forward and raised her face to his. Renno embraced her, and his fervent kiss told her all she wanted to know.

They moved apart, and for the first time he looked at the baby strapped to her back. The others, knowing this was a special moment, fell silent.

Renno reached for his son, then held him at arm's length and examined him critically. Solemn eyes that were precisely the same as his own, pale blue and intense, returned his stare.

"Renno, war chief of the Seneca and son of the Great Sachem, welcomes Ja-gonh to the Bear Clan and to the nation of the Seneca."

Betsy held her breath, hoping the baby wouldn't spoil the occasion by weeping, which would have been a bad omen.

The child was sturdy, Renno saw, and he was pleased to note that Betsy had made him a loincloth of buckskin to wear over his diaper. Drawing the baby closer, he cradled him in one arm and placed the middle finger of his free hand in the center of the infant's forehead. Completing the ritual of acceptance into the Seneca, he intoned, "Son of Ghonka's son, you will wear many scalps in your belt. You will be wise in council. You will show courage in combat."

Ja-gonh reached up, and his tiny hand closed around the man's strong finger. Renno tugged gently. The baby's grip tightened. Apparently he hadn't known what to make of this tall man who wore streaks of green and yellow paint. But Ja-gonh was enjoying the game and tried to stuff the man's finger into his mouth. A faint hint of a smile touched the corners of Renno's lips. At last Betsy relaxed. Now she knew for certain that Renno was pleased with their son.

All at once Ja-gonh exploded in laughter, which became louder and more shrill when the man who was holding him joined in the laugh. Betsy was afraid she would disgrace herself by weeping, but instead began to laugh, too.

The tension broken, everyone crowded around them, with Austin and Mary Ridley exchanging warm greetings with their son-in-law.

Only Consuelo was still nervous.

The carriage was too small to accommodate the entire party, and when Renno indicated that he would walk to the Watson house, Betsy moved up beside him, a mischievous twinkle in her eyes. "A war chief of the Seneca," she said, "does not carry a baby. That would not be seemly." She took Ja-gonh from him. "But the woman of Renno will walk with him," she added.

As they made their way to the house, their memories of their long separation faded, and they were contented, oblivious to the stares of passersby who gaped at the white family in Indian attire.

At the insistence of Renno and Ned, the shy Linnick joined the family group at the house, and Ned launched into a recital of the adventures they had experienced, beginning with the Spanish attack they had suffered while sailing to Cuba. Occasionally Consuelo interrupted him to add a few comments, particularly when he made light of his own exploits.

Renno said nothing, twice leaving the room quietly to peer in at Ja-gonh, who was now sleeping peacefully upstairs in the crib that Lucinda had obtained for him.

Everyone had questions. Consuelo, who was beginning to thaw, was drawn to Betsy, who bore such a strong family resemblance to Ned, and whispered to her, "I, too, would prefer to wear my deerskin clothes. Life in America is so much better—and simpler—than it was in Europe."

"I've never been in Europe, but I know what you mean," Betsy replied with a smile. Here was a kindred spirit.

Austin Ridley put his stamp of approval on Consuelo in his own way. "It strikes me, young lady," he said, "that you're an extraordinary person. I don't know of another girl, including my daughters, who could have done all that you did."

Only Anne would have asked the question that was in the minds of the whole party. "Consuelo," she demanded, "are you going to marry my brother?"

Consuelo turned scarlet.

Ned promptly came to her rescue. "I would prefer," he said, "that she gives me the answer to that question in private."

Relieved, Consuelo looked around the room. Only Ned's mother did not show her feelings. His father had made it plain that he liked her, and Anne had found a new heroine. Surely Betsy would become her friend. In fact, it was inconceivable that she would not become close to the wife of the man with whom she had endured so much.

Mary Ridley chose her own way to express herself, as always. When supper was announced, she made it her business to walk into the dining room beside Consuelo and murmured to her, "I hope you'll give Ned the answer that will make all of us happy."

After the meal, at the colonel's suggestion, the men remained behind at the table, although Renno and Linnick refused port. Austin learned all he could about the coming expedition from his son-in-law, and while he digested what they had told him he turned briefly to Linnick, whom he addressed in an Indian tongue. "Will you join those who will now fight the men of Spain?"

The reply was succinct. "Where Renno goes, there Linnick will go."

"Tomorrow morning, lads, I aim to have me a talk with Governor Moore, and I want you right there beside me."

Later, when Renno and Betsy adjourned to their bedchamber, they made love, sealing their reunion. They were so happy to be together again that they chatted far into the night.

"Do you think Consuelo will marry Ned?" Betsy asked.

The Seneca nodded. "She will, although she doesn't yet know it herself. She believes Ned feels sorry for her because otherwise she would be alone in the world. But soon he will convince her that he loves her. She also loves him."

"How can you be so sure?"

"There is one part of the story that Ned and Consuelo did not tell today," he said. "They have slept together since we were in Hispaniola."

Betsy giggled. "Well, their future is settled, then." She paused for a moment. "So is ours."

He chose his words with care. "It is important that Ja-gonh be taken soon to the land of the Seneca."

314

"Oh, I know. I'm the only one who can speak our language to him in Virginia. Now that you've joined us there will be two of us, of course, but the land of the Seneca is home, and the sooner we go there the better I'll like it!"

"It may be there will be a short delay," Renno said. "Governor Moore wants Ned and me to come with him to St. Augustine."

"That isn't fair! You've already done enough—" Betsy broke off abruptly in mid-sentence. "I'm sorry, Renno. It isn't my place to tell you what to do."

"I feel as you do," he said. "But when the English colonies are threatened and the nations of the Iroquois are threatened with them, what warrior dares to say he will not fight again?"

"Is this Florida campaign all that important?"

"I do not know." He frowned, and his eyes were troubled as he looked at her in the light cast by the small oil lamp burning on the bedside table. "Ned thinks it is important, but I know too little about the colonies to make up my own mind. I will wait until your father meets with Governor Moore tomorrow. I will ask his advice, and then I will decide."

Extinguishing the lamp and then returning his embrace, Betsy could only hope they would not be separated again.

"My overall plan is very simple, Colonel Ridley," James Moore said. "I'll be operating with slightly fewer than one thousand men. Our South Carolina militia will travel by sea, and we'll establish a rendezvous with the Tuscarora and Choctaw, who prefer to travel overland. These two," he went on, indicating Renno and Ned with a gesture, "have convinced me it would be foolish to attack by sea without the support of a strong Royal Navy squadron, so we won't brave the guns of the Castillo. Instead we'll enter St. Augustine by way of its unprotected rear."

"According to my son's report," Austin said, "your overall strength will be slightly less than that of the

Spanish defenders. Won't you be operating on too narrow a margin?"

"I think not," the governor replied. "I'm relying on the element of surprise to help us win the day."

The colonel spoke with care. "Your Excellency, that brings us to the crux of your campaign. I've been wondering what you hope to accomplish. Let's assume you seize all of St. Augustine. Spain will be certain to send enough reinforcements from Havana—including a naval armada—to drive you out again."

"I'm not stupid, sir," Moore replied with dignity. "I realize it would be impossible for a few hundred militiamen and their Indian allies to hold that fort if the forces of New Spain retaliated with all their might. Their Havana garrison could surround us in a siege, and the guns of their ships-of-the-line and frigates now stationed in Cuba could pound us to dust."

Austin did not mince words. "Precisely what is your aim, Your Excellency?"

"Your question surprises me," the governor said. "You lost the officers and crew of the ship that was supposed to carry these two to Cuba. You lost the ship itself, along with an expensive cargo."

"In all," the colonel replied, "my company has lost three ships to the Spaniards. To the Spanish navy, that is, masquerading as freebooters."

"There you have my answer, sir," Moore said with spirit. "London and Madrid are fencing, and neither wants a full-fledged war until the question of the Spanish succession is settled, which means all of Europe will continue to procrastinate until Louis of France decides how great a risk he wants to run. In the meantime the English colonies are suffering. South Carolina is suffering. So are you, Colonel Ridley!"

"I can't deny a word you're saying, Your Excellency," Austin murmured.

"There you have it, sir!" Moore was triumphant. "My aim is to accomplish no more than Drake and Davis did. And no less, certainly. I intend to reduce St. Augustine to rubble, and I'll evacuate the town before the viceroy in Havana can counterattack. But I'm not just going to pull the Spaniard's beard. I want to teach the viceroy a lesson. And I want to keep him so busy rebuilding his base at St. Augustine for the next few years that his warships will have no time to molest the merchant shipping on which the security and growth of the English colonies depends!"

"I agree completely with your objectives, Your Excellency," the colonel said. "By the time the Spaniards can rebuild St. Augustine, the major problem of whether the mother countries will go to war will have been decided. And I owe you an apology. I was afraid that by operating without our help and that of Massachusetts Bay you were going to indulge in some harebrained scheme. I find your plan sound in every respect, and I'll be delighted to submit a report accordingly to my own governor and to General Wilson in Massachusetts Bay."

James Moore shook his head. "The fault is mine, sir. My goals are so clear to me that I didn't think it necessary to spell them out!" He laughed, then said, "I'd be delighted to have you come with me on the expedition, Colonel."

"I wish I could." Austin's regret was sincere. "But my governor and the Burgesses wouldn't permit the commander of the Virginia militia to participate—even as an observer—in a campaign from which Virginia itself is being excluded."

The jealousies between the colonies was not new, and Moore could only say, "I'm sorry, too. I hope this doesn't mean that Captain Ridley must be left behind. I need him to guide Colonel Pomfret's men across terrain he knows."

"I see no problem," Austin said. "I'll simply assign him to temporary duty with the South Carolina militia."

Ned looked pleased.

"Thank you, sir." Moore looked across his desk at the Seneca. "Where does Renno stand?"

"Virginia has no control over the war chief of a

sovereign Indian nation, Your Excellency. Renno is free to make his own decision."

The governor appealed directly to the Seneca. "You have great influence with the Tuscarora and Choctaw, far more than I imagined. I need you not only to travel with them and lead them to the rendezvous with my militia, but your presence is vitally necessary to hold them in line. Every phase of my attack must be coordinated. And if you aren't on hand to command our allies, they may become undisciplined and do the wrong thing at the wrong time in the wrong way."

Renno listened carefully. He had heard nothing new, but without help he could not decide whether the campaign was as important as Governor Moore thought. He looked at his father-in-law.

Austin nodded slightly.

Facing the issue squarely, Renno knew he alone had to be responsible. He thought first of Betsy and Jagonh, then he conjured up a mental image of the stern-faced Ghonka, smoking his pipe in front of a supper fire. He knew what the Great Sachem would tell him to do. No escape from the call of duty was possible. "I will go," he said, knowing he would be separated again from his wife and child.

Betsy accepted Renno's decision with the calm expected of a Seneca warrior's wife. Concealing her hurt and dread, she nodded in silence when he told her he felt it necessary to take part in the expedition.

"This time," he told her, "we will be apart for no more than two or three weeks. I will march to St. Augustine with the Tuscarora and Choctaw. Then I will return on one of the transports after the raid."

His wife made no mention of the possibility that he might be killed or severely injured in the attack. True Seneca accepted such risks without comment.

That same evening, after supper, Ned made a point of asking Consuelo to stroll with him in the garden. He

was in no mood for small talk, and he spoke bluntly.
"When the troops leave for Florida, my parents are
going to sail back to Norfolk with Betsy, the baby, and
Anne. As they'll tell you themselves, they want you to
go with them."

Consuelo stopped near a rosebush and spread her
hands in a helpless gesture. "Do I have any choice?"

"Of course. You could stay here with Lucinda, if
you prefer. Or you could go anywhere else you please.
I'd prefer it if you go with my family." Ned paused,
then went on. "I don't want to belabor the issue," he
said, "but in any battle a man is exposed to danger. If
anything should happen to me, you'd have a home
with my parents, and they'd look after you."

"I see." She stood very still.

"Just today," he said, "I received a fairly substantial
sum of money from our Virginia regimental paymaster.
My wages for the entire time I spent in the Caribbean
and Florida. I hope I haven't spent the money foolishly." He began to search in a pocket.

"You spent it all?" Consuelo was surprised by his
unexpected extravagance.

Ned found a small object packed in a box, and he
grinned at her. "I know nothing about Spanish customs. But we English colonials follow an old British
tradition."

Consuelo took the box, opened it, and was surprised
to see a ring of yellow gold on which a clear, white
diamond sparkled.

"When a man and woman are going to be married,"
he said firmly, "the man gives his wife a ring as a sign
of their betrothal. By the way, if it doesn't fit proper-
ly," he added with assumed casualness, "the jeweler
will be glad to change the size."

She stared at the ring, then looked up at him.

"You'll note," he continued, "that I am no longer
proposing to you. I am no longer asking you to marry
me. There's been enough of all that. I'm damned if I'm
going back down to St. Augustine not knowing whether

you'll become my wife. So the question is settled now. Once and for all."

Consuelo assumed an air of mock humility. "Am I permitted to speak yet?"

Ned nodded, trying to conceal his apprehension.

"I was afraid your family might not like me or approve of me, but we feel very much at ease with each other, I am delighted to say. As for you, I have loved you for a long time—"

"Say that again!" he interrupted.

"You heard me." Her eyes were mischievous, and then she sobered. "I simply had to make sure you weren't taking pity on me. And I did not want you to feel you had to marry me because we have lived together. But now, if you are certain you want to marry me—"

Ned gave her no chance to finish the sentence, taking her into his arms and kissing her fervently. Consuelo responded with a passion that equalled his, and when he finally released her, she said quietly, "Please, I don't want to lose that expensive ring." It was clutched in her fist. Ned placed it on her finger, then kissed her again.

The entire family was elated when the beaming couple came into the parlor. The ring on Consuelo's finger spoke for itself, and there was no need for Ned to make an announcement.

Betsy embraced the girl who would become her sister-in-law. "After you're married," she said, "we'll want you to visit us in the land of the Seneca. Of course our living conditions aren't what you've had here or will find in Papa's house."

"After the way we have had to live since we escaped from Cuba," Consuelo replied with a slow smile, "I know I will enjoy myself. And tomorrow," she added, "I will wear my doeskins again. Now that I am going to become an English colonial—an American—I intend to look like one!"

In the following week the pace of preparations for

the invasion increased. Ships gathered in the Charleston harbor for the transportation of troops, and Austin Ridley decided to return to Norfolk at once so the sloop on which he and the women of his family would sail subsequently would be available to Governor Moore.

On their last morning together, Betsy unburdened herself to Renno. "I don't know that I'll ever be a good Seneca wife," she confessed. "I try so hard to be courageous, but I'm so afraid for you that sometimes I don't know if I can tolerate it any longer."

"You are a fine Seneca wife," he said. "All women fear for their men when a war comes. Just as the men, too, are afraid."

She was astonished. "You actually know fear? Surely Ghonka doesn't know the meaning of fear."

Renno shook his head in quiet disagreement. "The warrior who shows his fear is a coward who deserves to lose his life. The warrior who feels no fear surely will die in battle. His foolishness makes him so confident he will become careless. The true warrior always lives with fear. But he does not allow others to know what he feels because the fears of other warriors will become greater. These are the truths that Ghonka taught to his son. In seven winters Renno will teach them to Ja-gonh."

Betsy understood, and for his sake as well as her own she managed to hide her fears. A strange, almost unnatural feeling of peace gripped both of them as they walked to the Ridley and Watson piers.

Only at the last moment did Renno betray even a hint of emotion. He took his son in his arms and held him at arm's length, gazing at him intently. The tiny blue eyes returned the stare, and then Ja-gonh laughed merrily. It was an integral part of the game he played regularly with this tall, strong man who treated him so gently. Renno discarded his reserve, and his own laugh boomed across the water.

The antics of father and son dispelled the gloom of

321

parting. Consuelo's eyes were suspiciously moist as she said farewell to Renno and Linnick, then returned Ned's parting embrace. But she managed to smile easily, brightly, as she boarded the ship and stood at the rail beside her future parents-in-law, Betsy, and Anne. The men on the dock stood motionless as the ship slowly made her way out of the harbor.

"Now," Renno said grimly, "there is work to be done."

Two days later he and Ned attended a meeting of senior officers in the governor's office, and there James Moore made an announcement.

"I have decided," he said, "to take overall command of this expedition myself."

No one was surprised. In fact, some of those present couldn't help feeling that the principal purpose of the invasion was that of enhancing Moore's stature at Whitehall.

Certainly Renno and Ned would have preferred to wait until a much larger expedition could be mounted. The troops of the more heavily populated English colonies, with the strong support of the Royal Navy, not only would be able to conquer St. Augustine but to keep it. They had no voice in the matter, however, and were participating in the adventure only because their services were needed so badly.

"Colonel Pomfret will command the militia," Governor Moore said. "And I assume that Renno will command the forces of the Tuscarora and Choctaw."

Renno merely nodded, finding it too difficult to explain that the warriors of the two nations would serve under their respective chiefs, and that he would exercise the command function only by setting an example. It was obvious that Moore knew virtually nothing about the ways of Indians, so it was best to deal with him in terms he could comprehend.

"Captain Ridley," the governor went on, "I'll be obliged if—after you lead us to the rendezvous with the Indians—you'll act as my principal liaison officer between the two groups."

"Of course, sir."

The South Carolina armada would leave Charleston in another six days, but Renno's overland journey would be longer, so he and Linnick said goodbye to Lucinda Watson after supper that same evening, and the next morning they departed without fanfare at dawn, carrying only their weapons and emergency supplies of smoked meat and parched corn.

Ned saw them off, and his parting was brief. "We shall meet in New Spain," he said.

The streets were deserted as the Seneca and his Arawak companion made their way out of Charleston at a trot, followed the road to the southwest as far as they could, and then plunged into the pine forests.

Renno's talents as a warrior had been tested many times, but he was conscious of the fact that never before had he performed the duties of a war chief in battle. What was even more important, the Tuscarora and Choctaw would take their cue from him. He knew the prowess of the Choctaw only by reputation, and although they were known as competent, he had already made up his mind that he would rely more heavily on the Tuscarora, fellow members of the Iroquois League whose style of fighting was more nearly like his own.

For two days he and Linnick maintained a relentless pace, and at the end of their second day Renno slowed to a walk, then gave a shrill bird call. It was answered from a distance of only a few hundred yards by one of the Tuscarora outpost sentinels. Somehow, in ways that no Indian could ever explain to outsiders, Renno had sensed the presence of his allies.

That night he and Linnick ate a hearty meal at the campfire of Bro-al-gre, the grizzled Tuscarora war chief who had been given the command of his nation's warriors. At least fifteen years Renno's senior, he carried a score of scalps in his belt, proof that he had not won his high place by accident. Nevertheless he deferred to the Seneca.

They ate in polite silence, and after Bro-al-gre lighted his pipe he brought up several problems that were in his mind. "Will the sachem who leads the colonists of the English have anger in his heart if the Tuscarora take the scalps of their enemies at the town of the Spanish?"

It hadn't occurred to Renno to bring up the subject in his many talks with Governor Moore. But he knew all too well that even the best and most experienced warriors would fight half-heartedly if they were refused the legitimate spoils of battle. So he really didn't care what the self-styled commander in chief of the expedition thought. "Renno of the Seneca," he replied carefully, "will take the scalps of the enemies he kills in battle."

That was good enough for the Tuscarora war chief, whose quiet grunt indicated his pleasure. "What will be done with the firesticks and blankets and cooking pots of the Spanish?"

Booty was a legitimate spoil of war, too, but the capture of a foe's property could not be allowed to interfere with the main purpose of an attack. "The houses of the Spanish must be set on fire," Renno said. "Before the fires burn down the houses, the warriors of the Tuscarora may seize and keep all the belongings of the Spanish that they wish to gather. But any warrior who neglects to set fires because he is so busy collecting firesticks and blankets will be reported to the Great Council of the Iroquois. Then the sachems of all the nations will decide how he is to be punished."

It was clear to Bro-al-gre that this son of the Great Sachem would tolerate no warrior's failure to do his duty. Every Tuscarora in the expedition would be notified accordingly and would not regard the warning lightly.

"Will the Tuscarora take prisoners, war chief of the Seneca?"

Renno vividly recalled the cold-blooded murder of the master and crew of the merchantman taking him and Ned to Cuba. Never would he forget the torment of being chained in a Spanish dungeon, much less his disgust that a young woman had been accorded the same cruel treatment. "Renno," he replied, his voice harsh, "will take no prisoners."

Again the war chief of the Tuscarora grunted, and the light of the fire emphasized the anticipatory gleam in his eyes.

There was only one way to deal with the men of New Spain, Renno was convinced. They had to be treated as they treated their enemies until they gained respect for the people of other nations.

A day and a half later the scouts made contact with the vanguard of the Choctaw war party, and that evening the camps were made a short distance apart in the forest. Bro-al-gre immediately sent a junior warrior to invite Hamor, the Choctaw war chief, to eat supper with him.

The reply was startling. "Hamor, war chief of the Choctaw, says this land is the land of his people. So it is his wish that Bro-al-gre come to his fire."

The leader of the Tuscarora bristled, and a glance at Renno told him that the son of the Great Sachem shared his anger. "Say to Hamor that the war chief of the Seneca makes his camp with the Tuscarora and eats at the fire of Bro-al-gre."

The leader of the Choctaw changed his mind, and a short time later he made his appearance in the Tuscarora camp. He had seen thirty or more winters, and he carried himself with an air. Renno merely glanced at his gaudy war bonnet and knew his kind. No Seneca could abide a warrior who strutted and boasted. This man had to be put in his place before he could create complications.

Renno gave no indication that he was aware of Hamor's approach. Bro-al-gre followed his example, and he, too, stared steadily at the venison sizzling over the cooking fire.

The Choctaw was forced to speak first. "Hamor greets the war chiefs of the Seneca and the Tuscarora," he said, a surly note in his voice.

Renno's nod was lofty. Bro-al-gre waved the new-comer to a place beside the fire.

Hamor sat cross-legged and tried to gain the initiative. "Hamor of the Choctaw has fought in eleven battles," he said. "He has won all of them."

Renno turned to him, his pale eyes glittering. "It will be well if Hamor does not lose his twelfth battle," he said in a metallic voice.

The Choctaw was taken aback, but tried again. "How many battles has the war chief of the Seneca won?"

"The Seneca win all of their battles," Renno replied with aloof disdain. "So they do not count their victories. Nor," he added pointedly, "do they count their triumphs in hand-to-hand combat."

The message was clear. If Hamor continued to boast he would be challenged to a trial of strength by this lithe, muscular Seneca. He swallowed hard, then worded his reply carefully. "The warriors of the Choctaw," he said, "will have light hearts because they will follow the guidance of a war chief of the Seneca in the battle we will fight together."

His capitulation complete, Renno relented instantly, knowing that if he humiliated Hamor, the man's warriors would only go through the motions of doing battle. As the senior among peers it was Renno's privilege to remove the smoking meat from the fire. He did, but instead of keeping the dripping chunk that he cut off with his knife, he politely handed it to the Choctaw.

Hamor appreciated the courtesy of the gesture. His own importance recognized, his good humor was restored, but he took pains not to do any more boasting in the presence of this stern Seneca. As he ate he saw the scalps hanging from Renno's belt. No matter how great his own prowess, he had no desire to challenge a leader of the most feared of Indian nations.

Harmony established, Renno quietly told the Choctaw the outlines of the battle plan. The Indians would attack the town of St. Augustine first, killing the settlers and setting fire to their dwellings. The South Carolina militiamen would move forward through the ranks of their allies and would try to breach the defenses of the high-walled Castillo compound.

Neither Hamor nor Bro-al-gre liked the idea. "It may be," the former said, "that the soldiers of the English shoot well with their firesticks. But only Indian warriors can climb the walls of places where there are no ladders."

"The war chief of the Choctaw speaks the truth," Renno said. "But the sachem of the colonists wants his men to have the honor of being the first to enter the fort of the Spanish. We will let them try. Only if they fail will we take charge." He and Ned had discussed the problem at length and had concluded that, unless the Spanish garrison became panicky, the warriors ultimately would be responsible for breaking into the fort.

The combined parties encountered no difficulties on their march into Florida. Twice their vanguards encountered small bands of Seminole braves, who were killed on the spot. Under no circumstances could the high command at St. Augustine be allowed to learn that a large band of Indians was approaching.

The warriors reached the broad, unnamed river near the fort. Crossing in single file, they swam the considerable distance to the east bank, then proceeded southward with caution. As Renno had anticipated, however, no Spanish sentries ventured into these forests.

Reaching a point due west of St. Augustine and less than a day's march from the town, the columns of warriors halted, then spread out in the forest along the riverbank. Taking no chances of premature discovery, no cooking fires were lighted and the warriors were forbidden to engage in swimming races in the river. Even the junior warriors knew that the hour of battle was drawing nearer, and strict security precautions were observed.

After a rest of the better part of two days the

Choctaw, less disciplined than the Tuscarora, showed signs of restlessness. It was fortunate that, late in the afternoon, a Tuscarora sentry announced the approach of "many men." A man in buckskins was at the head of the column, the sentinel reported, so Renno knew that the South Carolinians were arriving. Word was passed to withhold all fire.

An hour later Renno and Ned were reunited. "We saw a few merchant ships from Virginia and Delaware," Ned reported, "but our lookouts could find no sign of Spanish sails anywhere. So far our plan is working."

The South Carolina militia made their camp adjacent to that of the Tuscarora to the northeast. Renno joined the high command, taking Bro-al-gre and Ham-or with him, and found it difficult to persuade Governor Moore to light no fires. The commander in chief, accustomed only to combat in Europe, knew nothing about New World fighting and agreed only after Colonel Pomfret added his voice to Renno's.

"How soon will your soldiers be ready for battle?" Renno asked.

"The men are tired after their march," Moore replied, unaware of the unfavorable impression he was making on the Tuscarora and Choctaw war chiefs. "They'll need to spend at least twenty-four hours at rest before they'll be ready."

Renno said something to Ned in Seneca.

"What was that?" the governor demanded.

"Every hour we spend this close to St. Augustine," Ned replied, trying to exercise diplomacy, "increases the risk of discovery. If we're to remain in camp here, the militiamen will have to learn the value of silence. There must be no pipe smoking, no clatter of metal, and no conversation. Talk carries farther than you realize in a quiet forest, Governor."

Lindsay Pomfret was relieved. The Virginian had given such good advice that he himself had been in no position to speak.

The militiamen did their best, but most were residents of Charleston and the plantations in the vicinity of the city. In years to come they would learn the principles of wilderness warfare, but they were still novices. They spoke in loud whispers, sometimes forgetting themselves and talking aloud. The cleaning of their muskets made sounds that echoed through the forest, and two of the new recruits ignored orders and lighted their pipes.

The leaders of the Tuscarora and Choctaw were in despair, and Renno grew increasingly apprehensive. Only the failure of the Spaniards to send patrols into the interior prevented the discovery of the invaders' presence.

The day dragged, the hours passing slowly, and about an hour after nightfall, Renno conferred privately with Ned and Colonel Pomfret. "We must move at once," he said.

The militia commander frowned. "The governor has given orders to advance at midnight."

Renno shook his head. "It will take longer than you think for your men to march quietly. And I'm afraid that if we wait much longer the Tuscarora and Choctaw will abandon the campaign and go off to their homes."

Pomfret flushed, although he knew the attitude of the Indians was fair, at least according to their own standards. "I'll go to Governor Moore right now," he said. "I'll tell him our allies will march without us, if they must, to spur him to change his order."

A quarter of an hour later the little army broke camp, and only the crashing of the boots of the militiamen in the underbrush gave warning of the column's approach to the strongest Spanish garrison on the North American continent.

Chapter XIII

An hour before dawn St. Augustine slept peacefully. Renno crouched with Ned behind the screen of trees at the edge of the cleared area, and only on the ramparts of the Castillo could he see any signs of life. Even there the silhouettes of the bored Spanish infantry sentries were silent and unmoving, making it apparent that the sentinels were dozing at their posts.

Renno waited until the first dirty gray streaks of dawn appeared in the dark sky, and then he nodded to Ned. They clasped forearms, Seneca-style, then went their separate ways. All Indians preferred this time of day to any other for a surprise assault.

The warriors surged forward in the dark, moving silently, their tomahawks in their hands, their arrows loosened in their quivers, their bows strung.

Renno halted near the outlying houses, then directed the streams of Tuscarora to his left and his right as they moved into the town. The senior warriors, who were in the lead, were instructed to penetrate as close to the high fortress wall as they could before launching their actual attack. The buildings closest to the forest would be the responsibility of the junior warriors.

It was difficult, at this climactic time, for Renno to refrain from joining in the assault himself. The handle of his tomahawk itched in the palm of his hand, but at this point his responsibility as a war chief was to command.

Scores of Spaniards, perhaps one or two hundred, died in their beds before they even knew the assault was taking place. The senior warriors burst into house after house, then swiftly dispatched the residents with their tomahawks and knives. The bounty of scalps was plentiful.

A high-pitched scream broke the quiet, and the terrified Spaniard who uttered the cry broke off suddenly, his throat slashed. A moment later a building near the Plaza Mayor caught fire, indicating the extent of the senior warriors' penetration. Then a house in the Choctaw sector caught fire, too, indicating that the warriors under Ned's direction were successful also.

Renno emitted a shrill whistle, and the South Carolina militiamen poured out of the forest, running toward the high wall, clearly outlined by the flames. It seemed an eternity before the defenders of the Castillo laid down a ragged barrage of musket fire, to which the South Carolinians responded.

Renno had no way of knowing whether the militiamen had entered the garrison or whether the troops there had closed the heavy metal gates in time to seal off the fortress. For the moment he was too busy to find out. Ranging from street to street at a trot, he had to admire the efficiency of the Tuscarora, although the carnage they wrought was frightful. The helpless Spanish civilians had little opportunity to use their pistols, swords, and knives. Swarms of warriors went from house to house, killing every occupant, then setting fires. The warriors were true to the Iroquois tradition, and no prisoners were taken.

The assault of the Choctaw was equally savage, even though their organization and discipline were more lax. They, too, killed and burned at will, and Hamor was in his glory, pausing frequently to add fresh scalps to his growing collection.

Ned, who was searching for Governor Moore, encountered Renno at a corner where the houses behind them and in front of them were burning. "I feel sorry for these poor people," Ned said. "They still don't quite know what's happening to them, and now they're cut off from their own garrison."

"The gates were closed?"

"The moment the alarm was sounded. Long before the militiamen arrived at the wall. You know the Spanish military, Renno. They don't give a damn for their own civilians. I reckon they figure they can always import more peasants."

As they went together to find Governor Moore, Renno was neither surprised nor disappointed to learn that the South Carolinians had been unable to break into the Castillo. He had anticipated that failure from the outset. What mattered now was that the Spanish garrison, at least one thousand strong, remain intact behind its high walls. They would need to be routed if the limited objectives of the attack were to be realized.

James Moore, conspicuous in his plumed brass helmet, with his scarlet sash of office across his chest, stood on a corner of the plaza opposite the closed metal gates of the Castillo, waving his sword as he urged the militiamen forward. He was an obvious target, and only the faulty marksmanship of the Spanish musketmen on the walls had spared him so far. Eventually, however, one of the defenders was certain to fell him.

"For God's sake, take cover, Governor!" Ned dragged the protesting Moore behind the stone wall of the church. Unaccustomed to such an indignity, the panting Moore struggled to regain his breath.

In a few moments they were joined by Colonel Pomfret. "I've ordered the battalion to seek protection on this side of the plaza," he said. "They can accomplish nothing by storming those gates, and they're easy targets for the infantrymen up yonder on the wall."

Governor Moore regained the use of his voice and shouted to make himself heard above the roar of musket fire, the crackle of burning houses, and the screams of civilians whom the warriors were still killing. "Would you have me abandon the attack, Pomfret?"

"Certainly not, sir. But we've got to devise some other method of breaching that wall. If we keep storming it our casualties will be horrendous, and we'll accomplish nothing."

Moore controlled his anger and turned to Ned for advice. The Virginian shrugged, then nodded in Renno's direction.

The Seneca war chief was paying no attention to the discussion. Crouching low, he was observing the Spanish infantrymen clustered on the wall, and he was so preoccupied that he totally ignored the others. Then he straightened, and pressing close to the stone wall of the church, he slowly and methodically worked his way around it so he could study the wall from the nearer side of the solidly built structure.

Even James Moore had the sense to ask no questions.

At last Renno returned. "Send runners to fetch Bro-al-gre and Hamor," he said. The situation made it necessary for him to take command himself, no matter how insulted others might be, and a Seneca never shirked his duty.

Some of the civilians had escaped and fled into the forest, where they were pursued by junior warriors eager to take more scalps. It was never possible to estimate the civilian death toll, but it was unlikely that more than a handful of the unfortunate residents survived.

Bro-al-gre soon arrived, saw Renno's mouth set in a firm, uncompromising line and waited for instructions. Then Hamor appeared, and Renno again moved around the church, followed by the two war chiefs.

The Spanish infantrymen had no targets now and

had stopped firing, but several hundred of them continued to line the wall in solid ranks. The three Indians made their way back to the place where Governor Moore and the others were waiting, and Ned signaled to Moore, urging him to be patient. War chiefs could not be pushed or bullied.

"Give Renno twenty of your senior warriors," the Senaca said to Bro-al-gre.

The Tuscarora grunted his assent.

"Also give Renno nine of your tallest and strongest warriors."

The war chief of the Tuscarora began to understand.

"We will climb the wall," Renno explained, "by making the ladder of the Mohawk."

A hint of pleasure appeared in Bro-al-gre's eyes.

"Let the other warriors of the Tuscarora wait where the enemy will not see them. When we reach the wall we will throw ropes to them. Let the ropes be strong enough to carry the weight of warriors."

"It will be done," the Tuscarora replied.

The Choctaw war chief had no idea what his colleagues meant, but awaited his turn.

"The Spanish in the fort may not yet know there are Indians in the town," Renno said to him. "Soon they will learn," he added, pointing off to the right. "The Choctaw will show themselves there, where the sun is rising higher. They will take care not to be killed by the firesticks of the Spanish. But they will send many arrows to kill the soldiers on the wall."

Hamor was confused. "Is it the wish of Renno that the Choctaw attack the Spanish?"

"The Choctaw will only pretend to attack. At first. The Choctaw will keep the Spanish busy while the Tuscarora climb the wall on the other side." Renno pointed toward the north. "But the Choctaw will have their chance to fight. They will take the scalps of many Spanish soldiers."

Governor Moore, unable to understand what was being said, lost patience. "Will someone be good enough to tell me what's being said? I can't make out this gibberish."

"The Choctaw are going to create a diversion while the Tuscarora climb the wall," Ned explained.

"How in the name of all that's holy are they going to get over the wall, Ridley?"

Ned shrugged. He had no idea what Renno meant by the ladder of the Mohawk.

Renno had not forgotten the man who had made himself the commander in chief of the expedition. "The warriors of the Iroquois," he said, "will open the gate for the militiamen." He moved off at a trot with Bro-al-gre.

Hamor vanished, too.

Governor Moore and Colonel Pomfret, with Ned beside them, watched as—on both flanks—the warriors of the two nations moved forward stealthily. The musket fire from the parapet had stopped, and the muskets of the South Carolinians had fallen silent, too. This caused the defenders to believe they had stemmed the advance of the invaders, and still more Spanish infantrymen appeared on the top of the wall.

All at once the Choctaw sent a hail of arrows into the midst of the defenders from the right flank. Caught by surprise, the Spanish commanders moved their main body in that direction. Several infantrymen were felled, and the others crouched low as they sprinted down the length of the wall.

The Choctaw fire increased.

Trumpets blew inside the Castillo, and reinforcements were sent to defend the positions taken by the Choctaw warriors, concealed behind piles of rubble, a stone warehouse that had suffered no damage, and the remains of still-burning houses. Occasionally the Spaniards caught a glimpse of a Choctaw warrior, and their officers ordered them to fire at will. The roar of muskets again filled the air, but the Choctaw remained hidden as they continued to let fly with their arrows.

This was the type of combat the Indians knew best. The Spaniards, trained only in European-style warfare, where opposing forces faced each other in the open, were frustrated by their inability to see their foes.

Ned pointed toward the left. Renno and a large number of Tuscarora on the left flank, which the defenders were ignoring, sprinted to the wall and flat-tended themselves against the base. Governor Moore and Colonel Pomfret were astonished when nine tall, husky warriors formed a human pyramid, with those on each succeeding level standing on the shoulders of those below them. The heads of those at the top reached almost to the parapet.

The instant the pyramid was formed, Renno scaled the human ladder. Bro-al-gre was close behind him, and they were followed by twenty senior warriors of the Tuscarora. They moved so swiftly, with such agili-ty, that they reached the walk at the top of the wall before any Spaniards were even aware of their pres-ence.

A junior Spanish officer was the first to see them, but before he could call out a warning, Renno let fly with an arrow that caught him in the throat. He straightened for an instant, then toppled to the ground inside the wall.

Tuscarora continued to pour up the human ladder, and once the first wave of twenty warriors was up, ropes were thrown down so that still more warriors could clamber up the walls.

Renno and Bro-al-gre led the attack, racing at top speed toward the arch that stood above the closed metal gates. It was their intention to reach a point as close to the gates as they could. By now the Spanish were becoming aware of this new threat and turned to open fire on the unexpected invaders.

Renno and Bro-al-gre leaped to the ground inside the wall. The senior warriors instantly followed them, while the two remaining groups of warriors who had also scaled the wall stayed on the top to provide cover for their comrades still climbing up from below.

Scores of Spanish troops were stationed on the

ground inside the wall, and they scattered in alarm as Renno and Bro-al-gre hacked a path for themselves with their tomahawks and knives, smashing and cutting left and right. Soldiers who tried to take aim at them were shot down by the warriors who had remained on the wall, while the twenty who had accompanied the two war chiefs moved forward and shielded them.

Renno reached the inside of the gate and began to tug at the heavy oak log that served as a bolt. Bro-al-gre joined him, but they needed the help of one of the senior warriors before the log began to move.

The arrows of the warriors on the wall and the tomahawks of the senior warriors who had penetrated the fort held the Spaniards at bay. The troops on the wall were afraid to fire at the Indians inside the compound for fear of hitting their own comrades.

In the confusion Renno and the two Tuscarora succeeded in hauling the log out of place, and the twin metal gates began to open.

That was the only signal Hamor needed. Eager not to be denied his share of glory, he emitted a blood curdling war cry and raced forward, with his entire force strung out behind him. The bulk of the Tuscarora army raced toward the open gates, too, and within moments scores of warriors were entering the supposedly impregnable Castillo compound.

Governor Moore was so startled by the developments that he could only stare open-mouthed at the scene.

"Sir," Ned Ridley shouted to Colonel Pomfret above the uproar, "I suggest your militiamen open fire on the Spaniards still on the wall to the south!"

Pomfret gave the order instantly, and the South Carolinians began to pick off the enemy troops who were isolated on the parapet.

Meanwhile, Renno and Bro-al-gre, their initial goal achieved, raced into the Castillo itself, the senior warriors on their heels and other Indians eagerly following. Here was the opportunity that both the Tuscarora and

Choctaw had awaited. Promotions depended in large
part on the scalps a warrior accumulated, and the
Indians were not to be denied.

The Spanish troops, even the garrison veterans, had
no experience in hand-to-hand combat. Their military
lives consisted of formal drill and equally formal fighting in battles waged at opposite ends of large fields.
Now, suddenly, they were being attacked by painted,
half-naked savages wielding knives and tomahawks,
and they were almost incapable of defending themselves. Occasionally a soldier staved off disaster—for
the moment—by firing his musket at an attacker, but
the few Indians who fell were replaced by hordes of
others, all of them equally bloodthirsty.

The carnage was frightful. The warriors continued
to pour into the fort, spreading out as they ran, each of
them searching for enemies in yellow and red uniforms.

The cannon of the Spaniards, which without exception were emplaced facing the sea, were useless. There
was no time to move them, and even if it had been
possible to turn them so they could be fired inland, all
of the attackers had already entered the compound.

The militiamen were the last to make their way
through the gates. The Spanish soldiers on the wall
were outnumbered, their marksmanship was far less
accurate than the South Carolinians, and they had to
abandon the unequal struggle. Before they could surrender to the English colonists, however, they were
slaughtered by the warriors.

Ned Ridley ran toward the front of the Castillo,
following the walk that circled the stone structure.
There he saw a scene of wild confusion. The better
part of the defending force had given up the struggle
and was trying to escape to the safety of a frigate and a
barque-of-war that lay at anchor in the harbor. The
warships had sent all of their boats to aid in the
evacuation, and troops were almost swamping the gigs
and dinghies as sailors rowed survivors to the ships,
then returned to the shore for more.

The garrison commander and members of his staff had been among the first to flee. They and the captains of the ships were helpless. The frigate was armed with thirty-six cannon, but these guns could not be fired at the fort without damaging the Castillo itself.

Many of the defenders, too terrified to wait for the boats, jumped into the water. Those who could swim made their way slowly out to the ships, but many others drowned.

A courageous rear guard of about one hundred men remained on the shore to protect the flight of their comrades. At least one in five was a brass-helmeted officer, and this group appeared to be comprised of veterans who refused to panic. When Ned and the South Carolinians who accompanied him opened fire, the Spaniards held their ground and returned the fire. Thanks in part to their ancient, clumsy weapons, their marksmanship was far less than accurate, but they managed to prevent their foes from making a headlong rush and driving them and the troops they were protecting into the water.

Colonel Pomfret led the main body of militia around the Castillo from the other side. When he saw what was happening he gave the order for every man to fire at will.

The Spaniards were hemmed in on both sides now, but they stubbornly continued to return the fire of their enemies as one boatload after another of their comrades reached the warships safely.

Abandoning the protective bulk of the massive stone building, Ned led the militiamen of the vanguard forward little by little. Using the technique perfected by his father's marksmen in Virginia, he ran forward a few paces, dropped to one knee as he fired, then reloaded as he moved forward again.

By now all but the rear guard had been evacuated, and Ned was prepared to let them escape, too. The ground was already littered with Spanish dead, and the victory Governor Moore had sought was virtually complete.

Then, suddenly, he recognized the Spanish lieutenant who had made advances to Consuelo. Not pausing to consider the consequences, he drew his sword and ran toward the officer.

The Spaniard stared at him for a long moment, then knew him, too, and drew his own blade.

The astonished South Carolinians, afraid they might strike the reckless Virginian, were forced to hold their fire.

"We meet again," the lieutenant called in heavily accented English as Ned approached him. "I should have guessed who you were and killed you then. I will make up for that act of carelessness now."

As Ned came within reach, the Spaniard lunged at him. Barely managing to deflect the thrust, Ned knew he had met his match. He was a powerful swordsman, but he lacked the subtlety of a member of the European gentry who had been taught the art of dueling since early boyhood.

Men on both sides held their fire now and watched the pair who were circling cautiously as each sought an opening.

The Spaniard feinted, then lunged again. This time his footwork betrayed him. Ned deflected the blow without difficulty, then thrust at his opponent's heart. The lieutenant knocked his blade aside and recovered quickly, but had lost the initiative.

Ned was determined to maintain the offensive and tried to use brute strength to knock his opponent's sword from his hand. The Spaniard retreated slowly toward the waterfront.

The boats were returning from the warships to pick up the rear guard, the oarsmen rowing with all their might as the small craft leaped across the placid waters of the harbor.

All at once Ned caught himself. He and Consuelo had already outwitted this man, and there was no real need for him to obtain further personal vengeance. The attackers had achieved their aim, and he would kill or be killed without purpose.

He leaped backward, out of his foe's range, and raised his sword in salute. The Spanish officer gaped at him for an instant. Then he returned the salute, smiling sardonically as he turned and ran toward the boats that were just arriving on the shore.

Colonel Pomfret came up beside Ned. "What the devil was that all about, Ridley?" he demanded.

"I had a private score to settle, Colonel, but I decided enough blood has been shed today."

"More than enough." Pomfret called an order to his men to continue to hold their fire, and he watched the soldiers of the Spanish rear guard clambering into the gigs and dinghies. "Nothing will be gained that we haven't already won. These poor devils will have trouble enough when they try to explain their defeat to the high command in Havana."

Ned often wished that, in battle, he could be as ruthless and unforgiving as Renno. But he wasn't sorry now that he had spared the lieutenant. The day's triumph became sweeter.

The militiamen would have had to work for a long time to destroy the Castillo, which the Indians were already ransacking. Instead the South Carolinians spiked the cannon, rendering them useless.

They were elated when a platoon discovered huge quantities of gunpowder in the inner recesses of the great fort. Some of the men wanted to blow up the whole magazine, totally destroying the fort. Colonel Pomfret refused to permit it. Powder was far too precious a commodity. Keg after keg was hauled away, most of it to be taken back to South Carolina, with the rest given to the Indian allies as a reward. The job of emptying the magazine was enormous, but the men worked furiously in spite of their exhaustion.

It was afternoon by the time they finished the task. The warriors of both the Tuscarora and Choctaw had returned to the civilian town and were looting the houses that had escaped destruction. Here and there they encountered Spaniards who had been wounded and immediately dispatched them without mercy.

Not one prisoner was taken. Colonel Pomfret estimated that approximately five hundred men out of the total Spanish garrison of about one thousand had escaped. Those who had been killed lost their scalps as well as their lives.

Complete order was not restored until late afternoon, when the Tuscarora regrouped and Bro-al-gre bade farewell to Renno, who intended to return to the English colonies on one of the South Carolina merchant ships lying at anchor somewhere to the north. The Choctaw departed, too, with Hamor and his warriors laden with all the booty they could carry.

James Moore was well pleased with the results of the invasion. New Spain had been dealt a catastrophic blow. The civilian town of St. Augustine would have to be rebuilt, and the spiked cannon would need to be replaced before the Castillo would become formidable again. The Spaniards would be able to reoccupy St. Augustine, to be sure, but would be required to work for at least a year or two before the base that had been their most powerful on the North American mainland once again would be able to threaten the English colonies.

The governor couldn't help preening as he marched beside the South Carolina militia commander as the troops headed in the direction of their waiting transports. His name would go down in history beside those of Drake and Davis as a conqueror of St. Augustine.

Therefore, he reflected, he was prepared to be generous. "Pomfret," he said, "when I send my report of this battle to King William, I'm going to credit our Indian allies for the assistance they gave us."

Colonel Pomfret nodded, then averted his face so the governor wouldn't see his smile. Renno had been the real conqueror of the Spaniards, but Moore would mention him only in passing and would claim the lion's share of the glory for himself.

To be sure, Renno was indifferent to the report that would be dispatched to Whitehall. He knew what he had accomplished, fresh scalps were hanging from his belt, and both the Tuscarora and the Choctaw had been forced to acknowledge the leadership of the Seneca. There was no more that a war chief could ask.

The sloop that carried Renno, Ned, and Linnick to Norfolk from Charleston put into port before dawn, and Linnick immediately collected the scalps he had left on the deck to dry. He had fought well, disdaining to collect any booty after the battle, and Renno's brief words of praise had given him a deep sense of gratification. Now, as always, the Arawak was content to follow his friend anywhere.

It was so early in the morning that Norfolk was not yet stirring. The only public stable hadn't yet opened its doors for the day, and the trio who had just arrived decided to walk to the Ridley estate.

The family was eating breakfast when they arrived. It happened that Ja-gonh was seated in Betsy's lap so that he faced the dining room entrance. His cry of glee when he saw Renno, part squeal and part a crowing sound, delighted all.

The meal was forgotten and grew so cold that the cook had to prepare more food for everyone. Renno, seated beside a quietly contented Betsy and their son, was the first to realize that Austin Ridley was not present.

"Where is the colonel?" he asked.

Mary Ridley frowned. "He received a message after supper last night and had to hurry off to militia headquarters."

"It sounds serious," Ned said as he and Consuelo held hands under the table.

His mother shrugged. "All I know is that he told me he might not be home until sometime today."

Obviously something was amiss. Ned and Renno exchanged quick glances but made no comment. They wanted nothing to intrude on their homecoming.

It was late morning when a haggard Austin Ridley finally rode his horse to the stable, dismounted, and walked slowly to the house. His spirits revived when he learned that Ned and Renno had returned, and he promptly took them to his study, closing the door.

Always methodical, he questioned them at length about the attack on St. Augustine, scribbling notes so he could make a full report to the militia commanders of the other English colonies and the governor of Virginia. Not until the subject had been exhausted did he turn to the matter that was foremost in his own mind.

"Lads," he said, "you've come back here at a critical time for Norfolk."

"We knew there was trouble," Ned said.

His father nodded grimly. "Last night I received a message that wasn't confirmed at headquarters until this morning, when a Pimlico warrior who spent a year in our school arrived in town. The news is bad. Si-de-lo, the principal medicine man of the Pimlico, had the sachem murdered and has intimidated the tribe into electing him the new sachem."

Renno stiffened, his expression wooden. He vividly recalled the Pimlico who had been responsible for the kidnapping of little Anne, the cunning, ambitious medicine man whose son he had challenged and killed in personal combat in order to win the child's freedom.

"Si-de-lo has always hated the Virginia colonists," Austin said, "and he hopes to consolidate his position by making war against us. He's trying to incite other tribes of the area to join him. In fact, we learned of his plans through the Chickahominy, who are being faithful to their peace treaty with us. According to the warrior who arrived this morning, Si-de-lo is determined to attack us, even if the Pimlico must act without the help of any other tribe."

"Then this is damned serious," Ned said.

"He can put at least a thousand warriors in the field, perhaps as many as fifteen hundred. I can't muster more than half that number to face him. Our muskets may succeed in driving them off. I rather suspect we will. But once Pimlico are killed, a blood feud will be started, and the whole western frontier won't be safe for years and years to come."

"They haven't yet declared war, sir?" Ned asked.

His father shook his head. "You know that isn't their way. They'll start by burning our outlying farms."

"The Pimlico are not an evil people," Renno said. "It may be they will listen to words of peace."

"Right," Ned declared. "We should send a mission to them at once. Large enough to let them know we mean business, but small enough not to frighten them."

Colonel Ridley smiled sourly. "We've discussed little else all night. But the Pimlico warrior who came to us this morning says that Si-de-lo has already anticipated just such a gesture on our part. His sentry outposts have been strengthened, and he's ordered that any party from Norfolk, civilian or military, is to be killed on sight. In short, he's refusing to deal with us."

"This is a nasty situation," Ned agreed.

Renno, deep in thought, folded his arms across his chest. "Si-de-lo may refuse to talk with the colonists of Virginia," he said. "But he cannot refuse to talk with a war chief of the Seneca."

"The moment I knew you had returned I hoped you'd find some way to neutralize him," Austin said.

Renno continued to ponder. "I cannot tell him the Seneca and the other nations of the Iroquois League will go to war with the Pimlico if he attacks you. He knows the ways of Indian nations, so he realizes that such a decision could be made only at a meeting of the Grand Council called by the Great Sachem. But I can remind Si-de-lo that the Seneca and the other nations of the Iroquois have a special treaty with the English colonies. I can remind him that their enemies are our enemies. He will know I do not make idle talk such as a woman makes. He knows that if he attacks you, I will go to the Grand Council of the Iroquois and will throw the black wampum of war into the Council fire. So, if he is not foolish, if he has not lost his reason, he will listen to me."

"When do we leave?" Ned asked.

"I will go to the land of the Pimlico, but I will go alone," Renno replied. "You heard the words of your father. If you come with me the sentries of the Pimlico will know that a delegation from Norfolk is coming to them, and they will try to kill us. So you will stay behind."

Austin was worried. "Will you be safe if you go alone?"

Renno smiled to reassure him. "The warriors of all nations know the green and yellow paint of the Seneca. Only the Erie, the Huron, and the Ottawa, our enemies, would be foolish enough to put an arrow into the heart of a war chief of the Seneca."

Ned had seen for himself the universal respect in which the Seneca were held and nodded.

"I must confess I don't like the idea," Austin said.

Renno had made up his mind and decided to end the discussion. "Si-de-lo will strike soon if he wishes to strike. So I will go to him at once."

He left the room abruptly, then went off to shave his head on either side of his scalp lock, apply fresh paint to his face and torso, and obtain provisions from the cook for a few days of travel.

Linnick came to him and did not speak, but there was a question in his eyes. Renno explained the situation in a few words.

"Renno will take Linnick with him?"

"Renno will go alone. Linnick will stay here and keep watch over Ja-gonh, the son of Renno." That ended the discussion, and Renno went in search of Betsy.

Her father had already broken the news to her, and she was finding it difficult to remain calm. "Will these crises never end? Will you be called away again and again? I want to go home to the land of the Seneca with you and the baby as soon as Ned and Consuelo are married!"

"The very day that Ned and Consuelo are married we will leave for our home," Renno promised her. "I know we have been separated for too long, but I will be away for only two nights. No more than three, if I

346

stay as a guest of the Pimlico in their town. A separation of only two or three more days is not too much to ask of us when the safety of Norfolk and of all Virginia is at stake."

Betsy knew she had no right to protest. She sighed and fell silent.

"Soon the snow and cold will come," Renno told her. "We will build another room on our house for Ja-gonh, and I will spend so much time sitting beside you at the fire that you will be happy to be rid of me when the time comes for me to hunt and fish again."

"I'll never grow tired of your company," she said.

There were times, he knew, when he had to deal with her as a colonist rather than an Indian, so he kissed her, then held her for a long time before he released her.

Austin was waiting for a final word with him. "I hope you can convince Si-de-lo that a campaign against us won't be worth the price he'll have to pay."

Renno inclined his head and was anxious to leave. "I hope to bring you more white wampum from the Pimlico in two days."

"That soon?"

"When a Seneca travels alone, he moves quickly." Renno exchanged forearm clasps with his father-in-law and left at a trot, not wasting time by bidding farewell to other members of the family.

This journey, as he saw it, was a necessary nuisance. He knew that Si-de-lo bore no affection for the warrior who had killed his son. But they had fought in fair combat. And now that Si-de-lo had made himself sachem of the Pimlico, surely he was intelligent enough not to run the risk of having the entire Iroquois League go to war against his small tribe. If that should happen, as the former medicine man undoubtedly realized, then all his warriors would be killed, while their women and children would be enslaved. Other tribes had met a similar fate, and not even the Huron and Ottawa, nations far larger and more powerful than the Pimlico, dared to engage in open warfare with the Iroquois.

Anxious to conclude this last mission as soon as he could, Renno trotted into the forest and kept up his same, even pace for the rest of the day. He made no particular effort to proceed silently, and he took no special precautions when he paused briefly, late at night, to eat a little of the food he had brought with him and drink water from a small stream. In fact he was trying to advertise his approach to the sentries of the Pimlico.

As he ran, tirelessly, for the rest of the night, he formulated a simple plan. As one who had achieved a high place in the Iroquois councils, he had no desire to arouse the fears of the Pimlico. So, he decided, he would invite Si-de-lo to meet with him privately in the forest, beyond the palisades of the town. Only if the new sachem proved unreasonable, unyielding in his insistence on going to war against the Virginia colonists, would the Seneca demand that he be allowed to address the council of the Pimlico. Not even a violently antagonistic sachem would have the temerity to deny him that privilege.

Occasionally, as Renno trotted, he could hear someone behind him, maintaining his distance, and he was amused. The Pimlico were already trailing him, but he gave no indication that he was aware of their surveillance.

In mid-morning he was not surprised when three warriors of the Pimlico appeared at the far side of a small clearing, near a meandering brook. Renno halted at once and raised his hand in greeting.

The trio saluted him in return, taking care to identify him by his war paint, and he neither knew nor cared if they recognized him as the warrior who had killed the son of their new sachem.

"Renno, war chief of the mighty Seneca, brings the greetings of his people to the people of the Pimlico," he said. "It is the wish of Renno to parley in private with the new sachem of the Pimlico. Let Si-de-lo come to him at this place, so that they may speak words to each other that no one else will hear."

The request was somewhat unusual, although such private conferences in the forest were not unknown, and the Pimlico, only one of them a senior warrior, had no intention of disputing the demand of a high-ranking Seneca.

The senior warrior again raised his hand. "The new sachem of the Pimlico will be told the words of the Seneca," he said, and promptly disappeared into the forest behind him, with the two junior warriors hastily following.

There was a chill in the air, so Renno gathered some dead wood, then made himself a small fire and ate lightly before he stretched out in the high grass to rest. He estimated that he was a two-hour march from the Pimlico town, so it would be at least four hours, more likely five, before Si-de-lo joined him. He would use that interval to sleep, certain that at least one sentry of the Pimlico—and possibly more—would be keeping watch over him. He placed his weapons beside him, knowing he would be awake instantly if any sentry came within striking distance.

His sleep was undisturbed, and he awakened refreshed. Building up his fire again, he sat cross-legged in front of it, certain that he would not have too long a wait.

At sundown he heard approaching footsteps. Renno stood up and he noted with approval that the man was making no attempt to maintain even a semblance of silence. Si-de-lo came into the clearing, wearing a feathered cloak and an elaborate bonnet that were symbols of his new, exalted rank.

Raising a hand in greeting, as befitted one who was lower in rank, Renno instantly saw that the new sachem of the Pimlico carried no weapon other than a stone knife in his belt. There were probably enough of his subordinates in the vicinity to protect him in the event of trouble.

Si-de-lo returned the salute, then seated himself at one side of the small fire. Renno lowered himself to a sitting position opposite the sachem and waited for him to speak.

"It is the wish of the Seneca to parley in private," Si-de-lo said, his voice grating, his eyes cold.

"It is." Ordinarily it would have been customary to observe an elaborate ritual, but Renno dispensed with formalities. "It is said that the Pimlico will break their treaty with the English colonists. It is said they will go to war against the men of Virginia."

The sachem inclined his head, but made no reply.

"Let the warriors of the Pimlico remember that the men of Virginia are the friends of the Seneca, friends of all the Iroquois." Renno spoke harshly, too.

Si-de-lo sneered openly. "The woman of the Seneca war chief is a woman of Virginia. Her father is the war chief of Virginia. It may be that other Seneca do not feel as Renno feels."

"The sachem of the Pimlico does not know the Seneca," was the swift response. "The treaty that binds the Iroquois and the colonists of the English was made before Renno married his wife. The white wampum was exchanged before—"

He broke off sharply and leaped to his feet as he heard sounds behind him. Automatically reaching for an arrow from his quiver, he strung it in his bow as he whirled. Creeping toward him, a tomahawk in hand, was a burly Pimlico warrior.

Before Renno could strike, a light arrow fired from the edge of the clearing penetrated the Pimlico's forehead, and he died instantly. Linnick came into the open, his bow still in his hand.

All at once Renno realized that the sounds he had heard on the trail during his march from Norfolk had been made by his friend following him.

A tomahawk sailed through the air and cut Linnick down, sending him sprawling on the grass. In a cold fury Renno drew back his bow, then let fly at the half-hidden shape he saw in the trees behind the clearing. A second Pimlico warrior died without making a sound.

It was obvious that the new sachem of the Pimlico had laid a trap for the Seneca war chief and had tried to dispose of him while they conferred. Si-de-lo had jumped to his feet, too, and stood with his stone knife in his hand, prepared to defend himself.

Renno felt a deep sense of contempt for the two-faced man who had violated the sacred code of Indian hospitality. Certainly Si-de-lo, many years his senior, was no match for him in personal combat. He had no intention of doing the man the honor of treating him as an equal.

Si-de-lo saw the icy rage in the eyes of the Seneca he had tried to trick and took a half-step backward.

"Die, son of a swine and father of a swine," Renno said in a toneless voice, and hurled his tomahawk.

The weapon decapitated Si-de-lo, his blood forming a crimson pool in the grass as he sank slowly to the ground. Renno quickly retrieved his weapon, turning slowly to peer into the forest at each side of the clearing, listening for even the faintest sound that might indicate the presence of other enemies.

He could hear and see nothing and concluded that Si-de-lo's escort had consisted only of the two warriors who were now dead.

Only now could he turn his attention to Linnick, and he dropped to one knee beside his friend. The Arawak was still alive, but his breathing was shallow and labored, and it was apparent that his life was slipping away rapidly. He smiled faintly as he looked up at the man who had saved his life and become his good friend. "Linnick has paid his debt to Renno," he murmured, his voice barely audible.

"Sleep in peace, Arawak," Renno replied, unable to get rid of the lump that formed in his throat. "May Linnick find happiness for all time in the land of his ancestors." Unable to do anything else for the dying warrior, he clasped the Arawak's forearm.

Linnick stopped breathing, the half-smile still on his

lips. Renno gently closed his eyelids and rose slowly to his feet, his cold fury unabated. In the distance he heard the sounds of approaching footsteps, and he was prepared, if necessary, to fight as many warriors as he had to. They well might kill him if he was outnumbered, but he would teach them how a Seneca died, and they would pay a terrible price for their victory.

To his surprise the Pimlico war chief who came into the clearing, followed by a score of warriors, raised his arm in a greeting of peace. Looking at the bodies of the dead that littered the ground, he spoke in a sorrowful, sincere voice. "Tan-ga, war chief of the Pimlico, greets his brother of the Seneca. Too late Tan-ga learned of the treachery that Si-de-lo planned for the Seneca." In a gesture of disgust he kicked the body of the sachem.

The kick reassured Renno. Only a warrior, living or dead, who was being disowned by members of his own tribe was subjected to the indignity of a kick.

Tan-ga turned to the warriors behind him. "Take his body and the bodies of those who followed Si-de-lo," he said. "Throw them in the open place where the vultures will come. Let their bones lie until the sun turns them white and crumbles them to dust."

The bodies of the dead Pimlico were stripped and carried away. Si-de-lo's bonnet was blood-soaked, so it was cast aside, but Tan-ga picked up the feathered cloak, which was intact. After examining it he threw it over his own shoulders.

None of the warriors clustered behind him objected, which meant they accepted him as their new sachem.

"Tan-ga, the new sachem of the Pimlico," he intoned, "will come in five days to the town of the English colonists. There he will exchange new white wampum with them."

The tragic journey into the interior that had cost Linnick his life had not been made in vain.

Renno addressed him for the first time. "Renno, war chief of the Seneca, will carry the good words of Tan-ga to the colonists of the English," he replied.

Tan-ga inclined his head, then gestured toward the body of Linnick. "Who was this warrior?"

"The friend of Renno."

"Is it the wish of Renno that he be given honorable burial?"

"It is."

A litter was made, and four senior warriors carried the body of Linnick through the forest to the town of the Pimlico. Tan-ga led the procession with Renno, who carried the dead Arawak's weapons, directly behind him.

The people of the town came from their houses and fields to watch the marchers, and Renno, although still grieving for his friend, was quick to note that the warriors and elders of the nation were pleased to see Tan-ga wearing the feathered cloak of the sachem.

The funeral ceremonies were simple and, at Renno's request, followed the Seneca customs. A grave was dug, and the body of Linnick was placed in it, with venison, parched corn, and a container of water to provide his spirit with sustenance on the journey to the land of his ancestors. Renno bent down to place the Arawak's weapons beside him, and the body was covered by a thick layer of dirt. Knowing nothing about the gods of the Arawak, Renno appealed to the gods and manitous of the Seneca to speed Linnick on his journey and see him safely to his destination.

At Tan-ga's insistence Renno stayed until the following morning as the honored guest of the Pimlico, and at dawn the next day he was provided with an escort of six warriors for his journey back to Norfolk.

Renno would have preferred to travel alone because he could have covered the distance in a fraction of the time, but it would have been a discourtesy to refuse. Consequently he did not reach the outskirts of Norfolk until late the following morning.

Austin Ridley was inspecting his late tobacco crop when he saw his son-in-law approaching, the mere presence of the Pimlico indicating that he brought good news.

Renno confirmed his guess, brought him up to date, and hurried off to the house, leaving the colonel to offer the warriors a meal.

Betsy saw her husband's approach from a window and chose to wait for him in their bedchamber, where they could be reunited in private.

"May the manitous hear my pledge," he told her as they embraced, "we will not be separated again before Ja-gonh can walk and talk."

Later, at dinner, Consuelo wept when Renno told the family the story of Linnick's death. "He had his own faith, whatever it may have been," she said. "But I will feel better if I go to church to pray for him."

Betsy and Ned accompanied her, and that evening she said, "Linnick did so much for us that we would not have survived on our long and terrible journey without him. I shall name my first son for him."

Three days later Consuelo and Ned were married in the presence of dozens of the Ridleys' friends and neighbors. Betsy and Renno, both in proper English attire, acted as matron of honor and best man. Anne participated in the ceremony as flower girl, and only Ja-gonh was left at home.

A reception followed at the Ridley estate, where tables laden with food and a punch of rum and tea were placed in the garden. The bride and groom were toasted, and then Colonel Ridley offered a fervent toast to a lasting peace with the Pimlico. He gave full credit to his son-in-law, but Renno was nowhere to be seen.

Soon thereafter Renno reappeared with his wife and baby son, all of them in buckskins for the long overland journey to the land of the Seneca. Renno had not forgotten his promise to leave the day that Consuelo and Ned were married.

They exchanged farewells, and Ned hoped that he and Consuelo would visit the town of the Seneca in the spring. Austin Ridley walked to the gate with his daughter, her husband, and their child.

"In twelve moons' time," Renno said, "we will come

back here. We will not allow Ja-gonh to forget that he is an English colonist as well as a Seneca."

Austin wanted to warn him to be careful in the wilderness, but he knew that such advice was unnecessary. The young Seneca war chief was better equipped than any other man to protect the wife and child he loved.

Watching them as they walked toward the deep forest—the heavily armed Renno matching Betsy's stride as the happy Ja-gonh, strapped to his mother's back, jabbered—Austin saw in them the hope for the future. Someday the wars between Great Britain and the other nations trying to establish permanent colonies in America would come to an end. Indians and whites would continue to intermarry. Ja-gonh was the symbol of all that his parents and grandparents were striving to accomplish, and he, in his time, would make America a safer, more prosperous, and happier land.

Read the thrilling Book IV
in the magnificent
WHITE INDIAN SERIES

THE SACHEM
by Donald Clayton Porter

In THE SACHEM, Renno is made acting leader (Sachem) of the Seneca while Ghonka and Renno's wife Betsy journey to England to plead for help against the French in America. But Renno's position is soon threatened by Colonel Alain de Gramont who, bent on revenge against Renno, secretly joins up with the French. The Spanish, headed by two schemers, Don Diego de Bernard and his daughter Beatriz, also see Renno's leadership as a threat to their ruthless ambitions. All of these turbulent forces build to a violent confrontation.

★ WAGONS WEST ★

A series of unforgettable books that trace the lives of a dauntless band of pioneering men, women, and children as they brave the hazards of an untamed land in their trek across America. This legendary caravan of people forge a new link in the wilderness. They are Americans from the North and the South, alongside immigrants, Blacks, and Indians, who wage fierce daily battles for survival on this uncompromising journey—each to their private destinies as they fulfill their greatest dreams.

☐	24408	**INDEPENDENCE!**	$3.95
☐	24651	**NEBRASKA!**	$3.95
☐	24229	**WYOMING!**	$3.95
☐	24088	**OREGON!**	$3.95
☐	23168	**TEXAS!**	$3.50
☐	24655	**CALIFORNIA!**	$3.95
☐	24694	**COLORADO!**	$3.95
☐	20174	**NEVADA!**	$3.50
☐	20919	**WASHINGTON!**	$3.50
☐	22925	**MONTANA!**	$3.95
☐	23572	**DAKOTA!**	$3.95
☐	23921	**UTAH!**	$3.95
☐	24256	**IDAHO!**	$3.95

TALES OF BOLD ADVENTURE AND PASSIONATE ROMANCE FROM THE PRODUCER OF WAGONS WEST

A SAGA OF THE SOUTHWEST
by Leigh Franklin James

The American Southwest in the early 19th century, a turbulent land ravaged by fortune seekers and marked by the legacy of European aristocracy, is the setting for this series of thrilling and memorable novels. You will meet a group of bold, headstrong people who come to carve a lasting place in the untamed wilderness.

☐	23170	Hawk and the Dove #1	$3.50
☐	23171	Wings of the Hawk #2	$3.50
☐	20096	Revenge of the Hawk #3	$3.25
☐	22578	Flight of The Hawk #4	$3.50
☐	23482	Night of The Hawk #5	$3.50
☐	24361	Cry of The Hawk #6	$3.50

Prices and availability subject to change without notice.

SPECIAL
MONEY SAVING
OFFER

Now you can have an up-to-date listing of Bantam's hundreds of titles plus take advantage of our unique and exciting bonus book offer. A special offer which gives you the opportunity to purchase a Bantam book for only 50¢. Here's how!

By ordering any five books at the regular price per order, you can also choose any other single book listed (up to a $4.95 value) for just 50¢. Some restrictions do apply, but for further details why not send for Bantam's listing of titles today!

Just send us your name and address plus 50¢ to defray the postage and handling costs.